HE WILL LOVE HER TILL THE ENDS OF FOREVER

DEATH DUE US

TILL DEATH DUE US PART

ALIAH DARKROSE

The characters and events portrayed in this book are fictitious. Any similarity to real persons, living or dead, is coincidental and not intended by the author.

No part of this publication may be reproduced, distributed, transmitted, or resold in any form or by any means, including photography, recording, or other electronic or mechanical methods, or stored in any database or retrieval system without the prior written consent of the author, except in the case of brief quotations embodied in critical reviews and certain other non-commercial uses permitted by law.

Copyright © 2025 Aliah Darkrose All rights reserved.

Edited by BrooksFormatting
Proofread by BrooksFormatting
eBook Formatted by Aliah Darkrose
Cover by Amy at Coversbyamy
First Edition 2023

This standalone is written in UK English.

PLAYLIST

2 Wicky - Hooverphonic
Shades Of Cool - Lana Del Ray
Cold Hearted Woman - Magic Slim
Emotions - Brenda Lee
Desert Rose - Lolo Zouaï
Moments in Love - The Art Of Noise
Only You - Portished
Glory Box - Portished
Playground Love - Air, Gordon Tracks
S'en Allaer - Swing, Angèle
Safe In Your Skin - Title Fight
I Love You - Cillie Eilish
All I Need - Bille Eilish
All I Need - Radiohead
La Petite Fille De La Mer - Vangelis

1:00   4:00

◀   ❚❚   ▶

ALIAH DARKROSE

WARNING

THE PAGES HOLD DESCRIPTIVE ACCOUNTS OF THE FOLLOWING

Sexual Assault

Gore

Extreme Violence

Child Abuse

Sadistic Behaviour

Self-Harm

Bipolar

Blood Play

Incest

Pregnancy Murder

Suicide

AND OTHER DEEPLY DISTURBING THEMES. THIS IS A WORK OF FICTION, AND ANY
GLORIFICATION OF THESE DARK TOPICS IS STRONGLY DISCOURAGED.

IF YOU ARE EASILY TRIGGERED OR SUSPECTION TO TRAUMA, I URGE YOU TO
REFRAIN FROM READING THIS BOOK.

YOU HAVE BEEN WARNED

ALIAH DARKROSE

DEDICATION

FOR THE WOMEN WHO WHISPERED "I DO" AND
LATER WHISPERED "I HAVE TO DO THIS ALONE."

WHO TUCKED THIER CHILDREN WHILE TUCKING
AWAY THEIR PAIN. MARRIED IN UNITY,
MOTHERING IN SOLITUDE.

YOU DID IT. YOU FOUGHT.
AND THAT IS EVERYTHING.

AUTHOR'S NOTE

MOST OF YOU ARE PROBABLY FAMILIAR WITH THIS BOOK, SOME OF YOU AREN'T. EITHER WAY, WELCOME GORGEOUS, THANK YOU FOR PICKING UP 'DEATH DUE US' AND CHOOSING INTERNAL DAMAGE.

I AM NOT APOLOGIZING BUT I HOPE THIS BOOK CAUSES YOUR MASCARA TO RUN, AND YOUR EYES BLOODSHOT RED. SO PLEASE DON'T RATE THIS BOOK A NEGATIVE REVIEW KNOWING THAT I HAVE WARNED YOU ABAOUT THE SAD ENDING.

BUT DON'T WORRY THERE IS ALSO AN ALTERNATIVE ENDING.

MUCH LOVE,

ADDITIONAL NOTE

THIS BOOK WAS ORIGINALLY PUBLISHED UNDER THE TITLE HOUSEWIFE BEFORE BEING RENAMED TO DEATH DUE US. THE STORY, THEMES, AND CHARACTERS REMAIN THE SAME, BUT THE TITLE HAS BEEN CHANGED TO BETTER REFLECT THE DIRECTION AND TONE OF THE WORK.

THANK YOU FOR YOUR CONTINUED SUPPORT AND UNDERSTANDING.

Aliah
DARKROSE

PART ONE

WE ALL RUN FROM SOMETHING,
UNTIL IT CONSUMES US AND TURNS
YOU INTO THE PERSON YOU NEVER
THOUGHT YOU'D BECOME.

PROLOGUE

Till death do us part.

I find that saying a bit humorous.

The memory of that day still burns inside me. The day I walked down the aisle, only to have my freedom ripped from me. All those unfamiliar eyes, piercing, staring into the deepest part of my soul as I whispered those damning words: "I do."

I screamed inside, wishing I could rip my own heart out. From that moment on, I was no longer a person but a hollow shell, trapped in a prison my uncle had crafted. My reason to live, to love, to even breathe was stolen. Every breath felt like a burden, every day a fight for an escape that seemed impossible.

But the more I fought, the more I drowned in despair, until I was no longer me. But today—today, it ends. I'm standing on the brink of reclaiming what's mine.

Fucking freedom. As the blade slides against the steel, sharpening with each pass, the metallic ring hums in the air. My eyes are locked on his portrait hanging above the mantle, his dead eyes staring back at me, a perfect reflection of the life he trapped me in.

Six long years of agony. Six long years of his abuse. I begged for help, but they turned their backs and sneered at me as if my suffering was a joke. A tear escapes, falling silently into the cold counter.

The timer dings and my heart pounds with anticipation. The rich scent of roasted garlic and butter fills the room. I set the knife down and move toward the oven, slipping on my mitts, and feeling the weight of what's about to happen.

Just as I pull the chicken from the oven, I hear the front door slam shut. My pulse quickens with excitement. He's home. Heavy footsteps echo through the hall, growing louder. I feel his eyes boring into my back. Smiling, I turn to greet him, my voice warm and inviting, "Just in time for dinner."

His eyes narrow, suspicion brewing in those darkened pupils. His hair, thin and lifeless, clings to his scalp like old straw left out in the sun. His face, wrinkled and weary, tells stories of a life I no longer care about. As he slips off his jacket and loosens his tie, a storm brews inside me. Rage, fear, hatred. But I swallow it down. He walks away, not saying a word leaving me alone in the kitchen. My grip tightens on the oven mitts.

I could end it right now, strangle him until every ounce of life is gone. But no, I have a better plan.

I open the drawer, my fingers brushing against the tiny bottle of cyanide salt. For years, I've been collecting the seeds…apple seeds. How many apples do you ask? Three-hundred apples. Innocent enough on their own, but when crushed? Deadly. With a calm smile, I tuck the bottle into my apron and move to the dining room, setting the chicken down on the table.

The room is set with candles flickering softly, casting long shadows over the pristine white tablecloth. The smell of vanilla mixes with the savoury food, creating an air of serenity. I plate the food carefully, each dish crafted from scratch. Everything is perfect.

And then, with a flick of my wrist, I sprinkle the cyanide onto

his portion, not wasting a single grain. The sound of his footsteps pulls me back, and I quickly tuck the bottle away, moving to the far end of the table.

I peel off the apron, revealing the sleek black dress clinging to my body. Sitting down, I wait, my heart calm. He strolls in, now wearing a silk robe and a cigar clenched between his patched lips.

The glow of the cigar reflects in his eyes as he glares at me, but I don't flinch. I start eating, savouring the meal I've made. The flavours dance on my tongue, sweet, spicy and savoury, everything in perfect harmony. Lifting my glass of red wine, I meet his stare head-on, unfazed.

"Eat, before it gets cold," I say, smiling sweetly.

He watches me for a moment, then takes a final puff of his cigar before setting it aside. He cuts into the meat, his movements slow, deliberate. He chews carefully, his eyes flicking between the food and my face.

"How is it?" I ask, my voice casual.

"Good," he grunts and then begins eating faster, shovelling the food into his mouth like the hungry dog he is. I sip my wine, enjoying every second.

Thirty minutes pass, and then, I see it. His breathing changes. It was shallow, laboured. He clears his throat, again and again. His eyes widened with confusion and panic. "What the fuck is in this?" he rasps, his voice cracking in-between coughs.

I can't help it. A smirk creeps onto my lips as I casually cut another piece of chicken. "Maybe I went a little heavy on the paprika."

He gulps down the wine, but it only makes it worse. His face turns red, veins bulging on his face as his hands claw at his throat, desperate for air.

I lean back, watching the scene unfold, every moment more satisfying than the last. He tries to stand, but his legs give out, and he collapses back into the chair. My grin widens.

"Forgot to mention," I say, my voice dripping with mock sweetness, "I added a little something special for my dearest husband." I twirl my wine glass lazily, watching the crimson liquid swirl.

"Cyanide."

His eyes fill with horror and rage, but it's too late. His body convulses, his muscles jerking uncontrollably. I take another bite, savouring it as I watch the light fade from his eyes.

His body slumps forward, crashing onto the table with a dull thud.

The music continues to play softly in the background, an eerie calm settling over the room.

Unbothered, I finish my meal, taking my time. When my plate is empty, I pour myself another glass of wine. Raising it in a silent toast, I smile, my heart finally at peace.

"Happy Anniversary, skurwielu."

CHAPTER 1

IRENA NOWAK

The air was thick with the bittersweet scent of mourning The air was thick with the bittersweet scent of mourning as I scanned the sombre faces around me. Viktor, the man we had gathered to bid farewell to, had been a shadowy figure in life.

Yet in death, he was elevated to saint-like status, as if mourning a hero rather than a wretched soul. Observing the dark parade of mourners with tears streaming down their faces, a twisted satisfaction stirred within me.

There was something satisfying in seeing a man like Viktor finally pay for his sins. While no one deserves to die, Viktor's demise felt deserved. He had earned every bit of the slow, painful end I had inflicted upon him.

For today, at least, the world had one less monster of a man lurking in its shadows. What should have been a sombre, dreary day cloaked in sorrow was instead radiant with a brilliant blue sky and the lively sounds of songbirds and buzzing bees. Nature seemed openly happy about Viktor's death. Seemingly celebrating the day with me instead of mourning.

My uncles sat stoically on one side, their faces as hard as stone.

Their scowls bore not sadness but a fierce resentment, furious that Viktor was gone.

They puzzled over how a man with no known medical issues could suffer a fatal heart attack. Unlike my uncles, I struggled to conceal my happiness. I forced tears down my cheeks, putting on a façade of grief as a grieving widow should, even fooling my uncles, who chose to ignore Viktor's abusive behaviour, leaving me alone in silent suffering.

But I refused to let them see me crack. Suspicious, Uncle Krzysztof caught my gaze, but I remained stoic, guarding my true feelings. The mourners' cries added to the heavy atmosphere, and I yearned for the funeral to end so I could begin rebuilding my broken life.

Though what makes me special. Everyone's life is broken somehow. I'm no one special.

The priest concluded, calling for others to speak. Originally, Viktor's deceased parents were to speak, but with no siblings and only distant cousins and extended family present, I was chosen to speak on his behalf as his wife.

Standing, the weight of his absence draped over me like a leaden cloak. I smoothed my black silk dress with trembling hands and approached the stage. All eyes turned to me, ranging from sympathy to curiosity. Gripping the microphone, my nerves buzzed like live wires.

Looking out at the faces, déjà vu struck the same crowd that witnessed Viktor and I exchange vows. But now, it was a sombre farewell, not a celebration. My voice faltered as I began. "Viktor will be missed," I managed to say, words catching in my throat, struggling to feign emotion.

He will, in fact, not be missed.

"The loss of a spouse is like no other," I continued, my voice trailing off into silence. The truth of those words washed over me, but I felt no sadness or heartache. Instead, I felt freedom.

"It changes everything…my habits, confidence, and sense of self. Viktor's death transformed me. And sadly, you're not here for me to thank you."

If only they knew the weight of my words.

"I wish I could see you again," I whisper, biding my time. Because when I do see you again, it will be to witness the beautiful way you suffocate and die like the pathetic man that you are.

"I..." I choke out, voice quivering, tears flowing down my cheeks, embodying the anger and hatred I feel for Viktor.

The priest comes to my side, leading me away from the spotlight to sit next to my uncle. The room fills with suffocating silence, my heart pounding non-stop. But I refuse to drop my façade, staring boldly at those around me. Finally, as the funeral continues, it is time to bury the one who caused me so much pain. We file out quietly, solemnly following the coffin into the warm outdoors.

Each step toward his grave makes my heart dance with glee. Solemn guests form a semicircle around the grave; heads bowed, tears shed. The air is heavy with grief as if the ground mourns beneath us. Clad in black, family and friends gently lay flowers before the headstone. A church bell tolls mournfully in the distance, echoing across the graveyard at six o'clock, adding gravity to the moment.

Silently, I watch as his casket is buried six feet under, a small smile playing on my lips.

Twisted satisfaction rushes through me like a drug, a euphoria I never thought possible. Who knew witnessing a burial could bring such blissful joy? Beside my late husband's grave, sympathetic individuals approach with condolences, sharing their petty woes. They try to empathise with my agony, but their words feel hollow and insincere.

Walking away, they carelessly passed by the other graves as if they were meaningless, just another pile of dirt.

For a whole I stood there alone, gazing at the tombstone with a mix of emotions in my heart. And as much as I wish I could say I felt a bit of guilt for what I have done. I would lie to myself.

I despise this man with every living fibre of my being for the pain and abuse he had caused in my life. Perhaps the only solace I can find at this moment is wishing the same suffering on the very men who prey on women. The very same men who possess the same rotten spirit as Viktor.

My entire existence has been a futile attempt to appease men like him, my uncles, friends, men on the street, my uncle's friends.

The list fucking goes on.

I discarded my own identity as a woman to submit my soul and physical self to be a sex slave and punching bag to men who think with their little shrivelled dicks.

They never apologized for hurting me, but I had to apologize a dozen times for being angry about it.

I firmly believe that taking your life was righteous of me. I simply couldn't imagine surviving another year of your merciless abuse. How much more heartbreak could I sustain, five, ten, twenty more years of constant mockery and assault for merely being a woman?!

No.

I had to do it. I had to save myself.

After what you've done to me?

You deserve to burn in eternal hell.

CHAPTER 2

IRENA NOWAK

One year later

"Let go of me you bastard!" I griped, my voice echoing through the hallways as they dragged me towards my future husband.

It had been a year since Viktor's passing, and life had been anything but peaceful.

Desperate to escape my fate, I kicked and screamed as the guard hauled me down the stairs and into one of my uncle's studies. The impact of hitting the wooden floor vibrated through my aching body.

After the door closed, I felt discouraged. I had enjoyed a year of freedom from abuse and control, but now I was trapped and facing yet another familiar situation.

The door creaked open, and I tensed, bracing for what would come. The two figures that entered were cloaked in black, their presence ominous.

"Time to go," the man with piercing brown eyes stared coldly and firmly. But I refused to budge.

Curling into myself protectively the two men exchanged a knowing look before closing in on me. Desperately, I scooted away, clutching the desk with all my strength. "No! Don't touch me!" I screamed.

The man with icy blue eyes snatched my hands, twisting my arm effortlessly. I cried out in pain, unable to resist any longer. A brown-eyed man imprisoned my arms as panic surged through me. They hoisted me up, defying my writhing resistance.

"Let me go!" I roared. Due to my trauma, I do not like being touched. It's triggering, especially by a man.

They marched me down the corridor, tightening their grip with each laboured breath.

"I said, let me go!!" My struggle only seemed to excite them. With a swift kick, the door gave way, and I was hurled onto the ground again.

Despite the pain, I sprang to my feet and lunged for the door, desperate to escape. But the chilling sound of my uncle's voice stopped me cold.

"Enough with this nonsense, Irena!"

Tears streaming down my face, I looked down at my bare feet, feeling exposed and vulnerable. My once-perfect dark hair was now tangled, half covering my face, and my ruined makeup stung from salty tears. I felt like a prisoner in my skin in a figure-hugging pink dress and black heels, well heels. One of my heels was lost in the chaos, scattered in the house where I'd been carried against my will.

Trying to catch my breath, I lifted my head and locked eyes with my cold-hearted Uncle Grzegorz. His dark brown eyes burned into mine, standing tall and imposing in his navy-blue suit despite his neatly groomed salt and pepper beard and sunburn patches.

Uncle Anatol's unblinking gaze fixed on me; his fingers wrapped around a Cuban cigar. Despite his imposing figure and youthful age of thirty-three, his clean-shaven face gave him a boyish look, complemented by striking blue eyes and dark blonde hair. His impeccable black suit spoke of dominance within our elite family.

Unbeknownst to me, Grzegorz approached with a menacing stride, simmering with rage.

"You little brat!" His thick Polish accent snarled as his palm connected with my cheek, jolting my head sharply to the side.

"Your fiancé is within earshot, yet you're out here acting like a wild woman," he continued with venomous malice. "Men do not like untrained women."

"Do you know what disgrace you're bringing upon our family name?"

"If your dim-witted guards hadn't laid a hand on me, I wouldn't have created a scene!" I retorted defiantly, anger festering like a volcano.

Our argument halted with the abrupt entrance of Uncle Krzysztof and a stranger, though Grzegorz's attention shifted to them.

His fingers tightened around my arm like a vice, warning me not to move an inch. Unease churned in my stomach as I watched the interaction.

Glancing down at my bare feet, I wished to disappear. The room's tension was suffocating. "Saint," Grzegorz's voice broke through, yanking me towards Krzysztof and the stranger.

"Grzegorz," a voice as cold as ice replied, sending a shiver down my spine. I lifted my gaze to meet theirs.

The piercing stare of the speaker froze me. Before me lay a wasteland devoid of feeling or life. "Saint." Grzegorz called out.

His jaw tightens, sharp enough to cut. His storm green eyes scanned the room as if he had already figured out every secret hiding in the corners. There was something about him…something dangerous. A storm restrained behind his demeanour. A promise of ruin. He doesn't just look at me; he studies, he calculates, he takes as if he already owns the space between us.

Men like him don't ask. They take. And God help me if I want to be taken by this man.

Despite my attempts to break free, Grzegorz's grip tightened around me, sending pain through my body.

"Why does she look like she's been scavenged from the streets?" Saint questioned, directing his stare at Grzegorz.

Grzegorz's lips contorted into a firm line as he fixed his gaze on Saint. "Forgive us, Saint. We're having a complicated morning with Miss Nowak. She's in a rebellious mood; it seems to be her time of the month," he muttered the last part under his breath. I furrowed my brows in perplexity.

Liar.

Saint's jaw tightened; his gaze sharp on Grzegorz. "Your apology falls flat Grzegorz. You promised me a clean and well-mannered woman not someone who looks like she lost in a cat fight. Leaving your words empty as a fucking dry well." Saint declared sharply, stepping menacingly toward Grzegorz.

"Is this your plan to humiliate and disrespect me?" Saint probed, eyes piercing. Grzegorz jolted back, nervously laughing in response.

As I watched, I saw a rare sight: my uncles showing fear, no longer playing the dominant role in a situation. To Saint, they are nothing. They respect him as if he holds some royal title.

"No, I didn't mean to—"

"Why are you touching her like that?" His words cut through me, making me look down at the hand still gripping my arm tightly.

His concern was like a dark cloud, and his brows furrowed in worry. Grzegorz's hold on me fell away when our eyes locked as if it were a distant memory.

I distanced myself from Grzegorz and his men and rubbed my sore arm, anticipating a bruise. Saint's fiery gaze burned into Grzegorz as he justified his actions, claiming I was a brat and needed to be put in my place. Despite the tension in the room, I felt a sense of deep discomfort and unease as all eyes were on me.

These men were notorious for their cruelty and power. Women like me didn't belong in these grimy, nefarious businesses, but we were always drawn in like moths to a flame. It was a dirty, dangerous lifestyle, yet we couldn't escape it.

The mafia blood ran thick in my veins. My mother, born into poverty in Tanzania, knew this too well. Her eldest brother, Fadoul, suggested she work night shifts at nightclubs to support their struggling family. Despite the criminals and paedophiles, she worked there for three years until she met my father, Dominik Nowak.

Dominik charmed my mother, and soon she fell in love, unaware he was part of the Polish American crime organisation.

After three years together, they decided to move to Poland where I was born. My mother tried to flee my father's dangerous connections but was killed. My father, devastated by her death, died soon after, leaving me orphaned at five.

Raised by my uncles, I was homeschooled and isolated, always the shy girl. I found brief moments of joy with friends and a boyfriend in my teenage years, but heartbreak followed. My uncles took me out of high school, and years later, I married Viktor.

Now, trembling in front of Saint and Grzegorz, I felt alone and violated. Despite my fear, I knew I had to be strong, for myself and anyone who might come after me.

"You've been troubling your uncles," he says, his voice deep and velvety with a light French accent.

I feel vulnerable and defensive. My heart races as his words remind me of the pain and hardships these men have caused me. But I refuse to cower before him, regardless of our marital status. I will always stand up for myself.

"Why?" Saint demands. His once-easy demeanour grows cold, and his jaw clenches in frustration. I stand in silence, determined not to give him the satisfaction of knowing the truth. Saint's expression darkens, and his voice grows hoarse with annoyance. "Irena, I'm talking to you."

The tension between us crackles with unspoken words. My heart pounds like a thunderstorm, and I wish I could disappear. Before me stands my soon-to-be husband.

The thought of speaking makes my head spin. Silence seems safer. I can handle my uncle's wrath, but Saint's fury is another story. I do not know the man. I do not know what he is capable of. As Saint's gaze shifts to my uncle's, a shiver runs down my spine. "Does this woman even speak?" His tone is laced with annoyance, making my heart race.

I look down at my pedicured toes, hoping to vanish. Uncle Krzysztof chuckles, and the tension between us crackles with unspoken words. My heart pounds like a thunderstorm.

"Don't be fooled by her quiet demeanour, Saint," he teases. "She talks enough to give us all a headache. You'll see once she gets comfortable." Saint's piercing stare bore into me. Half of me wants to curl up and give in; the other half is determined to prove my worth.

"Look at me," Saint commands, his voice low and menacing.

I force myself to meet his intimidating gaze.

"Leave," he orders the others, never breaking eye contact. My heart pounds like drums of war.

I desperately want my uncles to stay, to shield me from this dangerous man. But even with them here, I feel like a lamb among wolves. I trust no one, least of all Saint. His name alone sends shivers down my spine. My uncles may have my blood, but they would sell me for gold. No one leaves, leaving Saint more irritated. "Are you all fucking deaf? Leave."

After my uncles left, I stood before Saint, and I felt their full betrayal. As the room empties, leaving just us, unease washes over me.

Suddenly, Saint grabs my neck and pulls me close, his minty breath intoxicating and menacing. His dark eyes watching me, making my skin crawl. My disgust is evident, and he frowns.

"Did your uncles forget to teach you manners woman?" Saint's voice is calm, but his grip suffocates me. My body freezes, mind black as his fingers sink deeper into my neck, cutting off my breath.

"Answer me," he demands, tightening his grip. My heart races, and tears blur my vision. I try to push him away, but his hold tightens, pulling me to the brink of unconsciousness.

Instinct kicks in, and I claw at his face, drawing blood. He releases me, and I gasp for air.

He snarls in fury, covering his bleeding eye with a vengeful hand. My heart races as I catch my breath, rubbing my sore neck. The battle is uneven, but I won't back down. Saint clenches his jaw, revealing blood trickling down his face.

My eyes widen at the jagged gash from his eye to his cheek. The implications of my actions hit me hard; this scar would stay with him.

Saint produces a pristine handkerchief, dabbing at the blood on his face. I brace for his wrath, expecting a violent outburst.

But instead, a sinister smile curls his lips, sending chills down my spine. It's the haunting grin of a demon, a warning of the darkness in his eyes.

As I avoid his gaze, my eyes wander down his chiselled physique and pause in realization at the sight, my pupils dilate in disbelief.

Saint's erection.

It was large through the fabric of his pants, yearning to be released. The sight left me completely flabbergasted, and I could feel the heat rising to my cheeks.

I felt a chill as I looked at the bulge between his legs in disgust. His gaze was disturbing and animalistic.

Saint folded the handkerchief, tucking it back into his blazer and silently left the room with purpose, leaving me feeling uneasy and cold.

CHAPTER 3

SAINT DÉ LEON

"Did your uncles forget to teach you manners woman?" I ask.

Why is she not talking?

Is she fucking deaf?

Or slow?

My hand tightened around her delicate neck, waiting for her to cry out. But her eyes sparkled with wetness, as my free hand caresses down her caramel-coloured skin.

I do not care if it takes me to crush her windpipe.

I need to hear her voice.

She is like a silent bunny, when you wrap your hand around their necks, and they just dangle in the air. Not uttering a single squeal.

"Answer me," I snapped, tightening my grip further. Her skin is soft, her breath quick and shallow as she fights against my hold.

I study her face as I cut off her air supply. Fear etches into her features; her full two toned lips part in a desperate plea for oxygen. Her wide eyes stare into mine, silently begging for a reprieve.

There it is — *the fear I was looking for.*

She tried to resist, but I stayed determined. Her hands found their way onto my face as she tried to push me away. Just when I thought she had stopped, her long nails clawed into my flesh, scratching me and drawing out blood.

I winced in pain and stepped back, my hold slipping. Sweat dripped down my lower back as I focused on the wound on my face.

I felt a sudden shift of emotion inside of me. Anger.

I wanted to rip her off with all the innocence she could provide. Ruin her, destroy her, turn her into my little sinner.

My dick in my pants pulsed with an intensity that threatened to betray my emotions.

The damn thought of her hurting me.

Her innocence radiating from her.

Her breathtaking features.

Woke my body with a burning rage of intoxication for this woman.

I reached into my pocket and pulled out a handkerchief as I wiped away the blood.

Our eyes met again, her gaze falling shamelessly to my growing dick, igniting a passion I could not resist.

I noticed her blushing cheeks as I walked towards the exit. She quickly looked away when I caught her eye. My fingers itched to explore her natural curves, but I held back my desire.

I left her in one of her uncle's offices and was met by Grzegorz, who seemed calm despite being upset.

"She does not talk." I blurted out.

As I looked at Grzegorz, he noticed the cut on my skin and looked concerned, asking me about it. "Did she do that?"

I narrowed my eyes, holding back the words that wanted to come out.

It was clear that his stubborn niece was to blame.

I couldn't believe this foolish man's audacity to even ask.

"You can be a real dumbass sometimes."

It's hard to believe that this dickwad is even related to Dominik.

My mind was racing with questions.

Why was she so quiet?

Is she a mute?

I can't be with someone who can't communicate. It would feel like being with a child.

"She's not always like this, so don't worry, Saint. Irena is usually a chatterbox. You must be intimidating her," he quipped, his arms crossed smugly.

I glared at the wretched creature before me, analysing his every move. The charged atmosphere crackled with tension as Grzegorz, and I locked eyes. I could barely contain my fury, itching to smash his thick skull until it broke. But before I could move, my trusty companion, Prince, strode up to us and broke the silence. "Saint," Prince said, his voice even and unwavering. "They're ready to talk about Irena Nowak."

I gave him a curt nod, flicking my eyes towards Grzegorz one last time before Prince left. With him gone, I stepped forward, closing the gap between Grzegorz and myself. "I want to make one thing clear, Grzegorz," I spat, my voice low and dangerous.

"The only thing keeping you alive right now is your dead brother. You're a disorganised, two-faced coward, and you're nothing to me. Just because I haven't killed you yet doesn't mean you have my trust or respect. Got it?"

Grzegorz bristled, his eyes flashing with a desperate need for control.

But he knew, and I knew, who was truly in charge.

"Got it," he muttered grudgingly.

I agreed to the arranged marriage proposal because of its potential benefits and fairness. I don't owe any of the Nowak brothers a favour.

After a brief pause, I joined the other men in the office, feeling the weight of responsibility on my shoulders.

"Let's talk about Miss. Nowak?" Anatol's voice broke the silence.

IRENA NOWAK

As time passed, I was stuck in Anatol's study, thinking only of Saint.

The memory of his hands around my neck made me feel sick.

Despite his violent grip, he hadn't harmed me...yet.

I wondered if he would be a better or worse abuser than Viktor, the thought left me shivering with anxiety.

For as long as I can remember, I have yearned for the bittersweet taste of freedom. The kind that fills your lungs with the crisp scent of adventure and ignites a burning desire to chase after whatever sets your soul on fire.

It is an insatiable thirst that follows me everywhere I go, urging me to run away from this life and never look back.

If fate allows and luck is on my side, I hope to make my dream a pianist come true. I want to awe my audience with my music expressing myself through each pressing key.

But here I am, feeling trapped by dangerous men nearby. I knew I could not survive in this lifestyle any longer.

As I picked up the book, memories from my past came rushing back - memories of fear, feeling trapped and giving away my freedom. My heart raced as I held onto the book tightly. But what caught my eye were the golden roses on the spine.

Roses have always captured my heart, especially when they are pure and white. Since I was a young girl, I have been enchanted by their magical charm. I see roses as a symbol of good luck and hope that with determination, I will one day write the happy ending to my fairy tale and find my own happily ever after.

I read an old book and felt a sense of freedom and hope. Anatol entered the room, and I was brought back to reality. He poured himself a drink and gave me a cold glance. As he poured more amber liquid into a glass, I felt my heart race in anticipation. I silently prayed for protection from any trouble. I accidentally bumped into a shelf as I moved back, but Anatol didn't seem bothered.

He stood still, staring at me intensely with a drink in hand and one hand in his pocket.

"You should be getting a lecture from Grzegorz, not me," he said bitterly. I felt nervous and swallowed hard.

"Now, why don't you explain to me why you felt the need to act like a spoiled brat today," Anatol continued, his frustration clear in his tone. I struggled to respond, intimidated by his intense stare and hidden emotions. Despite his calm exterior, I could see the anger in his eyes.

"So, Irena, I'm waiting," he said. I licked my lips, my heart beating faster than ever before.

"Answer me, Irena!" In a fit of rage, he threw a glass across the room, the sound of it shattering adding to my fear.

I flinched and tried to avoid his gaze, but he forced me to look at him. I closed my eyes, bracing myself for the outburst.

"Thanks to you, Saint extended the contract. Now we're cursed to tolerate your presence for two fucking months. Two months of teaching a grown woman some godforsaken manners!" he bellows, spittle flying from his lips. My stomach roils in disgust, my lips quivering helplessly.

"If it wasn't for Saint's protection, I swear—I swear, I would have..."

Anatol's breath caught in his throat as he released his grip on my face and angrily left his study.

This action prompted two guards to enter the room and grab me by the arm. I tried to break free, but their stronghold dragged me through the house's halls.

When we reached my room, they pushed me inside and slammed the door, locking it behind them. The sound of the lock clicking filled the room as the guards' footsteps faded. Darkness surrounded me, mirroring the shadows in my heart.

I tasted metal in my mouth as tears rolled down my cheeks, glistening in the faint light. I leaned against the door, finding no comfort in its coolness. There was no solace to be found.

Why do they hate me so much?

My family's hurtful words and actions hurt more than any enemy.

I wonder what I did to deserve this pain. I cry out my sorrow, but there are no answers. Anger builds inside me until I can't hold it in, and I scream out, feeling trapped in a world where love has turned sour.

CHAPTER 4

IRENA NOWAK

Two months passed quickly with endless tears, screaming, and sleepless nights leading up to my wedding day on *August 22nd.*

The last time I saw Saint was when he almost suffocated me, and since then, he was gone.

No one in the house mentions his name, as if it's taboo to do so, without his presence. I look in the mirror and see a lost girl staring back at me. Krzysztof, the vague middle Nowak brother, picked out the special dress I was wearing for the occasion.

The white dress fits my curves well and has a flattering silhouette with off-the-shoulder sleeves. I decided to keep my makeup simple, using blush, concealer, mascara, and rosewood lipstick to compliment my caramel skin.

My uncles complimented me on looking innocent and obedient to my husband. Now, I must act the part of a submissive housewife.

Eyeing the mirror made me nervous on what should have been the happiest day of my life. Anatol was teaching me how to be a "mafia wife" emphasising obedience, silence, sweetness, purity, and physical beauty.

Feeling suffocated by rigid expectations, I knew the consequences of not meeting them would be severe.

I suppressed my emotions and played my role in a dangerous game, reluctantly becoming a pawn to avoid trouble. My happiness was disregarded as I prioritised my husband's ego. I was seen as a tool for his pleasure, with my own needs ignored.

Lost in contemplation, my thoughts are interrupted by a gentle knock on the door.

"Come in," I called out wearily. Gloria, an elderly woman with white hair and tired eyes appeared in the doorway. She looked frail but wore pristine clothes. She approached me in thick sandals, telling me it was time for the ceremony to begin. Her voice shook with fragility, and I felt defeated.

"Don't worry, Gloria. I'll be there in a minute," I reassured her, giving her a warm smile that softened her tired eyes. "You look simply radiant ma. Mr. Dé Leon is a lucky man," Gloria beamed, making my heart flutter with venom. "Thank you, Gloria. You're too kind," I replied, feeling my cheeks flush with gratitude as she closed the door behind her.

After gathering my thoughts once more, I finally gained the courage to step out of the room. Every step felt like a journey towards my destiny, the moment I would say "I do" and start anew.

I tightly held the bouquet, too nervous to look at the crowd. The song Le Cygne played added to my anxiety. The doors opened slowly, showing the way to my future husband. Grzegorz warned me not to make any mistakes with a threatening touch on my arm.

I felt scared and anxious as I walked down the dark aisle. The guests were talking quietly, but I tried to stay strong and keep my composure.

I focused my attention on the bouquet that I'm clutching tightly between my hands as I felt tears building in my eyes. The hum of the music mocked the pain burning in my chest, and my throat tightens from the tense moment among the people.

This day was meant to be a joyful celebration of love, but instead, I feel overwhelmed by sadness and the loss of my freedom. As Grzegorz takes my hand, lifts my veil, and kisses my forehead, I fight the urge to pull away. The sensation of violation consumes me, making it hard to contain my emotions. Suddenly, Saint appears and guides me with a supportive arm around me as we approach the priest.

But inside, I am falling apart.

"Today, we come together to witness the holy bond between Saint Dé Leon and Irena Rabia Nowak," the priest announces.

I hear a fuzzy hum in my ears despite the words being spoken. Time passes as my heart beats. The seconds slip away like sand through an hourglass.

I look at my partner, and tears blur my vision. The world fades into shadow as my heart aches. My stomach tightens, tears roll down my cheeks, and my breathing becomes fast and harsh.

I focus on the man standing before me.

Saint.

The way the light plays on the scar that stretches across his face amplifies his already daunting aura.

Realisation dawns on me in that moment—I am responsible for that scar. The priest's voice breaks my trance-like state, and I hear him utter the words that shake me to the core.

"Saint, repeat after me."

"I, Saint Dé Leon, take thee, Irena Rabia Nowak, to be my wedded wife, to have and to hold, for poorer, for richer, in sickness and in health, to love and cherish. Till death do us part."

As he finishes, he seems threatening, and I feel like he's making a dark promise. I can't imagine following through with it. His intense gaze and harsh appearance make him seem dangerous. Tears fall down my face as I stand at the altar, feeling his stare as a heavy burden. I know he enjoys my suffering and wants to make my life miserable. The priest's words make me feel trapped in a spell, causing me to recite vows that will forever bind me to this man.

Saint's eyes glinted with an emotion I couldn't discern as I uttered the fateful words, "Till death do us part."

His silence hangs heavy in the air, a question hovering between us. "Do you take Irena Rabia Nowak as your wife?" the priest repeats, breaking the silence.

We're frozen in time for a moment, staring at each other. I can feel his gaze boring into me, searching for something I can't quite name. And then, with a slow nod, he speaks the words that will seal both our fates.

"I do."

"I do."

The holy man raised his voice, his words ringing with finality, "I now declare you husband and wife! Amen!"

The congregation cheered as my new husband, Saint, touched my shoulders and kissed me. The tears dried and I felt mixed emotions, including fury and disgust. Saint noticed my reaction and looked at me curiously.

"Smile, Doe; I wouldn't want everyone to notice that the bride is in a sour mood," he murmured, enfolding his arm around my waist.

I recoiled with rage, shaking off his touch. "Don't you dare touch me," I spat at him. Saint arched an eyebrow, looking amused.

"Well, well, the little bird does have a voice," he teases. "Burn in hell," I fumed, turning to leave him waiting at the altar, unfazed by the attention from everyone.

All I wanted at that moment was to escape, to be as far away from the crowd as possible.

Especially from my new husband.

CHAPTER 5

IRENA NOWAK

"Drink. You look tense." Saint's honeyed voice caresses my ears like a lullaby, as he slides me his drink.

Cast in a sea of jabbering guests, I feel choked.

"I hate these things," I remark coldly, relishing the stony look on Saint's face.

"Why are you staying if this lifestyle is such an agony to you? You could run away," he said calmly.

My lips pressed together as I looked at him intently. "It's not that easy, Saint. I don't have the luxury like you do."

Without paying attention to his retort, I snatched the drink from his hands and downed it in one swift gulp. The burning sensation trickled down my neck, and I savoured every bit of it. Crossing my arms, I continued to glare at the guests, ignoring Saint's presence.

Awkward silence loomed over us as we sat at the bridal table, staring at the folks who attended this cursed wedding. Suddenly, a male voice exclaimed,

"There's the star of the night!" I turned to look at Saint, only to find a man with a beaming smile headed our way.

His shiny hair is slicked back, highlighting his captivating green eyes, which exude confidence. His strong jawline and light facial hair make him look a lot like Saint, showing they are related.

"That's my younger brother, Abel," Saint tells me quietly as Abel approaches.

Abel greets Saint and tries to kiss my cheek, I avoid it, confusing him. I feel uncomfortable as I nervously wet my lips with my tongue.

"I'm a germaphobe," I mumble sheepishly while Abel stares at me dumbfounded.

And all the while, I feel Saint's watchful gaze fixed on me with a solid intensity.

Abel's attention shifted sharply as he turned to Saint, his once-soft features distorted into a stern mask. "What's the matter?"

"I need to speak with you in private," Abel declares before turning to me. "Don't worry sis, I'll bring him back."

Saint stood up, adjusting his tie tightly before walking away. I'm now alone at the imposing dining table, boredly fiddling with my fork.

With a deep sigh, I muttered, "I can't wait to die on my bed after this."

I lounged in my own company, then noticed Grzegorz sauntering my way. His fake smile is ready to deceive anyone. Playing out an Iago if you ask me.

His fixed gaze however betrayed his intentions as he stopped right in front of me and clenched his jaw.

"Where's Saint?" he inquired.

I glared at him, my voice dripping with animosity. "He's not here, so go bother someone else." Grzegorz's grip on his wine glass tightened as his jaw twitched.

"Irena," he warned, inching closer to me. I couldn't help but roll my eyes. "I don't know where he is," I emphasised bluntly.

He lowered to my face, his breath spraying alcohol fumes at me. "Listen here girl, if you don't tell me where Saint is, I will-" My eyes went wide when Grzegorz was snatched away from me by his neck.

"You must have some massive balls to threaten my wife," Saint warned softly.

Yet his eyes, dark and penetrating, promised a level of violence that would make the bravest man tremble.

Saint leaned in, everyone around us forming a semicircle as they witnessed the sight unfolding.

"Threaten her again, and I will show you just how little those fat fingers of yours matter," It was then that I realized something that chilled me even more.

Saint did not merely tolerate pain-he relished it, revelled in it. The knowledge that he enjoyed the sight of suffering made my heart stutter and my palms slick with sweat.

The memory of that night in the study two months ago still terrifies me. I remember how he held my neck tightly and seemed to enjoy feeling my pulse. When I tried to fight back, he seemed pleased by my pain.

That event was a near death experience for me and this man found pleasure in it.

Talk about disturbing.

Now, as I see him threatening Grzegorz with a disturbing look in his eyes, I am disgusted and afraid. The idea that he finds pleasure in causing harm sends chills down my spine.

Saint is a sadist.

The darkness within him is far more twisted than I ever imageable.

"I wasn't threatening her. I-I was asking for you," Grzegorz stammered, his voice quivering. "Saint, back off," I ordered, guarding Grzegorz from further harm.

Although I would pay a million bucks to see my uncle suffer. I am just helping myself for future outcomes because I know my uncle would not let this slide, "I told you to let him go." I seethed.

The hush of onlookers lingered in the air, witnessing our intense confrontation. Saint readjusted his jacket and struck him across the face, causing him to fall onto the tiled floor, blood spewing from his mouth.

"But I did let him go," he teased. "Saint, he's my uncle!" I howled in anger.

Great, now I'm going to pay the consequences in the future.

Saint loomed over me; his presence almost suffocating. I couldn't help but inhale his intoxicating scent, a heady blend of spicy smoke and musk. My mouth watered, and I fought to keep composure under his intense gaze. His eyes darkened, and he spoke with a low, dangerous edge. "I do not like him, and no one threatens my wife and lives to see another day."

I trembled slightly, caught off guard by his sudden protectiveness. But before I could reply, he added, "And don't you fucking dare raise your voice at me Irena."

Saint silenced my protest with a swift glare, his stern gaze enough to make my words wither away on my tongue. He acted fast, shedding his jacket and draping it over me, shielding me from the icy air. I couldn't help but notice how he seemed to avoid any contact with my skin.

"Let's go," his voice cut through the tense atmosphere, commanding me to follow him. I took one last look at Grzegorz, sprawled on the floor, and fought the urge to laugh.

With a shaky breath, I stepped behind Saint as we made our way out of the ballroom. The weight of countless eyes followed us, and their judgement was palpable.

I cleared my throat nervously. Stepping into the bitter winter air of Poland, I pulled Saint's coat closer around me, his scent invading my nose. The sky above was a vast expanse of midnight blue, with twinkling stars that seemed to dance and a bright moon that shone like a heavenly eye.

We were met by two muscle-bound guards.

One had long, flowing hair styled in a risky mullet, while the other boasted a wild mane of ginger curls. "Your flight to French Polynesia is ready, sir," the ginger-haired guard announced, his Irish accent adding a hint of charm to his words. Saint quickly took charge, pulling out his phone and issuing orders.

"Take Mrs. Dé Leon with you," he instructed. "I have some important business to attend to, but I'll catch up with you later."

"One last thing. Don't touch her."

My eyebrows furrow in response to his declaration, a subtle sign that he remembers the smallest details about me. Of course, it's not every day that you confess to being a germaphobe to someone you barely know. But as far as he's concerned, I'm a woman who values hygiene above all else. Little does he know; it is just a white lie, covering the abuse that I endured.

As we stand there, two powerful SUVs glide up, bringing two of Saint's most reliable and trusted men. His voice cuts through the air before I can process what's happening. "Noel and Tyler will keep you safe. We'll meet at the airport," he assures me, not giving me a chance to argue. And just like that, he's gone, leaving me in wonder as the car carrying him disappears.

"Let's go, Mrs. Dé Leon," the brunette guard enunciated, trying to take charge of the situation. I can't help but scrunch my nose at how he addresses me. Who knew that a simple title could be so off-putting? "I am Tyler, and that is Noel."

"Nice to meet you, Tyler," I say with a gentle tilt of my head. On the other hand, Noel shuffled eyerolls like a deck of cards before climbing into the vehicle. "Enough with the tea party manners, let's go," he barked, slamming the door.

Tyler coughs apologetically to break the ice. "Don't take him personally. He's about as sociable as a brick wall," I slide into the backseat, gratefully thanking him as I fasten my safety belt. As Tyler takes his spot, Noel abandons the curb and peels out of the parking lot. With a heavy sigh, I glance at the towering brick building. It represented one of my worst days ever. I relax my shoulders and rest my tired head on the cool glass window, hoping for a brief break. Soon, I drift off to sleep, seeking temporary escape from my troubles.

CHAPTER 6

IRENA NOWAK

My eyes slowly opened as a loud noise interrupted my sleep.

I covered my face to block out the light and yawned. Noel held the door open as I got out of the vehicle. My heart raced as Tyler appeared next to me, pointing to a fancy jet in the distance.

"Mr. Dé Leon awaits your arrival," he announced solemnly. Nodding, I thanked the watchful guards and followed the crew member into the private jet.

The luxury inside the airplane made me feel like I was in a different world. The plush leather seats, shiny floors, and elegant wood walls created a lavish atmosphere. The gentle lighting added to the opulence. Despite being impressed by the surroundings, a familiar scent caught my attention.

"I didn't ask for a drink," I uttered, my eyes still fixed on the outside world.

"I'm aware, but your expression told me otherwise," he remarked bluntly, causing me to roll my eyes in annoyance. "Why did you lie?"

With a furrowed brow, I turned to face him, ready to end this conversation. "What?" I asked, my mind racing with questions. Saint shot me a sly glance before speaking, casting a shadow over our once playful banter. "At the wedding, you disrespected my brother," he said, his words sharp and calculated.

My arms wrapped tightly around me. I licked my lips nervously, taken aback by his sudden coldness. "What are you talking about?"

With a slow and deliberate sip of his drink, Saint's eyes never left mine.

"You know exactly what I'm talking about, Irena," he said, his tone heavy with disappointment. "If we want this marriage to work, we need to be honest with each other. And your behaviour is going to be a problem."

"You'll have to be more specific, Saint."

"You avoided my brother's greeting at the wedding," he said, his voice carrying a sense of curiosity. "I told you already, I'm a germaphobe." He raised an eyebrow, sceptical. "You call yourself a germaphobe, yet you had no problems drinking from my glass earlier." He set the drinking glass on the table and began loosening his tie. "So, what is going on, petite biche?"

Nervously, I tucked a strand of hair behind my ear and looked away. His gaze was intimidating, to say the least. "I just don't like being touched," I murmured. He leaned in, his voice deepening with interest. "Why not?" I shut down the conversation as quickly as it had started. "I just don't like it," I snapped, my thoughts lingering on my previous husband and the abuse I had endured at his hands. Saint's piercing gaze met mine, and I lost myself again in his striking features. His scar only added to his rugged allure.

"You like pain," I blurted out, my eyes locked on his. He took a long sip from his glass, his jaw tight with frustration. "Who said I like pain?" he retorted; his voice laced with annoyance.

With a scoff and eye roll, I brush off his question. "Saint, do not mistake my appearance for ignorance. Remember our first encounter when you nearly killed me? It is that very moment that defines you-"

"I did not *almost* kill you, Irena. Don't insult me like that; I was simply putting you to sleep." He shrugs.

Putting me to sleep while crushing my windpipe? *He cannot be serious.*

I looked at the intimidating person in front of me and felt disgusted and angry. I decided I wouldn't stay near him. I unbuckled my seatbelt and walked to the other end of the plane, looking for a way out.

I found a seat far away from him.

It was time to assert my strength and independence. This man might be my supposed "better half," but he couldn't control me like a puppet on a string.

I deserved more than that. I deserved respect, adoration, love, everything that bubbled inside me but it all withered in his presence.

He might be a ruthless mobster, but I wouldn't let that diminish the fire within me. Not now, not ever. And so I vowed to stand up to this bully - not just for myself, but for every woman who had been burned by toxic masculinity. History would not repeat itself.

Not again.

Someday, Saint will wake up and realise that I am not some meek little housewife to be bossed around.

"You are something else, Irena," he states, his voice grating on my nerves. I try to ignore him, but he continues to loom over me, taking a seat with all the grace of a bull in a China shop. "I don't want you here," I spit out, my patience wearing thin. A wicked glint flashes in his eyes.

"People who give me attitude tend to end up with broken bones," he warns. "Well, I guess I'm lucky then," I spit back, refusing to be intimidated.

"Should I also get on my knees and start thanking you like some god for your generous offer not to fracture my bones?"

Saint's jaw tightened as he impatiently flicked back his unruly hair. "I'm trying to have a civilised conversation with you, but you're acting like an obnoxious child," he growled with frustration.

Huffing incredulously, I shot him a withering look. "Do you ever stop to think that I didn't sign up for this? That there is nothing in this world that would make me want to be married to you?

Nothing! But here we are, and I am stuck in this arrangement.

So, pardon me Saint almighty if I'm not skipping around, singing your praises. You want me to kiss your ass just because we're married? Fine. But don't expect me to be happy about it. Because none of this makes me happy!"

Hot tears split down my cheeks as I vented my frustrations, betraying my true emotions. Saint observed me in silence, his expression unreadable.

I quickly wiped away the evidence of my vulnerability, refusing to meet his gaze.

As I sat there, broken and messed up, I couldn't help but feel embarrassed when his eyes met mine. My heart ached with shame as I whispered, "Ju-just leave me alone." At that moment, all I wanted was to curl up and die.

Without a word, Saint rose from his seat and walked away, leaving me to drown in my feelings.

CHAPTER 7

IRENA NOWAK

The journey to Bora Bora was daunting. The atmosphere on the plane was tense, with the cabin crew ignoring me. Even Saint stayed away, but his presence felt ominous. When our eyes met, it was like looking into a mystery I couldn't figure out. His pull on me was like the moon's gravity, making me feel stuck in my emotions.

As the plane landed, I felt the warmth of the sun through the window. Stepping outside, a warm breeze made me shiver. I saw a black Mercedes pull up, and a man in a tuxedo with buzzed hair got out. He smelled like woodsy cologne. As I approached him, his mysterious words intrigued me.

"By the way, you're not as ignorant as you claim yourself to be," Saint said in a deep voice, striding past me to the waiting car. My eyes never left him until he disappeared inside, leaving me to ponder the mysteries ahead.

Absorbed in a web of emotions, I instinctively climb into Saint's car. Before I realise it, I'm already sitting in the passenger seat, slamming the door shut without a second thought.

As the engine roars to life under Saint's control, I feel the power coursing through the car. Without a word, he shifts gears and starts down the road, leaving me to brood in silence.

My mind is fogged by anger, fear, and regret, making it impossible to express my thoughts without consequence.

So, I choose to keep my mouth shut and bear the ride.

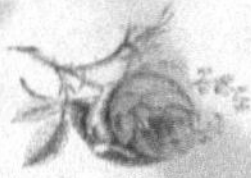

The sky has transformed, a mesmerizing blend of midnight blue merging into burnt amber.

After a long, winding drive, we finally arrived at our destination. As we stepped foot onto the resort, I followed Saint, who led me to his private yacht. My heart raced with excitement and anticipation.

As the pristine sail unfolds and rises higher, the water sparkles and casts a bewitching glow. The breeze sweeps through my hair while my dress gently sways to its rhythm. Suddenly, Saint appears beside me, offering a chilled martini. I accepted it without a word, my eyes glued to the skyline.

I felt the weight of his gaze on me, but I couldn't bring myself to look at him.

Although my instincts told me to flee, my feet felt as though they were rooted to the ground. I watched as the yacht groaned and heaved, launching itself off the dry dock and into the ocean's depths, its bow cutting through the waves with a sharp and urgent grace. With a martini, I rested my elbow on the edge of the yacht. Where I sat on the couch.

Suddenly, I blurted out a question. "Why did you marry me?"

He lowered his gaze, studying me carefully as he weighed his response. After a moment of silence, he finally replied.

"I didn't have a choice," he said, causing my brow to furrow in confusion. "What do you mean?" I pressed, but Saint remained silent.

With narrowed eyes, I tore my gaze away from him, intent on soaking up the awe-inspiring scenery. A gentle breeze worked through my hair, kissing my face with a chilly nip.

But my attention was divided. His silence was debatable, refusing to spin out his intentions like a spider's web. It was as if he had buried his truth beyond my reach.

Saint: the enigmatic French don.

"You said lies would fail us," I spoke, my voice trailing off before adding firmly. "I say it's secrets."

Without another word, I spun on my heel and strode off.

As we arrived at our secluded retreat, Saint graciously ushered our suitcases into the Waterhouse lodge.

Once inside, I was immediately overcome with a serene aura soaking every inch of the hut. The sweet fragrance of vanilla infused the air, causing me to let out a contented sigh as I admired the furnishings and the surrounding natural elements.

I kicked off my heels and walked towards the bedroom. As I pushed open the door, a gasp escaped my lips. The sight before me was breathtaking and unsettling - the bed was overdone with a blanket of red petals, and a chilled bottle of champagne, complete with two wine glasses, sat expectantly on the dresser. But as the realisation washed over me, a sudden panic set in.

There was only one bed—

Of course there was only one bed, this is your honeymoon.

But the mere thought of sharing a bed with Saint sends shivers down my spine.

It's been far too long since I've slept beside anyone. The last time was with Viktor when he took my celibacy. After that, Viktor and I slept in separate rooms. I couldn't bear being near that monster, not even in his slumber. After all the horrors and evils, he tautened upon me during our marriage, I couldn't trust him.

But now, as I enter the room and spot my suitcase beside the bed, I realise there's no avoiding it.

I can feel dryness in my mouth, like sandpaper scraping against my tongue. I know what I have to do.

I'll have to sleep on the couch. I drop my shoes by the door and kneel before the suitcase, unzipping it and pulling out my white lace robe. I let it rest on the bed before slipping out of my clothing, leaving me in just my lacy bra and panties. As I unclip my bra, my shoulders relax in sweet relief when my full breasts fall into their natural, comfortable drop. They're not too big or small, just perfect.

With a deep breath, I tie the robe securely around my body. I run my fingers through my hair and gently massage my scalp, hoping it will ease my stress.

My hair is naturally curly due to my African roots, but my uncles forced me to straighten it, saying that it makes me look more appealing. Now that they are technically out of my life, I'll return my hair to its natural state.

I walk over to the glass window and slide the door open, stepping out of the room as the ocean breeze tickles my skin. I inhale deeply. Silently enjoying my own company, drowning in the darkness of the night.

CHAPTER 8

SAINT DÉ LEON

A vicious spark ignites my blood.

Her Amazonian figure sat well on her pear-shaped body. Her skin is the hues of the rich oak in spring rains. Her thick median arched brows eased down gently to her languid eyelashes of velvet-black followed by her adorable bulb nose resting on her face. Her full two toned lips positively drooled with goodness. Her hair is a glorious tumble of light upon the night sea. Black strands glowing like a sweet poet's ink and quill and her virility-brown eyes set my heart a thump.

Christ, Irena was carefully built with perfection. Not a single flaw in sight.

As I lean against the door frame, I quietly watch. She unclips her bra, slipping the straps off her shoulders then tossing the bra onto the bed. My gaze admiringly lingers on her full breasts. The itching urge to reach out and hold them, suck them; the feeling is tormenting me. Irena slips her night gown on then walks over to the glass window, sliding it open as she steps outside.

I ran my fingers through my hair, letting out a breath I did not know I was holding up until she left the room. Without thinking I find myself removing my shirt before accompanying her outside. When I appeared beside Irena she didn't bother to look my way as her gaze was glued onto the midnight ocean. The moonlight's shine kissing the waters as it glimmers like crystal dancing and twinkling all about.

It is clear as day that Irena is not so fond of me. I do not blame her. I'm not so fond of myself either.

Wind swept across the ocean with a bold honesty. The smell of Irena's sweetness gently caressed the tip of my nose, my hand tightening against the wooden rails. Instantly I grow addicted to the scent. Turning to face her. Irena's skin glows under the moonlight like a dream.

She pulls her bottom lip between her teeth briefly. "How long are we staying here?"

I inhale a lungful of the salty air. "One week." I answer. My eyes still fixed on her.

I'm staring at her like she's one of the most interesting art works at a museum on display but she's not one of them. She is the only one.

Her quietness draws my attention like she's the only woman I've ever seen in my life. Her beauty is breathtaking. A mixture of her Polish side and African roots make a great combination enhancing her features.

"So it will be one full week of you staring at me like a creep?" She pointed out. "Hmm." I trail off.

A light breeze tosses her hair across one eye and a violent need to reach out and sweep it aside, to let my fingers taste her skin. Stirs in my veins.

"Irena." Her name is a guttural command that gains her full attention.

She raises her face towards mine, her chest rising and falling with control breaths. "Are you afraid of me?" I inquired my brows knitted together, staring into those hues of brown eyes that have now darkened due to no natural light.

She doesn't respond immediately. Silence spills between us as she disappears somewhere inside herself. Again, I'm tempted to explore her mind. The famished hunger disgustingly grows in me. Consuming me with each passing second. I want to explore the parts of her that she keeps hidden.

The deepest darkest parts.

I want its secrets.

Finally, she opens her mouth and says, "I'm not afraid of you Saint." Nervousness drips from her sweet-like voice.

She pulls her bottom lip between her teeth, a subconscious act I've picked up on her when she is nervous, anxious and scared or all of the above.

I take a step closer to her, my towering height casting a shadow over her small figure compared to mine.

Her eyes flash a glimpse of fear. My eyes darted to her neck witnessing her pulse thumping against her flesh like the rhythm of her heart beat I wish to hear.

My fragile little doe.

Reaching my left hand out, Irena tries to step back but I'm quick to grab a fistful of her hair, a small whimper escapes her lips. Pulling her closer towards me but not to close where we touch. Leaning in, I take a whiff of her divine scent. Honey and vanilla.

Dear God, this woman smells mouthwatering. *Literally.*

Her eyes grow wide in fear, lips parted as her breath quickens.

"Why do you lie Irena?" I question softly. Staring into the depths of her soul.

She remains silent.

Why does she do that?

Is it her way of self-defence, when she feels threatened, her body freezes and she becomes mute.

"Are you afraid of me?" I asked again, this time my voice was low. Annoyance spilling out into the crack of my bones.

My grip tightened, tugging her hair harder as her head was slightly jerked back, her neck fully exposed to me. "Are you afraid of me to the point where touching you like this makes you sick to the stomach."

"Come on, tell me." I whisper, voice low and deliberate, the words coiling around her like smoke. "Does being this close make your lungs forget how to breathe? Stomach twisting like it's trying to crawl out of you? That fragile little heart of yours pounding so hard I can almost hear the cracks forming in your ribs." I inch closer, my breath ghosting over her skin, just shy of contact. "Your mouth's gone dry, hasn't it? Swallowing feels like sand. Hands slick, body trembling… like a rabbit caught in the wolf's jaw." My lips hover at her neck, cold and patient. "Tell me, little doe…do I make you feel like you're about to die?"

Her snap of anger disappeared in a blink of an eye. I see fear harboured behind her large brown eyes. She doesn't want to be afraid of me but she can't contain her emotions.

She's so transparent and raw with her emotions. I fucking love it.

Tugging her head further back I whisper. "Answer me."

Tears welled up in her eyes, she blinked then it slipped out of her eyes caressing down her cheek, a shock of heat licked my skin when my gaze silently followed the movement of her tears.

I felt the hairs of my neck lift away from my skin, darting my tongue out my subconscious takes over as I lick her tears away, the taste of salt lingers on my tongue. Irena shuts her eyes , her body quivering in fear. The sight of her trembling sent a twisted apprehension sinking down to my bones.

"Y-You're sick." She managed to say through her uneven breaths.

I've been called worse my little doe.

A charged pulse ignites a fire beneath my palm. The air, volatile and tense, suspends time for a mere blink, allowing my body to ravenously absorb the feel of her where I've only permitted my eyes to touch. Letting her go she stumbles back, glaring at me while her arms are wrapped around herself as a way of shielding herself from me.

The fear in her eyes. She's looking at me like I'm some sort of monster awakening from her nightmares as a child, yet there's something else...

Irena shakes her head in disbelief, with one quick glance she scatters back into the room, my eyes following her every move until she's no longer in the eyes view.

My breath stalls, every nerve in my body cored tight. The thought of her makes me feral. Even her name. Her sweet, delicate name chants in my head like a forbidden promise.

Irena.

Irena.

Irena...

Irena. Irena. Irena. Irena. Irena. Irena. Irena. Irena. Irena. Irena. Irena. Irena.
Irena. Irena. Irena. Irena. Irena. Irena. Irena. Irena. Irena. Irena. Irena. Irena.
Irena. Irena. Irena. Irena. Irena. Irena. Irena. Irena. Irena. Irena. Irena. Irena.
Irena. Irena. Irena. Irena. Irena. Irena. Irena. Irena. Irena. Irena. Irena. Irena.
rena. Irena. Irena. Irena. Irena. Irena. Irena. Irena. Irena. Irena. Irena. Iren
Irena. Irena. Irena. Irena. Irena. Irena. Irena. Irena. Irena. Irena. Irena. Iren
Irena. Irena. Irena. Irena. Irena. Irena. Irena. Irena. Irena. Irena. Irend. Iren
Irena. Irena. Irena. Irena. Irena. Irena. Irena. Irena. Irena. Irena. Irena. Iren
Irena. Irena. Irena. Irena. Irena. Irena. Irena. rena. Irena. Irena. Irena. Iren
Irena. Irena. Irena. Irena. Irena. Irena. Irena. Irena. Irena. Irena. Irena. Iren
Irena. Irena. Irena. Irena. Irena. Irena. Irena. Irena. Irena. Irena. Irena. Iren
Irena. Irena. Irena. Irena. Irena. Irena. Irena. Irena. Irena. Irena. Irena. Iren
Irena. Irena. Irena. Irena. Irena. Irena. Irena. Irena. Irena. Irena. Irena. Iron
Irena. Irena. Irena. Irena. Irena. Irena. Irena. Irena. Irena. Irena. Irena. Iren
Irena. Irena. Irena. Irena. Irena. Irena. Irena. Irena. Irena. Irena. Irena. Iren
Irena. Irena. Irena. Irena. Irena. Irena. Irena. Irena. Irena. Irena. Irena. Iren
rena. Irena. Irena. Irena. Irena. Irena. Irena. Irena. Irena. Irena. Irena. Iren
Irena. Irena. Irena. Irena. Irena. Irena. Irena. Irena. Irena. Irena. Irena. Iren
Irena. Irena. Irena. Irena. Irena. Irena. Irena. Irena. Irena. Irena. Irena. Iren
Irena. Irena. Irena. Irena. Irena. Irena. Irena. Irena. Irena. Irena. Irena. Iren
Irena. Irena. Irena. Irena. Irena. Irena. Irena. rena. Irena. Irena. Irena. Iren
Irena. Irena. Irena. Irena. Irena. Irena. Irena. Irena. Irena. Irena. Irena. Iren
Irena. Irena. Irena. Irena. Irena. Irena. Irena. Irena. Irena. Irena. Irena. Iren
Irena. Irena. Irena. Irena. Irena. Irena. Irena. Irena. Irena. Irena. Irena. Iren
Irena. Irena. Irena. Irena. Irena. Irena. Irena. Irena. Irena. Irena. Irena. Ire
rena. rena. Irena. Irena. Irena. Irena. Irena. Irena. Irena. Irena. Irena. Ire
Irena. Irena. Irena. Irena. Irena. Irena. Irena. Irena. Irena. Irena. Irena. Iren
Irena. Irena. Irena. Irena. Irena. Irena. Irena. Irena. Irena. Irena. Irena. Iren
Irena. Irena. Irena. Irena. Irena. Irena. Irena. Irena. Irena. Irena. Irena. Iren
Irena. Irena. Irena. Irena. Irena. Irena. Irena. Irena. rena. Irena. Irena. Iren
Irena. Irena. Irena. Irena. Irena. Irena. Irena. Irena. Irena. Irena. Irena. Iren
Irena. Irena. Irena. Irena. Irena. Irena. Irena. Irena. Irena. Irena. Irena. Iren

Fucking Irena.
The name echoes in my head like a mantra, driving me insane with longing and frustration.

My patience with her is on thin ice. The destructive urge to ruin her innocent nature is growing stronger, deeper, hungrier.

I want to ruin her, bit by bit like a hungry dog chewing on his bone with no mercy until there is nothing left to save for later.

I burn with an insatiable hunger to break her.

IRENA NOWAK

I feel like my heart is racing and my veins are on fire, causing me intense pain. I struggle to breathe, and my chest is heavy with anxiety. I feel like I'm being tortured by something unseen, pushing me to the edge of my sanity. I feel dread as I walk to the bathroom and cry while throwing up. I can't hold back my inner turmoil as memories from my past flood my mind.

Putting on my apron like the dutiful wife I am. I'm excited to surprise Viktor with a cake. We've had some arguments recently, but I am determined to make things right. With our first anniversary and his birthday approaching, I've decided to start fresh and move past any past disagreements. What better way to do that than with a delicious cake that can help mend any lingering animosity? As the sweet smell of butter wafts from the oven, I focus on decorating the cake.

I even added the number 30 as a tribute to his age.

Out of nowhere, the front door bursts open, and within five swift steps, I can hear his heavy footsteps approaching the kitchen. He wasn't supposed to be back for at least another hour!

My excitement quickly turns to panic, my heart racing as I frantically hide the decorations in the cabinets.

Crap, the cake isn't ready yet.

Taking a deep breath, I carefully slide my hand under the freshly baked cake, lifting it off the counter with anticipation. It's a secret I must keep a little while longer. As I cautiously make my way towards the fridge, keeping an eye out for him, an unexpected obstacle appears before me. I collide with someone, and my precious cake is crushed under their designer clothes.

My heart plummeted in my chest. How was I going to hide the cake now?

A chill rippled through me when I gazed up at him, rendering me frozen in his icy glare.

His clenched jaw and seething fury consumed everything around him at the speed of light. "I-I'm sorry, Viktor," I stammered, my heart pounding in my ears. But his wrath burned brighter than the sun. "You fucking dumb woman! Do you not have eyes?" he bellowed, making me shrink back in terror. "This suit. Do you understand how much it costs!?"

With a violent shove, he sent me hurtling toward the oven, and the sharp handle dug into my back, stealing my breath away. I fought back tears, begging my eyes not to betray me.

Not now, not in front of him.

I couldn't risk upsetting him any further than he already was. My heart sank as I watched Viktor smugly toss his jacket onto the marble countertop. His piercing gaze met mine, and I knew I was in trouble. Tears streamed down my face, I hastily attempted to wipe them away before he noticed them but it was too late.

"Are you crying?" He scoffed, the corners of his mouth turning up in a cruel smile. I shook my head, my eyes downcast before I scrambled to clean up the mess of the ruined cake.

Suddenly, his shoes came into view, his hand grasping my chin roughly. "You ruin my suit, and you are fucking crying!" His voice was low and menacing.

With trembling lips, I tried to explain. "It was not my intention; I-I just wanted to do something nice for your birthday." But my words were lost in a sea of tears that never ended.

"My day was already fucked up, and I come home to a brat called my wife," he hissed, his grip on my chin tightening. I couldn't bear to look at him any longer and turned away, feeling defeated and small.

With a dry laugh, Viktor shakes his head and grins maliciously.

"Oh, I'll give you something to fucking cry about."

The next thing I know, he's yanking me by the hair, dragging me out of the kitchen like a rag doll. I struggle to break free, but his grip is unyielding, and he easily pulls me along.

When we reach the living room, I try to plead with him, but my terror-filled voice falls on deaf ears. "Please, Viktor, don't do this, I said sorry, I'll clean up your suit or even buy you a new one!" I whimper. But he slams me onto the couch, cutting off my words with a fierce slap across the head.

I scoot away from him as fast as I can, but his strong grip latches on my ankle, dragging me back towards him. I scream and struggle; my prostrate form remains transfixed on the ground, tears spilling in a steady waterfall down my face.

The coldness in his eyes sends chills down my spine, and my hair stands on end like spikes.

As the fabric rips apart, a blood-curdling sound screeches through my ears, making me freeze. There it is, the ruin of my dress, exposing my chest to the wind and the merciless gaze of Viktor. He hovers over me like a vulture, his eyes darkening and his tongue flicking over his lips with a pang of predatory hunger. Tears prick my eyes and I realise what's about to happen. But he's not done with me yet.

"You wanted to do something nice for me, didn't you?"

He purrs with twisted, mocking humour. I feel bile rising in my throat. My lips tremble as I try to answer. But he cuts me off with a mocking, condescending tone.

"Be a good little bitch of a wife, keep quiet, and be still." His words slither over me like a snake's venom, making me feel weak and powerless.

And then I hear the sound of a zipper, and my heart nearly stops.

Oh no. Not him. Not now. Not like this.

But I'm frozen, helpless, and at his mercy. Images flipping in my head, again and again. His face, his twisted voice, his rough hands, his dirty mouth, his cold body. I cannot bear it anymore.

I want to scream, I want to run, I want to fight back. But there is nothing I can do.

He has me in his grasp, and I am his toy to play with, destroy, use, and abuse.

I shut my eyes tight, preparing myself for what will happen next.

Seeking revenge against my oppressor brought me a sense of peace, but some might wonder why I didn't speak up earlier. The reality is it was not a straightforward decision. When I initially sought help from my uncles, they disregarded my suffering and chose to believe the false claims of my abuser. This abandonment was shattering, but I now understand that my feelings are a result of a society that distorts standards for women. I refuse to be confined by this society and opt to transcend societal norms. Instead of succumbing to harmful impulses, I am resolute in creating a new path filled with optimism, resilience, and self-compassion.

As a woman, I've been conditioned to hide certain behaviours, but I'm aware that society holds women to different standards than men.

Despite this, I'll continue to fight for equality and make my voice heard, even if it echoes in empty halls.

CHAPTER 9

IRENA NOWAK

I've been avoiding him for the past 3 days.

Call me crazy, but I can't be around a man who makes me feel some type of way. I don't like the way he makes me feel, I don't like how he finds joy in my suffering.

The way my heart speeds up, thumping like thunder against my chest, the way my hairs on the back of my neck rise, the way goosebumps travel all over my body, how I forget to breath, to speak, to move.

I don't like it at all. So the best way to avoid the feeling is to keep distance from Saint.

I felt like all eyes were on me as Saint and I sat quietly at our breakfast table. It's a special occasion where couples that are on their honeymoon have an all eat breakfast buffet.

All I took was an apple, pomegranate seeds and pineapple slices. I was not in the mood for anything heavy. Saint was the opposite. He filled his plate with two croissants, strawberries and a bowl of Greek yogurt with a cup of black coffee. *Just like his soul.*

This is the closest I've been to Saint. When it's time for bedtime. I sleep on the couch and he sleeps in the master bedroom. The first night he noticed how I didn't sleep in the same bed with him but he didn't bother to comment on it. Which I'm glad for.

Since it's our 4th day here Saint and I have to attend this evening party that's happening. I tried to avoid it but it's one of the things that comes with the honeymoon specialties.

So yay me.

I take a bite of my apple, a phone alerts us and my gaze lifts up to Saint's.

He sets down his cup of coffee then he reaches in his pocket, pulling out his phone. He looks at the screen before he steals one quick glance at me then answers, placing the device on his ear so that he can hear.

"Ne vous ai-je pas dit de ne pas appeler pendant ma lune de miel?" The way his voice lowers as he speaks his mother tongue language. It's deep and silky, the tone of his voice kissing each nerve in my body. Blessing my ears.

No, stop it Irena.

I must admit…Saint sounds hot when he speaks French.

I push back the unwanted thoughts of Saint, clearing my throat as my gaze falls back onto my plate whilst my ears are mainly focused on the conversation even though I have no idea what he is saying.

Silent spills between us as he listens to the other person over the phone.

I take another bite of my apple, lifting my gaze once more to catch Saint staring at me while he listens to his caller.

"She's here with me, biting into her apple." He lets out casually, purposely speaking English so that I can understand. I dart my tongue out, licking my lips nervously before biting into the apple and placing it back onto the plate.

Saint lifts his mini coffee mug, his lips touching the rim of the cup as he sips the hot bitter beverage, staring deep into my soul, reading me like an open book full of unsolved mysteries.

Now, I've realized that there are two paths with my feelings towards Saint.

No. 1 Kill him.

No. 2 Fuck him.

Or maybe both.

Yes he is an asshole but his assholeness is what makes me want to know more about him and I'm scared of him, terrified but also intrigued.

Does that make me okay to even think about such?

"Call me back in an hour." He declares before hanging up, placing his phone back into his pocket.

I have the itching urge to ask him who was on the phone but managed to bite down the curious question.

"You can't ignore me forever Irena." He suddenly blurts out catching my attention. I opened my mouth to bite back at him but closed them again, slouching in my chair then picking at the pomegranate seeds.

I'm self-aware that I am acting like a stubborn child. But do I need to remind you that he licked my tears away…

Who on earth does that?

"No matter how hard you fight it. You and I both know that you can't." He adds, like pouring gas into an outraged fire purposely wanting it to grow. Destroy and corrupt anything in its path.

That's exactly what Saint is doing.

He's pushing the right buttons. He wants me to explode. He wants to see my dark side.

He would like me to be furious and destructive.

Pushing my chair back , I rise from the seat and soothe the non-existent wrinkles on my white noodle strapped dress.

I walk away, leaving him all alone at the table.

Once again, I felt like all eyes were on me.

Wandering through the closet, my eyes search through every dress I have that I could wear to this stupid honeymoon evening date or whatever it's called.

All of my dresses either reveal too much skin or don't fit the occasion.

Now, if I wear a dress that reveals too much, I know I'll hear a fit from Saint and if I don't I'll be the odd one out.

Sigh.

I pull out a black lace dress where it's backless and has noodle straps. It's thigh length...

Saint for sure will lose his shit.

A small smile curls onto my lips, turning to the mirror as I press the dress against my body, picturing how I would look in it.

I love it.

Let's get ready I guess.

When I apply a thin layer of mascara I hear soft footsteps entering the room. Closing the tube of mascara I throw it in my makeup bag and notice Saint leaning against the door as he stares at me.

"Are you wearing that dress?" Saint questioned, walking further into the room.

I adjust my curly hair before meeting Saint's intimidating gaze through the mirror. "Is it a problem?" I asked.

Knowing his answer. I can't wait to hear him argue knowing that I'm wearing it either way.

Just the thought of pissing him off almost makes me smile.

He walked right up to me, got close enough I could smell the woodsy scent of his cologne. His green eyes captured mine. I stood there silently, staring into his face.

I looked small compared to him. He is tall and muscular, I'm the opposite.

He leans dangerously close, the hairs on the nape of my neck rise when I feel his warm breath caressing my skin. "No. I want you to wear it. So everyone can admire you, knowing that you're all mine and I'm the one whose fucking you at the end of the day." He whispers before pulling back.

My cheeks heat up and my mouth dries up.
What–

Without realizing it I turn around, lifting my hand and I slap him across the face, his head jerking to the side.

Fury burning into me.

"Downgrade me again, and you better make sure you sleep with one eye open." I snapped. His eyes gleam with dark desire, dangerously observing me.

Ugh…of course me slapping him turns him on.

Dark tension sparked between us, as we both glared at each other. The air between us is so brittle it could snap, if not then I would.

Call me crazy, but the way Saint is looking at me, It was like I felt his gaze as a touch. What's scary is that I almost allowed myself to get lost in them.

But what's even more terrifying is that I liked what I did. He liked what I did, scratch that *loved.*

This is weird, I'm starting to freak out.

I clear my throat then quickly brush past Saint making my way out of the room but actually I'm distancing myself from him. For my sake.

"I want you to wear it. So everyone can admire you, knowing that you're all mine and I'm the one whose fucking you."

Heat licks my bones at the thought of Saint inside of me.

I don't want to admit it, but I liked the way he casually spoke down on me.

God, what is happening to me?!

Is this a way of discovering hidden kinks about myself, it's quite disturbing.

I pause in my tracks when the sudden realization hits me.

All my life I was taught to be someone who is not me. Now that I've spent a few days with Saint I noticed how he's trying to pull out the real me. The destructive part of me.

And the more I fight him, the more I'm slowly allowing him to have the upper advantage.

He wants the fight and I'm giving it to him without knowing.

It's time for things to change. I have to have the upper hand or he will eat me alive and spit me out.

CHAPTER 10

IRENA NOWAK

I stared at the soothing yet vibrant streaks of colour that had filled the canvas of the sky. Strokes of pink and orange resembled the soft, supple skin of a perfectly ripened peach. The setting sun's radiant face is mirrored by the shimmering clear blue waves of the ocean.

Music fills the air without effort, like the waves filling holes in beach sand; the sound rushing in and around every person in the room. Some react to the beat, others continue in chatter.

The distinctive scent of grilled meat and chicken along with the fusion of tangy spices of lemon and chilli aroused my taste buds. It came from the kitchen inside the club restaurant, table and chairs lined up inside and a few outside, with rose petals scattered all over the wooden floorboards as mini lava lamps are placed on each table for light and to also set the romantic mood.

I took a sip of my martini, the gentle wind brushing against my skin. I stood at the edge of the wooden dock, the waters gleaming with soft light just below me.

I could jump, drown myself if I wanted to but I don't.

I just stand there, picturing my own death during this beautiful evening.

Saint is sitting just across from the dock, staring at me. I can feel his gaze burning into my back like laser beams. The minute we arrived here I ordered myself a drink and another and another and another. I lost count after four. I'm even surprised how I'm still standing. I couldn't allow myself to sit next to Saint while there's tension between us. Our waiter even caught it. She would give me pity looks each time she brought my drink while Saint was typing away on his phone to God knows who. Probably my uncles, complaining how I'm not entertaining him or about my sour moods and rude comments. Either way, I don't care. I just want this honeymoon to be over and done with. So that Saint can go back to his life and so do I. Only problem is that I'll be seeing him every day.

I'm pulled away from my thoughts when a man appears beside me. I look at the stranger from the corner of my eye, his olive tone skin kissed by the sunset. His hair is straight as a few strands brush his forehead, athlete body beneath his white t-shirt and jeans. He turned his head to face me and I focused my gaze back into the sunset.

"I've noticed you've been standing here alone for a very long time." The stranger suddenly says, breaking the silence.

That's when I realized that I've been standing alone for the past half an hour.

Taking another sip of my drink, I reply. "So you've been watching me like a stalker." My gaze was still glued to the view. He chuckles, his voice low and soothing like a bedtime story. "If you put it that way, then it sounds bad," he admits. I turned to face him, my brows pulled together in suspicion. "You do realize this is an evening for newly *wedded couples* on their honeymoon right? Where is your wife?"

His hooded brown eyes caught my gaze. "We got into a fight then she scattered away crying." he explains, his expression natural. "So, instead of following her you decided to talk to a stranger, a woman to be more specific." I pointed out, folding my arms. "Where's your husband?" he questions changing the subject.

Turning my head, I found the chair that was occupied by Saint empty, I sigh then face the stranger. "Busy." I simply answer, taking another sip of my drink. Then the man brushes his fingers through his hair before a small smile tugs his lips. "So I guess both our partners ditched on us."

"I guess so." I mumble.

The stranger stretches out his arm, I stare at his welcoming hand raising my gaze back on him. "Andrew." He says. I smile awkwardly. "Irena." I replied.

Andrew's smile fades when I don't shake his hand and he lowers his arm. Then awkwardly clears his throat. "Go check on your wife." I suggest. Andrew shakes his head. "She looked pretty pissed, I think it's best to give her space." he explains. I cock a brow. "Did she say she wanted some space?" I inquired, purposely trapping him in the spotlight. "She did, I tried to go after her but she stopped me."

"Well, women tend to do that but actually we want you guys to run after us. It shows us that you care." I point out.

We can be complicated sometimes.

He chuckles, with a trace of humour as it ends as quick as it started. "With her it's a different story."

I fold my arm, nibbling my bottom lip with my teeth watching as the sun sets and the moon ready to take over its nightly shift.

We remain in silence, wandering in our own thoughts. The sound of the gentle waters falling to sleep and light chatters with soft music humming in the air set me at ease. I could stand here all evening. I would catch a few stares from Andrew but casually brushed it under the rug not thinking much about it.

"Sooo, are we just going to be standing here?" he asked, breaking the peaceful silence. Shaking my head a small smile creeps onto my lips. "There is no *we* Andrew. I did not ask for your company, you're more than welcome to leave. Might be doing us both a favour." I proclaimed. He clicks his tongue. "Okay, no need to show off your lady claws now." he teases and I roll my eyes.

Glancing at my empty glass I sigh in disappointment. Turning on my heel I walk over to the table that was once occupied by Saint who somehow vanished. Confusion tingles my bones when I see Andrew catching up on my trail. "Are you following me?"

"No." he chuckles when he's beside me.

"You're following me." I mumbled.

I take a seat and scan the open restaurant until I spot a waiter and wave her over. The woman comes rushing in her steps, a polite smile stretched across her wide full lips. "Is everything alright?" She questions.

"Could I please have two of your strongest drinks." I politely say. The woman's amber eyes darted between Andrew and me. "No worries, I'll be back in a few." She dismisses herself and rushes back to the bar. Turning to Andrew my brows shot up when I watched him getting comfortable in Saint's seat.

Where is that banana anyway?

Now, the best thing for me to do is to get rid of Andrew but he's too clingy and won't take the hint and I myself is too exhausted by this honeymoon to cause any drama. I mean he hasn't sent any inappropriate signals towards me and maybe he's actually just being friendly. Occupying himself while his upset wife calms down.

But Saint could be back any minute and catch me with another man which will look bad concerning we are on our honeymoon. He will kill him then me or as messed up as he is, Saint will kill him and force me to watch.

And he will purposely make it a slow, painful gruesome death. That thought gives me the chills.

So why am I still entertaining this man knowing the outcomes to it? *I don't know.*

"So kind of you to order me a drink." he blurts out, pulling me out of my thoughts. Blinking back I frown. "What do you mean?" I asked. Andrew chuckles before saying. "You ordered two drinks."

Oh.

"Yeahh no, they are for me." I explain. Andrew's smile slowly fades, he clears his throat. "I–well..."

"I have a lot on my mind and tonight I just want to relax." I added. "If you don't mind me asking Irena. How many drinks have you had?"

I shrug. "I lost count."

He frowns. "Your husband is okay with you drinking that much?"

I shrug again.

"To hell on what he thinks." I say casually.

I mean, he's not here so why should I care about what he thinks about my drinking. I'm on my honeymoon right now, the least I could do is to enjoy myself even if it includes the use of substances and blackouts.

Right now I'm on a fuck Saint mindset. And I will make every use of it.

The waiter comes back with a tray of two glasses filled with unknown drinks. If it's strong and will make me temporarily happy then I'm okay with it.

She sets the glasses on our table before walking away without saying another word. I take one glass, analysing the gold liquor with a dash of blue floating on top.

I open my mouth, the liquor pooling into my mouth. My eyes screw such when I swallow as it leaves a burning trail on my tongue to my throat then finally my stomach.

Woah, that is definitely strong.

Andrew watches me with awareness as I devour the glasses of strong liquor, both now empty.

"You haven't seen a woman drink before?" I point out bitterly. Andrew shakes his head whilst laughing nervously as if he's been asked about something he's done that is embarrassing to say aloud.

"Actually, no. The woman in my life usually drink champagne or wine-"

"Your wife?" I cut him off. "No." He answers truthfully. My brows furrowed in interest. "What about smoking?" I ask and he shakes his head denying his wife participating in intoxication. "I don't believe that." I speak my mind. "Why not?" He inquired, his tone dropping low as he found offence on my comment.

I flicked my tongue over my lips, leaning forward with my elbows on the table. My fingers laced together beneath my chin as I stared at Andrew.

"When we hear 'intoxication,' we think of drugs or alcohol — acts of self-destruction, harming the body or mind. But Andrew, it's not just that. You can be intoxicated by sex, by overworking, by pain, even by porn. One way or another, we all poison ourselves. Whether it's physical or mental, we all have our vice." I project, my tone relaxed.

Stretching out my arms I smile. "But that's just my opinion."

"For a drunk person, you say some interesting things," he remarks.

A chuckle escapes my lips sensing the warmth growing in my cheeks. I stood up and immediately regretted the decision when my whole body felt a wave of rush. A fuzzy feeling tingling on my skin, the room more vibrant with colours and the soft music ticking my brain.

I stand corrected. *I am drunk.*

Andrew jumps out of his seat to help me but I stop him. Not wanting him to touch me. "I'm okay." I reassure him but he doesn't fall for it.

Grabbing my purse, I stumbled on my feet almost falling but I was caught in huge arms. My eyes grow wide, as I feel arms wrapped around my waist and a hand tightly gripped onto my wrist.

I met Andrew's soft eyes.

I bite back the disgusting feeling prickling under my skin. The urge to recoil danced in my stomach. I could almost taste the bitterness in my tongue. Without wasting any second I quickly untangle myself from him, stepping away as I kept a safe distance.

Suddenly annoyance spikes in my veins. "I told you I'm okay."

Andrew features relax, his no longer smiling. "Well, you didn't seem okay when you lost balance two seconds ago," he protested.

I opened my mouth to argue back but stopped when I felt warmth brushing up against me. The woodsy scent kissing the tip of my nose.

Saint.

Andrew's expression is now replaced with confusion and fear. I turn around, lifting my head to find Saint standing in front of me.

He meets my gaze before glaring at Andrew.

"Who's this?" Is the first thing that leaves his mouth. His voice was low and threatening.

Brushing past Saint, I mumble. "No one."

He steps in front of me, blocking my way. Saint's gaze darkened, his jaw clenched as he glared down on me as if he was about to unleash hell upon this Earth.

"Move out of my way." I demand. "Who is that *thing* that you were talking with?" bitterness lacing in his tone.

I cringe at the way he addressed Andrew as a thing.

Ignoring him I side step him and walk away, sensing him burning up my trail. My heels slapping hard against the docks, It's night time now, the full moon shining bright onto the cold crystal waters.

"Irena!" I hear Saint call out after me.

I speed up my pace trying my best to walk straight. My ears are buzzing and my head is spinning.

I start to regret the choice of over drinking.

"Irena." He calls out again, his voice no longer sounding distant. Turning my head I noticed that Saint was two steps from catching up to me. Not watching my next step I twist my ankle, losing my balance as I almost fall into the water but luckily Saint reaches out and grabs me by the arm.

Goosebumps coating my skin as the hairs on the nape of my neck rise.

The feeling is back again.

"What the hell is wrong with you? I asked you a question and you ignore me then fucking walk away." he points out, anger dripping from his tone.

Unfuckingbelievable.

"What the hell is wrong with me? What the hell is wrong with you? Ditching me to God knows where for hours only for you to return with your sour ass attitude." I bark back.

Saint pulls me toward him, his gaze narrows as he studies my face. "You're drunk." he simply states.

Ignoring him I try to pry free from his grip but he doesn't budge. "Let go of me." I demand anger fuelling up on me like hot lava.

"Not until you answer my question. Who the fuck was that man?"

The anger building up inside me is ready to explode any minute if this man continues to push my buttons.

"Like I said. Nobody. Now let me go!" I yell and he ignores me. His expression closed up but you could see the anger swirling in his eyes. "Irena if you don't tell me who that man was I will find out myself and we both know it won't be so pleasant." he growled, I chuckled bitterly. "I don't know who he is. I met him today and he kept me company after your ass disappeared leaving me alone." I explain once more hoping it will make him let go of me.

I'm drunk. Furious and tired. Right now I'm not in the mood to argue over something dumb and small. I try again, prying free from his tight grasp but he only tightens his grip, a small pain creeping onto my flesh.

"Saint. Let go of me" I said through gritted teeth.

He smiles. "Okay."

My eyes grow wide when my body loses its balance and I plunge into the water.

The coldness drinking me up, every tired muscle in my body shocked with coldness.

I swim up to the surface, Gasping for air when my head pops out the water. My gaze catches Saint, staring down at me not fazed by me falling into water.

Ugh! I just want to strangle him!!!

I swam my way to the edge of the dock, leaning myself onto it then pulled myself out of the water. I'm soaking wet, the dress now pressed against my body like a second skin, my hard nipples poking through the dress.

And I'm not wearing any bra.

I turn my head, noticing that my heels are long gone, skinning to the bottom of the ocean. I look back at Saint, glaring at him as he does the same to me. The hatred between us radiates with pure darkness.

He wants to hurt me. I want to hurt him.

"You are the fucking worst." I spat before storming off to our water hut. I push the door open, throwing my purse on the ground making my way to the bedroom. I walked over to the dresser and grabbed the bottle of champagne. Popping the cap off, it sizzles as foam slowly oozes out of the bottle.

Without caring I gulp down the liquid like water.

Saint walks in, stopping in his tracks when he catches me drinking.

"There you go again with the alcohol." he comments. I lowered the bottle, wiping my mouth then a shiver escaped my lips when gentle wind tickled my skin. "You're the reason why I'm drowning myself with alcohol." I mumbled, setting the bottle on the nightstand before I strolled my way to the bathroom. I slip out of the wet dress, tossing it inside the bathtub. I'm left in my panties as my large breasts are now exposed, my brown nipples hard and pointy like it's capable of cutting through diamonds.

I grabbed the towel, hanging on the towel rags, wrapping the soft cloth around my body, securing it in place, then walked out of the bathroom to find Saint unbuttoning his shirt.

I caught him staring at me, silently as I worked my way around the room gathering all my stuff. Once I'm done I turn to face him. "This honeymoon is a disaster because of you." I told him. Saint chuckles softly, his laugh bitter and dark.

He lifts his head, his eyes meeting mine as he removes his shirt. "Because of me? Don't be delusional Irena." he asserted. I fold my arms, frowning. "Delusional?" I say as if it's my first time hearing the word. "May I remind you that you are the one who violated my personal space, hurt me, threatened other people, pushed me into the ocean-"

"Push you into the ocean? Get your mind fucking straight you fell into the water I didn't push you." he drawled out. "Either way I'm soaking wet and might catch a cold because of you."

"Says the woman who's drunk and flirting with other men." he murmurs, slipping out of his shoes.

I tug at the hem of my towel angrily. "Excuse me?"

"Flirting with other men?" I repeated, taking a step closer to Saint. "I was not flirting, I barely knew the guy." I protested. "Then please tell me, why the fuck did I see his hands all over you." he barks back, his gaze darkening. "He can touch you but I can't?"

I blink back, my jaw dropping in disbelief. "Well for starters Saint, obviously I felt uncomfortable that he touched me, I slipped and he caught me that's all to it. So let me make this clear: I don't like being touched whether it's you, my family, a stranger, whoever. I just don't like it and you left me for hours in a place where I'm unfamiliar with, I being the person I am, I've decided to entertain myself by talking to other people and it's not a crime!" I yelled, my hands curled into a ball beside me. "Don't raise your voice at me Irena." He clapped back, taking a threatening step closer to me.

"Or what Saint? Are you going to kill me? Torture me? Send me off back to my uncles, if so…be my fucking guest Saint!" I bolted angrily. "I'd rather you do that then stand here in this room wasting my breath arguing with you over the dumbest shit!"

The heated tension between us grew by the second.

He dares to step close, inches away from me. "Don't raise your voice at me." he said calmly.

"Or. What?"

CHAPTER 11

IRENA NOWAK

His eyes are entirely black and devoid of life.

As I stare into their empty nothingness. It is as if the abyss itself is staring back at me.

His features are sharp, topped with malice. A prickling sensation webs my nerves with fear yet conquered with interest eager to know what he might do.

Saint runs his tongue along the inside of his bottom lip. After a beat of tense silence he grabs my face, his face inches away from mine, heat and disgust licks my core as his warm breath laced with whiskey and mint kisses the tip of my nose.

"You're going to regret saying those words Doe." He whispers as it sends unwanted chills travelling throughout my body.

In a blink of an eye Saint spins me around, he forces both my hands behind my back, my brows furrowed in confusion to what he is about to do.

My questions are soon answered when I feel a fabric wrapping around my wrist till it's tightly in place. Trapping my hands from its ability to move.

I try to wiggle my hands free but it doesn't seem to work on how tight Saint tied them together. It's as if he went to a camp as a child specifically to learn how to tie perfect tight knots.

He pushes me onto the bed, flipping me over.

"W-what are you doing?" I ask, fear dripping in my tone. He ignores me.

Saint disappears into the bathroom then minutes later returns with something in his hands, my eyes watching his every movement. My breathing is slow yet my heart is racing as if it's participating in a marathon.

I'm so screwed.

Saint kneels in-front of me, clasping my legs together. I try my best to wiggle myself free but he's too strong compared to my strength. Saint ties my legs together, the same way he did to my hands. Rising to his feet, his enormous body hovers over me. Leaning so close his body heat radiates out to me.

I turn my head away from him, my lips quivering, body trembling, heart racing, skin prickling with goosebumps.

"I'm not going to hurt you Irena." He simply says, his voice modulated and low. Saint caught me by surprise when he kissed my forehead in such a gentle manner. "But someone is getting hurt tonight." He adds as it sends fear spilling into my veins from the crack of my bones.

Saint pulls away, his body heat disappearing which somehow makes me miss it?

What the hell Irena, this man literally is on the verge of torturing you.

I'm not sure if it's the alcohol making me react this way but I definitely don't like it. At. All.

Saint turns on his heel, his back now to me and my eyes widen at the sight. He's fully inked, every inch of skin a canvas of shadowy art I can't quite decipher in the dim light. His muscles ripple with each step as he moves toward the door, the tattoos shifting like secrets etched into flesh.

"Where are you going?" I ask. "Saint!?" I call out with my raucous voice.

He ignores me, leaving me all alone, tied up helplessly on the bed half naked. The towel is still wrapped around my body but it's loose which scares me that Saint might see me...

Naked.

And that might give him the chance to take advantage of me. Oh God I can't go through that again. Which is terrible because I'm drunk.

Although Saint is an ass, I pray that he's not like Viktor. He's probably worse but you get the point.

Oh my fucks what if it happens, but I doubt it because Saint mentioned that I will not be getting hurt but someone will.

The realization hits me. Someone is getting hurt, if not me then...

Andrew.

Remembering the threat Saint made earlier on the docks replayed in my head.

The thought of someone innocent getting hurt because of me sends guilt crashing into me like a powerful tsunami. I wiggle my hands side to side trying to loosen the fabric tightly wrapped around my hands which only causes friction heat in my flesh which will most definitely leave a bruise later.

The more I wiggle the more it tightens, my flesh burning like fire.

Giving up I sigh in defeat, my eyes wandering around the room hoping to find something to free me but I don't find any sharp objects whatsoever.

Ten minutes later of me trying to free myself I stop when I hear muffled noises and heavy footsteps approaching the bed room. My eyes glued to the door, curious to whom might come into view.

My theory is correct when a bruised Andrew is pushed into the bedroom, his body stumbling onto the floor. Saint walks in closing the door behind him, with something in his left hand.

Andrew lifts his head, his terrifying gaze meeting mine. "Irena?" He questions.

Guilty washes over me.

"Saint, whatever you're planning to do-"

"The more you talk the more he'll suffer." He declares, circling Andrew like a predator sizing up prey, then pulls out a blade pressing his thumb against its sharp edge without flinching. The steel kisses his skin, slicing it open with chilling ease. Saint lifts his hand into view, a thin stream of blood trailing down his thumb like a tear. His eyes find mine and without breaking the gaze, he brings the finger to his lips, licking the blood clean with slow, deliberate intent.

Oh my days, my uncle's married me off to a crazy man.

I averted my gaze and looked at Andrew. Sweat drips down his nose, mixing with the blood on his face, his hair damp from sweat sticking to his forehead.

"What the fuck is going on?" He cries out, body trembling with fear.

I pull myself up, scooting to the edge of the bed so that I can help Andrew but Saint stops me when he grabs Andrew from his hair, his head forcefully tilted back. His Adam's apple bobbing up and down.

"My little doe over there needs to learn how to maintain her temper when talking to me. Now she doesn't listen and when you don't listen you need to be disobeyed. I'm a man of old traditions." Saint explains to Andrew. "Also, you touched what's mine." He whispers to him.

Saint let's go of him, his glooming gaze finding mine.

"So let's have some fun."

CHAPTER 12

SAINT DÉ LEON

"So let's have some fun," I said, calm and cold.

Andrew whimpered, mouth twitching, eyes wide with terror. "Come on, man. I didn't do shit." His voice was thin. Snot ran down his face, mixing with blood and sweat.

I rolled my neck until it cracked, bone on bone, slow and deliberate. That familiar pop grounded me. Tonight would be a long one. I could feel it.

"Don't play dumb, Andrew." I tapped his cheek with the edge of the blade. Not enough to break skin. Just enough to remind him it was there.

Funny. I never imagined I'd be here, ready to take a life over something so small. But sometimes, the small things are the ones that break you.

Across the room, my wife was tied to the bed. Drunk. Useless. Watching.

Our marriage was already in shambles. A little madness wouldn't hurt. Not more than we'd already done to each other.

I met Irena's eyes. Her fear filled the space between us, raw and electric. That's what I wanted, for her to look at me and see the thing under the bed. The thing she couldn't run from. The man who could make her bleed and beg in the same breath.

And she would. Oh, she would.

Right now, she probably hates me. She should. But that hate? It'll turn into something else. Something darker. Something better. The kind of thing that burns through everything until all that's left is need.

"Saint, you can't do this!" Her voice cracked. I didn't look at her.

I grabbed Andrew's wrist, the same hand that touched what was mine, and pressed the knife against his skin. Slow. Deep. The blade glinted under the low light as it opened him up. Blood bloomed fast. Thick. Hot.

To anyone else, it might've looked horrific. To me, it was beautiful. Crimson on skin, the colour of power. Of ownership.

He screamed. Irena did too. But I was focused. Steady. This was about control.

"You're fucking crazy," Andrew rasped.

"Poor me," I said, smiling. I leaned in close, voice low. "But you gave me something I didn't know I needed, a reason."

He groaned, still trying to speak. "My wife will find me an—"

"Your wife's busy fucking the bartender," I cut him off. "She's not worried about you. She's worried about finally getting off."

He flinched. His eyes darted toward Irena, half-naked under a loose towel on the bed. That was enough.

I gripped his face and forced him to look at me. "Don't you ever look at her again." The threat was cold. Final.

I turned to Irena. "This is what happens when someone touches what's mine."

Then I took his hand and cut off every finger…one by one.

His screams tore through the air. Irena was frozen, tears brimming in her eyes, but I didn't stop. He collapsed, shaking in his own blood. All his cut fingers dropping to the floor from my hands. I walked to her. Slow. Knife still warm in my hand.

She tried to recoil, her body trembling. I dragged the blade gently along her skin, streaking her cheek with Andrew's blood, down to the curve of her breast. She didn't move. Didn't breathe.

I watched her. Beautiful. Terrified. *Forever mine.*

I wanted to fuck her. Right then there. Leave her breathless and broken under me, held together by nothing but my hands and her hate. But Andrew was still groaning. Still ruining the fucking moment.

I went back to him, hitting him hard on the face and he whined like a little bitch, blood flowing from his mouth with his tooth flying out. I smashed a lamp against the dresser, picked up the jagged edge, and drove it into his stomach. I twisted, pushing it deeper into his flesh. Tearing his organs from the inside out. Again, and again, and again.

Irena screamed and her voice cracked open something inside me. It was perfect.

I leaned over him again. Pulled his remaining hand out and stretched it wide. With a swift move I cut it off clean. His howls were muffled by my boot on his face. I held the severed limb. Swinging it in the air. Feeling it's useless weight.

Then I brought him close. Letting him hear my last words.

"Your wife's going to get a gift box," I whispered. "Wrapped real nice with bits of you inside."

And then I slit his throat.

His blood splattered across my face, letting go of him and he dropped like meat. I stood there for a moment. Breathing. Letting the quiet settle in.

Irena sobbed behind me.

The blade slipped from my fingers, clattering to the floor.

Her eyes were wild, mascara smeared like war paint. She tried to crawl away. "Don't you dare come near me!" she spat.

But I did. Slowly. Locking my eyes on her beautiful crying face.

She kicked. Screamed. Fought but I untied her anyway. Ignoring her tantrums.

When she tried to slap me, I caught her wrist and held it tight.

"Kick and claw all you like. Scream. Hit me. Curse the fuck out of me. You are mine, and nothing is going to change that, and I will kill any man who dares to come near you, look in your direction, touch you, or dare to even put a smile on your face." Every single word I spoke to her was filled with promise. I released her and walked out without another word. My phone was already in my hand as I stepped into the spare bathroom.

Three rings. Then Abel picked up. "How's the honeymoon, big brother?" he asked, amusement in his voice.

"We've got a problem," I said. I turned on the tap and set the phone on the sink.

Blood was still dripping down my face. My reflection stared back at me. Calm. Sharp-eyed. The kind of man who only feels alive when the world's burning around him.

Virtue. Vice. It didn't matter anymore.

Aliah Darkrose

I R E N A   N O W A K

His eyes cut through me like a hot knife through soft skin. It's cold, hollow, and hungry. I don't flinch, not really. I'm too frozen to move, too tangled in the blood pooling around my bare feet. It's warm, sticky, metallic. Deliciously grotesque.

He's dead. Still. His face twisted in that final flicker of agony. I can still hear his screams bouncing off my skull like a song stuck on a loop. Wet, guttural, begging. And I didn't stop. Hell, I might've even wanted it.

Then it hits like a flashing film reel. I see the moment his body was sliced open. I see it too clearly, like I'm watching a movie I've already memorized. Blood, air, then silence. The way it sprayed like red confetti... almost artistic.

And I shake. Not from fear…no, fear would mean I didn't sign my name on this sin but from something deeper. Guilt? Regret? Or just the cold hard truth that maybe I'm not the hero of this little tragedy. Maybe I never was.

Tears shimmer at the edges of my lashes, threatening to drop. I clench my teeth until my jaw aches. My heartbeat? A war drum in my ears. I hear them. The voices. Chanting. Mocking.

Murderer.

I swallow it down, all the bile and guilt and shame, but it claws its way back up. I gag on it. I choke on it.

Because I didn't stop him.

83

Saint did the dirty work but I let him. I watched. I nodded. I said nothing.

Does that make me worse?

Saint? He doesn't do rage. No, not him. He's...content like killing scratches and itches he was born with, makes him feel something. Or maybe nothing. Maybe he's just wired differently.

And that hard drive of his...

I don't even wanna know what's on it.

But here's the kicker...I let the devil in. I poured him a drink and asked him to stay. And now? I can't stop replaying it in my head like a broken record.

I peel myself from the bed. The floor is cold. The kind of cold that reminds you you're still alive, even if you wish you weren't. My stomach rolls. My vision spins. I make it halfway to the bathroom before I collapse next to the toilet like a discarded doll.

I puke.

Once.

Twice.

Until there's nothing left but guilt and vodka.

When it's over, I wipe my mouth, drag myself to the sink, and start scrubbing. Toothpaste, soap, a fresh face, clean on the outside, rotting on the inside. I pull on my robe, it's silk, black, my second skin and slip into the hallway like a ghost on stilettos.

And then I see him.

Saint.

Back turned, bare skin covered in ink. That tiger... fierce. Scarred. Staring back at me like it knows what I did. Oleander flowers wrap around the edges. The ink looks beautiful, poisonous, just like him.

His voice slices the tension. "She'll be out shortly."

He knows I'm watching.

"Why is he here?" I snap, my voice sharp like a blade.

He doesn't even blink. "Because he's taking you home."

Behind him, Abel grins like he's won the sickest lottery. "Enjoying the honeymoon Irena," he teases. Sleaze wrapped in silk. Saint's eyes meet mine. Calm. Cold. That killer calm look.

"You'll stay with Abel. When I get back, I'll show you our new home."

I don't ask what he's doing. I already know.

Cleaning up the mess. Killing again.

Saint doesn't leave things unfinished.

"Of course you're going to act as if you didn't just traumatize me." I hissed.

He stands up and closes the distance between us. I can smell the danger on him, like smoke, blood, and something greener, like the woods just after it rains.

"Careful," he murmurs. "You remember what happened last time you opened that pretty mouth?" He says, referring to killing a man in front of me like it's sunshine and rainbows.

I tilt my chin, smiling slowly. "I remember. Threaten me again, you'll be the one regretting it."

He grins. That damn dimple flashes like a warning light. "You really don't know me woman."

"I don't have to."

My fury simmers. I lean in. "Just because I'm your wife doesn't mean I won't stab you in your sleep."

One brow arches, amused. He hums like I just told him bedtime poetry. "Oh, is that a threat, Irena? Because I'll let you in on a little secret—thinking of you covered in my blood?" He leans down, breath hot against my skin. "Is my dirty little fantasy."

My heart skips. My fist clenches.

"You're a psychopath."

He shrugs. "I prefer creative."

I express my disbelief with a scoff. I choose to ignore him, and as I leave the house, I resist the urge to turn back and face Saint, walking away with my back towards him.

My mind kept on repeating the gore scene of Andrew. Each time I closed my eyes I could see him and only him. Pleading with his eyes to be set free. Dear God I wonder how his wife will react when he finds out her husband went missing on their honeymoon. And the mention of Saint saying that he will make sure he delivers him to his wife in pieces only makes my stomach twist in disgust.

I know that Saint is capable.

Staring out the plane window, I twirl the glass of red wine in my hands.

I know, alcohol is the last thing I should drink right now but it's the only thing keeping me sane. I haven't eaten in hours and I'm starving but sadly after watching someone being killed. I don't have the appetite. Pulling my gaze away from the window I watch as the red wine gracefully twirls in the glass. A reminder of Andrew's blood.

The sickening scene of his hand being cut off, and throat being slit replays in my mind. It's so vivid I cannot push the dark memory away.

I am damaged myself but I never met someone as ruined as Saint. He knows how to make hell home. He wears the smell of blood and death like perfume. Which made me think how dark can Saints' past be to turn him into a heartless monster?

I'm pulled away from my thoughts when Abel sits in front of me. We haven't said a word to each other ever since I left the water house. Once we arrived at the private jet, one of the workers approached me and handed me a black dress and heels. The most embarrassing part was that a lace panty also came with the package and it was my exact size. Without questioning I took it and immediately changed before we took the lift off.

My lips found the rim of the glass as I took a small amount of wine. My questionable gaze glued onto Abel. His eyes never leave mine when he takes a sip of his drink.

Maybe I will ask Abel about Saint's past. I might have an open mind to what Saint is the way he is.

"You've been quiet lately," he says. "Considering the fact that your brother traumatised me, you out of all people should understand my silence." I imply and he smiles, nodding before taking another sip. A beat of silence passes.

Peeling my eyes away from Abel, I watch the wine twirl in the glass. "When did you start drinking?" Abel questions. My gaze lifts to his.

I swallow, fighting back the bad memories of the past. "When I was 16." I answer truthfully. If I'm going to ask questions about his brother I should also share a little bit about myself.

Let him loosen up a little and his drinking will only make this easier.

He frowns. "Mind me asking why?"

I adjust myself in the seat. "I had a lot of panic attacks during my teens years. It would get so bad that I would black out. I told my uncles about it but they never took my mental health seriously. So one day I sneaked into one of my uncle's studies to get a book from his collection and saw a bottle of scotch just sitting on his desk. Being the curious girl I am, I drank about two glasses. It tasted like shit but as time passed it kicked in and I liked the way it made me feel. So in some fucked up way alcohol is a coping mechanism for my anxiety." I explain.

Abel watches me carefully as if he is watching an unsolved crime documentary. "There might be more to you then I thought Irena." He simply says and I shrug taking another sip of my wine.

There is more to me than you think Abel.

"What about you?" I inquired. "I just like getting wasted. No dark story to it." He proclaims. "And Saint, is there a dark story implied about his behaviour?"

Abel pauses, his eyes narrowed in suspicion. "Curious." I add. "Mhm." He hums.

"Well..." he trails off. "If you're wondering. Saint's background is dark, very dark and I personally think he should be the storyteller, not me."

What he says only triggers my curiosity on Saint. So there is a dark story behind Saints action.

I guess we both have something in common, we can bond over our traumas like any other married couple. Nibbling on my bottom lip I ask this question without thinking. "Has he ever been in love?"

Abel chuckles humorously as if I told the joke of the year. "Saint is not capable of loving Irena."

I frown, setting the glass of wine on the table in-front of us. "Everyone is capable of love." I say. "Not my brother."

It's impossible but we speaking about Saint for crying out loud. If his own brother says that he is not capable of love then I might believe him. Which is quite sad to think about. Is he destroyed and filled with a void of emptiness that he even rejects human emotions.

"What if he is, then how would you describe it?" I ask. "I'd say, if Saint is capable of loving someone. It will not be as pretty and light as people describe the way to being in love is. Saint's love will come out as chaotic and dark as his soul. I mean if he's this crazy imagine him when he's drugged by loving someone else. It's going to be ugly, possessive, dark, dangerous and wild, and whoever is responsible for making him feel that way, they better run as fast as they can before it destroys them. That's how I picture Saint loving someone with his coal-like heart." he proclaims, tracing the rim of the glass with his fingertip. "There's nothing human left in Saint. No good, no kindness, no love. Only a monster." He states casually.

"You're making it sound like a nightmare." I mumble. "It's worse than a nightmare, Irena," he says.

"Saint falling in love with you is basically facing death itself."

CHAPTER 13

IRENA NOWAK

Laughter rippled through the air like poisoned thick honey, cloying, impossible to ignore. I placed the silver tray down with practiced grace, the fruit glistening like jewelled blood under the chandelier's dim sway. The room was awash in smoke and arrogance, and beneath the veneer of celebration, something vile slithered.

Tobacco and musk, overripe and feral, curled into my senses. I hated that it still made my skin crawl.

"A blessing, truly. Corruption in the force." One of Viktor's lecherous comrades boomed, his voice a thunderclap wrapped in molasses. His face flushed like aged wine, and his greying hair was slicked back with the desperation of a man terrified of irrelevance. He choked on his cigarette mid-sentence, coughing like the devil had reached up to tug at his lungs. I flinched, despite myself.

"They'd sell their badge and balls for a roll of bills," the one next to him grunted, his voice scraping along my spine. I felt his eyes before I saw them dripping down the neckline of my dress like oil.

I reached for the empty tray like it was a shield, keeping my expression blank as our eyes met. He smiled, all teeth and sleaze.

His stare clung to me like a parasite as I turned, stalking me with every step. I kept my movements fluid, feline. Controlled.

But then—

"Where'd you get her, Viktor?" The pig asked, with a wet laugh. "She's too polished for your taste."

The room quieted just enough to hear my stomach turn.

Viktor didn't miss a beat. "She's a Nowak," he drawled, swirling his whiskey with cruel amusement. "Married her for a fat stack of daddy's inheritance."

Laughter again. This time, it curdled in my ears.

I felt it rise, the rage, ancient and coiled, pounding against my ribs like it wanted out. Every year, his touches grew bolder. Every joke, filthier. The bruises, less hidden. I've flirted with death more times than I've been kissed gently.

When I finally spoke out, I thought I'd be heard. Silly girl.

They wanted proof. Photographs. Witnesses. Fingerprints of pain stamped in technicolour. As if a woman's breaking point needs receipts.

And Viktor, he smiled. That smug, syrupy smile.

"With tits like that," he chuckled now, swatting my ass with his stubby fingers, "you'd think she'd have half a brain."

I didn't flinch this time. I looked at him, really looked and imagined the sizzle of boiling oil on his bare chest, imagining sipping wine while he screamed himself raw.

Now that would've been comedy.

I clenched the tray, white-knuckled and composed. Walking away before the demons in me started dancing.

The moon draped across my bed like silk stolen from a crime scene.

I blinked slowly, sleeping a lost cause.

Viktor. Again. In dreams, he wore my memories like a skin suit, leering and endless. I exhaled. One long, trembling breath.

It had been eight months since I buried him and stitched on my grieving widow's face. It has been a year since I watched the casket drop and smiled behind my veil.

No remorse. Only peace, dark and quiet buried in the grave he now calls home.

I swung my legs over the bed, greeted by cold marble and the whisper of nightmares still clawing at the edges of my mind. My thoughts refused silence. And Saint…he hadn't been home in a week. His absence was a relief.

The house was still, except for the flickering glow seeping from the kitchen like a secret. I moved toward it, barefoot and restless.

And there she was.

Nirali.

A ghost in white lace, haloed by fridge light and elegance. Her nightgown clung to her like a scandal. Her ink-dark hair cascaded in loose waves, making her look like a painting that had learned to breathe.

"Nirali?" I whispered, caught between awe and caution.

She turned slowly, like a poem unravelling. Her face brown skin kissed with white patches, artful and rare, met mine with quiet grace.

"Sorry," I murmured. "Didn't mean to interrupt your midnight snack."

She smiled, something soft and knowing. "Can't sleep?"

"Just woke up." I watched her retrieve a bottle of wine with the elegance of a woman who knows exactly how the night should taste. She poured generously, the red gleaming like sin between us.

I took the glass, mesmerized by her.

"I had a nightmare." I announce. "Of my dead husband."

"Do you dream of him often?" she asked gently, her voice a melodic ache.

I hesitated. "Not for months. But he visited tonight." My words were thorns wrapped in velvet.

She sipped, slow and reverent. "Maybe he's haunting you." Her lips curled slightly over the rim. I let out a breathless laugh.

"Why are you up?" I asked.

She looked down at her hands like they held answers she hadn't earned yet. "Abel is gone. I can't sleep without him." Her confession was soft, a whispered bruise.

I tilted my head. "What do you mean?"

"If you don't mind me asking."

She drew a breath that trembled. "I'm not ready to share the whole truth. But nightmares…they come for me too. And Abel keeps them away." Her voice cracked. "When he's here, I sleep. When he's not, sadly I can't fall asleep."

"And when I try…" She half laughs, "I'm literally just closing my eyes."

I nodded, sipping. "You're lucky," I murmured. "He loves you."

Nirali smiled, fragile and radiant. "He was patient with me. Even when I didn't speak for months."

"You didn't speak for months?" I exclaimed. "How long?"

"Five." She admits and my eyebrows shoot up.

"Saint would've left after five minutes."

She laughed, surprised. "He's not exactly gentle, is he?"

"He smiles like it's a sin," I said. "Rare and never sweet."

"You've seen it?" she gasped.

"Not the kind that softens a room."

She leaned closer, eyes gleaming. "Even that is a miracle. Abel's tried for years to make him laugh. But ever since he—"

She stopped. Froze.

"Ever since he what?" I asked, sharp as a scalpel.

But Nirali recoiled. Her gaze dropped. Silence thickened, slithering between us. I studied her carefully. This family, it wears secrets like designer cologne. Heavy. Expensive. Suffocating.

"What do you really know about Saint Nirali?" My voice was honey dipped in suspicion.

She hesitated. "Only what Abel told me." A pause. Then, softer, "I'm worried about you, Irena."

I took another sip. Let the wine do the talking.

But even its warmth couldn't drown the scream in my head.

What have my uncle's done?

And what the hell have they handed me over?

CHAPTER 14

IRENA NOWAK

The sun is a fading disk in a violet sky, casting splinters of neon blue and orange over the tweed France sky.

Nirali appears beside me as my luggage is standing beside her. "Thank you, love."

She smiles softly, handing over the black luggage to me. I took it from her grasp and sighed.

"Irena." Nirali calls out, I lift my gaze meeting her tender eyes. She reaches out to me but stops realising that I don't like being touched. She quickly lowers her hands and blush creeps up into her cheeks. "Call me when you need anything. Anything at all." She announces. "You're too kind." I declare and she shakes her head. "Don't even worry about it. We are a family now. We have to take care of each other."

After my talk with Nirali earlier today, 3 hours later Abel came back. He didn't look like his friendly self. He has his poker face on and would glare at me occasionally but made sure Nirali didn't notice. He informed me that Saint is back and I should get ready to leave.

I sensed something bad was going to happen due to the sudden change of mood as soon as he stepped foot into those double oak doors.

I wanted to confront him about it. Asking him what's the problem but the little voice at the back of my head told me not to. That it would be better to remain silent. Like I always do.

Now I'm standing in front of Abel's mansion beside his wife Nirali as I prepare myself to enter Saint's driver's car. I want the ground to swallow me whole.

"When you feel like it, contact me so we can hang out together. I need to get out of this house." She suggested, chuckling lightly. I smile and nod. "I will."

A man dressed in a white and black suit approached us, his 6,2 foot figure hovered over us. I meet his icy cold gaze. "Mrs. Dé Leon, are you ready?" His hoarse voice sends shivers up my spine. Darting my tongue out to lick my lips I nod, turning my attention to Nirali I smile. "See you later?"

"Looking forward to that." She replies and I wave at her before brushing past the large man and entering the black SUV. I shut the door and buckle myself in place. Waiting patiently for the man to load my luggage.

Once he's done he rounds the car and enters the driver's seat. Pushing the start button as the engine purrs to life.

I share a quick glance at Nirali who watches me as we pull out of their long driveway. Waving one lady goodbye at her I sigh. Resting my head on the cool window watching the trees pass by.

Whatever this negative gut feeling I'm having. I sure am not looking forward to face it.

Saint's mansion was a fortress carved from silence, its regal, untouchable, like a palace built not for comfort but command. Forty minutes from Abel's home, it stood twice the size, twice the presence. Twice the secrets.

I knew it was big. What I didn't expect was how cold it felt. Not in temperature, no the marble radiated warmth under sunlight but in aura. It was the kind of cold that wrapped around your bones like a warning. This kind of cold only leaves power behind. I stepped through the grand entrance, my heels tapping out a slow rhythm across the marble like a ticking clock. There was no welcome. Just open vast space and echoing with the ghosts of unspoken things. It wasn't empty. It was restraint. A house that didn't bother to beg for company.

The sunlight streamed in through the wall-wide windows at the end of the foyer, casting everything in gold and glass. Below, the Eiffel Tower stood like a monument to sin, framed perfectly by Saint's unbothered opulence. Lush greenery draped the walls in quiet defiance. Art whispered from every corner. Nothing loud. Nothing desperate. Just taste. Just power.

I let out a breath. Long. Controlled.

To my left, the minimalist living room flexed its wealth like a muscle with sleek black sofa, cool grey vases, a wide TV that likely cost more than most people's cars. A grand coffee table gleamed like lacquered obsidian, overlooking a view that would make the Louvre weep.

As I wandered deeper, the kitchen met me with the scent of freshly baked bread and something spiced, simmering on the stove. Sunlight kissed the polished marble countertops, danced over the dark oak cabinets, and caught the edges of an eclectic wooden table. I could already picture Saint sitting quietly, calculating, cutting his food like he carves people down to size.

Further in, my heels led me to a wine cellar. It stirred something warm in my chest. Not softness, pleasure. This was my room. Cool, shadowed, lined with vintage temptation. My fingers trailed across the bottles like I was choosing a weapon. I picked one with an aged label and no remorse.

Bottle in hand, I made my way upstairs. The master bedroom was black and white. Its aesthetic was minimal, masculine, and utterly indulgent. The bed was wide enough to swallow sins whole. The bathroom, a different story entirely.

Marble, chrome, a freestanding tub that dared you to feel vulnerable in it. I didn't flinch. I filled it with warm water, lavender oil, and soft candlelight. The scent curled into the air like perfume on skin.

I poured my wine. Slipped out of my clothes. Sank into the bath like a woman who's done running.

This place was cold. But so was I.

Let the house learn.

Let it adjust to me.

A whiff of ripe berries and betrayal greets me as the wine reaches my lips. The first sip soothes down my throat like fire melting into a warm hum in my chest. I take another, then another, until the smooth swirl of crimson becomes a rhythm, one that numbs everything else. I'm floating. Unbothered. Free.

Each sip makes the room a little less real. A little more mine. Colours blur, and my sense of gravity slips like a silk dress off bare skin. I don't feel drunk, I feel delightfully uninhibited.

The bottle is half-empty when my skin begins to spark. That's when the music starts playing—no, wait. That's just the pounding in my chest when I hear the front door slam and heavy steps start cutting across the floor.

My body tenses. Not from fear. From anticipation.

A second later, Saint walks into the kitchen, his white shirt splattered in blood, sleeves rolled up, forearms flexing with each clenched step. He's carved from shadow and tension, and he's pissed. Really fucking pissed.

I take another sip. Let him boil.

His eyes land on the empty bottle like it insulted his ancestors.

"You didn't cook?" he grunts, voice low, like gravel dragged over silk.

I lift an eyebrow and give him a look. "You weren't home."

Saint's jaw ticks, his anger simmering just below the surface. "You know what your role is. Wife means responsibility. That includes dinner, whether I'm home or not."

I let out a short, humourless laugh. "Hire a chef if you're so pressed, Gordon Ramsay maybe. I'm not wasting food or effort on a ghost."

He's in front of me in two strides. Close. Too damn close.

"Don't test me," he warns, voice a hiss, eyes scanning my face like he's looking for cracks.

"Why not?" I breathe, tilting my head. "Worried I'll push back?"

Our eyes lock, vicious, charged, magnetic. The tension crackles, thick as honey and just as sticky. His hand twitches like he wants to grab me, shake me, or something else.

"You're drunk," he mutters.

I smirk. "Thank you, Captain Obvious. And you're bloody. Again. Matching uniforms?"

Saint snatches the wine glass from my hand and pours the rest down the sink. I gasp like he just shot my puppy.

"What was the point of that!?" I yell, leaping up.

"The point," he sneers, stepping even closer, "was to get your attention."

"Well, you've got it now," I whisper. His breath is hot against my cheek.

"I don't want to come home to this," he says. "Drunk wife. Cold kitchen. Smart mouth."

"Too bad." I say. "Because I am all of those things. And I look good doing it."

His eyes darken, something unholy glinting in them. "You want to test how far you can push me?"

"I'm counting on it."

"Keep on counting on it Doe and you won't have the voice to even reach ten," his jaw clenched, "You'd be lost from the feeling of my dick hitting the back of your throat."

We're nose-to-nose now. If I leaned in half an inch, I could bite his lip. I don't. Yet.

Though I want to, till he fucking bleeds and whines like a little bitch.

"Don't call me Doe," I say quietly, the heat of my fury making my voice drop to a simmer. "My name is Irena. And I'm not your housewife. I'm not your pet. And I'm sure as hell not your problem to fix."

"You're my something," he urges deeply. "I haven't figured out what. But I will."

"You want obedience?" I sneer. "You should've married a corpse. I bite."

He steps back. Saint's lips twitch, an almost smile. Almost.

"You know, for someone who drinks to forget, you sure don't shut up."

"And for someone who kills for a living, you're awfully slow at handling me."

That does it. He takes a breath, sharp, biting it back.

"You are infuriating," he says.

"You say that like it's not why you married me."

Saint moves swiftly when he pulls me by the arm and takes a seat on one of the stools before bending me over his lap, lifting my skirt and spanking me hard.

I let out a yelp and he does it again, and again.

"Watch."

Spank.

"You're"

Spank.

"Damn."

Spank.

"Mouth when you're talking to me."

Spank, spank, spank.

Tears now shimmer at the corner of my eyes from the burning sensation of my ass. My pussy pulses with a feeling I do not want to acknowledge.

Saint gently lifts me off his lap before grabbing my face and pulling me closer to his. "Next time I want dinner ready or else you won't get a gentle spanking."

Then let's go of my face and walks away, leaving me flustered and drunk out of my mind.

CHAPTER 15

IRENA NOWAK

Saint underestimated me—a stupid mistake.

The sting on my ass had barely faded by the time I woke up the next morning, wrapped in my rage like a silk robe. He hadn't just spanked me, the motherfucker declared war. I waited. I bided my time, quiet as a snake in tall grass. I let him think he'd won, that I was just his drunk, disobedient wife with a smart mouth and a sore behind. But three days later, I served him hell. It started with dinner. Not the metaphorical dinner he demanded, no, I meant literal dinner. The kind you plan like an ambush. The kind you plate like seduction. The kind you make for a man you intend to ruin.

Saint liked his steak rare, bloody, barely kissed by heat. Said it reminded him of control. I called it ego on a plate.

But tonight, I cooked it just right, let it sizzle in garlic butter and thyme until the scent filled the kitchen like a siren song. Rosemary potatoes, golden and crisp. Grilled asparagus drizzled with olive oil and the tiniest touch of lemon zest. I even lit candles, three of them as they cast soft gold shadows across the marble countertops like a lover's whisper.

Wine decanted, glasses chilled just enough. Everything is perfect. Everything laced with vengeance. I wore a white sundress. Saint has a weakness when I wear white dresses. And my closet is filled with them thanks to him. A silk slip dress that draped over my curves like a secret, thin enough to make him wonder if I wore anything beneath. I didn't.

My hair curled over one shoulder in soft waves. Lips bloodstained, eyes smoky. A vision of domestic bliss with a devil in her smile. Saint walked in just as I was lighting the last candle. White shirt open at the collar, sleeves rolled, the top buttons undone.

Tired. Tense. Hungry. Good.

His eyes swept over me, slow and possessive, like he had already tasted victory. "Smells like submission," he said, loosening his tie with a smirk. I turned to him, a glass of red in my hand, the smile on my face sweet and venom-laced. "Smells like delusion," I murmured, and handed him the glass.

We silently sat across from one another while dining. He took another bite, chewed, and swallowed before speaking. "Didn't know you had this in you. This whole…wife thing."

I smile thinly. "I can play the part, but you're always pissing me off."

Saint leans back, glass in hand. "Are you still mad about the spanking?" My jaw tightens at how casually he says it. "You didn't spank me. You humiliated me. I'm still sore."

Saint chuckles darkly, "That's rich coming from a woman who tried to claw my face off in front of a room full of diplomats."

"You think this is funny?"

"I think you're angry and desperate to matter." He stands now, towering over the table. "And all this? The dress, the food? A weak play of control. You'll learn eventually who holds the leash in this marriage."

My breath stills for a moment, the air in the room turns razor-sharp, provoking the anger that simmers inside of me.

"You're right. I do need to learn."

I rise slowly with controlled movements. A soft smile still plastered onto my face before stepping out of the dining room and making my way toward the kitchen. My heels clicked softly against the floor like a ticking bomb.

I open a drawer quietly. My fingers wrapped around the cool metal handle of a steel pan. I then make my way back into the dining room to find Saint comfortably seated while he takes another sip of his wine. He felt my presence and spoke up. "What, no comeback this time?"

"Oh I've got one."

Crack.

The pan connects with the side of his skull. Hard. The sound is sickening and final. Saint drops to the floor like a felled god, limbs heavy with the wine glass shattering beside him.

Then, silence falls after.

I stand over his body, my chest rising and falling. My eyes are calm now…too calm. I lower the pan with my white dress catching the candlelight when I kneel beside him.

"You look cute when you're half dead," I whisper, leaning in, then plant a soft kiss on his temple.

Saint was no longer in the dining room.

He was tied to a chair in the center of his bedroom, his shirt gone, shoes off, muscles straining subtly against thick velvet ropes I had bought six months ago out of curiosity. Guess they paid off.

Though I won't lie. Dragging him out the dining room, stripping him and tying him up was a lot of work.

He stirred, head lolling before his eyes blinked open. The chandelier sparkled above us like a crown of stars, casting shadows across his sharp cheekbones and furious scowl.

His voice was low, raw. "Irena."

"Welcome back," I said cheerfully, crossing one stilettoed leg over the other as I perched on the edge of the bed, watching him struggle. "You've been out for a bit."

"What?"

"The fuck? Irena what did you do?"

"Hit you with a frying pan." I lied.

"You what—"

"Don't be dramatic. Cast iron. It barely left a dent." I stood slowly, heels clicking across the floor. "Let's call it karma."

"Irena, you think this is funny?" His jaw clenched. "Untie me. Now."

"No."

I stopped in front of him, running a single finger down the center of his chest, where a light sheen of sweat glistened. His skin jumped beneath my touch. I smirked.

"Oh, I'm not laughing," I whispered, leaning in, "but I'm having a great time."

His breathing sharpened. "You think this makes us even?"

"Oh no, sweetheart." I climbed into his lap, straddling him without touching anything that would give him relief. "This is just an appetizer."

I traced his lip with my thumb. "You want to dominate? Humiliate? Break me? You forgot one little thing…"

He growled through gritted teeth. "What's that?"

"I bite back."

CHAPTER 16

IRENA NOWAK

Saint hated not being in control.

Which is exactly why I gave him nothing.

Day one began with silence.

I let him wake up tied, his arms flexing and failing against the ropes every hour or so. I watched him from the armchair by the window, curled up in one of his crisp white shirts, oversized, unbuttoned just enough to be distracting. My legs crossed, one knee bouncing lazily as I read a book like he wasn't glaring at me from across the room like a caged predator.

"You're gonna regret this," he said with his rasped voice.

I turned a page. "You said that after you threw me in the ocean. And after the spanking. Yet here we are. Dry and cozy."

"You don't know what you're doing."

I looked up at him then, slowly dragging my eyes from his face down his chest, where his muscles strained from the tension in his body, glistening slightly with sweat. He was gorgeous like that, all angry, tied up, helpless.

"Oh, baby," I purred, "I know exactly what I'm doing."

He went still at the sound of my voice. It was low, velvet-wrapped, and dangerous.

I stood and walked over to him, slow on purpose. Every sway of my hips was calculated, every glance meant to provoke. I straddled his lap again, lips brushing his jaw but never giving him more than a breath.

His breath hitched.

I pressed the softest kiss against the corner of his mouth. "Hungry?" I asked sweetly.

"For food or for you?" he asked, the annoyance and anger still lingering in his tone.

I smiled and leaned closer, lips brushing the shell of his ear.

"Both," I whispered, and just like that I felt his erection pressing between my legs. Teasing my heated core, "but you're not getting either."

I got up, leaving him with a hard-on and a temper.

He hadn't said a word since sunrise.

Not when I cracked the window to let the morning breeze chill the sweat off his skin. Not when I wandered around in one of his shirts, hem brushing high on my thighs, the faint smell of him clinging to the fabric like a warning.

Not even when I brought breakfast.

I could feel him watching me, watching everything. Every flick of my wrist, every sway of my hips, every bite I took before bringing something to his mouth. He was tied, but regal, like a lion in a cage who knew it was only a matter of time before the door broke off its hinges.

Good. Let him simmer.

I walked barefoot, the sound of my steps quiet against the floor, my body draped in silk the colour of spilled blush and bad intentions. No bra. No underwear. Just skin, barely concealed. I liked the way his jaw clenched when he realized that. The way his fingers curled around the ropes like they were the only thing keeping him grounded.

His eyes were a storm, hungry, dangerous, dark enough to drown in. And I? I was the siren with no interest in rescue.

I stopped in front of him, holding a peeled clementine between my fingers.

"Open," I said, my voice sugar-laced, honeyed.

He didn't. He just stared.

I tilted my head, letting a slow smirk rise to my lips. "Don't be difficult."

He opened his mouth. Not for me. For the game.

I placed the fruit on his tongue. Watched the way his mouth closed, the way his throat moved when he swallowed. It felt oddly... intimate. Watching him take what I gave him. Knowing I had the power now.

"You're quieter today," I murmured, brushing my fingers along his jaw as I lifted a slice of toast to his lips. "Not like you."

He chewed in silence, eyes locked on mine.

"Plotting?" I teased.

"Always."

I smiled, letting my fingers linger at the corner of his mouth, wiping a non-existent crumb. His skin was hot beneath my touch. Tense. Electric.

I wanted him to snap.

Not because I feared it, because I wanted to feel it.

I turned, ever so slowly, to refill his glass. Bent forward just enough to make sure he could see the curve of my ass beneath the hem of my shirt. I didn't have to look to know he was watching. His breath hitched loud enough for me to catch.

"You're playing with fire," he said, voice low and hoarse, like gravel dragged through honey.

I straightened and turned back to him, glass in hand, smile slow and lethal.

"Is that so," I purred, stepping closer. "What if I like to burn?"

I bent at the waist, offering him the glass, close enough that my breath grazed his cheek. As he leaned forward, I let my fingers drag along his jawline, feather-light.

That's when he snapped.

His head turned fast, catching my wrist in his teeth. Not biting. Not breaking skin. Just holding. A threat. A promise.

My heart punched against my ribs.

Oh, he was definitely still in there.

His eyes burned up at me, primal and smug.

I pulled back slowly, letting the tension stretch like a rubber band about to break, my wrist slipping free from his mouth, leaving behind a ghost of heat. I was trembling slightly, but I wouldn't give him the satisfaction.

I smirked. "Oh, you're still in there."

"You haven't seen shit yet," he growled, arms flexing against the ropes again.

"Let me out," he rasped, "and I'll show you just how much."

There it was...the edge. That simmering fury. That's what I want.

That Saint.

I leaned in, placing both hands on the arms of the chair, pinning him with a gaze that said mine, even if I didn't say the words. My lips brushed against his, but I didn't kiss him. I just let the heat between us choke the air.

"Maybe tomorrow," I whispered, breath ghosting over his mouth like a kiss he didn't earn yet.

He groaned, deep and raw, like the sound was torn from his chest.

I walked away without looking back. But inside? I was burning too.

He hadn't begged.

Not with words.

But Saint didn't need a voice to scream, I saw it in the way he shifted in his seat, how his fists clenched around nothing, how his throat bobbed with every breath he swallowed like poison. He was burning, and I was the match that lit him.

So I gave him what he thought he wanted.

Mercy. Or something that looked like it.

The ropes slid off his skin like silk sins, slow and deliberate, each pulling a silent dare. His arms were marked where I'd tied him, faint red indentations, evidence of restraint and lust and control. I traced one with a fingertip, and he didn't flinch. Didn't move.

He sat still, naked power coiled beneath his skin, breathing like a man who'd just survived something… or was preparing to destroy it.

"You think this gives you the upper hand?" His voice was low, broken gravel with the edge of a blade.

I said nothing. Just straddled him, letting my knees sink into the mattress on either side of his thighs. My silk robe slid apart as I settled on his lap, exposing bare skin. He was already hard beneath me, pulse thrumming through denim and threat.

My hands rested on his shoulders as I leaned in, lips brushing the curve of his neck. I let my tongue flick his pulse point. He hissed through his teeth.

"No," I whispered, barely a breath between us. "I think this makes us even."

I ground down slowly, letting the heat between my legs press into the thick line of him through his briefs. Just one slow, sinful roll of my hips, calculated. Designed to wreck him.

He cursed low, the sound guttural.

Then he moved.

Saint surged forward, his arms snapping around me like they were born to own me. The air rushed from my lungs as he lifted, flipped, and pinned me onto the mattress in one brutal, practiced motion. My wrists hit the headboard, caught in his hand, the pressure sharp enough to sting.

He hovered over me, eyes wild, breathing fire and brimstone. His mouth was just inches from mine, and I could feel him, his need, his fury, the weight of three days chained inside his chest.

"You want revenge?" he growled. "You've had your fun. Now it's my turn."

I met his gaze, breathless, smiling like the devil's favourite daughter. My thighs spread wider on instinct, teasing. Daring. Fucking Welcoming.

"Then make it hurt, Saint."

He paused.

Just for a moment.

Like a wolf savouring the kill.

Then he smiled, slow, wide, a sharp edge hidden beneath charm. That look that reminded me exactly who he was when he wasn't tied to a chair. Dangerous. Unforgiving.

"Oh," he whispered against my lips. "It will."

Then he pulled away, climbing off the bed and silently made his way to the bathroom as if he didn't just threaten me. My eyes watched as his ink on his back flexed from the nudge of his muscle before he walked in and shut the door behind him.

CHAPTER 17

IRENA NOWAK

For the past two and a half weeks, I've dutifully followed Saint's request and played the part of a submissive wife. But my behaviour is not a mere act; it's a calculated strategy. You see, there's a method to my apparent madness. I'm biding my time, waiting for the right moment to take Saint out. And this time, I won't use apples; that would take too long. No, I've got something much more sinister in mind…Wolfsbane.

Wolfsbane was a top contender when I researched ways to kill someone without arousing suspicion. But I had to exercise patience with Viktor. With Saint, however, I don't need to hold back. I'll play the perfect housewife until the time comes to strike.

Once he's dead, I'll disappear to Africa, emptying his bank account. My uncles will never find me there.

After taking the life of Viktor, I yearned to disappear without a trace.

Unfortunately, I lacked the funds to vanish like a phantom since Viktor had stripped me of everything, including access to his bank account. However, my fortunes had changed with Saint. Unlike Viktor, Saint was a beneficent husband who didn't hoard wealth. Though during our last argument, Saint attempted to pacify me with his credit card, without realizing it only provoked me further. Nevertheless, his folly made me contemplate how I could exploit it. Now, armed with his pin, all that remained was to obtain the combinations to his other accounts.

It may surprise you, but I had a friend when I first plotted Viktor's death. The origin of the scheme wasn't mine but rather the brainchild of a former maid in Viktor's employ named Jennet.

At first, I thought about killing Viktor by just stabbing him, a swift and brutal end to him. But wise and cunning Jennet suggested a more elegant approach, a method that would make the bastard suffer. Suffer so deeply that death would feel like mercy.

Of course, Jennet didn't just hand me a guidebook on how to murder my husband and get away with it. Instead, she whispered secrets about potent herbal mixtures and poisonous brews.

The allure of Wolfsbane was irresistible. Its venomous toxins could destroy a heart's rhythm, a single taste enough to cripple a man's stomach. But what sparked pure joy in my veins was the knowledge that even the slightest touch could lead to death. How delicious it would be to end Saint's life slowly and with a faint smile on my lips.

As the water trickled out of the pot's punctured holes, I watched the soil surge to life with fresh, verdant greenery sprouting from the surface. The wolfsbane seeds were not easy to come by, but I was determined to get them. I stumbled upon an old lady selling them online in a stroke of luck. The price was steep, but to me, it was a small price to pay for the chance to live my life.

I nurtured the seeds with devoted tenderness for two weeks before finally bringing them out onto the balcony to flourish. Though the brisk fall wind howled, the hardy plants persevered, visibly thriving in their new surroundings.

Their full growth signalled my liberation, the end of my struggles, and the beginning of a new chapter in my life.

As I gaze ahead, my gaze fixates on the sturdy SUV halting gracefully right in front of the mansion, where burly guards are seen patrolling around. Eyeing the vehicle like a hawk, my suspicious mind gradually kicks into analytical gear as the doors swing open and Saint, closely trailed by Abel, effortlessly steps out of the driver's and passenger's seats.

A gnawing anticipation rushes through me as I ponder the reason for Saint's abrupt return. Surely, he wasn't scheduled to return until another hour. Placing the water pot delicately on the table, I give my hands a quick dusting before retreating into the comforts of the house. A glance in the mirror reveals a few stray wisps of hair, and with a deft touch. With a breath of contentment, I take a step forward, leaving the sanctity of my bedroom behind me.

Thank heavens Saint and I are not forced to share a room.

Having a spare bedroom is a Godsend, though it's frustrating that I can't make use of the delights of the master bedroom's bathroom.

I've got to admit. I'm quite the explorer. I've scoured every nook and cranny of the house except the garage and one mysterious room at the far end of the downstairs hall. Though I've tried countless times to gain entry, the door remains firmly locked, with the key nowhere to be found.

The curiosity is eating away at me: what secrets are kept behind the door?

As I descend the stairs, I bump into Saint. Our gazes lock, pausing our movements in time, at least for a few bewitching seconds.

There's something about Saint that triggers a deep-seated animosity within me.

He has a way of coaxing out the darkest corners of my soul, parts I had no idea existed. My inner demon was always a whisper, but with Saint, it's a deafening chant that sends chills down my spine.

When I was with Viktor, that voice only filled me with shame and drained me of life. But with Saint, it's a new, sinister voice that sings of violent thoughts, making me uneasy.

I loathe him for the way he makes me feel. I despise him for how he treats me. And above all, I detest his mere existence on this planet.

"Why are you back so early?" I snap, bitterness coating my words.

"I'm not in the mood for your demands and bullshit lectures about me being a useless fucking wife."

With a slight tilt of his head, Saint fixes his eyes on me. His sharp gaze scrutinizes me as if trying to unveil my deepest secrets.

"Although your lips are as beautiful as a sunrise, you seem to have a dirty tongue," he quips. I can't resist an amused eye roll in reaction to his playful tease. "What is it, Saint?" I ask, making my way through our home to the dining room. There, Abel lounges on the couch, sipping bourbon and tapping away on his phone with a sly grin.

I can feel it in my bones, he's talking to Nirali. "I am hosting a poker game tonight, and some of my business partners will be attending. Would you mind preparing some snacks for them?" he asked. I halted and turned to face him. "So, I'll be serving these men snacks all night as they yell and reek of smoke and alcohol until they pass out?" I inquired, and his brows creased.

Recollections of serving snacks to Viktor's friends flooded my mind, causing my heart to race and the hairs on the back of my neck to stand up. I swallowed hard, pushing back the anxiety that threatened to overwhelm me. I nearly revealed my emotions in front of Saint, and I could sense that he wanted to ask about it, but he chose to let the matter go.

I take a deep breath, slicking my hair back with a graceful hand swipe.

"Say it how you want. Just feed them and mind your business," he argues, his eyes piercing mine as we lock in a heated stare.

"Jesus fucking Christ, you two are smothering your sour mood on me. My aura can't handle it. Go do your heated eye fucking somewhere else." Scolds Abel, interrupting the intense staring contest between Saint and me.

"This is my house, Abel." Saint retorts, but Abel dismisses him with a flick of his wrist while fixated on his phone. "Whatever," he mutters, and Saint gives up, returning his focus to me.

"The guest will arrive at 9 pm," he informs me before turning to follow Abel.

My frustration simmered beneath my skin, and I stormed out of the dining room and towards the kitchen.

Saint is just—ugh!

I feel a mix of strong emotions, but he just seems to use them for his own pleasure. I can't stand his insensitivity, it only makes me more upset.

I went into the wine room and picked out a nice bottle of red wine. As I held my glass in hand, I ran into Saint, who looked at me suspiciously.

I held my head high, refusing to let his judgement affect me. "You wanted me to be a good little wife, right?" I quipped, brandishing the bottle and glass-like weapons. "Well, how about this? I'll pour myself a little happiness and play the obedient little puppet in front of your friends. It is a win-win for both of us. How's that sound?"

Saint scoffed, correcting me with his usual precision. "They're not my friends, they're my business associates."

I rolled my eyes, dismissing his pedantry. "Whatever they are, I don't care." With a huff, I brushed past him, feeling his eyes bore into my back as I stormed out of the kitchen.

"Now excuse me," I called over my shoulder, "I've got some primping to do." I left him standing there, watching me with fascination and frustration. But I didn't look back. I had other things to worry about like becoming the perfect submissive wife.

CHAPTER 18

SAINT DÉ LEON

I hate it when Irena drinks.

There's something about the way she loses herself in liquor, like it's a game, like it's freedom. But to me, it's a ghost. A memory soaked in stale whiskey and a childhood I've tried to outrun. The poker room was cloaked in shadow, the amber swirl in my glass is the only thing reflecting the low, blood-warm light above me. It burned, but not enough. Not like she did.

Her drunken laughter used to echo through the house like a haunting with stumbling steps and slurred apologies. When Irena gets drunk she reminds me of my mother. Of the nights I'd curl into myself while the woman who birthed me drank herself into oblivion. But Irena never really listened. Or maybe she did, and just didn't care. Either way, her drinking lit a match, and I was a man who walked with gasoline in his veins.

Still, I sat. Watching. Silent. A predator in tailored black, cold to the bone, and deadly when provoked.

Cards shuffled. Chips clicked. The table was full, the air heavy with silent calculations and suppressed egos. Abel sat across from me, impassive as stone. Don, the fool, bet like he had a death wish and a wallet to match. Roy, all sharp angles and sharper instincts, played as if the world owed him something. And maybe it did. But not tonight.

The game progressed. Smiles were lies, and every glance was a threat. I played them like I played the world, carefully, quietly, and with enough force to crush when needed. The poker table was just a mirror of life. Bluffs. Alliances. Betrayals. And the unspoken knowledge that only one of us would leave feeling like a god.

Then Don opened his mouth.

"Mafia," he said, like a child telling ghost stories in the dark. "Have you ever dealt with them?"

Abel's eyes flicked to mine, and I met his look with cool indifference. Just another mask.

"I've heard stories," I replied, my voice calm, smooth. "Nasty ones."

Roy grinned. "They get what they want. No second chances."

I nodded, swirling the whiskey in my glass. "So they say."

They all nodded along, thinking themselves wise, unaware that the devil they feared was sitting right across the table. I've built empires with blood money and charm, turned a billion-dollar company into the perfect mask for the French underworld. And tonight, they were nothing more than pawns in a game I'd already won.

The door creaked.

Every head turned. Silence bloomed like poison.

Irena entered, wrapped in a pink sundress that clung to her like sin. She didn't belong in this room of wolves, and yet she owned it the moment she stepped inside. Her skin, soft as caramel, gleamed beneath the light, and her dark hair cascaded down her back like liquid night. She was dangerous. Not because she tried to be but because she didn't have to.

She placed a tray on the table, a flicker of discomfort in her movements, and that's when Roy touched her.

A slap on the ass and she squeals.

And then silence.

Roy's voice cut through it, ignorant and bold. "Who's the pretty maid?"

I didn't move. Didn't flinch. Just spoke.

"That's my wife."

"Oh wow, she certainly does not look like the woman I expected you to marry," he chuckled. We all laughed, except for Abel, and Irena watched awkwardly.

"Roy," I called out, raising my gun and taking aim at his head before pulling the trigger. Blood splattered the wall and table as Roy's lifeless body crumpled to the ground. The once-lively room fell silent as the other men gaped in disbelief, their faces drained of colour and their expressions conveying utter terror.

The group collectively turned to face me, their countenances now riddled with fear.

"What?" I ask.

"Y-you just killed a man in cold blood." He states fearfully.

I place the gun on the table, adjusting myself to the seat.

"Just a reminder," I said, voice low and smooth, "to watch your filthy hands. Especially when it comes to my wife. None is allowed to touch her."

I chuckle to myself, tracing the rim of my glass with the tip of my finger.

Don succumbed to nausea and vomited violently, staining the floor with chunks of his dinner. Abel winced while Irena stood by the door, crinkling her nose in disgust. "Jesus fucking Christ," I muttered under my breath. Kai tried to speak, but his words came out as incoherent gibberish. "Don't bother, Kai," I interrupted, sipping the fiery liquor that scorched my throat. "I won't kill you. Not unless you give me a reason to."

Don wiped his mouth, trembling with embarrassment as he tried to regain his composure. I rubbed my temples, feeling the headache creeping in. If losing one of my most prized investors due to a foolish mistake wasn't enough, now they all knew about my ties to the mafia. This night had turned into a disaster. I am curious about how they will react when they find out I am the Don of the French mafia.

"Kai, clean the tiles from your piss. We don't want the maids to be overwhelmed with Don's puke," Abel blurts out, abandoning his chair swiftly. Tugging off his leather jacket and smoothing back his hair, he levels a reproachful gaze in my direction. "As usual, I'm left to clean up your mess." Sighing, he whips out his cellular device, navigating to his calls.

"Zoltan, I need you at Saint's home, accompanied by the morticians," he conveyed before ending the call.

He then directed his attention towards the two apprehensive individuals.

"Please accept my apologies on behalf of my brother," Abel paused, glancing at the lifeless body of

Roy, "and him," as he indicated towards Roy with a nod of his head.

Observing the situation, I stood up from my seat. "His wife will ask about his sudden disappearance and demand a search party. But for now, the only facts are that you two shared a game of poker and wished each other goodnight. That's the story we're sticking to. Because if word leaks out that he's been murdered, rest assured, I'll be coming for every one of your family members until you're attending more funerals than birthdays. Clear?" I proclaim. Their heads nod in unison, sweat beading on their foreheads, and wide-eyed in fear.

"Excellent. Abel, you take care of the necessary arrangements. I'll attend to my wife." I gesture to Irena and open the door, escorting her out.

We walked down the hallway, I quickly closed the door behind us. Irena was ahead, heading towards the kitchen with her loud footsteps on the tile floor. I hurried to catch up, her words lingering in the air.

"You had no right to kill him." Her voice carried across the room, slicing through my thoughts like a serrated knife. I leaned casually against the counter, the cold metal piercing my skin as I reached for a water bottle, my thirst parching my throat like desert sands.

"But he touched you. You hate to be touched." I shrugged, the water half-gone in a single swig as my eyes locked onto hers.

"He had it coming, getting too close to what's mine."

Irena resolutely crossed her arms, making her chest jut out from the confines of her dress. I quickly jolted my eyes to meet hers and arched an eyebrow. "Death seems a steep punishment for his transgression. Killing every man that lays a hand on me is not the answer," she exclaimed, her voice etched with protest.

With an air of intrigue, I gingerly stuck out my tongue, licked my lips, and moved closer towards her. I towered over her curvy frame, and the tension between us grew darker with each passing moment.

"What did I tell you the first time someone dared to touch you?" I asked with a low, menacing tone. Irena's breathing deepened, and she nervously flicked her tongue across her lips as our eyes continued to lock in an intense, unspoken battle. "You have me, body, mind, and soul and no one will ever take that away from you. No man will ever lay a hand on me or even so much as smile in my direction without answering to you." My lips curl into a grin as I nod, feeling a sense of possessive desire burning within. Irena was mine, and nobody else's. "We're going to set something straight, Saint," she seethes, jabbing a finger pointedly at my chest. I meet her piercing stare and hold it. "I don't belong to anyone—not to men I encounter, not to you, not to my uncles," she declares with fiery conviction. I couldn't help but admire her strength, even as she attempted to exert her dominance over me.

My response was a simple grunt, which she took as compliance. However, I couldn't resist a small smirk that tugged at the corners of my mouth. I tilted my head, watching her with a ghostly smile, enjoying the tension of our unspoken power struggle.

"Understood?"

"Yes, ma'am."

My intriguing response left Irena visibly stunned. Her brow furrowed with suspicion, but deep down, she knew the truth, she belonged to me. However, as usual, my precious Doe denied it. With a subtle nod, Irena retreated, giving me a fleeting glance before disappearing from the kitchen.

Moments later, Abel strolled in and didn't mince his words. "You fucked up," he bluntly announced. I let out an exasperated sigh. "Thanks for the reminder, mother dearest," I quipped, the frustration seeping out. "But I know where I went wrong, Abel," I reassured him as he sat on a stool, rolling his eyes in response.

"I mentioned that they are not allowed to speak about what they witnessed,"

"That may be true, but the experience traumatized them greatly. I don't think we'll be able to hold poker night for a while." He expresses his confusion.

"We have bigger issues to tackle, and you're worrying about poker night?" I ask. Abel takes a moment to ponder before confirming, "Yes."

Although I wanted to object, I refrained from speaking and remained silent as I realized that there was no use. We fell into a period of silence, deep in thought. Suddenly, I broke the silence, stating, "I need you to help me out with something." Abel manoeuvres to face me and inquires, "What is it?"

"I want a full deep-dive on Irena. Background, connections, every secret she's ever tried to bury. Something tells me she's not just who she pretends to be."

CHAPTER 19

IRENA NOWAK

As I peeled my t-shirt off, my breasts leapt into view. Their soft, full curves bounced free, eager to taste the fresh air. Quickly, I relinquished my panties and slipped into the steaming bath.

The hot water beckoned to me like a long-lost lover, its soothing touch sending ripples of pleasure through my body.

My toes sank into the water, sending goosebumps crawling up my skin in delight. The steam swirled around me, enveloping me in a cloud of sensuality.

As the water swirled around my body, I felt my nipples harden in excitement. I reached down, cupping my pert breasts in my warm hands, savouring the exhilaration running through my veins.

I squeezed my breasts together, the soapy bubbles cascading down my body like a delicate necklace. I leaned back, lost in the sensuous pleasure of the moment.

Relaxing on my back, caressing my luscious tips until they formed a delicate froth, memories of Saint's voice echoed vividly in my mind.

"No, stop it, Irena." I warned myself. I envelop myself in a cocoon of solitude as I sink into the soothing embrace of the warm water. My usual preference for quick showers lies forgotten, overcome by an irresistible need for a luxurious, lingering soak. The serene silence is disrupted only by the clamour of my thoughts, racing like wild horses through the vast expanse of my mind. One tiny, treacherous voice whispers wickedly in my ear, tempting me to indulge in decadent pleasures.

I brush it aside, determined to purge my mind of all negativity.

But somehow, inexplicably, my musings drift towards Saint...

The first thing that comes to my mind is his stupid fucking voice, it's like warm honey drizzling over my senses. But I don't want to like the sound of his voice.

Ugh followed by his shitty eyes, they set my heart ablaze like a wildfire, alive and radiant with nature's wonder. The hue of his eyes almost beckons me to explore the unknown, to lose myself in a world of secrets and unspoken desires. A single glance and I'll find myself enchanted by the spellbinding magic of his gaze.

I then think about his stupid fucking lips, possessed by sin that they seemed to entice the devil himself. His mouth is a veritable portal to temptation and debauchery, with each syllable that escaped its confines stirring hedonistic desires in all who heard them. Saint's lips were full and pink and when they curved into a sly and seductive smile, one couldn't help but submit to their wicked charm.

I find myself shamefully submitting to Saint, my heart ablaze with a dangerous mix of both hatred and forbidden desire.

Gently caressing the insides of my parted thighs, the warm water lapped at my delicate folds. As my slippery fingers slid up my sudsy limbs, my body quivered with anticipation. Cupping my throbbing pussy in my hand, I reached around and teasingly circled my sweet spot. Gripping myself with fierce determination, I shuddered with desire.

Squeezing my fingers tightly on either side of my pulsating clit, a rush of pleasure shot through me. With each beat, my body begged for more, craving every touch, every flick.

Trembling with a mix of nerves and excitement, I wondered if this was really happening. But the fierce energy pulsing through me left no doubt in my mind. I was about to indulge in pure, unbridled pleasure.

I swiftly snatched up the wineglass, eagerly gulping down its chilled contents. The sensation of icy wine mixing with scorching liquid caused my head to spin. Hastily, I twisted the tap, relishing the jolt of cold on my skin. My pulse pounded in my chest like an insistent drumbeat, while the fragrance of my aroused essence overwhelmed my senses. Anticipation coiled within me, my pussy muscles clenching in excitement, fuelled only by promised pleasure, and the thrill of witnessing it afterwards. My fingers drifted down to my smooth and freshly shaven skin, plunging into the depths of my wet and fervent flesh.

My breath caught in a whimpering gasp, the shiver of desire running through my body. At this moment, I was consumed by the insatiable hunger of my primal urges.

As I traced delicate circles around my aching clit, my body quivered with anticipation. Imagining all the wicked ways he could ravage me, I arched my back and slipped two fingers inside.

The rhythm of my thrusts matched the fervour of my thumb on my clit, sending me careening towards a mind-bending release. My world dissolved into a kaleidoscope of electric pleasure, pulling me into a universe of ecstasy that left me breathless and gasping for air.

A faint moan escaped my lips as I opened my eyes, the reality slapping across the face.

I touched myself to Saint.

CHAPTER 20

IRENA NOWAK

"Okay, okay, how about this?" As Nirali emerged, clad in a crimson, shimmering, backless dress that hugged her curves, my words evaporated in awe.

"Marry me," I stammered, barely able to form a coherent thought. "So yes?" Her lips curled into a coy smile as she turned to survey herself in the mirror, analysing every angle. Abandoning my drink on the nearby table, I rose from the couch, unable to resist the urge to compliment her. "Darling, that dress was made for you," I gushed, admiring how it danced around her graceful legs.

A subtle blush crept across her cheeks as she locked eyes with me through the reflection, her gratitude in every inch of her being. "Thank you for agreeing to this last minute," I added, though she waved away my concerns with a dismissive flick of her wrist. "I'm available anytime, Reena." My brow furrowed in confusion as I uttered, "Reena?" But before I could finish, she let out an exasperated sigh.

"Your name is quite long. So, allow me to introduce you to your new nickname: Reena, Irena."

As her proclamation echoed in my mind, I couldn't help but let out a half-hearted chuckle. "Nirali, my name is not long to say, and Reena and Irena have the same number of letters." I pointed out.

But Nirali wasn't having it. "Oh, hush, Reena is a charming nickname, and I shall call you that from now on."

I shook my head, smiling, before stepping back to admire my friend in all her glory.

"Whatever you say, Nira," I replied with a smirk, lifting my hands in defensive playfulness as she turned to look my way. "You call me Reena, and I call you Nira. Besides, it rhymes," I added with a grin, watching the smile spread across her face as she turned back to fix her makeup.

"Reena, Nira."

Yearning to escape this suffocating atmosphere, I was grateful for Nirali's invitation to revisit the club she and Abel frequented back in the day - a surefire way to find some fresh air and forget our worries. Finally, I'd have the chance to let loose, drink, dance, and make the most of the night with my one true friend.

But first, I had to carefully select the perfect outfit for our evening out, laying on my bed wrapped in a silky robe, "I don't know what to wear." groaning over my lack of inspiration.

Nirali shoots me a sly look and arches a perfectly manicured brow. "Please, Reena. You've got a wardrobe full of gorgeous dresses just waiting to be worn," she announces, gesturing to my closet. I sit up straight, turning to face her. "Saint picked out half of them," I grumble. "Not bad taste for someone who's not even a fashionista," Nirali teases, her eyes dancing with mischief. I close my eyes and let out a deep sigh of frustration.

"Niraaaa, please help me. I want to look smoking hot tonight," I pleaded with her. She laughs softly. "Alright, alright. Don't get your panties in a twist. I'll find you something," she says, disappearing into my closet like a bright, shining light. As I wait for Nirali to work her magic, my mind wanders. I can't help but wonder how Saint will react when he finds out that I've left the house to go clubbing with my best friend. In my previous marriage, my husband never allowed me to go out, not even to fancy society events or dinners. I was a prisoner in my own home, barely allowed out for even a few hours each week. But not anymore. This time, I was determined to live my life on my terms.

As my eyes fell upon the stunning silver dress that Nirali presented, I couldn't help but feel a thrill of anticipation. I took the dress delicately from her outstretched hand, holding it to the light. My heart quickened as I took in its intricate, sparkling details.

"Where did you find this?" I ask incredulously, barely daring to believe my good fortune. Nirali's eyes twinkle with amusement.

"It was in your closet," she informs me with a smirk. "I'm willing to bet it's Saint's, the man has impeccable taste."

Without hesitation, I rush into the closet and strip off my robe, revealing my barely-there thong. I slip into the dress, feeling it hug my curves in all the right places. As I secure the spaghetti straps over my shoulders, I bask in how the fabric sparkles in the light. This dress flows flawlessly against every inch of my body, accentuating my feminine curves and emphasising my wide hips. The luminous silver fabric radiates with an ethereal sheen, elevating my beauty to unforeseen heights.

Subtly revealing yet charming, the spaghetti straps caress my toned shoulders while the daring plunge of the V-neckline draws the eye tantalizingly close. With its daring mid-thigh cut, the dress presents my strong, captivating legs with a breathtaking air of confidence and allure.

As I emerged from the closet, Nirali's eyes widened in awe. She flung her phone onto the plush bedspread and glided over to me, gasping in admiration.

"Girl, you look positively breathtaking," Nirali gushed, causing a rosy flush to bloom across my cheeks. "How did you look like a goddess in just a few minutes?"

I smiled, basking in the compliment, and thanked her. With swift movements, Nirali darted into the closet and emerged with two pairs of high heels. One was a shimmering silver that matched my dress, while the other was a fiery red that complemented Nirali's ensemble.

As she handed me the silver pair, I slid them on easily, and we gathered our essentials for the night ahead. Chirping and giggling, we descended the stairs, and Nirali's driver awaited us outside, ready to whisk us away to our adventures.

Nirali headed towards the car, but I halted in my tracks, informing her that I needed to get the keys to the house. As I reached the key holder, fate intervened, and I bumped into none other than Saint.

His eyes weighed heavily upon mine as he peered up from his phone before travelling down my frame, scrutinizing my ensemble. Curiosity piqued, I cocked my head to one side, studying his features.

"What?" I snapped. "Where are you going?" he questioned. "Clubbing with Nirali." I brace myself, prepared to fight back when he tries to restrict my freedom.

Saint remains silent, slipping his phone into his pocket, his tongue darting out to moisten his lips.

"What time will you be back?" I narrowed my eyes in suspicion. "I can't say for certain," I responded warily.

He nods but has an ominous warning. "Leroy and Nick will be keeping watch over you."

I swallow hard and clear my throat before responding. "I understand, but I'll be accompanied by Nirali's driver."

A tense energy crackles between us as he regards me sceptically. "That's fine," he replies. "Good."

"Good." Saint left without uttering a single phrase, leaving me perplexed. With a furrowed brow, I mouthed an unspoken "Okay" before stepping out of the house and shutting the door behind me.

As fall blew gusts of wind, the trees started losing their golden leaves, bidding adieu to the sun as it set into the sky. The moon and the stars prepared to take over the night, setting the perfect backdrop. Suddenly, out of nowhere, two soldiers appeared with a sleek black BMW sliding smoothly behind the SUV.

My thoughts immediately wandered to Leroy and Nick the second I caught sight of them. I hopped into the SUV, as Nirali was busy placing her small mirror into her bag, and questioned, "What took you so long?" We hit the streets as the car sped away from the driveway.

"I, uh-" Taking a moment to gather my thoughts, I summoned all the courage I had left and darted a glance at Nirali. With a smile, I whispered, "Nothing." She scrutinized me momentarily before wisely deciding not to pry any further.

"Are you excited?" she exclaimed, her eyes sparkling unbridled. I couldn't suppress a giggle. "More than you could imagine. I can't wait to bust out of this place and live a little," I declared with glee. Nirali tossed her dark tresses over her shoulder. "Well then, you're in luck," she teased, her eyes smouldering with a hidden promise. Just then, Nirali's phone buzzed, and she scrambled to answer it. A shy grin played over her lips as she read the message. "Sorry, it's Abel - do you mind if...?" she trailed off. Without a second thought, I threw up my hand dismissively. "Don't be silly. Go right ahead," I encouraged, and she quickly tapped out a response, giggling softly to herself.

As I gaze out the window, the rustling trees blur by in a verdant dream. I take a deep breath and rest my head against the supple leather seat. Saint's odd behaviour from earlier today still haunts my thoughts. He nodded and left without a disparagement or a huff, which is highly unusual.

Perhaps he has finally surrendered to my wishes? Regardless, I'm elated that we didn't clash in another fruitless argument that only results in sourness lingering till the next dawn. Nirali's words echo in my mind. This is the day to abandon my worries and relish the electrifying thrill I'll experience tonight.

The air was thick with anticipation as the doors to the nightclub swung open with a soft thud. The intoxicating aromas of perfumes, colognes, and smoke merged, forming a unique and heady scent that filled the senses. The dim lighting, the thumping beats of the music and the flashing strobe lights made it easy for one to get lost in the moment. The dance floor was alive with bodies, moving in sync with the rhythm of the night. The drinks flowed freely, glasses clinking, and laughter filled the air. The night was young and the possibilities endless, as the nightclub held an air of promise and excitement.

"Can you believe it?" I whisper excitedly to Nirali, my eyes roaming over the vibrant atmosphere of the club.

"I absolutely can't," Nirali breathes, her gaze hungrily devouring the scene before us as we settle down on a cozy couch.

As a waitress approaches, we lose ourselves in the beat of the club music before placing our drink orders.

Excitement bubbles within me as I confess to Nirali that I'm a first-time clubber. She gapes in disbelief, her eyes widening like saucers. "Are you serious?" she gasps, and I nod shyly, feeling like a newbie in the clubbing veterans. "I've never really had the chance to let loose before I married Saint," I explain, and a flicker of sadness darkens Nirali's face before she covers it up with a reassuring grin.

"Don't worry, love," she promises, her voice as sweet as honey. "You'll be a clubbing queen before you know it." With that, we're served our drinks and toast to a night of wild and crazy adventures.

As the music pulses through the club, Nirali and I take to the dance floor like we were born to boogie. Our hips sway in perfect sync, our bodies move like liquid fire, and our smiles light up the room like a disco ball. Soon enough, we've attracted a crowd of curious onlookers who can't seem to get enough of our killer moves.

Locking gazes, we exchange a silent vow to make this a night to remember - one filled with laughter, love, and a lot of shaking our booties.

Our VIP escapade was an absolute marvel, leaving us in utter awe. Dazzled. by the glittering lights of the club, we savoured the most exquisite drinks, from exotic cocktails to premium champagne, relishing the sheer opulence of it all. With each delectable course, our taste buds danced in delight as we rediscovered the sheer pleasure of indulgence with succulent appetizers and mouth-watering entrees.

But it was the company that made our VIP experience truly unforgettable.

We laughed, reminisced, and savoured the moment, lost in a world of luxury.

As the night waned, our feet tired but our spirits high, we danced until we could no longer revelling in the VIP treatment that left us utterly fulfilled and yearning for more.

I flopped down onto the plush couch, relishing in the cool fabric against my skin as the sweet taste of my drink danced on my tongue. My protectors, two looming shadow figures, stood guard behind me with steely gazes, just as Saint had promised they would. Nirali's hired guards kept a watchful eye from the sidelines, expertly concealing their presence in the room.

As Nirali and I chatted away, a striking figure caught our attention. He sauntered towards us in a dark blue shirt that flattered his chiselled frame, black jeans that hugged his waist in all the right places, and sneakers that whispered against the floor. His tapper hair was expertly styled, and his dark skin glowed under the neon lights. His muscular build was only accentuated by his full, pouty lips and siren-dark eyes, framed by full eyebrows and lashes that touched his cheeks with each blink.

I watched Nirali take in the newcomer with a quiet gulp of her drink while I couldn't help but be transfixed by his captivating presence.

"Bonsoir mesdames." The man addressed us with a deep and raspy voice, causing me to look up from my drink. "We don't speak French," I replied.

He nodded before sitting across from us, his legs wide open as his eyes scanned my figure. His French accent lingered in the air as he complimented us, saying, "You two ladies look beautiful."

Nirali, ever the inquisitive one, asked him who he was. The man chuckled, unfazed by her annoyed tone. "I couldn't help but notice you two from afar. Are you having a good time?" he asked, his eyes darting back and forth between us.

Wanting to keep the conversation light, I said, "Yes, we are. This place is gorgeous." As I took in the surroundings, I couldn't help but feel like the man was watching us too closely.

"Thank you," he exclaims, his proud gaze sweeping over his domain, and I share a quick look with Nirali, realizing he's the club's master. "You're the owner?" I inquire, unable to contain my curiosity as his eyes glitter with pride. "Aye, I am," he boasts, sweeping out his arm grandly. "I own three of the most illustrious nightclubs in Paris." His hand extends toward me. "Laurent Duval," he introduces himself charmingly, holding a winsome grin on his lips. I can't help but stare at his outstretched hand and then meet his piercing gaze before smiling poignantly. "Irena," I replied in turn. "Nirali," she jovially chimed in.

He noticed me declining his handshake; his smile stayed steadily fixed on his visage as he leaned back on the velvety couch with a regal air. His fingers flutter deftly, and a waitress waltzes over. "Fetch me the golden Moet Midnight," he commands, and the young lady hastens away to comply.

"So, what brings two gorgeous ladies like yourselves here with no date?" he inquired with friendly curiosity.

"We're on our lonesome tonight. Our husbands are busy, and we just wanted a girls' night out," Nirali explained, offering a satisfactory explanation for our presence. Laurent's gaze flitters to the gleaming wedding rings that envelope our fingers.

As Laurent's eyes flickered with a glint of disappointment, I couldn't help but notice how his charming personality quickly took over, masking any signs of sorrow.

"Your husbands must be fools," he said with a sly grin, "to leave two gorgeous ladies like yourselves here alone to hit the clubs." I shrugged nonchalantly. "We can take care of ourselves," I replied.

Laurent chuckled in response before rising from his seat and moving closer to me. As his warmth seeped through my skin, I noticed Nirali's watchful gaze and Saint's guards that he sent without informing me, eyeing the man suspiciously.

Uncomfortably, I tried to smile despite my skin prickling with apprehension. Suddenly, without any warning, Laurent leaned in, whispering into my ear, "Do you want me to come closer?"

My heart raced, and goosebumps covered my skin as I scooted away from him. "No, Laurent," I blurted out awkwardly, "I'm a married woman." But he shrugged nonchalantly, saying, "So what?"

"So, you'd be wise to steer clear of her. Believe me, crossing her path is not a game you want to play. Her husband is off the deep end." Nirali cautions.

Laurent lounged back, his piercing gaze scouring the club until it landed on me. "Seems her hubby's MIA. Unless you plan on ratting me out," he drawled, and I cringed.

Out of the corner of my eye, I see one of my guards striding away with an ominous air. The thick beat of my heart tells me that trouble's brewing.

"Nirali..." I cautioned, but my voice was heavy and foreboding. Nirali reaches for her phone with a sharp gasp. "We have to go," she declares, jumping up from the couch.

An instant later, the guard returns, sharing a meaningful glance with his companion.

In quick succession, Nirali and I grab our bags and exit. After what I'd been through with Andrew, I wasn't taking any chances with anyone.

Laurent rises, arms crossed, his demeanour giving nothing away. "So soon, ladies?" he inquires as we exit the VIP section, unaccompanied by our guards. I glance at the time on my phone - 11 PM.

"We're pretty wiped out," I reply. And with that, we vanish into the night, the tension palpable behind us.

I furrowed my brows in confusion as I wondered why they weren't taking any action. Although I expected them to intervene and remove Laurent's influence, they closely observed him without any reaction. Could it be possible that Saint instructed them to stand by and assess my allegiance deliberately?

Laurent's fingers clamped down on my arm like a vise, sending an electric jolt of anger coursing through me. I wrenched my arm away, fury simmering just under the surface.

"Mr. Duval, I suggest you leave before I take matters into my own hands," I said through gritted teeth, my warning falling on deaf ears. Laurent's dark gaze bored into me, a wicked smile playing at the corners of his lips.

"Is that a threat?" he taunted. I shook my head, refusing to be baited. "It's a warning," I spat out, my words razor-sharp. Without another glance, I turned on my heel and marched away, descending a flight of stairs with a purposeful stride.

As we emerged outside, I scanned the area for my guards, but they were nowhere to be found. Nirali's driver was waiting for us, and the towering shadows of her guards loomed behind them. The hairs on my neck stood on end, a sense of unease settling deep in my bones.

Strange.

The city's bustling streets were alive with energy, but our evening had been cruelly cut short by a persistent man who refused to accept "no" for an answer. As we climbed into the car, I slumped back into the seat, mulling over the incident in silence as the engine roared to life.

Turning to my friend Nirali, I made a plea. "Please, let's keep this to ourselves. Don't tell Abel." Confused, Nirali furrowed her brows and asked why. I let out a heavy sigh. "He'll tell Saint, and I'd rather he doesn't know what happened." Of course, I'm assuming that his security hadn't already alerted him. I cursed inwardly, hoping against hope that we wouldn't be dragged into the spotlight.

Nirali sighs and smiles weakly. "Oh, don't worry about it, my mouth is shut."

As I looked out the window, I couldn't help but smile at the sight of the moon resembling a bright giant eye and the stars twinkling like scattered salt on a dark surface. Nirali and I drove in silence until we reached at my—Saint's mansion. After an hour, I approached the door and unlocked it with my key. Upon entering, the foyer was completely silent, with a tense atmosphere. I carelessly threw my key into the nearby bowl.

"Hey, honey." A low voice called out. As I approached the dining room, a voice pierced through the silence, beckoning me forward. My heart raced as I followed the sound, each step echoing like thunder in my ears.

Suddenly, I froze in my tracks. "I'm glad you could join us sooner Doe." Saint's voice, rugged and raw, filled the room and I couldn't deny the shivers it sent down my spine. And there he was - Saint, his hair tousled and his face bruised, holding a pistol to the head of a man who cowered beside him.

My voice shook as I mustered up the courage to ask, "Saint, what is this?" He chuckles darkly, grabbing the man by the neck and lifting his head high; my eyes widen when I notice the man. It's Laurent.

"Remember your friend," he questions and my mouth instantly turns dry. "He touched what was mine," his words dripped with venom as he languorously traced the sharp contours of the metal gun against his neck. My gaze flickered towards a tablet resting uneasily on the table accompanied by a solitary button.

"Please, Saint," my voice trembled, but he remained steadfast. "You know the rules, Doe. No one crosses the line and lives to tell the tale."

With each passing moment, my throat constricted, making it hard to swallow.

"I-"

"Now, where did he touch you?" he questions. "Saint-" Saint's dark gaze locks onto me, his voice low and dangerous, "Irena, tell me. Where did he touch you?" I can feel his focus drilling into me as I whisper back, almost afraid to speak. "My arm."

A strange smile curves his lips, only adding to the threatening aura he emanates. As I watch in terror, his single dimple pops out.

Oh, how I wish I could look away, but his intense stare holds me captive.

"Did he make you feel uncomfortable?" he continues, and I can only nod mutely, my gaze darting nervously to Laurent, who is groaning in agony.

With a quick tap of the gun against Laurent's face, Saint manages to bring the man back to his senses. "You! What is this?" Laurent yells, trying to stand, but Saint pushes him back down. "Sorry to interrupt your slumber, Laurent. But we need to have a little chat with our guest here," Saint purrs, placing the gun on the table.

But it isn't until he picks up the tablet and reveals the three security cameras of different buildings that Laurent's eyes widen in horror. Suddenly, everything clicks into place, "Take a moment to truly see your babies," Saint's voice instils a sense of dread. "You wouldn't want any harm to come their way, would you?" His green eyes twinkle with a cruel pleasure as Laurent's pupils dilate in terror.

"Please, I beg of you, name your price," Laurent pleads for the safety of his cherished building. Saint scoffs, shaking his head in disgust. "Money is not what I desire from you, Laurent." His eyes blaze with an almost tangible fury. "I want you to experience the seething rage I feel when someone violates what is precious to them." He seizes the remote, and, with one push of a button, three buildings crumble into a cascade of debris, moments later I physically feel their echoes resonating through the air and ground.

As Laurent stares vacantly into space, his once-lively eyes drained of spirit, Saint saviours the pleasure of retaliation fulfilled.

A wave of fury boiled inside Laurent's chest as Saint's words hit him like a brick to the face. The thought of someone destroying what belonged to him was a bitter pill to swallow. "It's not a satisfying feeling knowing that someone touched and destroyed what is yours," Saint's voice trickled into his ear, stirring a fire within him.

Laurent gritted his teeth, feeling a mixture of despair and rage surge through him. "Y-you monster," he stuttered, fists clenched tightly at his sides. "You're all fucking monsters!" His voice thundered through the room, echoing off the walls. In a fit of desperation, he lunged for the gun on the table, finger hovering over the trigger.

I braced myself for the worst, shutting my eyes tightly, but nothing came. The gun clicked, but there was no explosion, only a smirk from Saint and a trembling Laurent, confused and frightened.

Saint's voice crooned smugly, "You didn't think I was that stupid to leave a loaded gun on the table with you untied, did you?"

"I-" A sinister chuckle escaped Saint before he revealed the weapon nestled in his pocket. The cold metal pressed against Laurent's flesh as a deafening pop echoed through the room, shattering my senses with a grotesque display of gore. He grabbed Laurent's head and smashed it on the table before breaking both his arms in one swift motion. I stood rooted to the spot, my mind reeling as I struggled to comprehend the carnage before me. As Laurent shivers on the floor while soft cries escape his lips, Saint calls out for one of his guards. Minutes later, they walk in and, without a word, drag Laurent's crippled body out of the room while he is still alive.

The stark reality of the situation hit me like a freight train - men were tortured or brutally killed because of their association with me.

The mere thought was enough to chill my bones. But more terrifying still was the realization that Saint brutality killed three men because of his twisted obsession with me.

And I couldn't help but find comfort in it.

CHAPTER 21

SAINT DÉ LEON

A twisted apprehension sinks to my marrow and pits out of my bones.

Staring down at the naked bum whimpering on the concrete floor. "The fuck are you crying for?" I question with annoyance. He trembles sniffing back the snot drooling out of his nostrils. "I-I didn't do it." He cries to himself pulling his legs up to his chest. "P-p-pleaseeee."

Of course, he did. I do not torture people for fun...

I torture them for the fucking pleasure. Okay maybe I do find the fun in it.

Crouching down to his level, I loosen the necktie around my neck. Cracking my tense muscle then satisfied when I hear the popping sounds of my bones.

Christ, I love the sound of breaking bones and soon, I will hear them.

"Didn't do what Angelo?" I question. He lifts his eyes, his haunted gaze meeting mine as I watch the fear swimming in his green pools. I push back the urge to sink my thumbs into his eye sockets. I have to be patient. "I didn't double cross you, Saint. I promise and devote my loya-"

I cut him off by slamming his head hard onto the ground. Grabbing him by his copper hair. Blood streaks down his face with his mouth hanging open in shock. Pulling him closer to me, I groan in frustration.

The fucker did double-cross me. I had a shipment coming from Japan for weapons that are illegal in France. Which cost over €500,000,000 on the dark web. I was ready to sell the weapons worldwide. Invest and triple the amount I bought them for. All my clients and workers are ready for the next process. Dealing with illegal weapons and selling them to corrupt officials, governments, etc...

It is one of the things I do to keep a roof over my head. I took over the arms-dealing organization after my father died 7 years ago. Originally it was supposed to be Abel but due to personal issues, I had to take over. He handles money laundering, operating a business for purposes, running gambling machines, restaurants, etc.

I do more of the dirty work which is no complaint from me. I enjoy it.

Now this fucking bum over here was in charge of transporting the weapons across the border, and come to my surprise the trucks are jumped by the fucking DST. One of the DST members bribed my people saying they will triple the number of their pay checks if they openly give up information and in return give them safety and lift all charges for their crimes.

The crimes the people have done for me are beyond lifting and just brushing it under a rug as if nothing happened and of course, dear Angelo was being a fucking airhead when he accepted the offer.

This brings us here. A pissed-off boss and an idiotic bastard paying for being a rat and a dumb, worthless piece of shit. We are collectively known as the French Mob and singularly known as Les beaux voyeurs.

One of the important rules that comes with working with me. Is that rats like Angelo will get punished for their sins. If anyone ever tries to double-cross me they better make sure I never find out or they will fucking regret it.

"Here's the thing about liars." I trail off slowly. "They piss me off and when I am pissed off." I pulled out my gun that was sitting in the back of my pants, turning the safety off. I point the weapon at his dick. "This happens." I say before firing. The gunshot echoes as Angelo's screams rumble within the walls. I silence his scream by shoving the gun in his mouth. Tears and sweat streamed down his face. "Now being the kind person I am. Let's start over."

The stench of iron and gunpowder trails up my nose and into my lungs. Inhaling deeply as a ghost smile creeps onto my lips. Letting go of Angelo I rise to my feet turning my attention to Prince and Abel as they watch from a distance.

"Ask Neal to bring the chainsaw." I ordered whoever was listening. Abel turns to Prince and he nods before strolling his way to the door. Knocking on the door, it opens and Neal appears. Prince mumbles to him then he walks away. Not a second later, Neal hands over the chainsaw to Prince before closing the metal door.

"Help him up." I demand. Prince and Abel rush to the naked bum. Each of them grabbed him by the arm and lifted him up. His head hung low as painful moans escaped his mouth.

Abel lifts his head and Angelo droopy eyes meeting mine. Locking the chain brake, I turn on the choke and push the primer button 4-6 times. I lay the chainsaw flat on the ground using my foot as I brace the chainsaw, leaning my weight on it to hold it in place then I pull the starter rope a few times until the engine starts. I bring the blade up to speed the sharp ends running, ready to cut through anything. The sound of the engine roaring consumes the silences. "Which one would you prefer me to slice off? Hands? Legs? Neck?" I suggest, listing all the above. Angelo swallows hard, soft whimpers escaping his lips as he pleads. I cast him a veiled glance, my eyes darting to all his limbs as I indecisively decided on which part I would like to remove.

Hmm?

Arms it is.

"Stretch out his arms."

Prince and Abel grasps Angelo's arms and stretches them out.

Terror overtook Angelo's face as I walked over to him. His chest rose and fell with rapid breaths while he used all his strength to fight Abel and Prince. Without wasting any second, I push the spinning sharp blade onto his withdrawn arm. His agonizing screams bless my ears, watching desirably as his flesh rips open, blood spraying out of his body, splattering onto my face and clothes as the deep red colours the blade that is gruesomely ripping into Angelo's face. The raucous sound of flesh ripping apart cuts through the deep, roaring sound of the rippling chainsaw, blending effectively with Angelo agonizing screams of pain. Pushing the heavy blade deeper into his flesh and finally I hear the sound of bones ripping apart like a butcher slicing the meat off and hitting the center of the animal's bones. The corner of my mouth quivered in satisfaction when his arm finally loosened from his body and fell to the ground. The thud of the arm brushed my ears. "Bloody hell." Prince mumbles, gawking at the penetrated arm. A thin layer of sweat beaded my forehead, caressing my tongue against my upper lip as I cocked my head to the side. "That's fucking disgusting," I snarled. Abel's forehead creased. "Yeah, no shit." Ignoring him, I continued, blinded by the gruesome anticipation of pain.

I promised him a slow and painful death. Knowing me. I am a man of my word.

"Angelo was not working alone." Abel declares, jamming his hands in his pockets. Prince walks out of the warehouse as he pulls out a cigarette from his pack, sliding the pack back into his jacket then lights it up. He inhales as the red cherry blares bright then pulls the cigarette from his mouth as he puffs out the smoke.

He stops right in front of us, his eyes scanning my body. "What?" I snapped at him. "The blood ruined your suit. There is no need to wash it, you should throw that shit away instead." He suggested, gesturing to my clothes covered in Angelo's blood that is now soaked into the fabric and has dried up. I stared down at myself and shrugged before turning my attention back to my brother. "Why do you say that?" I questioned, my gaze narrowed in suspicion. "We know he's jumped right, but people on the street are saying that Angelo was not the only one who has been offered to turn on you. Apparently other of our high-class workers have been approached. Nico, Chris, Marcello, Zo and Tobi have also been approached but not by the DST or any federal agents. It was someone else. Someone that's a part of the underworld crime families." He explains.

My shoulders tense.

So we have a bridge on our hands and possibly one of the crime families that's within my inner circle is fucking with my organization. They approach my men, manipulate them into going against me and when they deny the offer they jump to the next victim. Once they finally find an idiot to take the offer they purposely involve the federal agents, and from there shit goes down.

How the fuck did I not know this?

Groaning out of frustration, I pinch the bridge of my nose. "Do we know who it is?" I question in hope that Abel knows the snitch but deep down I already know the answer. Abel sighs and disappointedly shakes his head. "No but we are suspecting the Romano's." he answers. "Romano's? Why in the hell would the Italians go against us knowing that they are still in debt to us?" Prince asks, blowing out a puff of smoke. "I don't know, but the Romano family is the only lead we have. We are still working on it." Abel states.

Abel is also the smart one, who logically strategizes and gains information for me. He is the underboss and sacrifices blood, sweat and tears in his position.

A SUV pulls up in front of us and Prince tosses the cigarette on the dirty ground before turning the flame off with his foot.

"Call me when you get your facts straight." He asserts before he enters the car and it drives off leaving Abel and me in front of the warehouse's stretched landscape. "There's more," he blurts out. I frown. "It's about Irena. Remember when you told me to dig into her past relationship with her husband? I've been doing just that and actually found something interesting but it's ugly." He declares. I cock a brow allowing him to proceed.

"So, when I was chatting with the Nowak brothers, I found it a bit odd that they said Irena's marriage to Viktor was decent, even though it had its ups and downs. They shared a few little details about the marriage, so I decided to dig a bit deeper and look for the workers who used to clean and guard the house where Irena and Viktor lived. Irena was said to be really young, and Viktor, being older, totally used that to his advantage. The workers would just drop by the house now and then, and it was pretty rare to catch a glimpse of Irena. When they show up, she'll be all dressed up like she's trying to hide away and just chill in the background, kind of like a ghost. The cleaners were worried, but they figured it wasn't really their place to get involved. That just made me more curious, so I looked into it more. Eventually it got pretty rough, and Viktor ended up firing most of the staff who took care of the house. By the end, there was just one cleaner and a handful of guards left. The domestic worker had been with them for two years, but things took a turn when she caught Irena trying to hang herself. She managed to stop her and called Viktor, but when he got home, he just blew up at the maid and fired her without saying a word," he explains. Shaking his head as he sighs.

Irena tried to kill herself...

"This shit is all fucked up." he mumbles to himself. "What else did you find out?" I question, eager to know what dark secrets Irena has locked away.

"The very same worker who found Irena, her name is Jenette, a domestic worker that came from Mozambique, a rural town called Chokwe and moved to Poland at the age of 19 to live with her extended cousin so that she can earn money for her family." He continued. "A year later Irena unexpectedly appeared at her front doorstep all busted up. Her clothes were torn, her face was busted. Blood and bruises all over her body. Jenette told me that she was confused and surprised but helped Irena. She told her everything about Viktor and how he treated her and couldn't escape the marriage, so the only way to end it was to kill him and Jenette helped her. She gave her the safest and easiest way to switch him off."

"Kill him Abel, who the fuck says 'switch him off'?" I inquired, Abel rolled his eyes. "Anyway old fuck. They poisoned him but not just any poison she used apples." he conceded. "Apples?" I blink back in disbelief.

What is this? Snow white and the old witch with the poison apple, whatever the fuck kids watch these days.

"So you're telling me. Irena killed Viktor by using poisonous apples?" I snarled, "I got the same reaction but it's what is in the apples."

The seeds. I thought to myself.

"The seeds. They contain cyanide and somehow transform those seeds into cyanide salt. Which results in seizures, slow heart rate, shortness in breath and finally death. So it will play out as a casual heart attack." he blurts out, folding his arms.

"Irena killed her husband." I state the obvious aloud. "Yeah, and she did a fucking good job acting out her innocence as if she was not behind it. I mean using apple seeds, turning them into cyanide salt, sprinkle it on his food and the result leads to a heart attack...Fucking genius." he boasted. I run my fingers through my hair as I process the information.

My little doe is not so innocent after all.

"You better be alert because your wife might kill you and dear brother you certainly will not be expecting it." Abel teased and laughed, I shot him a glare and he instantly snapped shut. My brother might be an ass but he's onto something. If Irena killed

Viktor with no one suspecting her, what's going to stop her from killing me so that she can finally get her wish and escape?

CHAPTER 22

IRENA NOWAK

I slowly emerge from my slumber, I am greeted by a delicate
tune that resonates in the air. My senses are alert, and I listen closely, wondering where this symphony is coming from. My ears soon recognize the sweet sound of a piano, but my mind is puzzled. Since when did we own a piano?

I rise from my bed, hesitantly taking small steps towards the
source of the enigmatic music. The hardwood floor sends shivers, but the melody beckons me closer. Every step feels like a lifetime, my heart racing with anticipation.

The tune grows louder and more captivating. It's got me in its

grasp, and I'm powerless to resist. The enchanting melody consumes my spirit and takes me to a place I've never been.

A sudden jolt runs through my body as I reach the wooden

door that's been guarding my curiosity for far too long. My heart thumps wildly against my chest in anticipation of the unknown.

I take a deep breath and push the door open, only to be met by a haunting sight that freezes me in place.

My eyes are drawn to Saint, seated at the pristine white piano, his figure drenched in the deepest red. Blood. It's everywhere.

Yet, there's something intoxicatingly beautiful about how the

moon's soft light caresses his reddened skin, transforming the gruesome scene into a captivating work of art. Saint is lost in his music, his fingers dancing along the keys as the familiar melody fills the room.

From my vantage point, I can't help but marvel at the sheer

elegance of it all, the way every note seems to paint the air with a hauntingly sweet symphony. It's as if the world around me has faded into the background to make way for the stark beauty that unfolds before me.

The piano's sombre melody echoes through the room, a haunting lament of agony and despair. His fingers dance across the keys with a palpable sorrow that defies explanation. I watch

him, enraptured by the vulnerable moment he shares with me without him acknowledging me. The mood is poignant, a hushed tranquillity that heightens the sorrow as it creeps forward, swallowing the light inch by inch.

Suddenly, the notes stop, and the sudden quiet is deafening. It's as though all hell has broken loose, but no sound is heard, only the silent tension that crackles in the air.

"Saint?" I whisper, afraid to break the spell of this sorrowful moment. He turns to me, and his fierce gaze pierces me to the core, a reminder of the pain he carries within.

"Why did you kill your husband?"

My heart pounds against my chest when he prowls towards me. There's tension in my shoulders like thunderclouds swollen with rain.

How does he know?

What else does he know?

Is he going to kill me?

Of course he's going to kill you! The little voice at the back of my head yells.

"Answer the question Irena." He growls, with each step he takes my soul is being pulled out of my body. I couldn't find the voice even if I were to speak. I was frozen. Shocked. Terrified.

This man is insane and he uncovered my darkest secret far too easily. Around him, I'm never safe. He stops inches from me, his tall frame casting a shadow I can't step out of. I flinch at the stench he wears like cologne: blood and death. A scent he carries like a badge of honour.

Lifting my gaze to his, I instantly regret when I see the anger swimming in his magical pools of gold and emerald. It was beautiful, dangerous and terrifying.

"I didn't" I lied. His gaze darkened. "So not only are you a killer but also a liar." He draws out, taking another step forward and I'm forced to step back until my back hits the wall. I gasp. "I'm going to ask you again." He states, his voice deep, rich and silky as it sends unwanted shivers trailing up my spine.

"Why. Did. You. Kill. Viktor?" He questions slowly. A fiery ache lodges in my throat when I meet Saint's watchful gaze. Darting my tongue out I nervously lick my lips. "He hurt me." I whisper weakly. Saint's bloody hands cups my left cheek and I instantly cringe. Tears threaten to spill out my eyes as a tiny layer of sweat forms on my forehead. My breathing hitches when he leans dangerously close. His lips almost brushed against my ear. "How bad did he hurt you?" He whispers, the feeling of his breathing sends heat rushing to my core.

What the fuck Irena?

"Very bad." I uttered, biting down on my bottom lip stopping it from quivering. "So you killed him?" He clarifies. I nod. Shutting my eyes. "I'm going to need you to use your words Doe." He demands. "Yes." I breathe.

My heart plummets the moment I feel cold steel press against my temple, followed by the unmistakable click of the safety being released.

"Open your eyes, Irena," he commands, voice low and merciless.

Slowly, I do. My gaze locks with his. Out of the corner of my eye, I catch the unmistakable shape of the gun, still nestled against my skin like a threat whispered too close.

Oh God.

He's going to kill me.

"You're going to be a good girl and answer my questions. If you lie to me Irena…" He pauses leaning close to my ear. Goosebumps crawl on my skin as I feel his warm breath.

Without fighting, a soft whimper escapes my lips, tears pouring out of my eyes.

"I'm going to pull the trigger." He whispers.

Those haunting words danced in the air like a threatening thunderstorm ready to curse the lands with its wrath.

I swallow the lump in my throat, my heartbeat quickens as I feel the hairs on the nape of my neck lift away from my skin. An unsettling cool chill passes through my body like a ghost. "When did Viktor start abusing you?" he questioned, I inhaled an unsteady breath. I lift my gaze to Saint who no longer wears the sadistic grin. A prickling sensation webs my nerves, encasing me in a cold state of unease. "A year later into our marriage." I answer, beads of sweat prickling onto my forehead. Saint's sharp merciless gaze sweeps over the length of my body, then his eyes lock with mine again. It's not the seductive desirable way, it's the ruthless and painful kind. Nervously I dart my tongue out and lick my lips.

Keep calm Irena, he is not a lying detector. Just choose your words carefully. The little voice reassures me.

"You were what? Seventeen?"

I nod.

A low growl rumbles in his chest as he studies me carefully, I freeze. The feeling of the gun caressing down my jawline almost made me pee in my pants.

"You're trembling love."

"You're pointing a gun at me."

Dark eyebrows pinched together, he runs his tongue over his teeth.

"Did he abuse you with his words?" He calmly questions. My heart flutters and not the good kind. I close my eyes, pushing back the horrific memories of each time Viktor touched me. Sometimes I could still feel his rough hands on my skin, his hot breath tickling my neck as he whispered foul words to me. Pushing back the dark memories I reopen my eyes. "Yes." I answered, my voice flat as I maintained my cool. "Rape you?"

"Yes."

"Did you tell anyone?" He questions, his gaze darkening as I see the rage swimming in his hues of gold and green pools. I bite down on my lip. I hesitate to mention my uncles because I am aware that Saint is capable of confronting them about it and they will obviously deny which Saint will believe. That is what I'm telling myself but deep down I know that he will literally kill them for shutting me down all these years. Maybe I am delusional but I somehow sensed the concern in Saint. The curiosity and concern faintly clouded his closed up expression. I did not see any hint of pettiness or satisfaction. I saw something else. Apart from the anger if you look past it I can also see the pain. As if he too relates...

Like I said. Maybe it's just the delusions and my mind is messing with me since I'm in a vulnerable state right now.

"I told my uncles but they took Viktor's word over mine." I say breathlessly. The more he looks at me it's as if he is taking away my ability to breathe. He watches me closely, like there's something worth looking at.

"How did you cope?" he whispered, his eyes searching mine. I swallow the heavy lump in my throat. The questions Saint is asking me are all too much. Normally I would never answer such deep questions but right now I am forced to answer them. I am forced to trauma dump and in some fucked up way it makes me feel heard. After years of being silenced someone finally wants to hear my story and that someone is Saint.

Pointing a gun at me is irrational behaviour, but in Saint's mind it's the only way for me to talk about my past that I've been trying to bury deep inside my brain. That I've been running away from. That I've been in battle with since day one.

"Alcohol." I answer, telling him half the truth.

I never told anyone this apart from an old worker, Jenette. I would hurt myself. I don't know why but I did. Knowing that Viktor would hurt me I felt so unworthy as if I deserved to feel the pain so I would do it to myself. The first time I did was the third time Viktor raised his hands on me. I felt everything and nothing at the same time. I remember the day as if it was yesterday.

A younger me rushed to the bathroom, searching the cabinets until she found a needle. Confused and hurt to why she has the sudden thought to hurt herself, convincing herself that she deserves it. That she deserves the pain. Pricking the sharp needle into her fingertips watching as the blood lightly oozes out of her harmless wound on her fingertip.

It was harmless but did so much damage. One thing leads to another and she finds herself using the kitchen knife to slit her wrist. Ready to give herself up to death. Ready to give up on life. I was a girl who was trying to cope with something horrible that she should never have to live through. As I stand here forcefully confronting my darkest secrets to Saint.

I realized that I self-harmed myself because Viktor wouldn't let me cry. I cried because he wouldn't let me speak because they wouldn't let me speak. What scared me the most is that the phrase 'self-ham' never phased me; it only filtered in my head into 'punishing myself.'

A charged pulse ignites a fire beneath my palm, the air, volatile and tense. A flurry chaos swirled around us like a vortex.

Saint slowly trails the gun between the exposure of my breast. My chest rises and falls, heart beating like thunder, body trembling and beads of sweat forming on my forehead. "My little doe has been through so much in the past. I guess we have something in common. We can bond over our traumas." He chuckles darkly, the rich deep sound hits my chest as it faintly leaves a mark.

"I'd rather set myself on fire then bond with you." I snarled bitterly. "Trust me Irena, we are more alike than you think." he snapped. He tilts his head to the side, leaning so close his warm minty breath fans across my neck, his lips brushing against my ear lobe.

"You're stubborn, afraid and lost. You hate being touched and don't like many people. Your hair is nearly as black as the heart you want the world to think you have. In your own eyes, you are a monster, but what you don't know is that monsters aren't always what we imagine. Sometimes, they come in softer forms, like fairies with trembling wings and hearts too bruised to hope. The kind who flinch at love, not because they don't want it, but because they've never known it.

They call themselves unworthy, cursed, broken… but in truth, they're the ones who deserve love the most." He asserts, peering down at me. His voice is low and gentle.

He traces the gun across my cheek and I turn my head to the side avoiding his gaze. "No one knew the battle you fought inside every day, and when you finally got the courage to seek out for help they silenced you. All the anger and betrayal slowly growing inside of you–consuming. Eating you up until you left with nothing but darkness. Pain. Anger. Betrayal."

"You've bled in silence for so long that it became your favourite way of speaking." Saint drawls. The words sinking into my chest.

My breath stalls, every sinew in my body cored tight. My heart is kicking at my chest and speeding off.

No matter how much I try to deny or fight it. Saint is right. He took one look at me and knew the battles I've been facing my whole life. I refuse to believe that this man is more alike to me than I thought.

I refuse to believe that he actually sees the dark side of me that I've been burying for years. Holding back the chaotic emotions.

A single tear slips down my cheek. My heart clenches. "Why so quiet doe? Loss of words..." he trails off. He tucks a single strand of hair behind my ear with the tip of the gun. "No matter how much you try to deny it. We share the same demons."

"The only difference is that you haven't embraced them. You fight them every day because you're scared that once you let go." He pauses. My eyes grow wide and body startled when he pulled the trigger but the clicking sound of the gun nearly caused my life to flash before my eyes.

There were no bullets yet he still pulled the trigger!

"You will never be the same." He whispers.

I shake my head, pushing him away from me as I felt so closed up and having difficulty breathing. Walking out of the room I rush back upstairs and once I'm far away from him I try to calm down my anxiety before it triggers a panic attack.

And I'm no longer on my pills. My ears ring and vision blur as all the haunting memories of Viktor crash into me all at once.

I press my head against the hallway walls, holding myself as I slide down with defeat.

Allowing the gentle tears stream down my cheek.

I'm scared.

Scared that Saint can see me. See the part of me that's been silenced for years, scared that he knows the exact haunting emotions consuming from the inside out, scared that we share the same demons and somehow.

I find comfort in it.

It's now possible that I might betray myself by letting him in.

CHAPTER 23

IRENA NOWAK

The warm water gracefully hugs my body whilst soaking in it, easing the tensed muscles as the steam floats in the air. A thin layer of sweat prickled out of the pores on my forehead, my curly hair damped, sticking to my skin allowing the gentle tears to caress down my cheek. The smell of vanilla and honey lingers in the air rushing me comfort to the distress emotion that is consuming me from the inside out.

I've been in that bath for a while now. Lost in thought. Confused, collected, and confronted by Saint.

I have allowed myself to show a glimpse of my weakness, show him and share the dark secrets I have promised myself to take to my grave. Not knowing that one day a terrifying man will somehow and somewhat relate to me. What scared me was that he took one good look at me and read me like his favourite book. Word to word, specifying what I have been through, What I have hidden from the world.

I don't know how to feel about this.

Happy? Acknowledging that I am finally being heard not in the way I wanted to be but by someone — someone finally believes me and what is shocking is that they also can relate to the pain I am feeling.

Or...

Terrified. Knowing that this man can get anything out of me just by one conflicted look. He can bury my deepest, darkest secret and use it as a weapon to get anything from me. Anything that he desires. A loaded gun pressed to my temple as my heartbeat matches the ticking sound of the clock casually counting the seconds to my death.

It's all too much to bear.

But then, why would Saint want to hear my side of the story even though he already knew the truth and had proof of how I killed Viktor? There has to be valuable reasoning. Yes, the way he forced it out of me was fucked up but it also brought comfort to me because he forced it out of me...

I will never admit it out loud because I am ashamed but thrilled that I am finally being seen by the devil himself.

God, what am I thinking!?

I groan in frustration. Lying back in the tub, taking a deep breath as I completely submerge myself under the water.

My eyes closed and my heart was beating slowly. I hold my breath.

I've always wondered how it felt to drown. Is it painful?

The kind of pain that has you screaming in agony, praying to God that you would do anything to end the terrible feeling. Or is it peaceful?

Being underwater. The outside world of silence. Floating there as long as you can, slowly running out of oxygen but you still stay there. Listening to your heartbeat. Feeling your lungs being drowned away as it pleads for the one thing that will keep it alive and functional.

But in reality. I've always been drowning, suffocating by the darkness of my thoughts. Sacred as I try to overcome it. My body is tired. My soul is tired, empty with a numb void deep inside of me. Drowning in my tears. No matter what I do or how hard I try. The pain that's been inflicted upon me —

Just. Won't. Go. Away.

I open my eyes and my heart jumps when I see a shadow — a man heaving above the water. I quickly pull myself up, gasping for air and searching the bathroom with my eyes to find that it's only me.

I push my wet hair back and wipe the water from my face. Calming myself down.

It's all in your head. It's all in your head.

I calm myself by counting to ten. My shoulders fall in relief when I'm finally calm.

No matter how fast I run, I cannot escape my demons. No matter how hard I fight, I will never find peace.

When I swing the bedroom door open and step out I'm startled by Saint. *A shirtless Saint.*

His hair is not styled, it's messy and fluffy as a few strands fall onto his forehead. The black loose jogger he is wearing hangs dangerously low around his waist as it shows the V-line moulded with his defined abs. Old scars are plastered across his chest, a huge scar slashed across his chest, and a few bullet wounds here and there. I am eager to trace my fingers along those scars but I hold myself back.

I'm not sure how long I stayed in my room but all I know is that it's dark outside and all the main lights are off. The only light that's bleeding through the windows and into the house is the bright moonlight.

Saint tilted his head to the side, his eyes roaming my body before they met mine. My heart pounds against my chest.

His musky woodsy cologne kisses the tip of my nose with a hint of fresh soap, notifying me that he just came from taking a long shower. The smell of blood and death no more.

"You've been in there for a long time," Saint states with his deep husky voice that now has a huge effect on me. As it sends unwanted shivers traveling through my body.

"I was taking a relaxing long bath," I answered, not daring to look away. "Are you relaxed now?" He questions.

I press my lips together and nod, tugging the curls behind my ear. "I see you finally showered and got rid of the disgusting scent of blood." I point out. Saint's watchful gaze searches my eyes, the corner of his lips slightly twitching into a small smile. "Sadly, yes," he informs.

He walks right up to me, and I intentionally step back into the room. He got close enough that I could feel his body heat. I try to look away but I can't, feeling the unsettling touch coast my skin and the fine hairs on the nape of my neck rise.

"Why are you here Saint?" I snarled. "You should watch your tone when you talk to me because you wouldn't want to know what I might do to you." He blurts out. "Kill me..." I trailed off.

He steps closer. Inches away from me. "Why do you always assume I might kill you?"

I shrug. "You are a monster. You find joy and pleasure in seeing people suffer." I comment. "Because it's what you're capable of…because every time I look at you I just want to shove a knife down your throat." I admit half the truth.

"So when you have thoughts of killing me you assume I am thinking the same each time I look at you." he clarifies. "Am I not wrong?" I blabber back cocking a brow. He casually shrugs. "Maybe."

"Maybe is not an answer Saint." I declare. He tilts his head to the side, "No?"

"Then what do you want me to say?" Saint asks. This time it's my turn to shrug. "I want a straightforward answer." I state.

A ghost grin plastered across his face. He takes another step forward. Lips inches away from mine with his body heat colliding with mine. His addictive scent sends heat straight to my core.

"Each time I look at you. You make me sick with desire, with a desire to possess you, to have you around me…*always*. I want to kiss that soft skin of yours, kiss the scars away and replace it with mine." he pauses, leaning dangerously close to my ear. "That's what I think about when I look at you," he whispers then pulls back.

His gaze darkens, tension sparking between us. I hear my heart pounding against my chest and my core throbbing, begging to be touched.

I swallow.

I open my mouth to talk but the words fail to come out.

He smiles, that innocent dimple popping out again, with his eyes taking in the length of my body. "What if I don't want any of those things you mentioned?" I teased, keeping my tone calm. Saint lightly chuckles that it's barely audible. "You want those things. You are desperate for it. Irena, your body is a terrible liar than you are. I can catch how you breathe as your chest rises and falls rapidly. Your full lips parted. Your eyes wide staring back at me as if you're on your knees sucking my cock. Your fingers nervously fidget, fighting the itching urge to do something you might regret later. Your voice is soft and breathless. One look at you and your pulse quickens." he blurts out.

"You want me to fuck you. You just don't know it yet. You're in denial." he proclaims.

Stepping away from Saint, I fold my arms. "Goodnight Saint." I casually dismiss him, glaring at him with frustration. He traces his tongue across his bottom teeth, nodding as he pushes his hair back.

Not saying a single word, Saint heads for the door, shutting the wooden frame behind him leaving me all alone in my room.

Hot and wet.

My gaze is fixed on the vivid wolfsbane in front of me. Its blooms sway in the gentle breeze as my thoughts turn to the idea of poisoning Saint. Yet, a small voice within me urges restraint, warning me not to take his life.

Surprisingly, my hatred towards him is undergoing a transformation. Though still present, it's not as fiery as before, its intensity waning. The reason behind this change eludes me.

Perhaps it's due to what transpired last night, or maybe it's my refusal to surrender and accept his viewpoint. Whatever the cause, the only viable solution seems to be self-annihilation.

I pluck the plant and blend it into a sauce to use as dressing on Saint's plate. It's midday, but I've already prepared his dinner, setting the table with utmost care. When finished, I remove my apron and lay it in its place, neatly, in the kitchen.

As I enter the dining room, Saint is already lounging in his silk night robe, his toned abs on full display. Black sweats cling to his waist, tempting me to run my tongue along the creamy skin below. But as I take my seat, I force the sinful thoughts aside, not wanting to give in to the electric tension between us.

Pouring myself a drink, I catch Saint's watchful gaze as it lingers on me for a moment before darting back to his plate. The air crackles with anticipation, so thick you could cut it with a knife.

Suddenly, Saint picks up his fork and knife, inspecting his food with a careful eye. I take a sip of wine, watching him study each bite with a focused intensity.

Our eyes lock in an unspoken conversation, the unspoken words hanging heavy in the air between us. His gaze lifts to meet mine, his eyes alight with mischief as he tilts his head. A sly smile curves his lips, a wicked dimple popping out to play.

I take a bite of my vegetables, my focus still fixed on him. "What's wrong?" I ask, puzzled by his sudden hesitation to eat.

"Irena?" His voice is soft, a question in his tone. My brow arches in response, curious as to what he could want.

"Did you happen to do something to my food?" He asks, his tone laced with suspicion. I shrug, teasing him with a knowing smile. "What makes you think that?"

Saint stares at the food and back at me.

He rises from his seat, takes his plate, and approaches me. Cutting into the egg he brings the piece to my mouth.

"Eat," he demands and I look up at him, through hooded eyes. "The only way I will eat is if you take a bite," he explains and my heart quickens in my chest.

"I have my own food," I say. He shakes his head in disapproval.

"Do me a favour and take a bite. Unless, of course, you did something to my food," he demands, his voice dragging out each syllable.

Our eyes remain locked in a showdown of wills, the tension heavy enough to cut with a knife. I stand tall, refusing to back down from his challenge.

"No," I reply with a firm tone.

"I went to the trouble of cooking for you, so you should at least have a taste. And if you think I poisoned it, well, I guess you'll have to take the risk to find out," I retorted, adamant that my cooking skills deserve more respect.

Even though I did poison his food.

He stares at me, his eyes searching for any sign of weakness, but I hold his gaze without flinching.

"Remove the fork from my face. I'm trying to eat," I declared with fierce determination, despite feeling a surge of adrenaline coursing through my veins. Though timid on the inside, I refused to back down.

Saint arched an eyebrow, taken aback by my sudden confidence, and backed away as he delicately removed the instrument from my face.

With a satisfied grin, I nimbly bit into my toast and relished the burst of flavours that tantalized my taste buds. Meanwhile, Saint begrudgingly stormed out, leaving me to savour my hard-won victory.

Whether he eats my food, chooses to go hungry, or opts to dine out, the responsibility for his decision rests solely on him.

CHAPTER 24

SAINT DÉ LEON

Romano stepped out like he was walking into a scene he'd already written. Brushed off his jacket like the world owed him respect. I didn't move. Just watched.

"You're late," I said, low and deliberate, sharp enough to draw blood if needed.

He gave me that trademark smirk, the one that tried too hard to be charming. "I like to be dramatic."

I roll my eyes.

Of course he did.

Abel stood behind me with his arms crossed. The quiet one, but that silence held weight. We didn't speak unless it mattered. Romano always spoke like the world was a stage. That was his problem.

I turned without waiting and walked in. Let him decide whether he was coming or not.

Inside, the hall stretched long, lit gold and false. Oil paintings lined the walls with dead eyes staring at us, long forgotten. We moved into the meeting room. No windows. Velvet walls. One table. One decanter. Bourbon, untouched.

Romano stayed standing. Expected.

"I didn't authorize the drop in Marseille," he said. Flat and defensive. "Whoever used my name is either stupid, suicidal, or both."

I poured myself a drink. No rush. "Then we've got a ghost using your signature. A shipment with your organization's mark."

Abel's voice finally came through, it was rough and grounded. "If it wasn't you, it was someone close. That makes it your mess to clean."

Romano's jaw ticked. "You think I'd risk war over a shipment? I've got my own shit back home. The Russians are rotting everything they touch."

I looked him over. "You always had trouble keeping your house in order, Romano."

That made him step forward, shadow clashing into mine. "Say that again, Saint."

"You heard me."

Abel moved between us. "Enough."

Romano didn't back down. Most men know what I am. They watch their words, measure their breath. But not him. He never learned fear the way others did or maybe he just buried it better.

We go back, deep. Long before power turned us into wolves. When we were still just sons of kings, raised to inherit empires soaked in blood.

There was a time the Romano family was circling the drain. His father, Giancarlo was two steps from losing everything. Enemies at his gates, rats in his council, bodies dropping faster than they could be buried. The Russians had made a move. So had the Albanians. It was open season in Naples, and the Romano name was on the butcher's block.

Giancarlo called my father.

Not a meeting. Not a deal. A call. Old-school. One line, one request.

The Dé Leons answered.

We didn't come with lawyers. We came with men, cleaners, hitters, ghosts who spoke with bullets. We carved out a perimeter in Naples and turned it into a fortress. Blood for blood. That was the deal. No contracts. Just legacy.

The French saved the Italians that year. Quietly. Efficiently. And ever since, the Romanos have been in our pocket. Not by force. By oath.

Loyalty in our world is currency. You can't buy it. You earn it with your life. And when your family name gets saved from extinction, it binds you forever. Blood in, blood out.

That's why Romano's here. That's why we're still talking instead of burying bodies. But I never forget: his empire still stands because my family propped it back up. And every move he makes under our watch carries weight.

He might wear the crown now, but the gold's still tarnished with French fingerprints.

"If you think I'm going to eat the blame for something I didn't greenlight, you've forgotten who the fuck I am."

I set my glass down, harder than I needed to. "No," I said, voice like frost. "I remember exactly who you are. The outsider who got lucky. Who thinks obsession equals power."

He lunged. Abel caught him mid-step, palm flat to his chest.

"You want to swing on him in my house?" Abel snapped.

Romano's fist trembled. I didn't even flinch.

Then—

The door opened.

"I hope you're not about to start bleeding on my floors."

Nirali.

"Abel," she said, walking over to her husband. "Pour our guest a drink before your pride chokes the both of you."

Romano exhaled. "Good to see you, Nirali. Been a while."

He always softened for her. Everyone did.

"How've you been?" Nirali questions.

"Can't complain," he added.

She kissed Abel's cheek and turned to face us both. "You came all this way. Let's not waste it on testosterone and dick-measuring."

We locked eyes again, Romano and I. A truce passed unspoken between us. Not peace. Just history doing what it always does...binding the blood no matter how dry it runs.

He sighed. "We were ready to tear each other apart. But old blood runs deep. We don't have to see eye to eye to have each other's backs."

He offered his hand. I stared at it, then took it. Firm.

"If you're lying," I said, "I'll kill you."

Romano smiled. "There's the man I know. And no—it wasn't me. I've been off-grid for months. Anyone with half a brain knows that."

I let go of his hand, frowning. "Where?"

"Russia."

Abel blinked. "Still stuck on that girl?"

It's been five goddamn years with him stuck on Semion Lebedev's daughter.

Five years of silence, detours, and excuses. We've watched him walk through warzones with a pulse, but that girl—that girl is the one thing that broke him.

Nobody knows. Not the families, not the street, not even his own crew. Just Abel and me and obviously Nirali since her and my brother tell each other everything. But we know only because we caught him.

Wasn't planned.

We'd flown out to check on him. He'd been off the grid too long, no updates, no movements, just smoke. We figured maybe the Russians got to him, maybe he was dead in a ditch somewhere north of Novosibirsk. So we flew out just the two of us. With no guards or announcement. We landed in the middle of a snowstorm, went straight to that icy prison he called home.

We walked into the house and found him…Romano, the infamous heir, the street prince turned kingpin, kneeling like some sainted monk, pictures of a girl everywhere. It looked like he was on the hunt to find this girl. Nobody knew Semion had a daughter.

Not the Bratva. Not the FSB. Not even the old guard who used to kiss his rings and carry out his executions.

Semion Lebedev—the Butcher of Belgorod, the man who used piano wire and acid like most men use a handshake, wasn't supposed to have soft spots. He had a son, sure, maybe he's dead or disappeared. I don't know that tale, maybe they were just rumours. But a daughter? That was a myth. A fairytale told by traitors before they bled out in bathtubs.

So how the fuck Romano found her… that's still a mystery to me.

He's good, I'll give him that. Always had a nose for secrets, like a bloodhound raised in silence. But this? This was buried. Deep. Past layers of fake names, burned passports, hidden estates. And somehow he dug her out of whatever hole Semion shoved her in. Maybe she reached out to him. Maybe he found her by accident. Maybe he burned down half of Eastern Europe just to chase a name.

Whatever the truth is, he's not talking. And neither are we.

Because if the wrong people knew… if even a whisper got out that Romano found Semion's only blood…it wouldn't just start a war.

It would end everything.

The Bratva would rise out of the cracks like cockroaches. Every faction, every ghost loyal to Semion, would crawl out of hiding to claim her, kill her, or weaponize her.

The French hold power yes, but the Russians—they are gods in the crime industry.

Romano's obsession has a heartbeat. And that heartbeat is a loaded gun pointed at all of us.

Semion's daughter.

A living ghost. The one piece the world thought had burned in the war with the Bratva. Romano didn't say a word. Just stood between us and her like he'd take a bullet before letting us get too close.

We don't do human. We're built to bury, not to love. But there he was, already buried, and digging himself deeper just to keep her breathing.

We left without speaking of it that day. That was the deal. *Silence.*

But the weight never left the room.

Every time I look at him now, I see it. Not the man. Not the threat. Just the boy, still kneeling in that frozen house, wrapped in a war he refuses to end.

Romano shot Abel a look.

"You still haven't made a move?" Nirali asked.

He ran a hand through his hair. "It's more complicated than it looks."

Abel smirked. "Why? Does she give you scars?"

Romano frowned. "What?"

Nirali looked at me. "If you haven't noticed, Saint over here is also suffering from lady problems. His wife gave him his now signature scar on his face." Romano turned to me and I silently walked to the bar and refilled my glass.

"No shit," he said. "So it was your wife. I was going to come to the wedding, but you assholes didn't send an invite."

Abel shrugged. "Hard to invite a ghost. Man isolates himself for a woman and expects us to keep rolling out the red carpet."

"She's not just any woman dickhead," Romano snapped.

"She got you tucked away in Siberia like some sad monk. Tell me again how that ain't tragic?" Nirali lifts a brow, not impressed by my comment. "Do I need to separate you two like kids?" she said flatly. "Let him mourn. He's been chasing a ghost for five years."

"She's not a ghost." He argues.

"Then what is she?" I asked.

He didn't hesitate. "She's the reason I'm still breathing. You wouldn't get it though. You don't have a heart."

I scoffed and handed him a glass. "And you do?"

"For her? Yes." He looked me dead in the eye. "I do."

"Goddamn poets, the both of you." Abel mutters and Nirali chuckles beside him. "Let him be Abel. You would purposely get in fights for weeks when I left you in Milan."

Abel folds his arms in a defensive manner. "That's different Angel." Nirali smirks, "Sure it was."

I down my drink again, turning to face Romano. "Sooo. You went to Russia for her. You get what you came for?"

He shakes his head, "No, not yet."

"I'm patient with my girl, she needs a little time."

"You're close to pushing a decade with this girl. How long is it going to take?" Nirali questions.

"Still chasing." I answer for him. He sighs, "still bleeding."

Silence drapes the room. Heavy and familiar. Nirali clears her throat, "Alright, heartbreakers. Let's try not to burn down Paris with your tragic love stories and egos. Saint, refill that drink. Raph sit down. You boys have wars to plan, not just women to cry about." Abel chuckles under his breath. "I can never get bored with you Angel." He says to his wife and she smiles, planting a kiss on his cheek.

"You sure you're not the real boss of this place?" Romano asks aloud, regarding Nirali. Abel admits proudly, "She is." Nirali smirks and turns toward the hallway, her voice trailing like a velvet whip. "Try not to stab each other before lunch."

She disappears through the door, leaving behind a quiet laugh and a room of men forced to face their demons.

CHAPTER 25

SAINT DÉ LEON

I wake up to the smell of bacon and eggs.

Fluttering my eyes open, the newborn light instantly blinds me. Groaning in frustration I shut them tight—reopened them and forced myself out of bed. Pushing my hair out of my face I crack my neck, satisfied when I hear the popping sound of my bones.

I make my way to the bathroom and quickly brush my teeth then splash my face with cold water to wake me fully. Once I'm done doing my business in the bathroom I head downstairs and head straight to the kitchen.

I pause in my tracks when I see Irena's back facing me. Her thick curls bounce around as she slightly moves her body to her humming tunes. She's wearing a black lace dress that reaches just above her round ass. Her light brown-toned legs moved back and forth in harmony. Irena turns around and shrieks when she notices me.

"Pierdolic!" she yells in polish. I raise a brow, folding my arms in amusement. "Bonjour petite biche." I reply in French and she scoffs rolling her eyes as she sets the glass on the kitchen island. I walked further into the kitchen and took a seat on one of the stools. I watched her as she worked her way around the kitchen grabbing plates and utensils, and neatly placing them on the island followed by the food and a jar of orange juice.

When she's done with preparing breakfast for the both of us she takes a seat, two seats far from me. I wanted to comment on it but allowed the words to die on my tongue because right now I don't have the energy to argue and I am hungry as fuck, plus my wife prepared breakfast that looks too good to eat. So it's better to eat in a slightly happy mood than a grumpy one.

I pick up the fork and shovel the food off the plate before shoving it into my mouth. A low growl manages to escape my throat as the immaculate flavours burst on my taste buds. Darting my tongue out I lick the flavour off my lips. I feel Irena's stare, pausing. I turn to look at her. "The food is good," I simply say before proceeding to enjoy my breakfast. "Thank you." She mumbles then takes a small sip of her juice. We sat in silence for ten minutes straight eating out breakfast.

Once I'm done I slip off the stool and take my empty dishes then make my way to the sink. I turn the tap on before setting the dirty dishes into the sink. Irena appears beside me. Her sweet honey scent slapped my face with delight. She carefully placed the dishes into the sink and then took the soapy scrub from my hands. My breath stalls. "You don't have to wash the dishes." She lets out. Her chocolate eyes shimmer with her cresting trepidation. "I know, but you cook and I wash. A 50/50 relationship." I admit.

At a young age, I always saw how my father treated my mother and decided that I wouldn't do the same of carrying the sins of my father.

Irena blushes, biting down on her bottom lip as she rinses the plate under the running water before scrubbing it clean and setting it aside to air dry. "Who knew Saint Dé Leon had the gentlemen in him." Irena teased and I almost smiled. *Almost.* "Don't get used to it, Doe."

Irena pauses, and she turns to face me. Her brown's eyes stared deep into mine as she tried to read something that she could not understand. "Why do you call me that?" she questions as she looks at me, an imploring depth in her brown eyes. "You remind me of a doe." I pause and she frowns. "Why?"

"A doe represents a fighter, aware of its surroundings, smart, strategic, and secretly wild," I state. Irena inhales a deep breath, her full, shapely breasts rising to attract my notice. "You don't know what you're talking about." She declares as she pulls her gaze away from mine and scrubs the plate aggressively. I crane a brow. Taking my chances I stand close behind her and reach out for the scrub in her hands. Our arms brushed up against each other, she sighs with the impact of that touch.

And my heart skips a beat.

She's not moving away. She's allowing me to touch her. If I knew how to do a backflip, I would have done it by now.

"You know I'm right. You just cannot accept the fact that I can read you so easily, Irena." The gravelly rasp of my voice curls around the syllables of her name, intoxicating my tongue. She blinks back and spins around, her body tenses as she easily regrets the decision when her back is pressed up against mine. A low growl escapes my throat when I feel her huge soft ass pressing against my dick. Instantly blood rushes to it and hardens in a second. My breathing stalls whistle every sinew in my body intensified.

"God Irena." I breathe into the crook of her neck. "Saint," She warns, her voice sensual. The breathy cadence sinks beneath my skin. Dark energy pulses between Irena and me.

I'm tempted with a famished hunger to rip that t-shirt off her and fuck the living shit out of her. Her trained exhales reach my ears as she feels my erection pressing into her ass. Never in my life had I wanted a woman so bad as much as I wanted Irena right now. It's so bad that the little voice at the back of my head is telling me to fuck her boundaries and just slam my dick into her sweet pussy. I want to feel this woman inside of me, wrapped around me and filling me up with her sweet joyful cries of pleasure and pain. A remarkable combination for a woman, like Irena. This is the closest we have been without her fighting me, *She's so fucking close*. I can almost taste her dread. Leaving an addictive aftertaste of honey and vanilla. I never knew I would grow addicted until this woman came into my life. I lick my lips slowly, savouring the burn of her sweet desperate arousing scent as it stokes my senses.

I can't think straight when I'm around her.

I'm hooked.

Addicted.

Possessive over her.

Dangerously obsessed.

Every living fucking cell in her body belongs to me. It *will* belong to me, only me.

I push back the violent urge to take her and step aside. She takes a minute to collect herself before scurrying away, Leaving me in the kitchen.

Hovering over the sink I take a deep breath to calm myself down but it doesn't do shit so I do the one thing that will slightly ease my sexual frustration. I grab the plate from the sink and smash it on the floor as it shatters into a dozen pieces. Running my hand over my head, my jaw clenches as my gaze flicks to my throbbing length which is soon to grow painful.

I am fucked.

With each fiery punch and ferocious kick, my sweat-soaked locks clung to my skin in a maddening embrace, making it difficult to catch my breath.

"You're going to hurt yourself, take it easy," Abel interjected, but I remained deaf to his plea, giving the punching bag my all as I unleashed my pent-up turmoil.

I unleashed a double kick on the bag, sending it flying dangerously close to the screws that held it up. "I see someone woke up on the wrong side of the bed," he comments. "Unless you're going to be throwing childlike comments while I'm training I advise you to shut the fuck up or leave." I snapped with irritation, watching as he laughed lightly before rising to his feet.

"What the hell got your panties twisted?" he questions. My jaw clenched as I thought about Irena.

I give the punching bag one full blow before stepping back and cracking my neck, groaning in satisfaction when I hear a pop.

Abel tosses me the towel and I dry myself before grabbing the bottle of water.

"How do you make someone earn your trust?" I question, sipping on the water before closing the bottle with the cap.

"Woah, ar-are you coming to me for advice? The heavens have finally answered my prayers," he says as he wipes a fake tear from the corner of his eye. I roll my eyes. "I'm serious." I declare and he looks at me with a blank stare. "Oh,"

"May I ask why?" he questions, walking over to the pull bar, grabbing onto the pole as he begins to do pull-ups. "I want to earn Irena's trust. She and I have some complications." I explain and he laughs. "Yeah, like I noticed it."

"While considering the fact that you literally go around and kill people for her…and to clarify for the stupidest reasons, which is–I might say fucked up and psychotic. How could she possibly not trust you?"

"You know, if you're going to be bitching about it, then forget what I said." I snapped, walking over to my bag and removing my gloves before tossing them inside.

Abel groans as he does another pull-up. "Okay, fuck relax." he points out before letting go of the pole and landed on the floor. He raised his shirt and wiped away the sweat on his forehead before speaking.

"Is your situation similar to Nirali's and I?" he questions and I deeply think about it before nodding. "Yeah, something like that."

When Nirali and Abel met, she was a complete mute. Abel held her hostage after she was found sleeping in my train carriage which was loaded with cocaine. Obviously, at first, I thought she was a spy and wanted to kill her on the spot but Abel had a crush on her like a teenage boy and told me that she would be under his responsibility. Obviously, I was not taking care of some random woman who was found in one of my trains loaded with illegal goods for transportation. Eventually, he convinced me and he took her in. It has been months since she spoke. She didn't trust anyone, she didn't speak or leave the room.

I don't know what Abel did to gain her trust but she was slowly coming out of her shell. Well to him of course. The only time she started speaking to me was after eight months of knowing her.

So to summarise. My situation is similar to Abel's, which was seven years ago.

Instead of getting Irena's trust to talk to me like Abel did with Nirali. I want to gain her trust that I can touch her without her panicking or storming away from me.

"When Nirali was mute, I did not force her to talk to me, instead I gave her a reason."

"I would talk to her every day and clarify to her that I'm not talking to her because I want her to talk back to me, instead I told her because it's a way of me showing her that I trust her and she can trust me," he explains. "So with Irena…give her a reason to trust you with whatever is troubling you." he pauses, deep in thought for a moment before talking again. "Show her that you won't remind her of whatever she doesn't trust you with. Show her that you can be her escape," he explains and I began to think of all the things I could do for her to trust me.

"Also, be gentle and patient. Don't come off as strong and most in importantly don't come up with fucked up ideas in that sick head of yours. For once, just this once, Show her that you too can have that vanilla side."

"But I don't have the 'vanilla' side like you." I declare. "If you value her trust more than anything then trust me, you have that vanilla side I'm talking about." He approached me and stabbed me on my chest with his index finger. "All you have to do is dig deep in that tiny dark ashy heart of yours," he states before stepping back and patting me on the shoulder.

"If you ask me about this, maybe she's the one who can finally silence the demons you've been finding comfort in. You've helped me with this, now it's my turn to repay you," he says before walking away.

I watched him as he disappeared into the locker room. Once he shut the door behind me I sighed, running my hand through my hair.

All I have to do is dig deep…

IRENA NOWAK

His touch lingers on my skin, igniting a wildfire of sensations within me. Each breath, each whisper, and each caress fuels the unquenchable desires that consume me. Despite my best efforts to resist his advances, his lustful intentions leave me weak at the knees.

When his lips traced the outline of my ear and his hardened dick pressed against my backside, I was powerless to resist. The rush of desire that washed over me left me breathless and hungry for more.

But now, as I flee upstairs to escape the tantalizing temptation he presents, a fierce war rages within me. My hatred for him festers, yet it is at odds with my unbridled lust. Like a lioness, stalking its prey, I am consumed by the insatiable hunger that threatens to devour us both.

I feel like a blundering fool whenever I'm near him; my thoughts and words become muddled while my body vibrates with heat. But I refuse to succumb to this torment. Instead, I'll turn my cowardice into a clever ruse.

Hours later, I found myself weaving through the maze of shops at the mall, with Nirali leading the way like a shining beacon of distraction. Three of her beefy bodyguards and a pair of my own followed us, keeping a watchful eye on every corner.

Nirali's bright smile was contagious as we strolled through the crowds, and I couldn't help but smile back. "Thank you for saving me from the suffocating boredom of my bland existence," I joked with a laugh. Nirali's expression turned serious as she asked, "How is it living with him?"

Terrifying. Tensed.

Traumatizing.

"Appalling," I murmured, prompting a sympathetic sigh from Nirali. "I'm truly sorry. If you require some space, you're more than welcome to come and stay with me and Abel," she offered, causing me to feel tense. "I don't think that's a good idea. Your husband isn't very fond of me," I confessed. Rolling her eyes, Nirali responded, "Don't bother with him. He won't do anything. Though he might come across as cold-hearted, behind closed doors, he's the opposite. He practically worships me." She said it nonchalantly, flipping her dark hair over her shoulder.

If only I could be loved as wholeheartedly as Abel loves Nirali.

As Nirali and I stepped into the infamous Victoria's Secret, I couldn't help but notice the way her innocent gaze transformed into a heated desire. "I want to surprise Abel," she confessed, and I knew we were in for a wild ride. As we browsed the delicate garments, I couldn't help but sense the guards'

discomfort, their stern expressions, and their tensed shoulders as clear indicators of their unease.

But Nirali was on a mission, a devilish smirk playing on her lips as she sifted through the lacy fabric. "So many options," she purred, her fingers delicately tracing the delicate designs. But we were interrupted by a blonde- haired worker, her ocean-blue eyes questioning us with a hint of suspicion.

Nirali wasted no time and sought her assistance, and I couldn't help but notice the worker's soft features and nude lipstick. Her name tag read Amélie, and I tucked it away in my memory for future reference.

With a charming smile, Amélie shifts her attention to Nirali. "How can I assist you, my dear?" she inquires, her tone polite and gracious. Nirali leans in eagerly. "I'm looking for something that will knock my husband's socks off, something that's equal parts sexy and sweet." Amélie nods approvingly, her mind already working its magic. "Follow me," she commands, and we trot behind her like puppies, eager to see what wonders she has in store.

As we reach the storeroom, Amélie's eyes gleam with excitement. She vanishes for a moment before reappearing with a stunning, snow-white lingerie set cradled delicately in her arms. Nirali can hardly contain herself; her gasp of delight is followed by a rush of grateful words. Amélie's grin widens, and for a moment she appears to glow with pleasure at having fulfilled Nirali's request so perfectly.

As Nirali eagerly fingers the fabric, lost in thought, I can't help but giggle with glee. "That'll definitely drive Abel wild," I quip. Nirali turns to me, her eyes sparkling with excitement. "You know what? You should get one too, Irena."

My eyes widen with disbelief. "Who would I need that for?" I question in astonishment. She lets out a sigh and rolls her eyes in response. "For your husband, Saint," she mutters. I am left speechless, my eyebrows raising in shock. "Are you kidding me?" I exclaim. She folds her arms and scolds me with her gaze. "You'll regret it if you don't. I'll even pay for it," she teases, wiggling her eyebrows and shoulders enticingly. I nibble on my bottom lip, contemplating whether or not to indulge in the purchase of lingerie.

To wear. For Saint.

What's the harm in buying it? Even if we don't engage in physical contact, it could still be a thrilling indulgence.

Just imagining the look on Saint's face when he sees me wearing it, knowing he can't touch me, is enough to make me want to do it.

It's time to take a step out of my comfort zone and spice things up. "Fuck it." I sigh and Nirali claps her hands in joy like a child. "Yay."

"Hey, Amélie." I turn to my friend, a mischievous glint in my eyes. "Do you have anything that can turn her into a seductive vixen?"

My cheeks flush with embarrassment. But intrigued nonetheless.

Amélie struts away like she's on a secret mission. "You're gonna love this," Nirali can't contain her excitement. I'm sceptical, unsure if this idea is worth the trouble.

But Nirali sees something in me that I don't quite see yet. "You have the power to make Saint yours," she insists. "You have the looks, the charm, everything. All it takes is unleashing your inner Cleopatra and he won't know what hit him."

I'm silent, letting the words seep into my mind. Who knew a little confidence could be so deadly?

In a flash, Amélie slips into the room draped in the most seductive black lingerie and Nirali's jaw drops in disbelief. "Holy fucking wow!" she exclaims, unable to contain her shock. With a graceful gesture, Amélie hands me the lingerie and flashes a devilish grin, "This is perfect for your skin tone. It'll enhance the effect." Nirali bursts into giggles, all while I flash a sly smile, knowing deep down that I can hardly wait to taunt Saint with this new ensemble.

CHAPTER 26

IRENA NOWAK

With anticipation building, I slowly reached into the oven and pulled out the most mouthwatering biscuits I had ever seen. The aroma of toasted coconut and rich chocolate wafted through the air, filling every inch of my kitchen with a warm and inviting scent.

Hours had passed since I had last seen Saint and I relished in the solitude. As the clock inched towards 8 pm, I couldn't help but feel a sense of contentment from being alone. Honestly, I wouldn't have minded if one of his rivals had taken him out by now.

With the freshly baked cookies in hand, I indulged in a glass of wine. The feeling of being a little tipsy was quite welcome, especially in the silence of my own company.

As I returned my glass to the counter, I froze at the sight of Saint at the threshold of the kitchen. My heart skipped a beat and my voice escaped in a shriek. I hadn't expected him to return so soon.

My fingers grip the fabric of my ebony t-shirt, my heart racing as I try to catch my breath. Finally daring to ask, I whisper, "How long have you been standing here?"

His low voice sends a shiver down my spine as he responds, "Not long. Didn't you hear me come in?"

My laugh is shaky as I reply, "Jesus, no." Clumsily, I attempt to divert the attention away from my surprise. "Have you been baking?" he asks, eyeing the cookies on the counter.

Nodding, I admit, "Baking is one of the things I do when I'm distressed." My curls spill over my shoulder, my nervous habit of tucking them behind my ear all but forgotten.

Saint's gaze flickers between me and the glass of wine, curiosity etching into his perfectly sculpted features.

A light frown spreads across his face as he asks, "Are you intoxicated?" The embarrassment rises in me as I reply, "No." Catching his unsure expression, I explain, "I'm just a bit dizzy, but I'm mostly sober."

Saint approaches me, his black turtleneck showcasing his flexed muscles with every step. Standing inches from me, his eyes search mine, speaking a message beyond words. Gasping, I inquired, "What is it?"

"What are the other activities that you do when you're distressed?" he asks. "I take a bath, play the piano, or sometimes I just stare at white roses. Well, I used to do that a lot back in Poland." As I pause and collect my thoughts, memories of the past slowly resurface from the depths of my mind. "We used to have a wondrous garden, filled with the most beautiful roses, the white roses were my favourite" I speak softly, hoping to convey the emotions attached to those cherished moments, a flicker of curiosity lights up his emerald gaze. "You also play the piano?" he pointed out questionably, his interest piqued. "Yes, my uncle Anatol taught me," I confirm with a slight nod of my head.

While he may exude arrogance, his passion for classical music is unmistakable.

"Why are you distressed?" he asks, his voice carrying a gentle concern. And so, with my heart laid bare, I confess, "It's you, it's how you make me feel." Suddenly, I find myself uncertain.

Why am I telling him this? We aren't friends.

With his scent enveloping me, I find myself captivated, lost in the heady aroma of his cologne as it takes over my senses, evoking the flutter of a thousand butterflies in my belly.

No, don't you guys dare flap your wings or I will burn you by drinking hot sauce. Do not flap. Not for him! I mentally screamed at myself.

"What did I do?"

Where do I even begin Saint— "A lot of things."

He draws in closer, his warm breath tickling my earlobe and sending shivers down my spine. I'm ensnared by his gaze, searching for any hint of malice, but all I find is tenderness.

"Is there anything I can do to ease your mind? I take full responsibility for it," he murmurs, his lips grazing my skin in a tantalizing caress.

I'm at a loss for words, bewildered and yet, aroused.

"S-Saint, what is this?" I stammer, trying to make sense of all these confusing emotions.

He tilts his head, his expression one of genuine bewilderment. "What do you mean, Doe?"

I can feel my pulse quickening as he leans in even closer. "Your games... what are you up to?"

He shakes his head. "No games, Doe. It's just you and me now. I want to show you that I'm more than just anger and pain. I can be gentle and passionate, just for you," he declares, and with those words, my heart skips a beat.

Most young ladies would be smitten by Saint's charm, but I must confess, I have a more forbidden fixation. The darker side of him draws me in, as it's the only way for me to experience a significant rush of emotion all at once.

However, the inner child within me who longs for a fairytale romance can't help but rejoice at the thought of Saint's attention.

I let out a soft chuckle, "Since when have you cared about earning my trust? Since when have I meant anything to you?"

"Since the moment I realized I depend on you like a junkie yearning for his next fix. You're like a drug coursing through my veins that I just can't resist. There's something alluring about you, Irena, and I can't help but be drawn to discover its source," he declares, leaving my mouth agape and parched.

The tension between us crackles and sparks like a live wire as I lift my gaze to meet his. The intensity is palpable, coursing through me like a current and sending my heart rate racing.

"I want to believe you," I say, my voice betraying my uncertainty. "But how can I be sure you're not just playing with me...?"

"Words are just words, Saint."

He meets my gaze, unwavering and confident. "Words aren't just a collection of letters, Irena. They're a force to be reckoned with. They have the power to transform minds, to touch hearts, to evoke emotions that are beyond our grasp."

I lean closer, drawn in by his conviction. "You think so?" "Yes."

He smiles, slow and enigmatic. "Words can move mountains, Irena. They can stir the soul and ignite the imagination. And at this moment, they're all I have to prove to you that I mean every word."

The caress of his breath against my skin sent shivers down my spine, and I couldn't help but release a longing sigh.

"Words are intimate," Saint whispered, his gaze piercing mine intensely. "And tonight, Doe, I will reveal to you their most intimate secrets, if only you'd be willing to entrust me with your heart for one fleeting moment."

With a tantalizing flick of my tongue, I moistened my lips, my heart racing as I struggled to resist the temptation. But before I could second-guess myself, the treacherous word spilled out of my lips in a reckless impulse. "Yes."

A wave of caution swept over me, and I immediately added, "But that doesn't mean I trust you."

Saint retreats, his intense gaze fixed upon me. "Undress," he commands, his voice leaving me bewildered. Did he truly just ask that of me?

"What?" I ask, struggling to make sense of his words.

"Undress," he repeats tersely, his eyes filled with unwavering confidence. "You're entrusting me with your body for the night. Trust me when I say you need to undress."

I hesitate, my thoughts running wild as I try to decipher his intentions. Is he attempting to gain my trust, or is this merely a ploy to exploit me when my guard is down?

"Irena, I won't harm you," Saint reassures me, his words tumbling out in a soothing, genuine tone. "I promise."

"I–"

His piercing eyes meet mine, and suddenly, I am lost in their depths. A spell has taken hold of me, and I can do nothing but surrender. My shirt falls to the floor, a sacrifice to this irresistible force. I unbutton my jeans, inching them down, still under his hypnotic gaze.

Left standing before him, in nothing but my bra and panties, I am laid bare. All defences down, his scrutiny makes me feel like an exposed target. At this moment, I am no longer the carefully crafted mask I present to the world; I am simply Irena.

With a command, "Close your eyes," my heart races, and I follow his directive, abandoning sight for heightened senses. The world around me fades into pitch-blackness, and my anticipation builds.

Saint's warmth enveloped me from behind, sending shivers down my spine as a soft silk fabric brushed against my skin. Like a gentle embrace, the blindfold tightened as he secured it in place, leaving me in a state of anticipation.

"Saint?" I called out, my voice laced with both excitement and hesitation. "Trust me," he replied in a low, seductive tone, causing my heart to race.

As I steadied my breath, the sound of a belt being unbuckled heightened my senses. I held my breath, waiting for what was to come.

With gentle steps, Saint circled me, his presence permeating every inch of my being. His words washed over me, soothing and calming my nerves.

"Relax, Doe," he murmured, his voice having an almost magical effect on my body, making me surrender to his every command.

My entire body tenses with anticipation as the supple leather glides delicately across my shoulder. The sensation travels down my arm, sending prickles of excitement racing to my fingertips.

"Can you feel it?" he whispers, I moisten my lips and nod, barely able to articulate my response.

"It's like a serpent's gentle caress," I murmur.

He probes, curiosity written all over his tone. "Does it make you sick like other touches?"

I shake my head, surprised at the change in my usual reaction. "No, it's different. This touch doesn't bring back those memories."

His voice is low and charged with energy. "What memories?"

I grit my teeth, tasting venom on my tongue. "Viktor," I hissed.

Pressing in even closer, he taunts me with a sultry whisper against my neck. "And if I did this...?"

As he traces the soft leather belt along my stomach, I feel my body shiver with anticipation. The fabric glides upwards, grazing past the curve of my breasts, and I can't help but let out a soft sigh. His touch is gentle yet mesmerizing, and with each stroke, my skin tingles with excitement. His lips brush against my flesh like feathers, sending shivers down my spine and prickling goosebumps on my skin. I can feel the hair on the back of my neck rise as the sensation intensifies.

Every nerve in my body ignites. My heart races, and my breath quickens. "No," I gasp. "It's not the same."

"Imagine my lips trailing a map of sweet kisses across your skin, Irena." He murmurs softly. "Let my words wrap themselves around you like a gentle embrace, as they whisper the secrets of passion and desire to your soul. See the belt as a tantalizing dance, with my fingertips as your guide."

His voice is like a spell, enchanting and hypnotic. "Feel my words like the tingling warmth of soft kisses, let them reach deep within you and fill you with all the longing and yearning you've ever felt. Hear the rhythm of my voice and imagine it carrying you away to a place of pure bliss, where you can frolic with the angels in the gates of heaven."

My heart races as he steps closer, his breath mingling with mine as his lips graze my own. His touch is electric, sending shivers down my spine. This moment feels like it was crafted just for us, a perfect harmony of desire and passion.

"I know you view me as a man of destruction," he declares, his belt tracing a path down my quivering thigh before halting above my fervent core. "Let me show you that I can be more than that. For you. *Only for you.*"

"Tell me you desire sweetness and purity, and I'll submit myself to you. Ask for weakness and frailty, and I'll provide it. For you, I'll transform into the perfect partner. Your prince in shining armour or your valiant knight in the shadows."

Suddenly, the world around us vanishes, and I drift into another realm. His words have an alluring pull on me, magnetizing me away from reality. His voice, his phrasing, and his every touch have me enraptured, only focused on him alone.

Only Saint matters.

"My words to you are not mere utterances, Irena. I'll give you the world," he whispered, his lips just inches from mine. "The moon. The fucking stars. Anything you ask, it's yours. I'm yours."

"Only two things can have me. You and death itself."

As my lips tenderly part, my heart skips a beat, the words sinking into my soul like a hauntingly breathtaking vow — a promise cloaked in an alluring, twisted darkness.

As we bask in the comfortable stillness, it feels as if our very beings have merged into one. But beneath the calm surface, a fierce tension swirls like two planets on a collision course, destined to unleash a cataclysmic force.

"Just one touch," he utters. "Just one touch," I replied.

The belt hits the ground with a resonating thud, the sound echoing in the kitchen. My pulse quickens as Saint's fingertips begin to trace up my arm, sending shivers down my spine. I brace myself for the inevitable feeling of disgust, but instead, my skin ignites with a fiery sensation that leaves me speechless.

As Saint's lips brush against mine, a soft sigh escapes my lips. The spark

between us crackles, but now it's different. There's no longer any hatred or disgust between us, just a connection that I can't quite put into words. It's a feeling I dare not admit to myself or anyone else.

With anticipation building up inside me, Saint slowly takes off the blindfold and lets me open my eyes. I gaze into his soulful, tender eyes and the void that had once inhabited them is nowhere in sight. But there's something more pulsing behind those emerald orbs, something that sends electric currents down my spine. It's the unspoken language we communicate with our eyes, the storm brewing between us, threatening to consume us both.

"Just as simple as that." As he speaks, I'm transfixed by his gaze, scouring every inch of it for a hint of hidden emotion in his voice.

With a graceful motion, he plants a gentle kiss on my forehead and retreats with quiet dignity. "Go rest,

I'll handle the kitchen," he murmurs, his tone confident and reassuring.

Spellbound by the moment, I stand dumbstruck as he deftly steps past me to begin cleaning up after my culinary ravages. My mind races flooded with a deluge of confused feelings I struggle to put into words.

I can only hope the intoxication coursing through my veins isn't playing tricks on me, because what I just saw in Saint demands the impossible: a complete rethink of everything I thought I knew about him.

CHAPTER 27

IRENA NOWAK

I arrived home three hours ago after visiting Nirali.

I was home alone apart from the guards roaming outside the house. Since there was not much to do in this big house I decided to cook dinner for myself. Saint is not home so he will obviously make a plan.

I know that's not wifey material for me but I'm tired. Lame excuse but for some reason I am more comfortable with Saint then I was with Viktor.

I didn't cook anything hectic, just a small casual meal. Steak and vegetables. When it hit 11pm, I decided to take a long shower. Shaving from head to toe. Then the other times I spent in the shower was scrubbing myself and staring into nothing as I allowed the water to drain.

After my shower I did my night routine and dressed into my lacy night dress then finally collapsed on the bed and allowed sleep to take over.

Sadly it did not last long when I woke up in the middle of the night, I couldn't go back to sleep.

I checked my phone and the time read 3am.

I tried to force myself to sleep but my brain wouldn't allow it so I just slipped off the bed and roamed around the empty dark house. Saint isn't back. I don't know how I know but I can just feel it. Subconsciously my brain led me to the piano room.

I'm currently sitting in front of the white piano that was once occupied by Saint weeks ago. Chills travel all the way up to my spine at the thought of Saint playing the piano covered in someone else's blood.

My uncle Anatol taught me how to play the piano as a child. He stated that it's one of the elegant instruments that a lady could play. That it should be portrayed in one of her characters oddly enough I grew to love the classical instrument.

I haven't played it ever since I left Poland. So it's shocking to see one in Saint's house, and that he can also play it.

I take a deep breath, adjust my position on the white piano bench, ready my bare foot on the pedal. I steady my fingers on the black and white keys and start to play.

The soft music hums in the air.

Notes are swirling around in my head. The black and white keys flash before my eyes making my fingers respond to time and rhythm. Once I master a piece, my fingers fly on the piano playing challenging scales and chords that I did not know my hands could reach. The only time I feel peace and composure. The only time where I can be in control and feel free in my life.

I get lost in the music as my fingers weave the sad tales of my past.

I was so lost in playing the piano that I had not realized Saint was standing behind me until I felt his warmth.

"You play beautifully." He whispers and my body jerks as my fingers slam against the keys and cause an unpleasant sound. "Gosh, Saint, are you trying to scare me to death." I breathe as I try to catch my breath and calm my heart that's pounding against my chest. He ignores me and rounds the piano so that I can see him. The moonlight kisses his features as it bleeds through the windows. "Where were you?" I blurt out and instantly regret when I notice the ghost smirk haunting his lips. "Worried for me?" he teases. I roll my eyes. "I was busy taking care of something." he simply says, his expression turning cold and chills run through my body. I frown. "Why do I feel like this is something that I should know about?" I state. My eyes pull away from him and I realize the dirt covering his clothes. "Saint..." I warned. "It's cute how you seem worried thinking that I got myself into trouble. Love, I am the trouble." he states casually leaning against the piano.

I fold my arms. "Where were you?" I ask again. "I was visiting an ex family relative." he states casually. My frown deepens. "What do you mean by that?" I inquired suspiciously. Saint pushes himself off the piano and lurks towards me. "I paid my wishes to Viktor's grave."

My heart constantly flutters in my chest and not in a pleasant way.

"I burned his grave."

CHAPTER 28

IRENA NOWAK

The words hang in the air like haunted tunes dancing in the howling wind. I blink back, my mouth instantly went dry like sand.

"W–what do you mean?" I choke on my words.

Saint's captivating gaze shifted away from me, fixating on the glimmering piano keys.

"Should I paint you a vivid picture, or merely skim over the specifics?" Saint's voice was nonchalant, but his words held weight. I remained seated beside him, absorbing the information he had imparted.

He burned Viktor's grave? How does one even burn a grave?

Why-how did he even find the location of the cemetery he was buried at?

The mere thought of that track made me want to smack myself in disbelief. Saint, a true powerhouse, owned fear like no other. When he put his mind to something, nothing could stop him. I had always known Saint to be a bit off-killer: bipolar, narcissistic, manipulative, and selfish. But the extent of his chill-inducing ways were something else entirely. It never occurred to me that he could actually be capable of hurting someone, even in their resting bed.

"How..." I murmured, barely able to get the words out. "I had my guys do some digging, and they found his death certificate. Flew to Poland last night and took care of the rest," he explained, sparing me the gruesome details. I breathed a sigh of relief, grateful for small mercies.

With a sharp crack and a couple of pops, Saint readied himself for his chilling revelation. As he turned to face me, his eyes glinted with a sinister gleam.

"My men, they absolutely loved smoking his ashes," he revealed with a nonchalant shrug. My eyes widened with shock and disbelief. "Excuse me?"

Smoked his ashes?

Loved?

I couldn't help but wonder just how depraved Saint's loyal followers truly were. "Wait, are you telling me that they actually-" My words trailed off as the image of Viktor's remains being inhaled like a drug sent shivers down my spine.

The very thought of it was enough to turn my stomach and fill me with disgust, leaving me writhing in agony from the inside out.

Does that mean Saint also—

Oh my go—

"I did not smoke Doe." With a single utterance, he seemed to pluck the thoughts from my mind and expose them to the world. Relief washed over me as I realized he was not a participant in such a heinous act. But no word in the English language could articulate the level of evil and inhumanity it takes to carry out such deeds and still sleep soundly at night. Just when I thought I was safe, he added with a twisted smile, "but that doesn't mean I could not join in on the fun." Suddenly, every fibre of my being was on edge, bracing for the worst. As I waited for his next move, he toyed with my emotions by pushing back his hair and staring directly into my soul with a sinister smirk. "God, I love the way I have fun," he muttered under his breath.

My heart skipped a beat as I realized he was the devil incarnate.

Curiosity clawed at me as I observed Saint's every move. He reached into his suit jacket, tantalizingly slow, as though he relished the suspense. My eyes narrowed, desperate to glimpse what he would pull out.

Finally, Saint produced a small black box, sending my heart racing. I furrowed my brows in suspicion, confused and unsure of what was happening.

My confusion soon dissipated with the opening of the box. Three silver bullets gleamed in the dim light, arranged neatly at attention. My mind was a whirlwind of questions and panic.

"Bullets?" I whispered, barely able to form the words.

Saint's eyes were like steel, unwavering as he spoke. "I used what remained of his ashes to craft these bullets. And I hunted down his old friends…three of them still live."

Viktor's friends? The three men that took a part in destroying me? But how does he know about them?

The revelation made me shiver in revulsion, but another emotion began to stir, gratitude. Saint's fierce protectiveness made me feel warm, secure, and cherished.

"I nearly killed them with my bare hands," he confesses, his voice dark and dangerous. "But these bullets are for you."

I'm speechless.

"How do you know ab—"

"I know that he allowed his friends to take advantage of you. When I told you I've done some digging on Viktor. I fucking mean it. Just saying his name is like drinking acid. If God could give me one day with him..." He sucks in a sharp breath. Then smiles. "I'd brutally dismember that decrepit bastard in ways that would strip me of every shred of humanity until only death's shadow remained in my soul, assuming I even have one." His tongue slithers across his lips as his penetrating gaze bores into me.

I observe him, speechless but bursting with countless queries clamouring to be answered so my interest and anxiety could be quelled. I'm at a loss as to what to say, how to react, or even how to think.

He tips his head to one side, his dark locks cascading over his forehead.

With a heavy exhale, he spoke softly. "I'd do anything to know what goes on in that pretty little head of yours." Saint shut the case with a gentle click, placing it atop the grand piano with care. "Those bastards are a mess, barely clinging to their sad existences. When you're ready to face your darkest fears, Doe, I am here." He held a deep pause, sliding the case towards me with a knowing glance.

My thoughts swirled as I stared at my hands, pondering the web of complexities within. "You claim to relish in my pain, savouring every agonizing moment. So why do you offer this escape?" My question hung in the air.

Saint's reply was deliberate, each syllable laced with sincerity. "I know the demons that haunt you, Doe. And while your pain may be my pleasure, this kind of pain sparks a different fight within me...one in which I want to protect you from the monsters lurking in your mind."

"I hear you. But that's not the answer that will satisfy my curiosity," I confess, my eyes fixed firmly on his.

He tilts his head, studying me closely. "You want me to spill my guts, don't you? Reveal the darkest secrets of my past that led me down this path. But that's not something I'm willing to do."

I purse my lips, feeling a pang of disappointment. "I understand...but surely there's something you can tell me?"

Instead of answering, Saint leans in closer, his eyes locked on mine. "What you need to know is that I understand. I've been where you are. And that means a lot more than any tragic story I could tell you."

I can't help but chew nervously on my bottom lip. For a moment, we sit in silence, the air between us heavy with unspoken words and the weight of our situations.

Finally, I managed to whisper, "Thank you." But as I meet Saint's intense gaze, I realize there's so much more I want to say.

At that moment, I know I need to end this once and for all. My heart pounds wildly in my chest, Saint meets my gaze and for a moment, we simply stare at each other, neither of us speaking. But even though we're not saying anything, I can feel the tension between us rising with each passing second.

My fingers glide over the ivory keys of the piano, weaving a slow and sultry tune that hangs in the air like a phantom. By my side sits Saint, his eyes locked on me with an intensity that threatens to ignite a wildfire within me. But I keep my cool and continue to play on. The harmony between us is nothing short of magical, a dance of two souls intertwined, moving in perfect unison.

As the notes linger between us, I catch Saint stealing a glance at my lips and my fingers falter for just a moment. But then, in an unexpected move, Saint begins to play alongside me, his fingers finding their way to the keys with ease. Together, we create a melody that speaks volumes, full of unspoken words and raw emotions.

But as our fingers dance upon the piano, I can sense a brewing tension between us. We're both hiding something, a deep-seated desire that we're too afraid to confront. And as we collide and clash, I can feel a familiar fluttering in my stomach that sends shivers down my spine. It's a dangerous game we're playing, and one that I'm not sure I'm ready to face.

I ceased playing the piano, entranced by Saint's allure. My gaze deviated towards his lips, which possessed a magnetic quality. Their plush, rosy hue and soft texture mesmerized me.

As I refocused on his eyes, palpable electricity surged between us. Our words seemed inadequate to express the intensity of our mutual attraction.

Unconsciously drawn towards him, I leaned in hesitantly, observing as his expression remained nonchalant. Drawing ever closer, I caught a whiff of smoke and brimstone. Despite my reservations, my heart raced and my palms became moist.

Though a voice in my head urged me to reconsider, I disregarded it entirely. My eyes shut as I passionately joined my lips to his, revelling in the thrilling unknown.

His lips were like a gentle breeze on a humid summer night, tinged with the flavours of whiskey and mint. A daring impulse surged within me as I licked the dewy bottom lip, stirring something primal in him.

As he lifted me effortlessly onto the piano, the keys clashed in discord, but the chaos only heightened the intensity between us. Saint's hand instinctively sought my neck, but I pushed him away, fingers shaking as I took control of the kiss, holding his face tenderly.

"Don't touch me unless I say so," I murmured against his lips, feeling the frustration and longing emanating from his every pore.

My hand entwined with the back of his neck as our lips met again, this time with fire and passion, each of us vying for dominance. Saint held back, his knuckles turning white as he clung to the piano, the tension between us reaching unbearable heights.

"I need to touch you, please." Saint pleaded, but I clamped down on his lip with a ferocity that left him gasping.

"No," I breathed, my fingers trailing through his silky hair as his body pressed against mine, my legs hooking around his waist like a belt.

An unrestrained moan escaped my lips as his solid cock eagerly yearned for my touch. The temperature soared, my body blazing like a raging inferno. With lips as sweet as candy, Saint devoured me, ravishing every inch of me as I surrendered to his tempting touch. I was lost in him, disintegrating with the fervour from within. Suddenly, a ferocious growl erupted from the hollow of his chest, and his kiss consumed my being, overwhelming my senses. His lips were savage, his essence dripping with malicious sin, a punishment for something only he knew. A secret he kept to himself.

But as the voice echoed in my mind, Irena, what the hell are you doing? I was jolted back to reality.

What was I doing?

Oh, God.

As he gazed at me with greedy eyes, Saint threatened in a husky tone, "I'm so close to tearing you apart, Irena."

I forcefully pushed Saint away from me and collapsed onto the piano in frustration. "Fuck," I muttered under my breath, trying to calm down my racing heart. As I tugged at my hair, I turned towards Saint, my eyes wide and my lips parted, as if I had committed a heinous crime. "This was a mistake," I stammered, unsure of how else to approach the situation.

"Irena," he called to me, but I shook my head, refusing to face the consequences. "No, it was a mistake."

I mentally groaned at how foolish I had been. Without another word, I hastily made my way out of the room, feeling like I was living in a never ending loop. "Stupid, stupid, stupid," I repeatedly chanted to myself as I scurried to my bedroom.

As I closed my eyes, memories of Saint's lips flooded my mind, and I couldn't resist reaching up to lightly touch my mouth. My lips felt parched as I remembered how his tongue had slipped into my mouth and how I had savoured every moment of it.

In front of me were four beautiful strawberry tarts, their bright red berries glistening under the kitchen light. Without thinking, I reached into the hot oven, braving the intense heat against my skin. I carefully lifted the tray out, my eyes locked on the tempting treats. I set them down with a thud, the tarts wobbling slightly, and began arranging the strawberries on top in rose-like patterns. The sweet, buttery scent filled the air, wrapping around me like a warm hug.

Proud of my work, I stepped back and smiled. These little creations were as beautiful as they were delicious. I had spent the entire morning perfecting them…four hours of weighing ingredients, mixing, slicing fruit, and cleaning up. It was a lot, but I loved every second of it. Baking let me escape, if only for a while, from the chaos swirling around in my life.

Especially after yesterday's mistake. I had thrown myself at Saint on impulse, a bad habit of mine when someone gets past my defences and sees the real me. He had broken down my walls, and I let him in, thinking he was my knight in shining armour. But he wasn't the hero I thought he was, he was dangerous, chaotic, and the kind of man I should've run from. Now, I vowed not to give in to temptation again.

Today, I lost myself in baking, hoping to keep my mind off things. Nirali's voice broke my focus as she looked at the tarts, her eyes wide. "They're almost too perfect to eat," she said. I grinned. "I know, right?" I replied, turning to see her perched on a stool, looking stunning in a white floral dress and matching heels, with her long hair cascading around her face.

"So, dress shopping?" She asked, tracing her glass's rim with her finger. I gave her a confused look as I washed my hands. "When are we going?" She pressed. I blinked, clueless. "Saint didn't tell you?" she sighed, jumping off her stool and coming closer. "The crime families are hosting a charity event. It's all glitz and glamour on the surface, but trust me, things get darker as the night goes on."

I frowned, feeling uneasy. "Why even go?" I asked. She smirked.

"It's about appearances, Irena. Showing up sends a message, we're involved, and we're not to be messed with."

My stomach churned at the thought. "So we're just trophies, there to prop up our husbands' reputations?" I scoffed. Nirali shrugged. "Pretty much." I let my mind wander, thinking about the ball. It would be my first one, Viktor never took me to these events. He preferred the company of other women, leaving me alone, which suited me fine. My uncles always pressured me to go, saying I was a disappointment to the family, but I never cared.

Even with Viktor's unfaithfulness, at least he left me be.

I sighed, thinking aloud. "I guess I'll have to talk to Saint first. When is it?" I asked. Nirali shrugged. "Later this week." I nodded, realizing I had little time to prepare.

For once, I'd need Saint's help.

The front door creaked open with a soft push, and shadows flickered on the walls as muffled voices and footsteps moved closer to the living room. Nirali and I were curled up on the couch, enjoying the warm glow of the TV and a soothing glass of wine.

Suddenly, Nirali shot up, eyes wide with excitement. She set down her drink and rushed to the door where Abel and Saint had just walked in, along with a stranger who looked oddly familiar — the same man I met in Poland when I first met Saint. Nirali's eyes sparkled as she ran into Abel's arms, and he caught her effortlessly, his smile lighting up the room. They kissed passionately, and I quickly turned away, locking eyes with Saint. His piercing gaze and sharp features sent chills down my spine, making me squirm in my seat. I forced myself to look away and refocus on Nirali and Abel. "For God's sake, get a room," The man beside Saint grumbled, earning a scowl from Nirali as she broke away from Abel's kiss. "I missed you," she said, and Abel planted a soft kiss on her cheek. "I missed you more, Angel." The man gagged dramatically, then turned his attention to me. "Not too cozy with Saint, huh?" I shot him a cold glare as he teased Saint. "When was the last time fucked?" Saint brushed him off, ignoring the jab. Abel rolled his eyes, but the man continued, taunting me. "Not getting any love lately, Irena?" I ignored him and turned back to the TV. Nirali, curious, asked the man, "Did your mom ever love you?" He snapped back defensively, "What's my mom got to do with this?" Abel chimed in, "Just ignore Prince." I nodded, pretending to focus on the screen, though my thoughts were on Saint. With Nirali and Abel settled on the couch, Prince and I sat in tense silence, the only noise coming from the TV. Where was Saint? Now seemed like the right time to talk to him about the ball. I excused myself and headed to his lavish office. Standing at the double doors, I took a moment before knocking and stepping inside. Saint was busy sorting through papers. "I didn't say come in, shithead," he snapped, startling me. Did he just insult me? "Excuse me?" I shot back, crossing my arms defensively. Saint looked up, his intense stare making me shrink back. "Thought you were my brother or Prince. Sorry." I stood there awkwardly, caught off guard. "You can sit, Doe; I don't bite," he said with a smirk. Steeling myself, I got to the point.

"We need to talk, Saint." He leaned back, muscles flexing, and for a second, my mind wandered. I shook off the thought, trying to focus. "I'm listening."

"Why didn't you tell me about the ball?" I asked, meeting his
    eyes. His expression hardened, and he clenched his jaw. "I didn't tell you because you're not going," he said coldly.

CHAPTER 29

IRENA NOWAK

I arrived home three hours ago after visiting Nirali.

I was home alone apart from the guards roaming outside the house. Since there was not much to do in this big house I decided to cook dinner for myself. Saint is not home so he will obviously make a plan.

I know that's not wifey material for me but I'm tired. Lame excuse but for some reason I am more comfortable with Saint then I was with Viktor.

I didn't cook anything hectic, just a small casual meal. Steak and vegetables. When it hit 11pm, I decided to take a long shower. Shaving from head to toe. Then the other times I spent in the shower was scrubbing myself and staring into nothing as I allowed the water to drain.

After my shower I did my night routine and dressed into my lacy night dress then finally collapsed on the bed and allowed sleep to take over.

Sadly it did not last long when I woke up in the middle of the night, I couldn't go back to sleep.

I checked my phone and the time read 3am.

I tried to force myself to sleep but my brain wouldn't allow it so I just slipped off the bed and roamed around the empty dark house. Saint isn't back.

I don't know how I know but I can just feel it. Subconsciously my brain led me to the piano room.

I'm currently sitting in front of the white piano that was once occupied by Saint weeks ago. Chills travel all the way up to my spine at the thought of Saint playing the piano covered in someone else's blood.

My uncle Anatol taught me how to play the piano as a child. He stated that it's one of the elegant instruments that a lady could play. That it should be portrayed in one of her characters oddly enough I grew to love the classical instrument.

I haven't played it ever since I left Poland. So it's shocking to see one in Saint's house, and that he can also play it.

I take a deep breath, adjust my position on the white piano bench, ready my bare foot on the pedal. I steady my fingers on the black and white keys and start to play.

The soft music hums in the air.

Notes are swirling around in my head. The black and white keys flash before my eyes making my fingers respond to time and rhythm.

Once I master a piece, my fingers fly on the piano playing challenging scales and chords that I did not know my hands could reach. The only time I feel peace and composure. The only time where I can be in control and feel free in my life.

I get lost in the music as my fingers weave the sad tales of my past.

I was so lost in playing the piano that I had not realized Saint was standing behind me until I felt his warmth.

"You play beautifully." He whispers and my body jerks as my fingers slam against the keys and cause an unpleasant sound.

"Gosh, Saint, are you trying to scare me to death." I breathe as I try to catch my breath and calm my heart that's pounding against my chest. He ignores me and rounds the piano so that I can see him.

The moonlight kisses his features as it bleeds through the windows.

"Where were you?" I blurt out and instantly regret when I notice the ghost smirk haunting his lips. "Worried for me?" he teases. I roll my eyes.

"I was busy taking care of something." he simply says, his expression turning cold and chills run through my body. I frown.

"Why do I feel like this is something that I should know about?" I state. My eyes pull away from him and I realize the dirt covering his clothes.

"Saint..." I warned.

"It's cute how you seem worried thinking that I got myself into trouble. Love, I am the trouble." he states casually leaning against the piano.

I fold my arms. "Where were you?" I ask again.

"I was visiting an ex family relative." he states casually. My frown deepens.

"What do you mean by that?" I inquired suspiciously. Saint pushes himself off the piano and lurks towards me.

"I paid my wishes to Viktor's grave."

My heart constantly flutters in my chest and not in a pleasant way.

"I burned his grave."

CHAPTER 30

IRENA NOWAK

The words hang in the air like haunted tunes dancing in the howling wind. I blink back, my mouth instantly went dry like sand.

"W-what do you mean?" I choke on my words.

Saint's captivating gaze shifted away from me, fixating on the glimmering piano keys.

"Should I paint you a vivid picture, or merely skim over the specifics?" Saint's voice was nonchalant, but his words held weight. I remained seated beside him, absorbing the information he had imparted.

He burned Viktor's? How does one even burn a grave?

Why, how did he even find the location of the cemetery he was buried at?

The mere thought of that track made me want to smack myself in disbelief. Saint, a true powerhouse, owned fear like no other. When he put his mind to something, nothing could stop him. I had always known Saint to be a bit off-killer: bipolar, narcissistic, manipulative, and selfish. But the extent of his chill-inducing ways were something else entirely. It never occurred to me that he could actually be capable of hurting someone, even in their resting bed.

"How..." I murmured, barely able to get the words out. "I had my guys do some digging, and they found his death certificate. Flew to Poland last night and took care of the rest," he explained, sparing me the gruesome details. I breathed a sigh of relief, grateful for small mercies.

With a sharp crack and a couple of pops, Saint readied himself for his chilling revelation. As he turned to face me, his eyes glinted with a sinister gleam.

"My men, they absolutely loved smoking his ashes," he revealed with a nonchalant shrug. My eyes widened with shock and disbelief. "Excuse me?"

Smoked his ashes?

Loved?

I couldn't help but wonder just how depraved Saint's loyal followers truly were. "Wait, are you telling me that they actually-" My words trailed off as the image of Viktor's remains being inhaled like a drug sent shivers down my spine.

The very thought of it was enough to turn my stomach and fill me with disgust, leaving me writhing in agony from the inside out.

Does that mean Saint also—

Oh my go—

"I don't smoke Doe." With a single utterance, he seemed to pluck the thoughts from my mind and expose them to the world. Relief washed over me as I realized he was not a participant in such a heinous act. But no word in the English language could articulate the level of evil and inhumanity it takes to carry out such deeds and still sleep soundly at night. Just when I thought I was safe, he added with a twisted smile, "but that doesn't mean I could not join in on the amusement." Suddenly, every fibre of my being was on edge, bracing for the worst. As I waited for his next move, he toyed with my emotions by pushing back his hair and staring directly into my soul with a sinister smirk. "God, I love the way I have fun," he muttered under his breath.

My heart skipped a beat as I realized he was the devil incarnate.

Curiosity clawed at me as I observed Saint's every move. He reached into his suit jacket, tantalizingly slow, as though he relished the suspense. My eyes narrowed, desperate to glimpse what he would pull out.

Finally, Saint produced a small black box, sending my heart racing. I furrowed my brows in suspicion, confused and unsure of what was happening.

My confusion soon dissipated with the opening of the box. Three silver bullets gleamed in the dim light, arranged neatly at attention. My mind was a whirlwind of questions and panic.

"Bullets?" I whispered, barely able to form the words.

Saint's eyes were like steel, unwavering as he spoke. "I used what remained of his ashes to craft these bullets. And I hunted down his old friends…three of them still live."

Viktor's friends? The three men that took a part in destroying me? But how does he know about them?

The revelation made me shiver in revulsion, but another emotion began to stir, gratitude. Saint's fierce protectiveness made me feel warm, secure, and cherished.

"I nearly killed them with my bare hands," he confesses, his voice dark and dangerous. "But these bullets are for you."

I'm speechless.

"How do you know ab—"

"I know that he allowed his friends to take advantage of you. When I told you I've done some digging on Viktor. I fucking mean it. Just saying his name is like drinking acid. If God could give me one day with him..." He sucks in a sharp breath. Then smiles. "I'd brutally dismember that decrepit bastard in ways that would strip me of every shred of humanity until only death's shadow remained in my soul, assuming I even have one." His tongue slithers across his lips as his penetrating gaze bores into me.

I observe him, speechless but bursting with countless queries clamouring to be answered so my interest and anxiety could be quelled. I'm at a loss as to what to say, how to react, or even how to think.

He tips his head to one side, his dark locks cascading over his forehead.

With a heavy exhale, he spoke softly. "I'd do anything to know what goes on in that pretty little head of yours." Saint shut the case with a gentle click, placing it atop the grand piano with care. "Those bastards are a mess, barely clinging to their sad existences. When you're ready to face your darkest fears, Doe, I am here." He held a deep pause, sliding the case towards me with a knowing glance.

My thoughts swirled as I stared at my hands, pondering the web of complexities within. "You claim to relish in my pain, savouring every agonizing moment. So why do you offer this escape?" My question hung in the air.

Saint's reply was deliberate, each syllable laced with sincerity. "I know the demons that haunt you, Doe. And while your pain may be my pleasure, this kind of pain sparks a different fight within me...one in which I want to protect you from the monsters lurking in your mind."

"I hear you. But that's not the answer that will satisfy my curiosity," I confess, my eyes fixed firmly on his.

He tilts his head, studying me closely. "You want me to spill my guts, don't you? Reveal the darkest secrets of my past that led me down this path. But that's not something I'm willing to do."

I purse my lips, feeling a pang of disappointment. "I understand...but surely there's something you can tell me?"

Instead of answering, Saint leans in closer, his eyes locked on mine. "What you need to know is that I understand. I've been where you are. And that means a lot more than any tragic story I could tell you."

I can't help but chew nervously on my bottom lip. For a moment, we sit in silence, the air between us heavy with unspoken words and the weight of our situations.

Finally, I managed to whisper, "Thank you." But as I meet Saint's intense gaze, I realize there's so much more I want to say.

At that moment, I know I need to end this once and for all. My heart pounds wildly in my chest, Saint meets my gaze and for a moment, we simply stare at each other, neither of us speaking. But even though we're not saying anything, I can feel the tension between us rising with each passing second.

My fingers glide over the ivory keys of the piano, weaving a slow and sultry tune that hangs in the air like a phantom. By my side sits Saint, his eyes locked on me with an intensity that threatens to ignite a wildfire within me. But I keep my cool and continue to play on. The harmony between us is nothing short of magical, a dance of two souls intertwined, moving in perfect unison.

As the notes linger between us, I catch Saint stealing a glance at my lips and my fingers falter for just a moment. But then, in an unexpected move, Saint begins to play alongside me, his fingers finding their way to the keys with ease. Together, we create a melody that speaks volumes, full of unspoken words and raw emotions.

But as our fingers dance upon the piano, I can sense a brewing tension between us. We're both hiding something, a deep-seated desire that we're too afraid to confront. And as we collide and clash, I can feel a familiar fluttering in my stomach that sends shivers down my spine. It's a dangerous game we're playing, and one that I'm not sure I'm ready to face.

I ceased playing the piano, entranced by Saint's allure. My gaze deviated towards his lips, which possessed a magnetic quality. Their plush, rosy hue and soft texture mesmerized me.

As I refocused on his eyes, palpable electricity surged between us. Our words seemed inadequate to express the intensity of our mutual attraction.

Unconsciously drawn towards him, I leaned in hesitantly, observing as his expression remained nonchalant. Drawing ever closer, I caught a whiff of smoke and brimstone. Despite my reservations, my heart raced and my palms became moist.

Though a voice in my head urged me to reconsider, I disregarded it entirely. My eyes shut as I passionately joined my lips to his, revelling in the thrilling unknown.

His lips were like a gentle breeze on a humid summer night, tinged with the flavours of whiskey and mint. A daring impulse surged within me as I licked the dewy bottom lip, stirring something primal in him.

As he lifted me effortlessly onto the piano, the keys clashed in discord, but the chaos only heightened the intensity between us. Saint's hand instinctively sought my neck, but I pushed him away, fingers shaking as I took control of the kiss, holding his face tenderly.

"Don't touch me unless I say so," I murmured against his lips, feeling the frustration and longing emanating from his every pore.

My hand entwined with the back of his neck as our lips met again, this time with fire and passion, each of us vying for dominance. Saint held back, his knuckles turning white as he clung to the piano, the tension between us reaching unbearable heights.

"I need to touch you, please." Saint pleaded, but I clamped down on his lip with a ferocity that left him gasping.

"No," I breathed, my fingers trailing through his silky hair as his body pressed against mine, my legs hooking around his waist like a belt.

An unrestrained moan escaped my lips as his solid cock eagerly yearned for my touch. The temperature soared, my body blazing like a raging inferno. With lips as sweet as candy, Saint devoured me, ravishing every inch of me as I surrendered to his tempting touch. I was lost in him, disintegrating with the fervour from within. Suddenly, a ferocious growl erupted from the hollow of his chest, and his kiss consumed my being, overwhelming my senses. His lips were savage, his essence dripping with malicious sin, a punishment for something only he knew. A secret he kept to himself.

But as the voice echoed in my mind, Irena, what the hell are you doing? I was jolted back to reality.

What was I doing?

Oh, God.

As he gazed at me with greedy eyes, Saint threatened in a husky tone, "I'm so close to tearing you apart, Irena."

I forcefully pushed Saint away from me and collapsed onto the piano in frustration. "Fuck," I muttered under my breath, trying to calm down my racing heart. As I tugged at my hair, I turned towards Saint, my eyes wide and my lips parted, as if I had committed a heinous crime. "This was a mistake," I stammered, unsure of how else to approach the situation.

"Irena," he called to me, but I shook my head, refusing to face the consequences. "No, it was a mistake."

I mentally groaned at how foolish I had been. Without another word, I hastily made my way out of the room, feeling like I was living in a never ending loop. "Stupid, stupid, stupid," I repeatedly chanted to myself as I scurried to my bedroom.

As I closed my eyes, memories of Saint's lips flooded my mind, and I couldn't resist reaching up to lightly touch my mouth. My lips felt parched as I remembered how his tongue had slipped into my mouth and how I had savoured every moment of it.

In front of me were four beautiful strawberry tarts, their
bright red berries glistening under the kitchen light. Without
thinking, I reached into the hot oven, braving the intense heat against my skin. I carefully lifted the tray

out, my eyes locked on the tempting treats. I set them down with a thud, the tarts wobbling slightly, and began arranging the strawberries on top in rose-like patterns. The sweet, buttery scent filled the air, wrapping around me like a warm hug.

Proud of my work, I stepped back and smiled. These little creations were as beautiful as they were delicious. I had spent the entire morning perfecting them...four hours of weighing ingredients, mixing, slicing fruit, and cleaning up. It was a lot, but I loved every second of it. Baking let me escape, if only for a while, from the chaos swirling around in my life.

Especially after yesterday's mistake. I had thrown myself at

Saint on impulse, a bad habit of mine when someone gets past my defences and sees the real me. He had broken down my walls, and I let him in, thinking he was my knight in shining armour. But he wasn't the hero I thought he was, he was dangerous, chaotic, and the kind of man I should've run from. Now, I vowed not to give in to temptation again.

Today, I lost myself in baking, hoping to keep my mind off

things. Nirali's voice broke my focus as she looked at the tarts, her eyes wide. "They're almost too perfect to eat," she said. I grinned. "I know, right?" I replied, turning to see her perched on a stool, looking stunning in a white floral dress and matching heels, with her long hair cascading around her face.

"So, dress shopping?" She asked, tracing her glass's rim with her finger. I gave her a confused look as I washed my hands. "When are we going?" She pressed. I blinked, clueless. "Saint didn't tell you?" she sighed, jumping off her stool and coming closer. "The crime families are hosting a charity event. It's all glitz and glamour on the surface, but trust me, things get darker as the night goes on."

I frowned, feeling uneasy. "Why even go?" I asked. She smirked.

"It's about appearances, Irena. Showing up sends a message, we're involved, and we're not to be messed with."

My stomach churned at the thought. "So we're just trophies,

there to prop up our husbands' reputations?" I scoffed. Nirali

shrugged. "Pretty much." I let my mind wander, thinking about the ball. It would be my first one, Viktor never took me to these events. He preferred the company of other women, leaving me alone, which suited me fine. My uncles always pressured me to go, saying I was a disappointment to the family, but I never cared.

Even with Viktor's unfaithfulness, at least he left me be.

I sighed, thinking aloud. "I guess I'll have to talk to Saint first.

When is it?" I asked. Nirali shrugged. "Later this week." I nodded, realizing I had little time to prepare.

For once, I'd need Saint's help.

The front door creaked open with a soft push, and shadows

flickered on the walls as muffled voices and footsteps moved

closer to the living room. Nirali and I were curled up on the couch, enjoying the warm glow of the TV and a soothing glass of wine.

Suddenly, Nirali shot up, eyes wide with excitement. She set down her drink and rushed to the door where Abel and Saint had just walked in, along with a stranger who looked oddly familiar — the same man I met in Poland when I first met Saint. Nirali's eyes sparkled as she ran into Abel's arms, and he caught her effortlessly, his smile lighting up the room. They kissed passionately, and I quickly turned away, locking eyes with Saint. His piercing gaze and sharp features sent chills down my spine, making me squirm in my seat. I forced myself to look away and refocus on Nirali and Abel. "For God's sake, get a room," The man beside Saint grumbled, earning a scowl from Nirali as she broke away from Abel's kiss. "I missed you," she said, and Abel planted a soft kiss on her cheek.

"I missed you more, Angel." The man gagged dramatically, then turned his attention to me. "Not too cozy with Saint, huh?" I shot him a cold glare as he teased Saint. "When was the last time fucked?" Saint brushed him off, ignoring the jab. Abel rolled his eyes, but the man continued, taunting me. "Not getting any love lately, Irena?" I ignored him and turned back to the TV. Nirali, curious, asked the man, "Did your mom ever love you?" He snapped back defensively, "What's my mom got to do with this?" Abel chimed in, "Just ignore Prince." I nodded, pretending to focus on the screen, though my thoughts were on Saint. With Nirali and Abel settled on the couch, Prince and I sat in tense silence, the only noise coming from the TV. Where was Saint? Now seemed like the right time to talk to him about the ball. I excused myself and headed to his lavish office. Standing at the double doors, I took a moment before knocking and stepping inside. Saint was busy sorting through papers. "I didn't say come in, shithead," he snapped, startling me. Did he just insult me? "Excuse me?" I shot back, crossing my arms defensively. Saint looked up, his intense stare making me shrink back.

"Thought you were my brother or Prince. Sorry." I stood there awkwardly, caught off guard. "You can sit, Doe; I don't bite," he said with a smirk. Steeling myself, I got to the point.

"We need to talk, Saint." He leaned back, muscles flexing, and for a second, my mind wandered. I shook off the thought, trying to focus. "I'm listening."

"Why didn't you tell me about the ball?" I asked, meeting his

eyes. His expression hardened, and he clenched his jaw. "I didn't tell you because you're not going," he said coldly.

CHAPTER 31

IRENA NOWAK

"The hell do you mean I'm not going?" I protested, anger beginning to boil in my veins. "I don't want you to go, which means you aren't going. It's just a simple instruction to follow." He proclaimed as his gaze darkened.

Now usually in these types of situations, I would listen without a doubt, but Saint...

I don't want to listen. I don't want him to know that he has the upper hand and can control or make decisions for me. It's as if telling a student to stop talking and they do the opposite. It's a human nature act. You tell us to do this and we will do the opposite just to piss the person off. At first, I didn't want to go. That's the reason I came to talk to Saint but watching him sit behind his table talking to me with his big balls makes me want to go to the stupid fucked up ball.

I'm hyper-aware of how his heated gaze drags me over to him. "Understood Irena?" But the dark twist of his mouth implies how much he knows that I will not listen to him whatsoever.

"Why aren't I allowed to go? You're going and obviously if you don't attend the ball with a mistress you're setting a bad image on your name." I implied, not daring to break eye contact even though I am shaking on the inside. Saint tilts his head to the side, amusement flashing in his eyes. "Someone did their homework," he teases and I roll my eyes at his comment. "Just answer the goddamn question, Saint." I barked out of annoyances that began to spark in the crack of my bones.

Saint's jaw ticks before he rises from his seat and walks over to the mini bar at the far end of the office next to shelves stacked with vintage books. The room is silent; the only noise you could hear is Saint's faint footsteps. He grabs two glasses from the shelves above the table where a bottle of amber liquid sits and a bucket with ice I presume. I watched him quietly as he fixed himself a drink. Once he is done Saint turns on his heel and approaches me with two glasses of alcohol in both his hands.

He stops just a few inches away from him, stretching out his hand for me to take the glass and I do just that.

Our gazes are locked on each other as we take a sip of the alcohol. I nearly cringe at the burning taste of the liquid running down my throat. Clearing my throat I dart my tongue out to lick my lips and Saint gulps down the remaining amber liquid in the glass before placing the empty glass on the table behind me.

I quickly took a whiff of his masculine scent that I quickly grew to love.

Not being a creep or anything but my God Saint smells heavenly.

While staring into his divine beauty the brutality and sadistic manner dangerously shadows his features.

"If you go. The men over there will try to claim you in seconds and you know how I get when it comes to sharing." He states. I cringe, my brows narrowed in disgust. "Firstly Saint I am not an object to be tossed around by horny perverted men and secondly I make my own decisions so I would like to go to this ball." I spat bitterly. "Who said you're an object?" Saint questions casually.

No one but he did imply me as an object. Indirectly to be exact.

I remain silent.

"I'm going." I snapped.

"No, you're not." He barked back.

I have to curb my anger and respond with sensitivity. Although this man drives me crazy. He cannot know that in an act on my part, he makes me feel unstable.

Taking a step closer to him, I tilt my head back so that I can get a good look at him. "I am going Saint. You don't control me. You don't own me and you don't get to make decisions for me. Furthermore, don't you dare start with the "I'm protecting you" crap?" I spat back.

Saint smiles and quips with dark amusement with the face of an angel–yet a devil lurks beneath his shadows. He brushes past me and takes a seat behind his desk. Tilting his head, assessing me seriously.

"You amuse me little doe." He lets out while his mouth tips into the faintest, knowing smile. Locking my gaze with him I curiously watch as he brushes his fingers over the scar I gave him. "Really, amuse me," he adds slowly with his masculine deep voice. The way his gaze darkens, the defiant spark of hunger and malice igniting within the flinty shadows of his features makes me question what goes through this man's mind.

"Stop calling me little doe," I demand furiously. He chuckles unexpectedly and the deep sound hits my chest, unfurling in a light with a fluttering sensation.

"In any case, whether you approve or not, I'm going. If you're not okay with that, feel free to pucker up and kiss my ass," I say defiantly.

Saint's gaze drops, his head tilting as if he's contemplating the idea. "Oh, I will kiss that sweet ass, *soon*," he replies, his voice dripping with a calm certainty that sends a rush of heat to my cheeks.

This is why I cannot trust myself around him anymore. Besides my body being highly responsive to him, my hatred for him shrinks by the day being consumed by desire and I hate myself for feeling this way because I have no control over it.

Saint drums his fingers on the tabletop and I finally move toward the door. Pulling it open I stood for a moment, turned to face him, and finally exited the office, shutting the door behind me. I took a long deep breath and exhaled then rubbed my sweaty palms over my jeans.

"There you are!" A female voice called out from a distance. I turned my attention to where the sound came from and saw Nirali approaching me. "God, I thought you left me there all alone with them. They are such a handful." Nirali proclaims and I nervously smile. "I'm sorry, I had to talk to Saint," I told her as we both walked away from Saint's office and climbed down a flight of stairs. "What were you guys talking about?" She questions and I shrug. "About the ball, nothing important."

"Oh, well I'm glad you guys didn't bite each other's head off." Nirali jokes. "Yeah," I mumbled as we both entered the living room.

I don't know about him but I was close to strangling Saint.

The day of the grand ball has arrived.

Saint and I haven't revisited the issue of my attendance, but I refuse to let it dampen my spirits. Come hell or high water, I'll be gracing the occasion.

As I gaze into the mirror, I gently wipe away the mist to reveal my reflection. I radiate cleanliness, having recently emerged from a shower and pampered myself with moisturizer. Time to work on my hair and makeup.

Instead of approaching Saint with inquiries about the theme or dress code, I reached out to Nirali. Her skills prove invaluable--she's my guardian angel.

After finishing my makeup, I expertly pulled my hair back into a high, curly bun using gel, while leaving a few wispy curls framing my face. My look was complete with a touch of smoky eyeshadow, nude lips, and a pop of lip gloss for added drama.

As I pondered what to wear to the ball, I rifled through my closet, feeling a mix of anticipation and dread. Unfortunately, I couldn't find anything that fit the rose gold and black theme, despite my best efforts.

Annoyed with me for not asking for help, I almost gave up hope until a gentle knock interrupted my thoughts.

"Come in," I called out, the anticipation of the mystery within the door tantalizing me. The entrance creaked open and glided one of our household attendants cradling a mysterious black parcel.

"Mrs. Dé Leon," the gracious woman began, carefully placing the oblong parcel down upon my bed, "Your husband has tasked me with giving you this gift." I eyed her curiously as she departed, leaving me with the enigmatic parcel.

Trembling with excitement, I unzipped the velvety black cover and beheld a stunning dress wrapped neatly within. The sight of it prompted a visceral gasp to escape my lips, as my eyes drank in the exquisiteness of its gold and diamonds. The elegant form-fitting design, bedecked with trails of delicate silk and ornate lace, was simply breathtaking.

I was beyond honoured to receive such a sensational dress, so superbly crafted and worth a fortune, that my thoughts began to dance, surprised that I'll be wearing this beautiful gown. The golden hue complimented my complexion, and the dress hugged my curves like a second skin, making me feel both regal and seductive all at once. It felt like a true gift of royalty, exuding confidence and beauty far beyond anything I had ever worn before.

In a flash, I slipped into the dress and gazed at my reflection in the full–length mirror. The fabric caressed every curve, accentuating my cleavage with a subtle hint of seductive elegance. My golden mermaid dress pushed my chest out, begging to be noticed. The dress flowed out like blooming flowers, luxuriously laying against my legs as I twirled and took in every angle.

Eventually, my eyes shifted to the floor as I noticed my dilemma. With no time to spare, I contemplated which pair of heels to select, the sleek black pumps or the sentimental white heels from my wedding day. Finally, I surrendered to my heart and chose the white ones.

After spritzing myself with my favourite perfume and grabbing my purse, I gracefully made my way down the stairs, hoping and praying I wouldn't take a tumble.

My gracefulness can be a hit or miss, especially in towering heels. With careful precision, I descended the stairs and gently brushed my hand over my flowing dress, experiencing the rapid fluttering of my heart.

"Irena." A low voice spoke behind me. Slowly turning around, I was met with Saint's lustrous gaze. His eyes devoured me from head to toe, tilting his head in admiration. My cheeks grew hot as my breath became shallow, our eyes locked in an intense stare.

Dressed impeccably in a sleek black suit and smooth tie, Saint held a box I had failed to notice. With silent steps, he edged closer leaving behind a trail of his warm, masculine musk.

"You are stunning," he whispered and my cheeks blazed red in reply, "Thank you," I said, barely able to get the words out.

As Saint lowers himself before me, my heart flutters like a butterfly taking flight. The box he brings with him seems to hold secrets untold until he pulls back the lid revealing exquisite pencil heels adorned with glittering diamonds.

"May I?" he asks, his gaze locking onto mine. My head nods in silent agreement as he takes my right foot in his hands. Suddenly, the touch of his fingers against my skin ignites a flurry of stars across my body.

My senses are swept away as Saint deftly removes my current shoes and delicately slides the new ones onto my feet. The sensation of the soft straps against my skin lingers long after he rises to his feet. The heat of his body seems to wrap around me like a warm embrace, leaving me with goosebumps and a breathless ache in my chest.

"Please, turn around," he spoke softly, and I complied, feeling a shiver run through me. Something cold gently brushed against my skin, causing my breath to catch in my throat. As I tentatively traced my fingers over the object, I lowered my gaze and caught sight of glistening diamonds wrapped around my neck. I turned back to Saint, a stunned smile spreading across my lips. "Saint, this is simply beautiful." I gushed, but he merely glided his hand over my back, wordlessly guiding me out of the house. Though I longed to say more, I held myself back, biting my tongue and allowing the luxurious necklace to speak for itself.

With a sleek black SUV rolling to a stop in front of the house, the driver steps out and opens the door for Saint and me. As we approach the car, Saint graciously allows me to enter first, and I sink into the plush leather seat. The air inside is rich with a crisp, clean scent, and the car hums with an electric charge before the driver brings it roaring to life. The low growl reverberates through my frame as we set out from the long driveway and onto the street. I gaze out the window in awe as the sky transforms into a canvas of oranges, pinks, and purples, while the sparkling city in the distance begins to pulse with the anticipation of the night ahead.

The car ride was silent, a thick tension growing with each passing second as Saint and I exchanged uncomfortable glances. Even the driver seemed uneasy, stealing quick looks at us in the rearview mirror. Finally, we arrived at a towering brick building, a red carpet stretching out before us and flashing cameras threatening to blind me. Nirali had warned me about

the paparazzi, but the reality of their frenzy was overwhelming. They were ravenous for any glimpse of Saint and his new mistress, the billionaire and his forbidden flame.

My mind was left stunned and still when the public's accusations were thrown our way. Saint's empire spanned multiple countries, boasting a portfolio that included trendy hangouts and cutting-edge technology. But it was all a facade for his dirty little secret…laundering money. Dé Leon, his company, had burst onto the scene in the early 90s by investing in up-and- coming businesses that are now household names.

As we entered the colossal building, a sudden chill crept up my spine. The notion of turning tail and fleeing back to the safety of my home grew stronger with each step.

Saint draws near, his hand gently resting on the small of my back. "Stay by me," he whispers into my ear. A surge of emotion takes hold, and I gulp. "I'm feeling anxious," I admit, my gaze shifting to his face which is only a breath away from mine. "Don't be. I'll be here, always," he coos, his voice soothing my rattled nerves. In response, I nod.

As we approached the formidable doors, the imposing figure of the doorman observed us with a sharp eye. With a brisk nod, he swung the door open to reveal a maze of stairs leading to a destination unknown. My eyes drank in the ambiance of the interior as I alighted the first step. A classy, chic space with contemporary art adorning the walls and black tile flooring interspersed with pristine white walls. The crown jewel, a magnificent chandelier, suspended in the center of the ceiling, with luminous crystals that sparkled like the sun-kissed ocean waves. I inhaled deeply, taking in the grandeur and excitement of the moment, my heart pounding in my chest as I followed Saint. The winding stairs deposited us in a sumptuous ballroom aglow with the radiance of chandeliers hovering over the dance floor, casting an otherworldly gleam. The decorations were nothing short of awe-inspiring, with tables converging at each end of the ballroom swathed in black velvet, delicately arranged single gold roses, and dainty seating cards done in elegant calligraphy. Catching my breath, I stood in amazement as I watched people in their captivating finery and tuxedos talk, laugh, and dance to the soothing sounds of classical music wafting through the air.

As Saint and I took our seats at the elegantly adorned table, my eyes were drawn to the grandeur of the ballroom. The chandeliers sparkled like stars in the firmament, casting a warm glow over the room. Suddenly, a waiter came forth with two glasses of chilled white wine and placed them gently before us, before melting away like a ghost. I grasped my glass and took a sip, feeling a soothing chill run up my spine.

As the music faded away, an unexpected hush fell upon the room, signalling the arrival of a mysterious host who appeared on stage. He wore a sleek black suit and a shiny black mask that accentuated his sharp features, especially his prominent aquiline nose. But it was his piercing blue eyes that held the attention of the crowd, gleaming with darkness that evoked pure evil and left me quivering in fear. The very air seemed to shift as if a malevolent force was about to sweep over us, haunting our dreams long after the night was over.

As the evening unfurled, a thrilling announcement electrified the room, sparking a rush of excitement and joy. "Ladies and gentlemen, the moment we've all been waiting for has arrived! Thanks to your unwavering support and generosity, we've raised a staggering one million euros to sway the fate of the Alberta Cancer Foundation and the

World Food Programme. Oh, and guess what? We've tripled the amount we collected last season!" The crowd erupted into thunderous applause, causing an uproar of emotions. The man on stage continued, adding, "This season has seen some extraordinary businesses soaring high in the stock market."

Through the sea of dazzled faces, I caught Saint's gaze, and his eyes were fixed firmly on the stage.

"Unfortunately, we have encountered some obstacles, including traitors who have attempted to undermine one of our prominent crime families. We have apprehended those responsible and it is time to administer justice, demonstrating that we will not tolerate such conduct." With a cool and collected demeanour, the man before me flicks his head, beckoning a line of five hooded figures to be thrust onto the stage, and forced to kneel before the crowd.

"These five individuals stand before you today accused of theft and deceit against our family. For months, they have fraternized with the very law enforcement we seek to elude, exposing our trade secrets involving illicit firearms, narcotics, border crossings, and street wars. Our timely capture of these turncoats kept us in control of the situation." The man concludes.

With a flourish, he whips a gun out of his suit jacket and levels it at the first man, whose identity is hidden behind a bag that shrouds his head. The gunshot booms through the walls, and my body convulses in shock at the sudden noise. No trace of blood mars the victim's head as he crumples to the ground, lifeless. I stare, wide-eyed and incredulous, at the poker-faced crowd. They seem not to notice the carnage unfolding before them. One by one, the gun speaks with deadly force, until all of the targets drop. The man smiles a satisfied smile, tucking the pistol into his pocket with a quick, deft movement. With a graceful adjustment of his tie and collar, he turns on his heel and disappears into the milling crowd.

As I turned to look at Saint, I met his penetrating gaze. I was about to speak, but he beat me to it, his words delivering a sickening blow. "It's our tradition," he explained nonchalantly. "Once we discover you're a rat, we'll eliminate your whole family and you during one of our grand events, and if you happen to have a daughter of 17 or above, they become the property of lecherous and depraved old men."

A lump formed in my throat as I imagined helpless young girls being snatched from their lives and sold to the highest bidder. "What could possibly be the purpose of such a horrific tradition?" I asked with revulsion laced in my voice.

Saint simply shrugged, lifting his glass of white wine to his lips. "It's for fun, power, and wealth," he answered with a disturbing smirk. As I watched the aftermath of the latest assassination, my mouth went dry, and my stomach turned with abhorrence and disgust. This is going to be one hell of a night.

CHAPTER 32

IRENA NOWAK

I've been sitting at the table as I watched the people go wild.

Like Saint promised he hasn't left my side since we arrived. We haven't talked, just exchanged looks and I'd be Saint's shadow when random people would approach us to be specific, Saint.

The men would talk to Saint and crack dad jokes while their wives would awkwardly stand behind them. They would completely ignore me unless Saint would introduce me to them.

It's been an hour and all I've done was listen to men ramble about their business sports cars and sleeping around with hookers while their wives would just stand there and listen to their partners brag about being disloyal. Each time these sick twisted men would open their disgusting mouths and talk about unnecessary bullshit I had the urge to grab the fork on the table and repeatedly stab them in the eyes but that would just get me killed. So I'm as useless as they come.

"Ah and who's this lovely lady?" A tall man approached with pepper salt hair and a beard including a charming smile. "This is my wife," Saint simply states.

I'm grateful that he hasn't mentioned my name to any of these men that would notice me. "Well, you are some lucky man. I would sell my left ball sack to spend one night with her." The middle-aged man teased and sensed Saint's body tense beside me. "Carefully on how you speak about my wife Diego because I would gladly cut off both your balls while fucking my wife in front of your dying pathetic ass," Saint warned and Diego immediately stopped laughing.

Just the thought of Saint fucking me while watching a man dying sent heat straight to my core which widely made me uncomfortable.

Diego nervously cleared his throat and let out a nervous laugh. "Apologies Saint." Diego blurts out as fear swims in his green pools. "Don't apologize to me, apologize to her." Saint proclaimed. Diego met my gaze and I almost lagged when I noticed a thin layer of sweat forming on his forehead. "My apologies Mrs. Dé Leon. It was not my intention to disrespect you like that. I've had a lot-"

"Go away, you whining ass is giving me a headache," Saint demanded whilst pinching the bridge of his nose. Diego scatters away like a headless chicken not turning back knowing that he will regret it. "You don't have to be that cruel, the man almost pissed himself," I state letting out a light chuckle from the thought of a grown man peeing himself. Saint turned to face me with a cocked brow. "I've said it before and I'll say it again. No one fucking disrespects you and gets to live the following day," he growls.

I shift uncomfortably on the chair before taking a sip of my glass of red wine. I've lost count of how many glasses I've drank after the third. It's unhealthy to admit but alcohol is my coping mechanism, especially in events like these.

CHAPTER 33

SAINT DÉ LEON

The intense and alarming feeling I get when I'm around Irena bleeds all rational thoughts and reasons from my mind.

Most obsessions start off small, harmless like a tiny irk in the back of your mind. Then you underestimate the obsession until one day it grows and becomes addictive. We begin to pick and pick until the desire overwhelms you and have no choice but to rip it apart with razor-sharp claws.

Irena didn't start as a tiny exasperate. From day one, she flayed my flesh and buried herself deep inside of me and I can't stop scratching.

The itching desire to taste her, touch her, fuck her, kiss her, torture her. All channels into one destructive bomb. Ticking by the second until it explodes.

She's killing me, slowly.

I watch her closely as her gaze is fixed on the crowd watching couples dancing and chattering. We haven't left the table since we arrived at this ball. The only time I'd socialize is when some of my business partners would approach me and we would talk about useless shit for five minutes then they'd leave.

Abel and Nirali haven't arrived yet. I received a text from my brother earlier claiming that he will be late due to some emergency he had to handle.

He's lying out of his anus but I didn't call him out on it. He's obviously fucking the brains out of Nirali because he can't control himself around her. They both act like horny high school teenagers. When they have the opportunity to fuck they will take it without a doubt not caring that they'll get caught.

Sadly I am a victim myself of walking in on them fucking in Abel's office. I can never erase the image from my mind. It haunts me to this fucking day.

Irena has been awfully quiet. The only time we would speak is when she had questions about the ball. All she did was sit across from me and look like a sexy goddamn angel.

"How many glasses of wine did you drink Irena?" The gravelly rasp of my voice curls around the syllables of her name. She takes a sip of her wine and twirls the glass of wine. Her cheeks tinged with a slight shade of blush. Turning to face me, her glossy brown eyes meet mine and her plump glossy lips slightly curl up into a smirk she casually shrugs before answering. "I lost count."

I remain silent as my gaze skims her angelic features.

Now I would have stopped her in fact I wanted to but Irena is stubborn and when I tell her to do something she will do the complete opposite just to piss me off and I wouldn't want her to overdrink and do something that she will obviously regret later.

Not that I care. I'm just trying to protect my image. Wouldn't want everyone to think that I'm married to a fool.

Which is the complete opposite of what I personally think about Irena. She's ten times better than all the women here. She has one thing that the majority of the women here don't have. Brains.

Irena sighs. "I'm bored," she complains. "Then entertain yourself," I stated.

Irena gave me a black stare and rolled her eyes before taking another sip of her wine.

Staring at the couples who are dancing slow tunes an idea immediately pops up in my head. Now usually I wouldn't do this but for some reason, I wanted to, for her sake.

I rise from the chair and drag a hand through my slicked hair. A few loose strands creep over my eye but I ignore them. Irena questionably lifts a fine brow.

"Where are you going?" she inquired. "Dance with me." I let out. Irena's eyes slightly widen and she shakes her head. "I can't dance."

I shrug. "I'll teach you, it's very simple plus you did state that you're bored," I remarked. Irena nibbles on her bottom lip hesitant to accept my offer but a moment later she gives in when she rises from her chair.

I offer my hand to her and she ignores it and then brushes past me.

I nearly smiled at her sass then quickly caught up to her. When we reached the dance floor Irena looked around. Her chest rises and falls whistling, biting down on her bottom lip.

I had the urge to punish her for biting her lip so innocently. She might not see it as something big but whenever she does this I just want to punish her lips with mine.

Fuck this woman is driving me crazy.

I catch her by surprise when I gently place my hand on her lower back. I noticed how her body immediately reacted to my touch. She's slowly getting used to me. I just have to push her further until she's out of her comfort zone.

Soon her bubble will pop and she'll get addicted to my touch as much as I am addicted to her.

"Relax, I don't bite." I said and her body immediately relaxed. I slowly pull her closer to me and she tips her chin higher to get a good look at me. I gently lock our hands together and her mouth slightly parts as her pulse beats rapidly. "Just follow my lead okay." She nods instead of using her words.

I moved my left foot backward in a smooth motion, sliding across the slick floor and Irena slid her right foot forward chasing my retreating foot with hers. Dipping her forward I stared into those earthy hues that showed the depth of her soul. The way she looked at me, not in a cheesy romantic way that you'd read in those novels. She obsessively looked at me, lustful but with the kind of beauty that expands a moment into frozen time. My fingers tightened on her waist as her right foot came forward again. Surprising her foot I chase her again and she does the same. We stopped toe to toe and I purposely pulled her hips closer to mine.

Our faces are inches away. Her sweet intoxicating scent drove me wild. I lick my lips slowly, savouring the burn of her arousing scent as it webs my nerves. A mouthwatering combination of honey and vanilla, a unique scent that's well-suited for her. Threatening to brush my lips against hers, I looked to the left and she looked to the right and then to the right and she mimicked me. I pushed her away, spinning her out of my arms. Her grip tightened as she held onto my right arm. Then reeled her back in. Our bodies sway back and forth in sync.

My heart hammered against my chest. The way she effectively looked at me. Her eyes are large and luxurious, dark like the riches of an oak tree. They glistened and were beautiful. They were slowly trapping me. Everything stood existing but those lustful eyes of hers. Time ticked beyond count and everything around us collapsed. Stars dying as they scatter into the void, a gaze in a moment in a heartbeat, nothing else. Then it was broken. Irena slipped out my touch and time resumed and life carried on. Nothing changes. She frowns.

"I-excuse me," Irena utters before walking away and disappears into the crowd.

Without realizing it my feet quickly follow after her. I noticed her golden dress sparkling from a distance as I pushed the heavy double doors open and continued walking. I exit the ballroom and follow the sound of heels clinging to the tiles. I passed a few guards and they all greeted me with a curt nod.

"Irena!" I called out as I continued to chase her down the hall. She doesn't turn back, instead quickens her pace as she takes a right turn. I caught up to her and she stormed into the restroom before she could shut the door. I stopped her by blocking the door with my foot and pushed it open then entered.

"Why are you running away from me?" I inquired. I closed the door behind me and locked it after so that no one could disturb us. Irena hovered over the sink, lost in thought as she caught her breath. "Irena?"

"What!" she snapped. I remain calm.

Normally I would kill someone if they ever speak to me in that tone but when Irena is upset or bothered, cruel to admit but it turns me on. "Why are you running away from me?" I ask again with a gentle tone.

Irena ignores my question. "Saint, I would appreciate it if you'd give me some privacy. I need to be as far away from you as possible." Irena asserts.

"Is that so?" I tease as I take a threatening step forward and she steps back. "Yes, I can't trust myself around you right now." she proclaims softly. "Why? Is it because your body is desperately begging to be touched by me again..." I trailed off teasingly. Her mouth parts, as if I've said something to confirm my suspicion. She drops her gaze to the floor and I almost chuckle knowing that I'm right.

Us dancing was so tense for her that I caused her to be dripping wet for me. She's aroused and afraid to admit it. "Look at me Irena." I demand and step closer she steps back. "No." she breathes. "It's because you're a handful to be with. It's annoying and draining." She lies as she tries to convince herself and me that we both know that it isn't the truth. A charged pulse ignites a fire beneath my palm. The air is volatile and tense between us. Her chest rises with uneven breaths as she nibbles on her bottom lip, lifting her gaze once more. She crosses her arms, anxiously waiting for me to leave.

Which won't happen unless she comes with me. "Saint, please leave." Her strained swallow drags along the column of her throat that I wish to wrap my hand around.

I release a low chuckle, thoroughly amused. "You're adorable when you're nervous." I tell her and take two steps forward, she steps back but gasps when her back hits the wall.

She has nowhere to go. "Saint." Irena warns, desire and fear swimming her brown pulls. Her body tenses when I'm inches away from her. I could feel her warmth radiating towards me. I trap her with both my arms placed on each side, caging her in one place.

I lean in and whisper inside her ear. "Is my wife wet for me?" A flurry chaos swirled around her like a vortex. "Hmmm?"

I noticed how Irena clenched her thighs together. She glares at me angrily.

"When I look at you, I become dry like sand." She spat bitterly.

I chuckle, shaking my head at her insults which clearly had no effect on me. Reaching my hand out I part Irena's legs with my leg and brushed my finger tip against her damp panties and she gasped in shock.

"Your body is a terrible liar then you are, love."

I lean in the crook of her neck . "You're dripping wet for me."

"I-it's hot." she lies again and I shake my head in disappointment. "You know I hate it when that pretty mouth of yours lies to me."

"What are you going to do? Punish me?" she states pushing my buttons. I wrapped my hand around her waist and gave her a gentle squeeze. "You want me to punish you?" I questioned and she thought about it for a moment then nodded. "Either way, you wouldn't know how to handle me." Irena remarks, I arch a brow tilting my head to the side– amused by her comment.

"Baby I'll handle you in ways you couldn't imagine." I tell her and she scoffs. "I doubt it."

Those three simple words triggered something in me. In a blink of an eye I pick her up and place her on top of the sink.

My mouth grazes her shoulder in sinful pursuit to reach her earlobe. "I'm going to show you how a man handles his woman." I warned teasingly.

That fire was in his eyes and my breath caught. Saints hands cupped my face, capturing my lips with his. He used his size and strength to back me up against the mirror and kissed me hard. His tongue pushed into my mouth and I touched it with mine.

Arousal blazed through me and I sank against him, loving the feel of his body, strong and hard from all the physical work, pressed to mine. His lips feathered across my jaw and I tilted my head back, exposing my throat. Pushing my dress from my shoulders with his other hand, he dragged down the front, exposing my tits to his heated gaze. "I love it when you don't wear a bra," he murmured against my skin. I instantly blush.

I've obviously had too much to drink and the alcohol only hits now. All my senses are heightened.

He kissed my neck, the sensitive skin rising in goosebumps with every lick and nibble. Saint palmed my breast and pinched my already hardened nipple between his thumb and forefinger. The pinch was just the right amount of pleasure and pain and I gasped, my arousal ratcheting up another notch. "You have the most perfect tits I've ever seen," he growled. I bite down on my bottom lip unable to form a proper sentence without a moan escaping my lips. As our kisses deepened, Saint reached for my dress, dragging up the front, and then delving his hand between my thighs. His fingers brushed the front of my panties and I groaned and rocked my hips against his hand. my body has been secretly yearning for his touch in a way I'd never experienced before. It was as though my body craved him independently of my heart or soul—

though all of me had grown desperate for his presence with each passing day.

I crushed my breasts to his chest, gripping his shoulders with my fingers, smooth muscles beneath soft cotton.

Saint pushed my panties to one side, his index finger sliding between my folds, opening me up to him. He'd already found me wet and wanting, and he pushed one finger inside me, fingering me a couple of times, before adding a second. I stretched around him and grind my hips down on him, loving how he made me feel.

I was heady with pleasure, lost in the sensation of his mouth claiming mine. My inner muscles clamped around his fingers and a fresh gush of wetness readied my body for him.

"Oh God," I moan. "That's right, baby," he breathes against my skin. "To you, I am."

He ducked his head to my breast and sucked my nipple into his mouth. His teeth grated across the sensitive peak and I arched my back, pressing myself into him, wanting more.

His fingers continued to work me, curling to find that sensitive spot on the inside of my walls. My breathing grew faster, and I knotted my fingers in his hair while he feasted on my tit.

"Saint." I warned. "Hold it baby, just a little longer." He pleads. My eyes roll back as I feel my climax building by the second.

My world is shattered when I hear a knock on the door followed by an aggressive voice. "Hello! I know you in there I have to fucking pee." A male voice called out of frustration.

"Occupied." Saint annoyingly calls out as he continues to pump his fingers in and out of me. "Fuck- S-S-aint" I cried out.

Another bang on the door. "Hurry up!" The angry voice called out constantly banging on the door and I stared at Saint wide eyed.

"For fucks sakes." Saint mumbles under his breath before pulling out a gun from his pocket with his free hand, aimed for the door and pulled the trigger four times. Leaving bullet holes on the door.

My eyes grow wide as I feel my heart beating against my chest. I tried to process everything but couldn't because I was so high up in the sky reaching for my climax.

"Saint!" I warned again, biting down on my lip to the point it may bleed.

Saint chuckles lightly as he kisses the corner of my lips. "You can let go, baby. Let me taste you." He whispered.

The muscles in my belly and thighs tensed. His thumb found my clit, applying pressure with short, fast circles, and I unravelled around him. My body shook and shuddered as my orgasm rolled through me. I clung to his shoulders, my face buried against his neck, light-headed and gasping for breath. "Oh," I moaned into his ear.

He pulled out his finger and blushed when I saw my juices dripping down his finger. He locks gazes with me, opens his mouth, slides his fingers into his mouth and sucks hard on it. Watching me carefully as he licks his fingers clean.

"You taste better than I imagined doe."

"It's the last time you'll get to taste me." I blurt out, knowing that's it's lie.

He turned me around and yanked my skirt up over my ass. He delivered a quick sharp spank to my cheek, sending a pulse of pleasure and pain through my body. "Next time, I won't allow you to come." He growled.

After catching my breath and gaining back my senses. I quickly realised that Saint shot someone.

"Fuck, fuck, fuck." I panicked as I slipped off the sink and rushed to the door. Pulling the door open, my eyes grew wide when I saw a pool of blood on the floor and a man laying on the floor as he took his last breath. Saint appears beside me unbothered. "Look what you have done! You killed someone innocent and for something useless." I yell at him. He shoves his hands into his pocket and eyes the almost dead body.

"He annoyed me and wouldn't want to go away. Plus I didn't shoot him for something useless. If I wouldn't have stopped him from knocking you wouldn't have come." He explains casually and my cheeks grow red.

True but still!

Ignoring him I jumped over the body and walked as far away from Saint as possible.

I'm currently angry at myself and him.

CHAPTER 34

IRENA NOWAK

My feet pound the floor like an accelerating heartbeat as I flee down the hall. Saint's footsteps sound like a determined drum beat, relentlessly pursuing me.

"You sure do have this tendency of running away from me," Saint declares as he materializes beside me with a smirk.

I shoot him a stony glare. "And why shouldn't I? My husband is a lethal killing machine."

"You don't have to explain. But I could list a million reasons why you shouldn't," Saint boasts, brimming with confidence.

With an exasperated huff, I pick up the pace, but Saint's legs are like lasso ropes, drawing him ever closer.

Stopping beside a pair of burly guards, Saint barks out an order. "Check the restroom and send medical aid ASAP." The guards scurry away, and I continue towards the looming double doors that lead to the ballroom. My heart races like an earthquake, but the scene that greets me is calm and eerily normal.

The gunshots were deafening but it seemed like nobody around me noticed. My mind was racing with the possibility of danger lurking around every corner. Suddenly, a voice breaks my concentration, sending tingles down my spine.

"Something's troubling you," a male voice whispers seductively in my ear. My heart races as I turn around to face Saint. "No one heard the gunshots," I blurted out.

He sighs. "Most of the walls in this building are soundproof. It's a safety precaution apparently."

I furrow my eyebrows in frustration. "But what happens when we're randomly attacked or jumped by the police? This is ridiculous."

Saint shrugs before declaring, "I agree. Whoever owns this place is a complete idiot."

I trail behind him, content with being his shadow. As we walk, someone bumps into me. Ready to lash out, I suddenly recognize who it is.

"Abel."

As Abel's eyes lock with mine, a flicker of recognition dances across his chiselled features. His guard drops and a tender smile creeps onto his lips.

But before we can exchange any pleasantries, a blur of rose gold and curves materializes beside him. It's Nirali in a dress so stunning, it could make even the heavens gasp. The mermaid cut hugged her curves in all the right places and her makeup accentuated her natural beauty flawlessly.

As she glides towards me, I can't help but feel a twinge of envy. But my envy quickly fades as I realize just how genuinely happy I am to see her. And she clearly feels the same as she reaches out for a hug, only to restrain herself at the last second, mindful of my boundaries.

And as we stand there, basking in each other's radiance, Nirali erupts with a compliment so effusive, it ignites an inner glow within me. I jokingly fan myself, trying to hide my delight, but she sees right through me and returns the favour by acknowledging my own beauty. It's moments like these that make me appreciate her like a friend.

Nirali is quite the stunning woman. Abel is surely blessed to have her as his own. Suddenly, as if out of the blue, Saint creeped up behind me. My entire body tensed up at the surprise visit.

"I honestly thought your ugly ass wouldn't make it." Saint quipped. "I wasn't going to come but Nirali wouldn't stop bugging me because she wanted to see your crazy wife." He explains. Nirali let out a gasp and playfully nudged Abel's arm. "Don't call Irena crazy, it's mean."

Abel managed to sneak a quick glance in my direction before resuming his conversation with his wife. "My apologies, Angel, what I meant is psycho wife matched with psycho husband." Nirali's glare immediately fell upon Abel, causing him to shrug before planting a tender kiss on her forehead. Rolling her eyes, Nirali returned her attention to me.

"Has the auction already started?" Abel queried Saint, only to receive a shake of the head in response. "Not yet, but it will start shortly."

My features contort with a frown at the mention of an auction, causing all eyes to fixate on me like a swarm of curious bees. "What kind of auction?"

I inquired, my curiosity piqued. "It's centered around this year's theme, gambling." The response prompts an exchanged glance between Nirali, and I before she simply shrugs in response.

"Shall we?" Abel poses a query with an elegant hand gesture, inviting us to take our places. With a silent nod, they trail us to our designated seats adjacent to theirs. With poised composure, we settle in while the waiter gracefully delivers martinis to each of us before gliding off.

Abel's gaze slides to Irena's dress, an eyebrow quirked in curiosity. "I'll just bypass the blood stains on your dress, Irena," he comments, a sly hint of humour in his voice as he takes a gulp of his drink. Suddenly self-conscious, I blush and hastily adjust my dress. Nirali can't help but glance around the table, searching for answers. "What happened?" she inquires, her eyes darting between Saint and me, caught in a whirlwind of curiosity and suspense.

"You know Nirali, someone like you should not be asking such questions considering-" Saint's words are swiftly halted by Nirali's sharp retort. "You know Saint for you to try and bring my issues up shows that your heart is as cold as my room and I can't feel my toes in that room, so it's bloody cold." she snaps with a bitter edge. Exasperated, Saint rolls his eyes. "Your insults are akin to those of a child in nursery," he states without bother, much to Nirali's disgust as she takes a sip of her martini. "I'm fully convinced you never graduated kindergarten." she spits out disdainfully.

Abel and I couldn't contain our laughter as we watched the drama unfold between the two of them.

"I could eat a whole bowl of alphabet soup and shit out a smarter statement than whatever you just said." counters Saint with a bland expression, causing me to bite down on my lip to control my laughter. Nirali is quick to fire back, "I would tell you to go fuck yourself but that would be cruel and an unusual punishment." The atmosphere is tense between the two, but Abel and I can't help but find it all incredibly amusing.

Saint let out a heavy sigh and shook his head with disappointment. "Everyone is entitled to act and say stupid things once in a while Nirali, but you really abuse the privilege," he lamented. "Okay, you two should seriously get a time-out." Abel jumps in and Nirali and Sint glare at him. "Shut the fuck up Abel, can't you see I'm trying to have a mature conversation with your wife."

Abel sets his martini glass down on the table, breathing in deeply before he can even speak. Suddenly, a voice echoes through the room, demanding silence. "Looks like even fate wants you to zip it," Saint jests before turning his focus toward the stage.

I turn to him in quiet amusement, noting the childish behaviour of the trio. "You'd think with your reputation, you'd hold a little more maturity," I remarked quietly, my eyes fixed on the performance. Saint lets out a resigned sigh. "All I can say is that I had to endure these two for seven years including those other two imbeciles for most of my life," he states. I turn to look at him. "Are you referring to Prince?" I question and he nods. "Yes and another named Zoltan."

Before I could respond the man on the stage began to speak.

"Ladies and gentlemen, behold! The night we've all been waiting for has finally arrived. Tonight, our creme de la creme bachelorettes will grace the stage in all their glory, wowing the finest men in search of a wifely companion. From the most prestigious crime families across the world, these enchanting young ladies are sure to leave a lasting impression. Get ready to witness an unforgettable night, my friends!" The announcer's booming voice echoes through the room, riling up the men - with the exception of Abel and Saint.

"With great pleasure, allow me to introduce our first entrant - hailing from the lush landscapes of England, only 19 years of age and a proud member of the infamous Lyons Crime Family... It is with immense pride that we welcome Miss Freya Lyons!" With a flourish of his arm, the spotlight illuminated the beautiful blonde in a dazzling mermaid dress. But as she strutted proudly onto the stage, guarded by a dark-suited figure, the fear in her emerald eyes betrayed her apparent confidence.

"Behold, all the way from Nigeria, a young gem. At 17 years young, she is the pride of Black Axe, the fierce Abebi Axe!" The speaker announces with zeal, as the audience eagerly waits for the next girl. Suddenly, a woman with deep, rich ebony skin bursts onto the stage wearing a flamboyant red dress. With each step, her voluminous afro bounces to the rhythm of her stride, and a forced smile rests upon her lips, like the previous contestant. However, her eyes smoulder with an intense passion, shimmering with tears that threaten to cascade down her cheeks, unnoticed. A guard shadows her, like the girl before her.

As the speaker introduces each girl, every young woman dons a red dress and the same fixed smile. But their eyes reveal a story untold; pain, fear, indignation, and a vast array of emotions that go beyond what their smiles can convey.

As I scan the stage, my eyes take in the beauty and intensity of each of the twenty women on the platform. They all stand tall and proud, their ages varying from 17 to 20, but their undeniable spirit and resilience is a common thread connecting them all.

My stomach churned with revulsion as they commenced the auction of the ladies.

"Polina Sergei, now the property of the notorious drug lord Mr. Ruiz, for the staggering price of $1.5 million!" The words boomed through the room, eliciting cheers from some and sighs of disappointment from others.

When I turned to Saint for support, he was already watching me, his gaze intense. "This is beyond sickening," I muttered. Saint exhaled loudly. "These people are all deranged. The depths of the criminal underworld are much darker than you can imagine, Doe. And this auction is only the tip of the iceberg."

A shiver coursed down my spine at the thought of what unspeakable events must have taken place in prior years' balls. I was eager to ask more about such atrocities, but a voice in my head cautioned me against seeking out further knowledge. It was better, perhaps, to remain somewhat ignorant of the depths of human depravity.

As the auction stretched on for what felt like an eternity, the women were gradually claimed by the lecherous bidders with greedy smirks stretched across their faces. The air was thick with dread, and the room was illuminated only by dim, flickering candles.

Looking over at Nirali, her gaze was heavy with sorrow, a reflection of the wretchedness surrounding us. But as I observed her, it was clear that what lay beneath that sorrow was a sense of empathy. It was almost as though she felt each girl's pain on a personal level, making my curiosity about her only intensify.

After the horrific display, I couldn't wait to escape and seek solace in a different kind of drink. "Want to get a drink?" I asked and she nodded. "Yes please."

As I stood up from my seat, I informed Saint, "I'll be with Nirali." He nodded, understanding my need to console her. "I'll catch up with you after I speak with Abel."

Without another word, I made my way through the crowd and Nirali walked alongside me towards the bar.

"Since when does he care?" She asks as we take our seats on the bar stools. I shrug. "Not sure."

Nirali gave me a weird look. She opened her mouth to say something but was interrupted when a waiter asked for our orders.

The bartender takes down our drink orders and walks away to prepare them. "So why were you and Abel late?" I question. Nirali shifted on her seat as she pressed her lips into a thin line and looks anywhere apart from me. Her cheeks reddened and my eyes grew wide when I finally realized her delay to the ball.

"You naughty girl." I tease, she turns to face and she laughs nervously. "Is it that obvious?" Nirali questions folding her arms and I nod. "Tell me the fucking details!" I squeal excitedly like a high school girl. "Okay so, we fucked in the shower, he ate me out in my dress because I look so fucking hot in it. Anyways, we did it again in the car and I sucked him on our way here." She explains casually not giving the specific details. My jaw dropped as I stared at Nirali. "How aren't you tired!?"

"Irena, having sex with Abel is never tiring. I can't get enough of him and he can't get enough of me. We are equally addicted to each other. Sex with him is amazing. It's sloppy, choking, wet, heated all right up to the point of losing consciousness." Nirali groans as she bites down on her lips and slightly rolls her eyes.

The bartender awkwardly clears his throat as he hands us our drinks and walks away nervously as if he didn't overhear the conversation. Nirali and I both stared at each other and burst into laughter.

"You are one horny freak." I state, taking a sip of my cocktail. "Hey, if you're man knows what he's doing then honey you'll be horny 24/7. Craving the dick all day…every day."

I shook my head and the memory of Saint and I in the bathroom flashed in my mind. Blink back the memory.

"Yeah, well I wouldn't know." I proclaim. "That's because you're not making the first move." She whines and sips on her cocktail. I shrug. I open my mouth to talk but a familiar male voice beats me to it.

"Am I interrupting ladies."

My heart instantly drops when I recognize the voice.

Grzegorz.

PART TWO

"'TILL DEATH DO US PART' IS NOT JUST A VOW; IT'S A PROMISE OF
LOVE THAT ENDURES THE DARKNESS, DEFIES THE SCARS, AND
DARES EVEN DEATH TO TEAR US APART."

CHAPTER 35

IRENA NOWAK

Have you ever felt so much hate for someone that a single thought of them makes you wish all the terrible, most horrifying things to happen to them.

That looking in the depth of their eyes pulls out this other dark side of you. A side that makes you question your own sanity.

That's exactly how I feel as I stare into the depth of my uncle's rusty brown eyes.

"It's been a while Irena. Who's your lovely friend?" He questions, a friendly smile stretching across his face that I would love to stab over and over and over and over.

Nirali cast me a suspicious look and immediately noticed the tension and dislike I had for my uncle.

Ignoring his questions I straightened myself on the stool with one leg over the other and my hands sleeping on my lap. "It's not a surprise bumping into you Uncle Greg. Seeing that this ball is hosted and attended by sick men like you."

I immediately forced my mouth shut when I realized what I just said.

Where did that confidence come from?

Not sure if it's the alcohol talking or the fact that I've been spending a lot of time with Saint but I'm pretty sure that all the fear I had for this man just vanished in thin air.

I used to look at him with fear but now I feel nothing but anger.

And I love it.

Greg's smile fades and anger quickly swims in his brown pools. "I see someone has lost their lack of respect. Now that you're married off to someone one level higher than me you think everything revolves around you. You're still the pathetic little girl who's been neglected by her own father and was the cause of her mother's death."

My heart drops and everything around me falls away.

"*You're still the pathetic little girl who's been neglected by her own father and was the cause of her mother's death.*"

His words haunt my head like a record player.

Neglected by my father.

Cause of my mother's death.

He's just trying to get in your head and push your buttons. He's trying to gain back his empowerment over me.

I swallow the lump in my throat and blink back the tears that are threatening to spill out my eyes.

"Twisting and manipulating your words about my parents not loving me is very pathetic for a man like you Uncle Greg. My mother did everything in her power to protect me from a world like this and my father loved me unconditionally but unfortunately couldn't bear the heartache of my mother's death. If he was still alive today you would be nothing but his shadow. A piece of lint on his shoulder that he can easily flick away. All my life you've told me that I'm a disgrace, an embarrassment to the family name but looking at you now." I scoff. "You're nothing but a small man who tries to act tough but underneath all that fake act is just an insecure, foolish weak man who finds strength in picking fights with people who are weaker than you. It's depressing, embarrassing and pathetic." I arch a brow whilst stared at him with my best poker face.

Greg was raging with anger and embarrassment as his cheeks were flushed pink. Greg raised his arm, directing his hand toward me but stopped mid-air.

Someone firmly gripped on his wrist, stopping him from slapping me. My eyes followed the foreign masculine arm as it led to those familiar hues of every tree in the forest with rings of green threads circling his iris.

Saint.

Saint cocks a perfect brow and slightly tilts his head. "Were you about to slap my wife?" His voice is low, threatening as itself sent chills down my spine. Greg shifts his focus to Saint. Fear sparked in his eyes but he quickly masked it. "Saint, you know women like Irena need to be dealt with." He casually said as he tried to pry free from Saint who didn't budge.

Saint lightly laughs then shakes his head and glares at Greg. Greg suddenly whines in pain. "No I don't know Greg because I'm not a miserable old shit like you who beats women to boost their lack of confidence." Saint calmly remarks.

Saints calmness only ticked me to the edge. The brutality and coldness in those green eyes pierced through me like a bullet. His body language is collected and tone of voice controlled yet just staring into those green pools. He is unrecognizable. Like the devil in him has awoken. Anyone could tell that Saint was singly planning and picturing torturing Greg in ways that are unimaginable. All the sanity and humanity has been stripped away from him. "Clearly this isn't the first time you've laid your filthy hands on Irena." He states. "You've been abusing your power for too long, Greg," he adds.

In a blink of an eye the sound of bones snapping reaches my ears and I cringe in disgust. Saint snapped Greg's wrist followed by all his fingers. Greg's agonizing cries slices through the music and chatters from the crowd. The ball room goes silent as low murmurs and gasps whispers in the air. Twisting his arms Saint pushes him to the ground and presses his foot on Greg's now broken wrist and hands. He pushes all his weight to his foot as Greg's scream's pierced through my ears.

I couldn't look away. I don't want to look away.

Without realizing it, the corner of my lips slightly curled up into a grin.

The sight made my stomach roil but the sounds of Greg's agonizing cries, the terror and pain in his eyes? It got me high with satisfaction and joy...

"Oh my gosh." Nirali gagged beside me. Her eyes widen as her hands begin to tremble.

I was so focused on the gruesome scene in front of me that I've forgotten about Nirali's presence. Abel appears beside her and pulls her to his chest. He gently strokes her hair and whispers something in her ear followed by her nodding.

Abel meets my gaze. "Nirali can't handle the sight of people getting hurt. I'll be taking her elsewhere." Abel explains and I nod in understanding then he walks away with his wife in his arms and tries his best to comfort her.

I turn my attention back to Saint and Greg and Saint yanks Greg's hair. "You're one lucky bastard that I need you alive." He says through gritted teeth and slammed Greg's head on the ground before rising to his original height. Saint adjusts his suit and dust off the invisible dirt on his expensive suit jacket.

Greg's whimpers hummed in the air and everyone's gaze darted back and forth between Saint and I.

Saint turned his attention to the crowd and everyone looked away as if they hadn't witnessed Saint brutally snapping and breaking someone's bones with his bare hands. He turns his attention back on me.

He approaches me and I automatically step back which makes him pause on his tracks and analyze me. His gaze slightly softens. "Are you okay?" He questions with his low voice. I stand there and just watch him.

Am I okay?

I just smiled at my uncle who's been tortured in front of me — in front of dozens of people. I enjoyed watching him being in pain?

Normally I wouldn't support such acts but after today, the darkest parts of my brain are slowly consuming me.

"I know you're not going to hurt me." I quietly say. Holding with one arm whilst dozens of questions invade my mind.

His silent broodiness and black work suit added to the effect to trigger gossip in the ballroom.

"I just—being around you is not good. For the both of us. You're too violent and I'm—" I paused, sucking in a breath.

I'm slowly being influenced by you. I don't like it not one bit.

He waits for me to finish but I don't. I silently stare at him. Tension thickened between us.

I cleared my throat and shook my head. "Never mind." I say mostly to myself.

Saint peers down at me. His woodsy cologne kissed the tip of my nose. His body warmth radiating towards me, licking every nerve in my body. "Denying the truth will only make you go insane, Irena." He claims. I suck in a short breath as my heart takes a dramatic pause and continues to thump against my chest. Lifting my gaze to him I say. "There is nothing to deny Saint."

We both knew that I was lying to him and mostly to myself. There is everything to deny.

Deny the sudden shift of feelings I have towards Saint.

Deny the changes in my character ever since I've encountered myself with him.

Deny that for the first time in forever. I've become utterly addicted to something that I fear the most. His touch.

"Nothing." I force out not daring to look away from those piercing green eyes.

Saint looks down at me. Carefully studying my features before stepping back and finally I had the ability to breathe freely. He didn't say another word to me but his eyes spoke for him. A haunting grin blesses his lips before he nods then gestures his arm for me to follow him.

And just like that I've officially fallen into the pits of hell, corrupted by all his sins and something even more dangerous.

The ball was a disaster.

Saint and I did not stay long, neither did Abel and Nirali. We left thirty minutes after they did. We even skipped the betting auction with the young girls which I am secretly glad for. I was not looking forward to seeing young girls being sold off to cranky old men.

Once we arrived home I immediately stripped out of the dress, took a long shower and changed into my lacy nightgown then threw myself into the bed.

I closed my eyes and tried to force myself to sleep but I couldn't. I was fully awake and did not feel any tiredness swooping over me.

I groaned out of frustration and grabbed my phone from the night stand beside me. The screen flashes me showing me the time and it's past midnight. I twist and turn in bed, trying my best to fall asleep but nothing.

Why can't I fall asleep?

I knew why but I wouldn't answer that question. Instead I did the one thing that broke all the rules I've told myself to follow.

I pulled myself out of bed and exited my bedroom. The house was dark and quiet with each quiet step I took. My heart picked up its pace until I stopped in front of a door and everything stopped.

I reached my hand out and grabbed the door knob nervously licking my lips before I pushed the door open, noticing the dark room lit by the bright moon casting through the open slits of the thick black curtains.

I quietly enter the room and carefully shut the door making sure to not make a sound. Holding in my breath I tiptoed to the master bed and carefully pulled the covers away then slipped myself into the bed.

His scent kicks me to the curb and butterflies flutter in my stomach when I feel his body warmth. He was so close yet so out of reach.

I sigh and close my eyes, my body relaxing whilst I allow myself to fall asleep in Saint's bed with him beside me.

CHAPTER 36

SAINT DÉ LEON

As the morning sun seeps in through the curtains, its warm rays caress my skin, awakening my senses. I turn my head to the side to admire the sleeping beauty lying next to me. Irena, my stunning goddess, lies there. Her skin glowing like molten caramel in the gentle light. Her lashes flutter slightly, highlighting the curve of her cheekbone, and her lips are parted in a soft, contented sigh. Her luscious curls frame her face like a halo, the dark strands dancing in the morning breeze.

I can't help but lean closer, my nose filled with the intoxicating aroma of her vanilla perfume. Every inch of my body aches to reach out and touch her, to brush those curls from her peaceful face. But I stop myself, content to bask in her beauty and the tranquillity she brings. Here, in this moment, all the chaos of the world fades away, and there is only us and the rising sun.

So near was I to her that I could feel her breath, calm and steady. It was as though I wanted to cocoon her in my arms and shield her from all the harm of the world. To keep her with me for all of eternity.

I leaned in, placing a feather-soft kiss on her lips, and she stirred, her rich brown eyes gradually opening to meet mine. She searched my gaze for answers.

"Morning."

"Morning Doe."

"Last night," she said in a hoarse tone. "I came into your bed."

"Why?" I asked, puzzled.

She hesitated, trying to decide whether to reveal the truth to me or not. "I couldn't sleep," she whispered, casting her eyes downwards.

I eyed her, craving to touch her but I restrained myself by turning away. I closed my eyes, attempting to ignore the nagging need within me.

With her 'no-touch' policy, this woman had the power to throw me off balance.

A surge of electricity courses through my body at the slightest touch of her fingertips on my skin, sending shivers down my spine. As she traces the intricate designs of my tattoos, I find myself surrendering to her touch, my tense muscles loosening in an instant. With a contented sigh, I let out all the tension that's been building up in me.

She nudges me with a curious question, her voice soft and gentle. "Why the ink?"

As soon as the words leave her lips, I'm transported back to the dark, twisted memories of my past. Memories of the hours I spent being whipped at the hands of someone I once trusted. I can feel the heat of the agonizing pain on my flesh and the urge to scream as a little boy.

I turn my head and look into her eyes, trying to keep my emotions in check. "They cover up a part of me that I've been ashamed of for years."

Irena's lips brush against my back, leaving behind a trail of delicate kisses that set my skin on fire. The familiar chill that runs through me makes me shiver uncontrollably.

"What are you doing?" I asked, feeling the palpable unease that filled the room. "I'm trading your scars for kisses, hoping that someday they'll finally heal," she murmured, peppering my back with soft, gentle kisses. "You've taught me to stop letting my past wounds define me, to take up arms and fight my own battles. I want to be the one who finally silences your demons. Consider it a thank you." Her fingers danced lightly over the tattoos that adorned my skin, as I took a deep, cleansing breath, feeling the tension begin to slip away.

Unexpectedly, Irena seizes me, flipping me onto my back and mounting me with fierce determination. Her gaze pierces mine as she rests her palms on my chest, catching the frenzied rhythm of my heart. In the glowing morning light, her caramel-tinted brown skin radiates with a delicate shine. "I'm done fighting, Saint," she avows, locking her stare onto mine. "I'm done fighting with you, with myself, with everything. I'm just so tired." With a heavy exhale, she relinquishes her body to me.

With every fibre in my being, I focus solely on her, my nerves sparking with electric energy. "You're finally giving in," I say coolly, and her nervous smile gives way to a hesitant nod. "It may take some time for me to adjust," she proclaims, and I graciously nod in agreement. "You're absolutely torturing me, Irena Dé Leon," I exhale, my hair falling around my face.

"Am I really, Saint?" She lowers her voice, tracing the defined lines of my abs with her fingers. I reach out to hold her face but she catches my wrists and pins my arms above my head. She gets tantalizingly close, her body pressed against my pulsing erection, straining against my briefs.

My breaths come out in quick gasps as she teases me, moving sensually on top of me. "What did I say, Saint?" Her voice is soft and playful, her lips tantalizingly close to mine. I groan in frustration as she lowers her hips, adding subtle pressure to my throbbing dick.

I swear this woman has been playing with me like a cat with a wounded mouse, and I'm ready to combust in a frenzy of ecstasy. Who knew that a dominant goddess like Irena could ignite such a passionate fire within me? My desire has built to the point where it hurts, an undeniable urge that begs for release.

With a disapproving shake of her head, she admonishes me like a scolded child. "That I should ask before I touch you," I say, echoing her words from a week ago. "Exactly." Her voice trails away teasingly, causing frustration to churn in my gut. "Can I touch you?" I grumble, my voice barely concealing the desperation burning within me.

She raises a brow and I sigh. "Please Irena, can I-fuck, can I touch you?"

The fact that she's allowing me to beg is both maddening and intoxicating. She leans closer, her lips tantalizingly close to mine. I'm frozen, pinned under her gaze and the weight of her mesmerizing aura. "No," she whispers before pulling away, a sly grin playing on her lips. My hands remain immobile above my head, as though they're not even a part of me anymore.

In this moment, she's an unbridled craving that I cannot resist. I inhale the heady perfume of her being, revelling in the overwhelming power she holds over me. I am awestruck by her beauty and her dominance, lost in a world of hypnotic bliss.

Irena's movements are a slow, seductive dance, her hips swaying to a tantalizing beat. Each shift sends a jolt of pleasure through my body, my core tightening with desire. Her sinful drooling adds to the carnal atmosphere, making my blood flow faster and faster.

As she kisses my neck, her lips set me on fire, and her slow, steady grinding drives me wild. The dampness of her bare pussy sends through to my briefs, heightening the sensation even more. "Irena," I warn but she ignores me.

Moving down to my chest, she gives me a trail of wet, teasing licks, and I struggle to hold back my moans.

Irena's fingers trail up my thighs, inching closer and closer to the waistband of my briefs. Our eyes meet and the air crackles with an electric tension. Sin and desire dance in the depths of her dilated pupils, promising to deliver me into the abyss of pure pleasure. With deft hands, she tugs off my briefs and lifts my hips to discard them with a toss. My cock springs free, eager and ready for her. The tip glistens with my pre-cum, beckoning her to come closer. Irena's gaze lingers on my length, her head tilting slightly to assess the challenge before her. She ponders how best to accommodate my throbbing cock in the depths of her mouth.

Her mouth opens, tongue darting out, eager and hungry to savour me. I gasp, hands quivering above my head as I grip the pillow beneath me. As Irena draws me in, half of my length disappears into the wet suction of her lips. Her back arches sensually, her ass popping up with irresistible allure, surging blood driving me to the edge.

With her head bobbing up and down, her cheeks hollowed in delightful suction, she teases and tempts me with swirling tongues and playful flicks, sending shivers of pleasure skittering through my veins. I groan out loud, biting my lip to keep a lid on my wild climax. The sounds of her feasting on me, her moans of pleasure echoing through the room, are like a passionate symphony. In between sucking my cock like a queen, her free hands massage, fondle, tease, working their magic on every inch of my body.

"Fuck." I breathe. With a burst of speed, she quickens her steps as I bask in the glory of what's to come. Every muscle within me tenses as I draw nearer to true euphoria. I feel my jaw clenching tightly as I allow the climax to take over, my soul soaring higher and higher toward the open gates of heaven. My eyes roll back in sinful delight as I reach the peak and explode into Irena's mouth. The sensation leaves me gasping for air, while she keeps on sucking until there's nothing left to offer.

As my senses return to me, Irena's tongue cleanses me off, and I watch as tears streak her cheeks with remnants of my come still perched on her lips. She grins wickedly before wiping away the traces of my release.

She crawls up to me, and without hesitation, I lift my head and capture her lips onto mine. The taste of myself lingers on her tongue. She nibbles on my bottom lip, pinning my hands above my head as the tip of my dick teases her wet entrance.

She pulls back and smiles innocently.

"I'm going to take a shower and no, you cannot join me." She addresses me before pecking my lips and climbing off me then wordlessly steps out of the bed, leaving me in a state of such pure bliss I don't know what to do with myself.

CHAPTER 37

IRENA NOWAK

The phone rings three times and Nirali answers the call. "Hi?" She responds over the line and I lean against the balcony railing as I gaze into the driveway, observing the afternoon sun fade away while the chilly wind brushes against my skin. "Hey, I'm just checking in on you after yesterday." I trail off slowly.

There is a brief pause on the other end before Nirali speaks. "I'm fine, Irena. Abel made sure of it." She says with a gentle laugh.

"That's good, but I want to personally make sure you're alright." I pause, tracing my finger along the metal pole before letting out a soft sigh. "I heard Abel mention that you get anxious when you see violence. Would you mind telling me why?" I inquire quietly. I turn my head towards the room to make sure Saint is still in the shower. Nirali sighs. "Irena-" she trails off, her voice hesitant for a moment. "I know, I know. You feel more comfortable discussing your situation with Abel, but I'm here for you as your friend and you can confide in me. I'm just worried about you." I state, and she sighs. "It's not that I don't trust you, I just worry that you'll see me differently because when I told my parents what I've been through, they couldn't look at me the same way anymore." She explains, and my heart aches at the thought. I sigh, nibbling on my bottom lip. "You remember how my late husband Viktor died from a heart attack, right?" I explain, and she responds with a "Yes," allowing me to continue. "He didn't actually die from a heart attack. I poisoned him." I blurt out, and there is a moment of silence on the other end, which only heightens my anxiety. "Hello?" I question, hoping she is still on the line. "Nirali, are you-"

"I'm here Irena, I just had to digest that information." She reassures me. I hold my breath. "Why?" She asked softly. "He abused me, assaulted me. I sought help from my uncles but they dismissed me for some reason and believed him instead of me. I couldn't bear it anymore. Waking up every day not knowing what to expect from someone you live with and call your own husband. I couldn't handle the torment Nirali, so I had to take matters into my own hands." I finish and she sighs. "I'm so sorry you had to endure that for almost a decade. Although I don't support violence. You had every right. I just wish I had your strength..." she trails off and my eyebrows furrow in suspicion as I watch the grey cloud pass by. "Remember when I told you I was a mute when Abel found me?" She asks and I nod, realizing she can't see me, and reply with a "Yes."

She takes a deep breath, preparing for whatever she's about to tell me.

"Well, I come from an financially unstable background and I would always work extra shifts to earn additional money to support my family. So one day I worked a night shift and on my way home, I didn't realize I was being followed until I was abducted and trafficked to a foreign country to be a worker into hard labour. I've been abused, assaulted, and tortured by people for months until a girl and I took a risk and escaped. Sadly, she didn't make it because she lost her life while trying to save mine. She-she was only 16 and came from a family in Russia. So I found a train, hoping to make my way to the nearest police station so I could find my way back to India. Fate had other plans and the train belonged to Saint, and fast forward, Abel found me and decided to take care of me. That's when our love story began. Although my journey to him was tragic. I'm happy he's in my life and was my first love." My heart fills with happiness as she mentions the last part but aches with pain as I let the words of her story sink in.

She was a victim of human trafficking. I can't even begin to imagine the things she has witnessed and endured. The countless times she has felt that pain of being worthless and wanting to give up.

No wonder she doesn't tolerate violence because it triggers.

She truly is a survivor.

"You mentioned that you desire to be as strong as me. Never compare the hardships you've faced with someone else's nightmare. You are a survivor Nirali. Life has thrown a lot of challenges and messed up things your way, and yet here you are today, still standing with a smile on your face and your heart filled with love more than ever before." I tell her sincerely. "I apologize that you had to endure that, and I'm sorry that your parents can't meet your gaze after what you've been through. I'm also sorry that you had to witness the altercation between Viktor and Saint yesterday." I confess, and she lets out a light chuckle to lighten the mood. "You've apologized many times, knowing that it's not your fault," she asserts, and I offer a weak smile. "Out of everyone, you deserve an apology." I declare to her. "You too, Irena. I can't even imagine the betrayal and pain you've had to endure." Nirali sighs, and I do the same. "That was incredibly difficult." She points out, and I run my hands through my hair. "Yeah," I mutter under my breath. "But thank you for checking up on me. I really needed that from a friend." She states. "You would do the same for me," I respond. Before I can say anything else, I hear a male voice in the background, followed by Nirali's voice. "I have to go. Abel needs me for something." Nirali explains, and I bid her farewell before hanging up.

SAINT DÉ LEON

I've never enjoyed staying at home more than I do now. My wife's presence fills me with warmth and contentment. The clock shows one in the afternoon, and as I sit at the dining table, Irena invites me to lunch. The aroma of roasted chicken fills the air, paired with fragrant white rice and a refreshing avocado salad. Since we got married, Irena has been cooking for me, and she's truly talented at it.

As I take a bite, I can't help but admire how stunning she looks. Her long, curly hair frames her face beautifully, and her white floral dress adds an elegant touch. She sips her red wine, and her pearl earrings catch the light. Time seems to slow down, and all that matters is the delicious food in front of us and the company of my beautiful wife. I find myself staring at her until she catches my gaze. A blush creeps onto her cheeks.

"You're staring," she says.

"I know," I admit.

She's a mix of whiskey and honey—a tempting combination I can't resist. "This is my first time having a nice meal with someone," Irena says, munching on her vegetables. "I'm the first one?" I ask, and she nods. After wiping my mouth, I stand up, and Irena watches me with curiosity. "I want to show you something," I announce. She looks confused, but I assure her it's nothing scary.

"I promise," I add, and after a hesitant nod, she gets up to follow me. As we leave the dining hall, I notice her presence filling the air with a light vanilla and honey scent. We walk down the grand foyer, and an imposing door to the left catches my eye. I swing it open and gesture for Irena to go inside. I flick on the lights in the garage, revealing my collection of sports cars lined up neatly. Irena's eyes widen in amazement at the 34 different models, from cute convertibles to powerful supercars in various colours.

"Are these all yours?" she asks, disbelief in her voice.

"Well, as my wife, I like to think of them as ours," I reply, heading to the board where the keys hang.

"What?!" Irena exclaims, watching as I hand her a key. "These are mine too!?" she adds, laughter escaping her as she admires the cars.

I fold my arms, watching her elegantly move around the vehicles. "Choose your ride," I say with a grin. Without hesitation, she points to the sleek white Lamborghini. "Good choice baby," I affirm.

As I unlock the car, I open the passenger door for Irena, enjoying her grateful smile as she gets in. I slide into the driver's seat, inhaling the luxurious leather interior. With a click of my seatbelt, I bring the engine to life, its roar sending thrills through me. What a beautiful fucking roar. Second best sound. The first one is the sound of my wife's moans when I make her see stars.

Now that's something I could listen to religiously. The car zips forward, shifting into second gear with a jolt. I take a moment to breathe and open the garage door. Finally, I feel the freedom of the open road as I reverse out and onto the driveway. As the ramp approaches, I downshift for a powerful take-off. With the engine roaring, I eagerly hit the empty road, the wind in my hair and adventure in my veins. Irena's excitement is clear; she squeezes her eyes shut and grips the storage compartment tightly. I glance at Irena, her eyes shining with excitement. Her angelic face radiates courage and recklessness, making my heart race even more. I focus back on the road, pressing the pedal down. The wind whips around us as we speed up, reaching 140 km/h. With no one around, I grip the wheel tightly and shift into fourth gear, feeling the RPMs surge. I glance at Irena, and a mischievous smirk spreads across her face. "I want to try something," she says suddenly. Before I can respond, she unbuckles her seatbelt and leans out the window, letting the wind whip through her hair and clothes. Her laughter fills the air as we race forward, both of us caught in a thrilling rush. I can't help but grin at her joy. The speedometer climbs higher as I press down on the gas pedal. With the world blurring past, I feel alive, a wild dance with destiny. Hearing the engine roar like a beast, I slam the car into fifth gear, ready for more speed. "Get ready, Doe!" I shout over the wind. Grinning, she grips the door handles tightly, bracing herself. Together, we dive into the unknown, chasing the thrill with every fibre of our beings. As I shift gears smoothly, the speedometer reaches an astonishing 240 km/h. Adrenaline rushes through me, making my heart race.

"Do you remember when you said no one had ever shared a lunch with you?"

"Well, Doe, you're my first-ever passenger princess."

"Awh, Saint, and it's going to stay like that," she replies. I watch her fix her hair and buckle her seatbelt, her chest rising and falling with excitement. "I had no idea you were such a daredevil," I tease.

Irena raises an eyebrow. "What type did you think I was?"

With a grin, I pull over to the side of the road, revealing a breathtaking view of Paris. I flash her a cheeky smile.

"The psycho type." Irena playfully runs her fingers through her hair.

"That is your type — psycho ladies."

"Not quite," I reply firmly, catching her off guard. Suddenly, I slide my seat back, unfasten her seatbelt, and pull her onto my lap.

"My type is a bit more specific — my psycho wife is my one and only type." Irena's cheeks flush bright red, and I'm charmed by her cuteness.

"You've been grinning all day," she points out. I shrug. "My morning got off to quite the start." I wink, and her blush deepens. She silences me with a finger on my lips. Absolutely adorable.

"You're the first person to join me in my sports car. I'd love to take you for another ride sometime," I say. The tenderness in Irena's eyes softens her demeanour.

"Saint," she murmurs, pausing mid-sentence. My heart skips a beat as she leans in to kiss me, catching me off guard. Feeling remorseful, she quickly apologizes.

"Sorry, it just felt... right."

"Don't apologize, Doe. I'm not him. The only time I'll raise my hand to you is to wipe away your tears, and the only time you'll see my fist is when I grab your hair as you moan 'deeper' while I rearrange your insides," I say, each word heavy with truth.

The air between us crackles with tension as she clears her throat, her eyes locked onto mine. "Well, we must see about that rearranging part," she replies.

"As for that, Doe," I say, tracing her jawline with my fingers, "you'll never want to return to your old self once you've experienced my touch." Irena's breath catches as desire lights up her eyes. The heat between us grows, but I remain cool and collected. With a playful roll of her eyes, she gives me a smile that makes my heart race.

I know she's already hooked, and I can't wait to show her what I can really do.

"Tu es belle, Irena," I murmured, tracing her cheekbone. She leaned into my touch, her eyes fluttering closed.

"Saint," she whispered, her voice a soft plea. I leaned in, capturing her lips in a deep kiss. Our tongues danced, exploring each other's mouths. She moaned, a soft sound that went straight to my cock. I pulled back, my breath ragged.

"I want you, Irena," I growled, my hands roaming her body. She gasped as I cupped her breast underneath her shirt, my thumb brushing against her nipple. I could feel it hardening under my touch.

"Oui," she panted, "Je te veux aussi." She straddled me, her skirt riding up, revealing her lacy panties. I could feel the heat of her pussy through the thin fabric. I groaned, grinding my hips up, my cock straining against my jeans.

"Fuck, Irena," I hissed, "You're so fucking beautiful." She smiled, a wicked glint in her eye.

"You like that, Saint?" she teased, grinding down on me. I groaned, my hands gripping her ass.

"Yeah, I fucking love it," I replied, my voice hoarse. I leaned in, capturing her nipple through her shirt. She gasped, her hands tangling in my hair.

"Huh, Saint," she moaned, "That feels so good." I bit down gently, making her squeal. I soothed the bite with a lick, then switched to her other breast, pinching the nipple I'd just abandoned. She writhed on my lap, her breath coming in short gasps.

"Please, Saint," she begged, "I need more." I slipped my hand under her skirt, pushing her panties aside. I could feel her pussy, hot and wet. I slipped a finger inside, making her moan. I added another finger, pumping in and out, my thumb rubbing circles on her clit.

"Oh, fuck, Saint," she cried, her head thrown back. I could feel her pussy clenching around my fingers, her orgasm building.

"Not yet, Irena," I growled, pulling my fingers out. She whimpered, her eyes pleading. I brought my fingers to my mouth, sucking her juices off. She watched, her eyes wide.

"Delicious," I murmured, "Now, turn around. I want to taste that sweet pussy." She quickly turned, her ass in the air. I pushed her skirt up, revealing her glistening pussy. I leaned in, licking her from clit to asshole. She moaned, pushing back against my face. "Fuck, Saint," she panted, "That feels so good." I slipped a finger into her ass, making her gasp. I pumped it in and out, my tongue lapping at her pussy. She moaned, her orgasm building again. I could feel her pussy clenching, her asshole tightening around my finger.

"Come for me, Irena," I growled, sucking hard on her clit. She screamed, her orgasm ripping through her. I felt her pussy gush, her juices coating my face. I licked it up, savouring her taste. I unbuckled my jeans, pushing them down. My cock sprang free, hard and ready. Irena turned, her eyes hungry. She leaned in, taking my cock into her mouth. I groaned, my hands tangling in her hair. "Fuck, baby," I hissed, "That feels so good." She sucked hard, her tongue swirling around the head. I could feel my orgasm building. I pulled her off, flipping her onto her back. I pushed her legs apart, settling between them. I lined my cock up with her pussy, pushing in slowly. She moaned, her legs wrapping around me. I started to move, my hips snapping forward. She moaned, her nails digging into my back. I leaned down, capturing her nipple in my mouth. I bit down gently, making her squeal. "Harder, Saint," she panted, "Fuck me harder." I obliged, pounding into her. I could feel her pussy clenching around me, her orgasm building again. I reached between us, rubbing her clit. She screamed, her orgasm ripping through her. I felt her pussy gush, her juices coating my cock. I pulled out, flipping her onto her hands and knees. I lined my cock up with her asshole, pushing in slowly. She moaned, her head dropping forward. I started to move, my hips snapping forward. I could feel her asshole clenching around me, her orgasm building again. I reached around, rubbing her clit. She moaned, her orgasm ripping through her. I felt her asshole tighten, her orgasm milking my cock. I couldn't hold back any longer. I groaned, my orgasm ripping through me. I came hard, my cock pulsing in her ass. I collapsed on top of her, our bodies slick with sweat. We lay there for a moment, our breaths ragged. Then, Irena turned, a wicked grin on her face.

"Ready for round two?" she asked, her eyes sparkling. I laughed, my cock already hardening again.

"Always, Irena," I replied, pulling her into another deep kiss.

CHAPTER 38

SAINT DÉ LEON

The gates of my mansion swing open as I rev the engine of my sleek Lamborghini. I expertly guide the car through, my hand resting on the smooth white center console. As I pull up, I spot two guards patrolling the perimeter, smoke curling from their lips. *Where are the other three?* Suspicion fills my mind. I park and turn to Irena, who's sitting beside me. We've spent the morning cruising through Paris, and her driving skills have improved significantly. Concern etches her face as her brown eyes meet mine. "What's wrong?" she asks, her voice trembling with worry. "Just a feeling that something's not right," I reply, trying to make sense of my intuition. "Bad vibes?" she murmurs. "Yeah, but I'll investigate it. Don't leave my side, okay? Until I'm sure it's just my paranoia." She nods, and I step out, reaching for my gun in my jacket pocket. The cool metal offers me some comfort as I turn off the safety. I stride toward the guards, Irena trailing closely behind.

Mico and Sash stand like statues, their expressions guarded. "Where are the other three?" I ask bluntly. Sash frowns. "Aren't they supposed to be guarding the other side? We haven't seen them since this morning." "They were assigned to the front," I reply, unease creeping up my spine.

"But we received a new schedule from Zolton," Mico says, worry evident in his voice. "Something's off here. You two, scour every inch of this yard!" I demand. As we make our way up the porch steps, I grip my weapon and cautiously open the door. I silently assess each room, guiding Irena behind me for safety. The living area and kitchen seem clear, but I remain alert as I move through the foyer. Suddenly, I'm blindsided and knocked to the ground. "Irena, take cover!" I shout as I get up.

Before I can retrieve my firearm, an attacker yanks it from my grip. I face the shadowy figure, ready for a fight. He swings at me, and I block it, then jab him in the gut. He stumbles back, snarling, and pulls out a knife. I step in close, deflecting his swing and striking his arms.

The knife clatters to the floor. "You're a dead motherfucker," he hisses, and I smile. A flash of silver signals another attacker. I duck but feel a sharp sting as his blade slices my cheek. I grab him by the collar and hurl him against the pavement. But the first assailant scrambles to his feet and kicks my shoulder. Pain flares, but I won't fall. I twist his arm until his hand points skyward, then wrench it down, snapping it with a sickening crack. He howls in agony. I relish his weakness and land two punches to his nose, blood spraying everywhere. He reels, and I deliver a swift blow to his kneecap. He crumples to the ground. I scan the room for Irena and finally see her crouched behind the door, eyes wide with fear. I rush to her side, finding my gun on the floor. "Are you okay?" I murmur, checking for injuries. She shakes her head, still in shock. "I'm fine. Thank you."

"You're bleeding." I look down at my cheek. "It's just a small cut. I'll live." Before I can register the sting, Irena's warm thumb brushes my skin, sending shivers down my spine. "There," she says softly. "All better." Something unspoken passes between us in that moment. But then, a group of armed figures emerges from my office, drawing their weapons. I grab Irena and shield her, her trembling form against me. With their fingers on the triggers, I urge Irena to stay put as I rush toward them, using the door as my shield. I fire rapidly, hoping to hit my targets. They fire back relentlessly, their masks hiding their faces. When their guns click empty, I grab my loaded rifle and unleash a deadly rain of bullets, taking them down swiftly. After a moment of silence, I return to Irena's side. "Are they gone?" She asks, fear still lingering. "Yes," I reply. Trembling, I pull out my phone and call Zoltan. "Hitmen. I was attacked but took care of them," I say, pacing. "Where?" he asks. "My place."

"How many?"

"Maybe seven or eight."

"Did you get anything off them?" I shake my head. "No, they're all dead. Call Abel, Prince, and the cleanup team. I want everyone here in less than an hour." I disconnect and turn to Irena. "We can't stay here."

"Where do we go from here?" she asks. "To my brother's house. We'll stay there until the safe house is ready. I'll also triple your guards." Her brow furrows with questions. "Who do you think sent them?"

"I'm not sure. I have a lot of enemies. It could be anyone, even the people I trust." She lowers her gaze. "I'll do everything I can to keep you safe."

"I know," she mutters.

"For fuck's sake." Zoltan snickers as he surveys the bodies in my foyer. "You've done quite the job here, Saint." He pats my shoulder and starts directing the cleanup crew. "How did they get past security?" Abel asks, eyeing me with concern. "I'm trying to figure that out. One guard mentioned a new schedule, which explains why most of my men weren't on their posts. They were reassigned, making it easier for these bastards to get in," I explain to my brother. "Isn't Zoltan in charge of managing your security layout?" Prince questions and I nod.

"It's strange. Just before the attack, I saw three men leaving my office," I add, leading them back to my quarters. Everything looks in order, but I sense they were searching for something. I head straight for my desk and turn on my laptop, eager to check the security cameras. I trust my instincts and prefer to keep some things private; you never know what chaos could ensue if the wrong person learned about my precautions. I scrutinize the screen, on high alert.

My heart races as three shadowy figures enter the room, rifling through my books, clearly looking for something. Zoltan breaks the silence, asking if they've found anything. I shake my head, unable to look away from the monitor. Out of the corner of my eye, I see two of the men digging through my desk drawers. Suddenly, one pulls out a tool and unlocks a drawer that should have been secure. My breath catches as they pull out a black file, its ominous contents threatening to expose my hidden truths. Inside is the contract binding Irena and me in a facade of marriage. A shiver runs down my spine at the thought of it being revealed, the plans I carefully laid out crumbling before me. As one masked figure removes his mask to look at the contract, my heart races with anger and fear. It's Cal, one of the guards I assigned to watch the house—he shouldn't be here. I watch in disbelief as he takes pictures of the contract before putting it back and slipping it into my cabinet. The three of them exchange words, and it hits me: these were the guards who should have been on duty. I chuckle at the irony—Cal is part of Zoltan's team, yet Prince sent out a new schedule that disrupted our security. Either Zoltan or Prince is behind this. Taking a deep breath, I close my laptop and rise from my chair, my so-called loyal trio following me. As Abel presses for answers, I instruct my team, "Search their pockets for evidence, starting with their cell phones." I'm curious if any of them has a phone that might lead us to who's behind this. "No cell phones here, sir," one of the men reports.

My mind races. Someone higher up is pulling the strings. "Stay alert. If you see or hear anything strange, let me know," I instruct, though I know I have to stay on high alert myself. I can't trust anyone until we identify the mole. I'll triple the security, stay with Abel for now, and once the safe house is ready, I'll take Irena there until I find out who put her in danger. My priority is keeping her safe and hiding the contract, especially from her.

CHAPTER 39

IRENA NOWAK

The white roses were beautiful, their pale petals glistening with snow. The cold breeze brushed my face as I admired them, their resilience standing out in the frozen garden. Nirali's once-vibrant haven was now a wintry scene, but the white roses stood tall, a symbol of grace and hope. For the past two days, Nirali and Abel have been our hosts, though it hasn't been a relaxing stay. Saint is focused on tracking down the person behind the attack, leaving me alone with my thoughts. Abel has been busy too, but he finds time to be with his wife whenever possible. As I stand outside, lost in thought, Abel approaches. "You've been out here too long, Irena," he says, breaking my trance. I chuckle. "Yeah, it's freezing, but the peace is worth it." We stand together in silence, just enjoying each other's company in the cold. "Why the early return? And where's Saint?" I ask. Abel, his cheeks red from the cold, replies, "He's occupied."

"With what?" I press. "Killing people," I say bluntly, knowing the truth. "Do you feel remorse after taking a life?" I ask, watching him closely. Abel's expression grows thoughtful. "Once, I did. But now, I take comfort knowing they pay for their sins, though I'll join them soon enough."

"You don't enjoy it?" I question. He sighs.

"No. I'm not like my brother. I don't hurt for pleasure. My actions are driven by anger, not cruelty." I nod, understanding more about him.

"I don't harm the innocent," he continues. "I take what I need from the guilty, be it an object or a favour. I only do what's necessary." I have more questions but hold back, sensing the moment isn't right. The past few years have been a struggle, haunted by memories of the men who hurt me. But after the recent attack, something inside me has shifted. I'm ready to confront my demons. Living with someone capable of such violence has shown me I need to be stronger, both physically and emotionally. I'm determined to learn how to defend myself, starting with the men who stole my innocence. "Do you feel guilt after killing?" I ask Abel, my voice unsteady. He meets my gaze.

"Never. The more you do it, the less it bothers you. It becomes just another task." After a pause, he asks, "What brought this on, Irena?"

"I want to kill some people," I admit, staring at the roses. Abel turns to me. "Whose blood do you seek?"

"The men who took a part of me when I was young," I answer calmly. "Do you have the courage to go through with it?" he challenges. I pause, then answer, "Yes." He nods, and we both look back at the roses, the promise of violence lingering in the air.

"You never listen, do you?" I said, meeting his confused expression with a pointed look at his soaked clothes. He smiled sheepishly.

"I'm sorry," he muttered, kissing my forehead. I tried to fight a grin and bit my lip instead. "Let's get you cleaned up," I said, taking his hand and leading him to the guest bedroom. In the bathroom, I gestured for him to sit on the toilet while I rummaged through the cabinet for the first aid kit.

"Take off your shirt," I instructed, laying out the necessary supplies to tend to Saint's cuts and scrapes. A smug smirk crossed his lips.

"I like where this is headed," he quipped. With a mischievous glint in my eye, I couldn't resist rolling them as I quipped, "Shut up." When Saint peeled off his shirt, my heart skipped a beat as I stationed myself firmly between his long, masculine legs.

"This might sting a bit," I warned, gently dabbing his injured face with alcohol-soaked cotton. As I meticulously attended to his wounds, Saint rested there, silently observing my every move.

"I'll sleep with you tonight. Only because you've not been sleeping for the past few days." I told him as I continued to aid him. He chuckles lightly. "You can just say you enjoy being in bed with me." he teases, and I roll my eyes. I do, but I will not admit it out loud. "Says the guy who can't sleep without me." I let out, and he grins. "Touché." A stillness gripped the room, punctuated only by the gentle hum of the air conditioner. Suddenly, as if impelled by an unexplained force, Saint burst out, "You are beautiful,

Irena." I froze, my eyes meeting him as my cheeks turned rosy. "Where did that come from?" I managed to stutter out. But before I could say anything else, he reached over, his hand curling around my thigh, drawing me closer. "Who cares where it came from? Just know that you're beautiful." I couldn't help but smile, feeling a flutter in my chest at his words. "You're beautiful too, Saint," I murmured. He laughed, a twinkle in his eyes as he revealed his lone dimple. "Hardly. I'm not beautiful."

"But beauty comes in many forms," I replied, feeling a sudden surge of courage. "And you, Saint, are beautiful in your own dark and twisted way." He licked his lips, absorbing my words with solemn attention.

"You know what? You're something else," he finally said, releasing me from his grip. I gathered the wad of bloody cotton and tossed it into the trash. "Okay, I'm done," I declared, returning to him with a newfound lightness. Saint rises from his seat without uttering a sound, deftly removing his pants and stepping out of them. I'm left standing there, a bundle of nerves and desire, mesmerized by the sight of his chiselled back.

My eyes rove over the defined muscles, tracing the intricate tattoos that adorn his skin before landing somewhere they really shouldn't, on that perfectly sculpted ass. I can't help but tilt my head to one side, envisioning myself grabbing onto those firm curves as he pounds into me with abandon. But before I could get lost in my fantasies, I cleared my throat to remind him of my presence.

Saint turns his head, flashing me an innocent grin before stepping under the showerhead and letting the water cascade down his body. With a deep sigh and a satisfying neck crack, Saint's wet hair cascaded down his back as he tilted his head, lost in thought. With a sudden baldness, I cast my inhibitions to the side and slipped out of my clothes, sneaking into the steamy sanctuary of the shower. The water felt like a gentle weight on my skin, washing away the traces of the day. As I looked over Saint's body, I noticed the dry residue of blood and decided to take charge and tenderly scrub him clean. With every stroke of the scrub, my hands explored his body, making sure not to miss an inch. Saint turned around, offering me his rock-hard abs for my special attention. He took the scrub from me, rinsed it away, and started washing me with a new soap leather.

The warmth of the water washed away any awkwardness, allowing for comfortable silence between us. As Saint and I lock eyes, a magnetic force pulls us closer together. His gaze is intense, and he tilts my chin ever so slightly. My heart flutters as his warm breath caresses my lips, beckoning me toward him. The moment our lips meet, the world fades away. Our kiss is a slow burn, intensifying with each passing second. It's more than physical; it's emotional and intimate, and we both feel it. I cling to him, my fingers tangling in his wet hair, lost in the moment's passion. Saint's arousal is obvious, pressing against me, and I moan softly as he pulls me in closer. The taste of him fills my senses as our tongues dance together.

Our kiss becomes more intense and primal before Saint pulls away with a satisfied smile. I'm left breathless, longing for more. My heart aches to fully exude my emotions, but the words get stuck in my throat. "I want to, I do, but-." Before I could finish my sentence, he silenced me with a gentle touch of his lips against mine. I bask in the moment, feeling his warm breath on my skin as I lose myself in the kiss. Finally, we part, and he reassures me there's no need to explain. With a soft smile, I concede. I clutch him tightly, laying my ear on his chest to hear his heartbeat. We share in the sweet intimacy of the embrace, silently understanding each other's unspoken sentiments.

As I coolly survey the arsenal of bullets before me, my mind is a hive of fierce tactics on how best to bring them to their knees. Sure, Saint had inflicted critical harm, but I would ensure that my wrathful stamp would be the last thing they saw as they descended into the fiery abyss. Suddenly, the car grinds to a halt and my attention is drawn to a towering brick edifice before us. The yard is littered with a host of vehicles and burly guards pepper the perimeter, leaving no doubt to the unwavering, impregnable security in place.

As the purr of the engine faded to a halt, I snapped shut the small case and switched my focus to Saint. Before me stood a work of divine art. A white shirt clung to his every muscle, revealing biceps that threatened to burst free. His black pants and shoes were perfectly tailored, making him look like a Greek god gracing the mortal world. Dark hair lazily caressed his forehead, a look that defined him. And then there was the cologne. The woodsy scent tickled my nose and sent shivers down my spine. His stubble was trimmed to perfection, his lips plump and perfect. He was flawless, a fallen angel in human form. "You don't have to be afraid," he said, coaxing me out of my seat. I'll protect you."

"I have nothing to fear," I quipped, giving him a smirk before stepping out into the sunlight. My black pants suddenly felt too plain in comparison to his majestic presence. I smoothed out any wrinkles and admired the results in the car's window. My curly hair framed my face, and my light makeup added a hint of glamour.

I'd decided to go formal today. I'm wearing a white blouse with black pants, and heels to match. This was going to be a day to remember. Saint emerged from the car and strode towards me, exuding confidence and power. Together we made our way toward the warehouse, my heart pounding with anticipation. As we walked, I noticed two guards staring intently at us. But Saint's words rang in my ears: I am a queen here. The thought filled me with a newfound sense of authority and I held my head up high, a regal aura emanating from my every step. After all, as his wife, whatever was his was also mine. But as we entered the building, the air turned dank and frigid, the stench of death and blood wafting through the air.

We pressed on, ignoring the intimidating men strewn throughout the warehouse, each one bearing a gruesome scar that told a story of torture and pain. Finally, we reached our destination: a door guarded by two imposing figures who stood their ground, unwilling to let us pass. "Are they still alive?" Saint inquired of the guard.

"Affirmative, sir. Dr. Stone made certain of it," the soldier with the buzz cut replied. Saint gave a satisfied nod.

"Excellent," he murmured, his hand outstretched to receive the weapon the guard now proffered. Turning to me, his eyes gleamed with a sinister light. I hesitated for a moment before yielding him the case of bullets. As he deftly loaded the firearm, I could feel the pulsing darkness urging me to take matters into my own hands. But Saint held my gaze steadily, a loaded gun in his hand. "There are more weapons inside...if you want to take things further," he said coolly, his voice a low growl. My nod of acquiescence was all he needed. I whirled on my heel, my sights on the unyielding steel doors ahead.

"Open the door," Saint commands his sentinel as they hasten to extract the keys and insert them into the lock. The lock yields with a satisfying click, and the portal glides open in a rusty hinge with a dolorous groan. My heart races as I'm confronted with the pungent odour of blood and grime, but I steel myself against the instinct to recoil. A shiver runs down my spine as I enter the room from the dark, chilly air. Three naked men hang limply above me, their arms bound above their heads, and their heads hung low in surrender. The concrete floor is slick with eerie fluids, and the walls are spattered with dry blood.

A terrifying display of torturous tools adorns one wall. Though there is a single window, sunlight only trickles in and cannot brighten the shadowed corners of the room. To my left, a table gleams with deadly weapons, all polished and ready for use. The steady, dripping sound that echoes around me emanates from a single source - a leaky tap or a hole in the ceiling. Suddenly, Saint and two ominous guards enter, slamming the door shut behind them.

Every detail engraved itself into my mind. Their faces' twisted features, ominous names, and the putrid stench lingered in the air. Each moment of that fateful night feels as fresh as a dewy morning. Their rancid imprint on my body is still as tangible as ever. Their blood and fluids clung to me like a sickness. Cuts and bruises lined their bodies, open wounds oozing with disgust. It was evident that Saint showed them no mercy. "Wake them up." Saint's husky voice broke the eerie silence. One of the guards seized the hose that lay lifeless on the ground, turning it on with a vicious twist. The stream of frigid water struck the trio with brutal force, eliciting sharp gasps and feeble moans. They were now wide awake, writhing in agony.

Shane.

Mikolaj.

Piotr.

As I enter the dimly lit room, Shane's gaze is fixed on me like a hawk on its prey. His narrowed eyes betray his recognition of me, and my anger begins to boil like molten lava. Moving closer, I confront him with a steely glare.

"Remember me?" I challenge, my voice laced with venom. Shane's eyes widened in shock as I asserted my presence. "Yeah, you remember me."

As Shane struggles against his chains, I can't help but feel a sense of satisfaction at his plight.

"What do you want from me?" he pleads, desperation creeping into his voice.

"I told you-"

"Shut up, Shane, with your bullshit excuse." I snarl, cutting him off. My rage pulses through me like an adrenaline rush as Piotr coughs out blood in the corner.

"You know exactly why I'm here." Shane's eyes dart back and forth, searching for a way out. But there is none, and he knows it.

"Please," Piotr choked out weakly, "just kill me already." I smile, feeling the rush of power coursing through me as I contemplate my next move. This is just the beginning.

"Awh, Piotr. Remember when I begged just like you to stop? Please stop, I just want it all to end, and all you fuckers found it amusing to assault me." I started to move in a circular motion around them, my fingers gliding over the tip of the gun as I did.

"The pain, the cries, the humiliation you've caused me," I sneered, relishing the power in my voice. "But enough talk. I didn't come here to chat. I came to make you pay, to watch you beg for mercy as I did" With a flick, I signalled the men to free Shain. He would be my first victim.

"You fucking worthless dirty whore." Shain let out a guttural groan as he pressed his insistent fingers deeper into me, and I recoiled, the urge to escape almost overwhelming. My stomach clenched, and tears coursed down my cheeks as he pinned me mercilessly to the ground, his breath thick with the stench of alcohol. "Please," I begged, but my pleading voice only seemed to spur him on. His dry lips grazed my cheek as he sneered, "You want this, baby girl. I've seen the way you eye me up at dinner." A searing pain drove through me as he slammed his fingers into me harder, At that moment, the world around me faded into a blur of red, my mind cleaved clean. A switch flipped off inside me, a sudden white-out of everything I had ever cared about.

Nothing mattered anymore.

He groaned as a thunderous headache erupted in his skull, his eyes tightly shut against the dull pain. The throbbing was so intense it felt like a heartbreak of a whore, and he cursed under his breath, his hand instinctively reaching up to assess the damage. To his shock, his arms and legs were restrained, rendering him immobile and vulnerable.

He realized he was lying flat on his back as he tried to sit up. I yanked him by his shaggy hair, bubbling snot and tears streaming down his face like an ephemeral river.

"Irena, I'm sorry," he pleaded with infantile snivelling. "I've changed." But I was having none of it; I shoved the gun into his mouth, my eyes narrowing in menacing disdain.

"You silly, silly man," I said through gritted teeth, my innocent smile painting my luscious lips. And as he trembled and whimpered in fear, I remained collected and calm, basking in my power over him.

Every sound faded into silence, consumed by the insatiable hunger within me. With each passing moment, I swelled larger, towering over my helpless prey, who shrank before me. The bloodlust was all-consuming, a thick fog that suffocated reason and restraint.

Deep within my soul, something primal stirred, a force of untold power that surged through my veins. I felt invincible, unstoppable, driven by a strength I never knew I possessed. And I set my sights on one singular objective: to inflict upon this person a pain so severe, so profound, that it would be etched into their very being.

They would understand what it meant to lose something so vital and precious that it felt like an integral part of themselves had been torn away. "At least you're going to taste the ashes of your pathetic fucker of a friend who is surely rotting in hell." With a bitter taste in my mouth, I pulled the trigger, painting the room in a gruesome display of gore. The metallic stench of blood and the sound of muffled sobs filled the air as Shane's limp body hit the ground with a jarring thud. Piotr's desperate pleas for mercy were silenced by his parched throat, a testament to the inhumane treatment we had been subjected to. The rustling of fabric alerted me to someone's presence, but my focus remained unwaveringly fixed on the eerie scene, and I cried out in anguish.

How long had I been trapped in this nightmare? Hunger pangs gnawed at my gut, a cruel reminder of our grim reality as I struggled to stay alert.

Piotr tried to wrench his arms free and felt narrow straps dig into his flesh. He cried out in pain and kept battering at the straps with his forearms. They sawed in deeper and drew blood, but he was too far gone to notice it. His every instinct forced him to fight this unseen enemy. He snapped his head back, the impact dizzying him for a moment. "Crazy how parallel our lives are," I announce.

"No, stop it! Stop it!" My cries of agony were drowned out by Viktor's laughter as I watched the blood from my nose mix with my bitter tears. It was a scene straight out of a horror movie as Piotr slammed my head against the pool table, his hard bulge pushing against me from behind. My protests were met with his cruel advances, pushing me to play his twisted game.

"Aye, Viktor, bring it!" Piotr barked at the amused observer. I begged for mercy, pleading with Viktor to save me from the brute before me. But he only responded with a smirk, leaving me at the mercy of his sadistic friend. "It's just a game, Irena," Piotr sneered, his grip tightening on me. The taste of my fear was sweet to him as he leaned in to attack my willpower. With sick amusement, he praised my body, reducing me to nothing more than a sex toy for their entertainment. Piotr pushes deeper into me. Grinding against my butt as he bites my ear lobe. "You have the body of a porn star, do you know that? Viktor is a lucky man to have you. Good thing he's generous enough to share you because if I were him, I would be a greedy fuck."

"Ah, Jenet. Set it down for Piotr. We are about to play a special game with my dear wife." With an air of grandeur, Viktor exclaims, beaming from ear to ear. Jenet shoots me a heartbroken look as she sets a tray beside me, casting her gaze downward as she walks away. Viktor rises from the couch and places his empty glass by the pool table, his eyes like a dark abyss, drawing me in. My breath catches in my throat as he picks up an object, revealing a sharp, glinting blade.

Saint's men positioned a lavish table in front of me while Piotr, the only unchained one, quivered on the ground. He attempted to rise up and flee but the swift men intercepted him. With a firm grip on his hair, they threw him at my feet. I stood there, arms folded, staring down at him. I gripped his hair and commanded him to kneel. "Shall we relive that fateful night?" I proposed with a smirk. I took a step closer and whispered in his ear, "Do you want to play a game?" Piotr's eyes welled with tears as he shook his head. With a swift motion, I jerked his head backward, sending him into a dizzying spin. Then, with a fierce determination, I slammed his skull against the cold, metallic table again and again, heedless to his screams of fury and fear. The acrid tang of blood mingled with the putrid stench of excretion, decaying and corroding the air around us.

As the red fluid spattered my face, clothes, and hands, a frenzied bloodlust seethed through my veins, overwhelming reason and sanity. The man's gasping, ragged breaths invited the foul tastes back into his mouth, like a twisted, demented film of unspeakable cruelty. And in that gruesome moment, I called for the knife, eager to take my revenge.

"No...ba-..." he croaked as loud as he could.

"No... Don't..."

"Pull out his arm." With an unrelenting demand, I sprang into action. In one fluid movement, I seized Piotr's arm and held it outstretched.

"We're about to play our favourite game," Viktor explains coolly, "Five Finger Fillet. I'll have you place your hand palm down and I'll swiftly stab the spaces between your fingers, gradually increasing my speed. If I manage not to stab you, then Piotr here can have you for the night. If I do..." He trails off with a sinister grin.

"You'll be mine." I shake my head, struggling against Piotr. With a wicked chuckle, Viktor savours the sheer terror in my eyes as he stabs the sharp blade between my trembling fingers. Piotr pins me down, his hot breath on my neck as he grinds against my back, heightening the experience. My heart is a drum in my chest, pounding with anticipation and dread, and tears fall from my eyes as I plead silently for mercy.

Suddenly, a sob escapes my lips as the fear consumes me completely. I blink back to the traumatic memory.

"No," I declared with conviction. I aimed my weapon toward his dick with unwavering determination and pulled the trigger.

His screams resonated the memories of that fateful night flooded my mind, I mercilessly plunged my blade between the spaces of his fingers, gaining momentum with each passing second. Piotr's body trembled with fear, his eyes screwed shut in anticipation of the piercing pain that was soon to come.

His voice was hoarse from previous cries, his lips parched from thirst, only a gasp escaped from between them now. With unwavering strength, I thrust the blade into his flesh, rending a piercing scream from his lips. Piotr fell heavily against the cold metal surface, gasping for breath, his body wracked with pain.

"Ple-" I aim for his head, my finger tightening on the trigger. The bullet pierces the base of his skull with precision, unleashing a gory explosion of blood and brain matter that splatters across the table in gruesome glory.

My chest heaves with the adrenaline of the moment, my gaze cutting towards Mikolaj.

His eyes are filled with sorrow, but even they cannot mask his acceptance of his fate.

"No point in begging right?" His voice is cold and unfeeling, devoid of any hint of compassion.

A towering figure looms over me, a Cuban cigar perched in the corner of his lips. His head tilts and a devilish grin spreads across his face. I'm forced to my knees as he puffs out a cloud of smoke, the ashes falling like burning stars upon my skin. Silent tears stream down my face, but there's no use in begging. Viktor's gang of friends watch on from across the room as Mikolaj lurks closer, his eyes set on me. I'm left half-naked, my torn dress cast aside, and my body bears the marks of their torment…blood, sweat, cuts, and bruises. "You're nothing but a good-for nothing slut," Mikolaj growls in a raspy voice. "And you're going to take it all." With a gut-wrenching sound, he unbuckles his belt and unzips his pants to reveal his penis. Shudders of disgust rattle through me as he taps it on my face I cringe leaning back. I will not allow myself to suck such a thing. He groans in pleasure. My trembling body is met with the cold, hard steel of a gun pressed against my temple.

The air as a vivid light pierced through his eyes, devouring his nerves with ferocity. "I'd rather you bleed your dick out to death." Mikolaj writhed in agony, frothing at the mouth and succumbing to the darkness that slowly embraced him. I released the firearm from my grip, a weight lifted from my shoulders.

My tear filled eyes sparkled with liberation rather than sadness. The burden of anguish, guilt, and fury had been lifted; my demons could finally rest. I turned to face Saint, empowered and unafraid. I stood resolute, gazing into his cloaked expression illuminated by the evening twilight.

With each step he took towards me, I inhaled his woodsy cologne, his presence looming over me like a shadow.

"Everyone out." With one commanding gesture, Saint dismissed all the men without another syllable uttered. I couldn't help but keep my eyes glued on him, captivated by his indecipherable gaze. Suddenly, his eyes honed in on mine, and I shivered as I felt his power surge through me.

"You're breathtaking," he murmured, tenderly caressing my blood-stained cheek. At that moment, I saw the pure, unadulterated magic in his eyes. A dark and intoxicating brew that left me dizzy with desire. "The way that blood looks on your face... stunning. I'm beyond honoured to be your husband, and I'll carry that pride with me beyond death. Hell, I'll even brag to the demons about how an angelic beauty snared my soul without even setting foot in heaven."

His words cut deeply into my heart, carving out a place for him that another would never fill. I bit my lip, fixated on Saint with a passion that bordered on greed. He tilted his head, and his eyes roamed over every inch of me with a ravenous hunger that threatened to consume us both.

In one swift movement, he crushed his lips to mine, hoisting me up with ease and pressing me against the wall. My legs wrapped instinctively around him, clinging to him like his ultimate prize. As our bodies drew closer, a thrilling electric pulse ran through my skin. Saint's lips pressed against my neck, and I could feel the power and control emanating from his touch.

Our worlds collided, the boundaries between us disintegrating like the seams of a garment. The bitter taste of degradation was transformed into something intoxicating as Saint worshipped me.

The heat between us grew hotter, fuelled by desire and lust. His kiss was like a violent storm, taking over my senses and leaving me breathless. I was a willing victim, surrendering to his fierce and unforgiving embrace. My sins were like an invisible cloak, but he didn't shy away from them. Instead, he worshipped me with every fibre of his being.

"Look at them, Doe," he urged, trailing kisses down my neck. "Look at how much power and fucking control you have." Our worlds collided, merging into a single pulsating entity. The thought of him worshipping me, surrounded by those who had once mocked and humiliated me, fuelled an intense heat deep within me.

"Irena," I whispered, my voice hoarse with desire. "I want to fuck you." She looked up at me, her eyes wide. "Here?" she asked, her voice barely a whisper. "Yes," I growled, my hands already reaching for the hem of her dress. "Right here, right now." She bit her lip, her eyes flashing with excitement. "What about the bodies?" I started with her dress, pulling it up over her head. She wasn't wearing a bra, her breasts spilling out, her nipples already hard. I took one in my mouth, sucking hard, my teeth grazing her nipple. She gasped, her back arching off the wall.

"The bodies are least of my worries Doe." "I'm covered in blood." she adds on and I smile, "Yes, and I'll be fucking you, covered in the blood of those who did you wrong."

Her eyes widen with wildness lingering behind those brown eyes. She smiles wickedly, "You fucking insane."

"I love it." Her hands explored my chest, her nails raking down my skin. I moved down her body, my hands pushing her legs apart. She was wearing a thong, the fabric already damp. I hooked my fingers in the sides, pulling it down her legs. She lifted her hips, helping me. I tossed the thong aside, my eyes on her pussy. It was bare, her lips glistening with her arousal. I leaned down, my tongue finding her clit. She moaned, her hands fisting in my hair. I licked her, my tongue delving into her pussy, tasting her. She was sweet, her taste exploding on my tongue. I could feel her getting wetter, her hips moving in time with my tongue. The smell of blood and Irena's arousal was enough to make me go crazy. I was ready to fuck her like a deprived animal. I was ready to lay her on the dead bodies and fuck her brains out as she cries out not caring of those who can hear us outside this room.

"Fuck, Saint," she panted, her hands pulling at my hair. "I'm going to come." I pulled back, a wicked grin on my face.

"Not yet, you're not," I said, my hands moving to her thighs. I pushed her legs further apart, my thumbs spreading her lips. I leaned down, my tongue finding her asshole. I love tasing every inch of her. She gasped, her body tensing.

"What are you doing?" she asked, her voice breathless. "I'm exploring," I said, my tongue circling her hole. I could feel her relax, her body opening up to me. I pushed my tongue in, fucking her ass with my tongue.

"Oh, fuck," she moaned, her hands fisting the sheets.

"That feels so good." I pulled back, my fingers replacing my tongue. I pushed two fingers into her ass, fucking her slowly. She moaned, her body moving in time with my fingers. I added a third finger, stretching her, preparing her. "I want your cock in my ass," she said, her voice a low growl. "I want you to fuck me till my eyes roll back." I grinned, my cock throbbing at her words.

"Not yet," I said, my fingers still fucking her ass. "First, I want to taste you again." I moved back down her body, my tongue finding her clit again. I licked her, my fingers still fucking her ass. She moaned, her body writhing under me. I could feel her getting close again, her body tensing. "Come for me, Irena," I said, my voice a low growl.

"Come on my tongue baby." She screamed, her body convulsing as she came. I could feel her pussy pulsing, her juices flowing onto my tongue. I licked her, drinking her up, my fingers still fucking her ass while her legs trembled barely standing up. When she came down, I pulled back, my cock throbbing. I stripped off my pants, my cock springing free. I was rock hard, my cock aching to be inside her. Fuck it. We both hungrily kiss each other, our hands roaming all over each other's bodies.

Irena stumbled back, losing her balance as she trips backwards landing on one of the bodies taking me down with her.

The floor was covered in a pool of blood which soon stained us. from our hair, to face to hands to fucking feet. But I didn't care, we didn't care. I just wanted to feel her. My cock wanted to be home. Hovering over her, I pushed her legs apart, my cock finding her pussy.

I pushed in, my cock sliding into her wet heat. She moaned, her hands grabbing my ass, pulling me in deeper. She stares at me through hooded eyes, blood painting her face as she hungrily bites down on her lower lip.

God that sight alone could be enough to make me cream and fill her up. I started to move, my cock sliding in and out of her pussy. She moaned, her body moving in time with mine. I could feel her getting close again, her body tensing under me. "Come with me," she panted, her eyes on mine. "Come inside me baby." I grunted, my cock throbbing at her words. I could feel my orgasm building, my balls tightening. I pushed into her, my cock burying itself deep inside her pussy.

I came, my cock pulsing, my cum filling her.

I pulled out still hard. I wanted more, I wanted to fuck her ass. I wanted to fucker her pussy. I wanted to fuck her mouth. God I'm so fucking hungry for her. Her eyes quickly glance to the body lying beside us and she slightly panics but I slowly and gently force her head to face me.

"Focus on me Doe." I reassure, slicking up my cock. I peck her forehead as an apology before swiftly lifting her up and flipping her over. I pushed her onto her hands and knees, my cock finding her asshole, She arches divinely, her head pressed onto the corpse. Biting down on my lower lip, I spank her full juicy ass.

"Yes," she moaned, her body pushing back against me. "Fuck my ass, Saint. " I pushed in, my cock sliding into her ass. She moaned, her body tensing as she adjusted to my size. I started to move, my cock sliding in and out of her ass. She moaned, her body moving in against with mine. My knees ache at the friction of my skin grinning against the bloody concrete floor.

Though the pain was unbearable it added on to the pleasure. That alone, driving me feral. I reached around, my fingers finding her clit. I rubbed her, my fingers moving in time with my cock. She moaned, her body getting close again. "Come for me, Irena," I growled, my fingers rubbing her clit. "Come on my cock." She screamed, her body convulsing as she came.

I could feel her ass pulsing, her body milking my cock. I came too, my cock pulsing, my cum filling her ass. I pulled out, my body spent. I collapsed onto the ground beside her, pulling her into my arms. We lay there, our bodies slick with sweat and blood our hearts racing.

"You're going to be the death of me, won't you?" I murmured, my thumb gently brushing her cheek. "Does it scare you?" she ask.

"You know what? I couldn't be happier about it."

"You scare me, but it what makes you so irresistible." I pause, searching her eyes.

"And it fucking thrills me." As she lean in, a grin spreads across her face before she gently plant my lips on hers.

The energy between us ignites like a fireworks show, a glorious collision of passion that erupts like a supernova. Her mouth was plush, inviting, and parted to receive my exploring tongue. Bodies flush against each other.

We were a fiery inferno blazing wrapped in each other's arms on the floor. Our paced breathing, hot and rapid, only added to the intensity. I could taste our mingling breaths and feel our hearts pounding in perfect sync. Finally, Irena reluctantly pulled away from our explosive embrace.

"Good."

CHAPTER 40

SAINT DÉ LEON

"You should have seen her, Abel. I can't get enough of her," I exclaim, my mind was vividly conjuring images of her captivating beauty.

Abel recoils in horror, his eyes widening at the thought of this femme fatale. "No offense, but I think I'll pass on that kind of trauma. You both seem to be a harmonious duo of dysfunction."

He quips, flipping through the pages of his book. I let out a sigh, twirling my glass of amber liquid in my hand.

"You don't understand the magnetic allure of someone so alluringly dangerous," I confess, mesmerized by the idea of surrendering oneself to a lethal beauty like Irena. Yesterday, Irena was unlike any version of herself I had ever encountered before.

For months, she had presented a bittersweet demeanour…someone who exuded kindness and creativity. She played the piano, baked delectable treats, and adored white roses.

I found myself hopelessly drawn to her. But yesterday, a different Irena emerged. A side of her that had been lurking in the shadows. It was as if she had shed her skin, revealing a dark, twisted side. Sensing my conflicting thoughts, Abel discreetly interrupts my reverie with a throat clearing.

"Have you got any leads on our traitor?" he asks, and I let out a deflating sigh.

"No, they slip through my fingers when I'm close to collaring them, leaving me back at square one. It's as if they're a step ahead of me at every turn- leading me to believe that I'm dealing with a mastermind who knows all my tricks. I've got my money on Zoltan, that cunning devil who knows how to erase people from existence, but then there's Prince, who seems to know more than his fair share. It's a coin-flip situation," I confess while scratching my scruffy chin. Abel interjects with wisdom, "You must keep your cards close to your chest and remain tactical. We don't want to give away our hand too soon. This is a game of chess, and we won't make a move until we're one hundred alluring and complex beings.

"You just don't get it." I randomly blurt out to Abel, he chuckles gently in response. A being that secretly desired to dance with the devil and thirsted for revenge against those who had shattered her world. A being that craved the euphoria of pain and found pleasure in the scent of blood.

It was a juxtaposition of two beautiful yet divergent personalities that I found magnetizing. There were two sides of her that I could not help but be drawn to. "Saint, every time I lay my eyes on my wife, I discover another layer of my love for her. It's like an infinite odyssey," he gushes, radiating affection. "So I'm the last person who wouldn't understand." However, I refuse to entertain the idea that I am experiencing romance. "Abel, you're barking up the wrong tree. I am definitely not falling for anyone," I interject decisively, discouraging any notion of amorous involvement. His expression, that "look," tells me he isn't convinced.

Without hesitation, I repeat myself. "I'm telling you, I'm not." He raises his eyebrows and drops a knowing comment, "I hear ya, man." As he retreats into silence, I release a heavy breath and knead my forehead, grappling with my emotions. It's no secret that Irena is the most stunning woman I have ever laid eyes on, and I would go above and beyond to please her. But the question remains: do I love her the way Abel loves his wife? The answer is no. It is way more complex than that.

"Ah, but what of the binding agreement?" He probes suddenly, his voice taunting and rough. My eyes flick up to meet him, my jaw stiffening in response.

"I just have fulfilled my end of the bargain and if Irena found out, which she won't. It wouldn't matter," I reply, trying to keep my tone steady. Such is the life of a contract killer, I remind myself.

Abel leans forward, his piercing gaze drilling into mine. "You've got to see the big picture here, sweetheart," he advises, I recline slightly in my chair, swirling the whiskey around in its glass. Maybe he's right. Maybe I should focus on my end of the bargain and let that be the end of it. For now, though, my mind is consumed with finding out who's been playing me for a dumbass. And once I do, they'll wish they'd never crossed me.

For weeks now, Saint has been clinging to me like a tenacious vine, and I can't say I'm complaining. After standing up to the three of them, I felt like a new version of myself had been unleashed.

Irena 2.0, if you will.

Suddenly, I was brimming with newfound confidence and unexplored potential. And it's all thanks to Saint.

He's shown me a side of myself that I never even knew was there, and I'm grateful for it. Later that day, I proudly set down a sumptuous bowl of fresh salad that I had slaved over since the morning. After dusting off my hands and neatly tucking away my apron, I surveyed the room with a sense of satisfaction. We had just moved out of Nirali and Abel's home and into our very own safe house, and it was a milestone I couldn't help but revel in.

The sound of jingling keys catches my attention and I eagerly turn my head towards the door. As though sensing my excitement, Saint arrives just in time for dinner. I scurry to greet him, a wide smile stretching across my face as he steps inside. After casually shedding his jacket and loosening his tie, the sleeves of his shirt are rolled up, giving him a relaxed yet refined look. I can't help but admire him as he hangs his jacket on the coat stand and turns to me with a soft, knowing smile.

My brows furrow as I approach him, planting several light pecks on his lips. I feel his hands wrap around my waist in response, his touch sending a wave of comfort through me. "Rough day?" I whisper against his mouth, and he groans in response, pressing his forehead gently to mine. "You have no idea. I'm so close to catching the one who sent the hit men after me, but they always seem to be one step ahead."

With my hand gently caressing his stubble, I reassure him, "But you're Saint Dé Leon…there's nothing you can't handle." My heartfelt words put a genuine smile on his face as he chuckles, his dimple is now visible.

"It smells delicious," he comments, sniffing the air appreciatively. "Well, I prepared a feast. You know a small celebration of our relationship and how far we've come. Baby steps." I tell him.

"Yeah...?" He trailed off planting a single kiss on my lips. "Yeah," I whisper. He leans in to kiss me and I'm consumed by his fiery passion. His teeth graze across my lip and I gasp, feeling a heat swelling deep within me.

"Saint, the food will get cold," I manage to whimper as he continues to tease me with his mouth. "Tell me what you made." He demands.

Continuing to tease me with his mouth. Flushing with excitement, I clear my throat and begin to recite the delectable menu. "Chicken confit." My voice is low and sultry, tempting him with every word. "Mhm, what else?" Taking me by the waist, he leads me into the dining room, his arms still wrapped around my supple form. "And freshly baked bread," I purr, my lips dangerously close to his ear. "What else?" His lips trail down my neck, igniting my every desire. My nipples harden at the sensation, their tips straining against the soft cotton material of my dress. A soft sigh escapes me, as I struggle to keep my composure. "Mmm, s-salad."

"What else?" God, this man will be the death of me. His fingers slide down, shimmying under the fabric of my lace dress as he cups my ass. And as I gasp at his boldness, I am greeted with the bulge of his desire pressing insistently against my stomach.

I throw my head back, unlocking a sensual moan, as his tongue flicks out, teasing and tasting before sinking his teeth into my neck. A surefire way to leave behind a delicious bruise.

"Um... I made cheesecake for dessert." My voice comes out in a breathy whisper as I tug at Saint's locks. "Why don't we start there? I'm craving something sweet and warm." He growls into my ear before lifting me effortlessly and depositing me onto the sturdy table. With a deafening crash, the plates and salad bowl fall to the floor shattered into a million pieces.

"Saint!" I snap, glaring at him with flushed cheeks and wet panties. "The maids will clean everything in the morning," he replies with unsettling ease. But as he pulls back, his sinful gaze consumes me whole. The heat flooded my cheeks as Saint's voice drifted across my ear, sending a tingle down my spine. "I will claim you tonight, Doe," he breathed, his lips dangerously close to mine.

"I will ruin you in ways you never thought possible."

"Then ruin me." With a devilish grin on his lips, he slowly runs his tongue across his teeth.

"Irena, you've shown me all the dark and beautiful parts of you, including your thorns. But now it's my turn to show you that I'm not afraid to bleed when I touch them," he says, as he draws the blunt side of a knife across the base of my neck. His breath is hot against my ear as the adrenaline floods my system with the corrupted void of Saint's chaotic nature.

"Whenever you feel uncomfortable, just say stop," he declares. "Do you understand?" My nerves sing with frenzied energy as I nod, trying to quell the trembling of my hands. In the depths of Saint's eyes, I can see a devilish gleam that sends a shiver down my spine. "Undress," he orders, his voice rough and dark as the night. With a racing heart, I follow his command and strip off my dress, bra, and panties, leaving nothing but my heels. His gaze rakes over my naked form, and I feel exposed under his piercing stare. As he licks his lips, I catch sight of the knife in his hand and feel a sudden spike of desire. I should be repulsed by his crude demands, but instead, I feel my body thrummed with arousal. "You're going to fuck yourself and I'm going to watch then I'm going to mark you and after I'm going to fuck you senselessly," he says, his words full of raw aggression. It's vulgar, possessive, and disturbing, and yet, I can't help the heat building between my thighs. With a flick of his thumb against the blade, my desire is almost too much to bear.

As I teasingly run my hand over my belly, Saint steps back to fully appreciate the sight. My fingers descend over my wet folds and I can't help but pinch my clit, my hips involuntarily moving as I maintain eye contact with Saint. All the fragments of my life are jagged and haunting, and my darkness seems endless. It was this darkness that attracted Saint to me, as he delved into my soul like a serpent.

I was lost, shattered, and in constant agony until the devil himself discovered me. His evil allure called to me, and I responded, craving the thrill and bloodlust that made me feel alive. His fire ignited something within me, leading me to submit to his madness, and I'm slowly giving in. Saint creeps into my life like a shadowy figure, blending seamlessly into the dark abyss of night.

Under the cloak of anonymity, he brings with him a sense of danger that only adds to the thrill. Without hesitation, he takes hold of a sharp knife and slices his palm with delicate ease, blood gushing freely onto the hilt. My senses reel as I watch him, the edges of my mind blurring as I take in the raw power of his actions. "Saint, you're bleeding," I caution, my heart galloping in my chest. But he pays me no heed, lost in the all-encompassing rush of indulgence. "Touch yourself, Irena," he urges, his voice almost desperate. The chill of his words rocks through me, electrifying every inch of my being. As my body curves and stretches, my fingers navigate the wetness between my thighs, craving attention.

Our gaze remains fixed on each other, a mutual fire igniting a wild desire within us. His long thick erect length taunts me, and my body can barely contain its longing, whimpering uncontrollably. Suppressing the urge to scream out in pleasure, I sink my teeth into my lip and watch Saint stroke himself before me. As I cling to the wooden table, I spread myself wider, intensifying both the pleasure and pain. My fingers penetrate deeper within me, circling my aching clit, my heart racing in anticipation of the ultimate climax. Undeterred, Saint moves closer, his eyes lit with primal lust, ravenous for me. My fingers don't stop pleasuring me with fervent hunger, while he watches over me, biting his lip and groaning with each passing moment.

Our gaze continues to bind us as we both feel this feverish craving building up uncontrollably. He warms my skin as his fingers wrap around my neck, tracing down my collarbone to leave a mark with his blood. I bite his lip fiercely, causing a growl to escape from his throat, while he pinches my breast with cruelty and leaves a red mark on my skin. My mouth fills with the taste of his blood as our pleasure merges and my body shakes with an orgasmic release, but I do not bite hard enough to break his skin.

"Tonight, I devote myself to you, no matter the shift of the knife. Through blood and bone. I am yours, Irena," As he murmurs, the icy metal pricks my skin. The knife's edge glides between my breasts and enters my chest, causing a thin trail of blood to appear. The mix of agony and ecstasy produces an unearthly and powerful sensation. I bend my back and indulge in the experience. The blood on my flesh now shines, and the flickering firelight creates a playful sensuality that urges me to succumb to his impulses. His eyes become darker in colour as he feels a tumultuous emotion. His lovely grin envelops his face, rendering me defenceless against his enchanting enchantment. Suppressing a shiver I said.

"Stop looking at me like that."

"Like what?" He tilted his head and spoke softly in a teasing tone, questioning on one side.

"Like I'm dinner."

"Maybe I'm hungry." he pauses, "Now relax baby, and let me have my dessert." He gently lays me down on the table and kneels before me.

His clean fingers caress my warm folds, while our lips collide fiercely. I can't resist his touch, and he draws me closer, raising one of my legs over his shoulder.

Every time he touches my clit, I convulse towards him and utter throaty groans that reverberate through the night. As he bites my flesh, I surrender to the irresistible combination of pleasure and pain - like a star chasing a joyful dream. At this moment, I am wholly lost. His passionate kiss takes me higher, feeling like a heartless demon devouring my being. Strangely, I feel protected and secure in his arms.

My eyes widen in surprise as he removes his finger with a pop, sucking on them like a man possessed. My heart races as he teases my entrance with the butt of his knife. This is reckless, crazy, and utterly thrilling. I can't wait to see what he does next. My flesh sways to the irresistible ebb and flow of the sensual tide, while my innermost desires blossom in the dark recesses of my soul. I relish in Saint's ability to use my body as his own personal temple, pledging his worship on its hallowed grounds. The rubber rear bolster of the knife circles my entrance, its thick butt gliding against my skin. I quiver with anticipation, eager to indulge in his hedonistic desires. "You have no idea how much it thrills me to see my wife so damn wet," he murmurs, flashing me his feral gaze. As he thrusts the handle of the knife inside me, my words disintegrate into startled breaths.

A cruel grin illuminates his sharp features. "Go on, Doe, take it like the good wife you are." Mesmerized by his prowess, I watch him invade my being, every inch of my being pulsating with rapturous pleasure. Amidst the awakening of my secret desires, I come to a realization: this is happening, and I'm allowing it to happen. With a steady hand, Saint smoothly works the handle inside of me like his own cock, causing a blend of ecstasy and agony to ripple through my body.

An unexpected pause, and he tenderly kisses my inner thighs in apology, before ramming the entirety of it inside of me. Instantly, my back arches, my head involuntarily tilts back and a devilish moan escapes my lips. As the butt of the knife retreats, I gather my breath, but just as quickly the rear rubber slides in and out, to which I let out a guttural sound of satisfaction. My breath quickens, my head flings back and I can't help but think, "This is so wrong, but it feels oh so right."

"Who do I belong to?" He breathes, intensifying the rhythm with the handle of his blade as he devours my clit, his tongue swirling and teasing it like it's his favourite candy. Pleasure courses through me, making my core clench with satisfaction. "M-me," I managed to utter. "Oh, yes..." I moan, biting my lip but failing to contain the next wave of ecstasy. His knife thrusts drive me over the edge and I whimper with delight. But as I bask in the afterglow, a small voice echoes at the back of my mind, questioning my own pleasure. How can I relish this without feeling sick? Yet, I am craving more; every word, every touch makes me burn with desire.

The way he angles the knife's butt sends a shockwave through me, making my eyes roll back and a primal moan escapes my lips. A wave of ecstasy engulfs me, kissing the depths of my soul and unlocking my fleshly desires. I clench my fists as my legs shake involuntarily, surrendering to the heavenly sensation he brings. His skilled tongue flicks up and down, stroking me with the weapon until I'm left breathless and unable to think. I gasp when his teeth clamp down on my inner thigh, tears of pleasure stinging my eyes.

Saint pulls out the handle, savouring the creamy liquid that drips off the knife's edge. His primal growl fills the air as he stands, taking me in a fierce grip as he grips my thighs. His urgency is palpable as he lowers his pants, needing to be connected in the most primal way. The pink head of his penis glides smoothly against my wet entrance, causing my muscles to tense with excitement. He lifts me effortlessly, and my legs wrap around his hips as he pressed me against the glass window, which overlooks a backyard hidden by forest.

In the moonlight, our skin glows, and I feel a quick connection with him before he enters me with a sharp breath. I dig my nails into his flesh and whimper as he kisses my neck, his blood-stained hands tangled in my hair.

"Saint, I don't know if I can handle this," I gasp, overwhelmed by his size.

"Shhh...just a little bit more," he reassures me with a whispered shush. I am consumed by him as he plunges deep within me with one powerful move. An indescribable sensation overpowers me and I let out an unmistakable cry that echoes through the room. The feeling of being filled completely cannot be contained and my body shudders uncontrollably. Pain and pleasure collide, driving me into a frenzy of desire.

"Fuckk...you wrap around me so perfectly," he whimpers as he thrusts deep, unforgiving, and relentless. I try to accommodate him entirely, but he is too much for me to handle. His strength and skill overwhelm me completely as if I am but clay in the hands of an expert sculptor. The sound of his heavy breathing fills my ears as he continues his furious onslaught, his movement a symphony of muscular perfection.

With every motion, I am plunged deeper into a vortex of ecstasy, my senses overcome by bliss. He holds me close, dominating me with his unbridled passion, his rhythm increasing with every moment that passes. Finally, I surrender to him completely, falling headlong into a bottomless abyss of pleasure. He wants me as he fucks brutally, passionately, giving me what I pleaded for—fucking me right out of my mind.

Ruining me. I am a blaze of unbridled desire, searing with intense pleasure and insatiable lust. My body collides with the glass, each thrust deeper and harder than the last. Our limbs entwined like vines, I clutch his shoulders, my nails sinking into his flesh. The pain ignites a primal energy within him, driving him wild. He moans my name, biting my neck in ecstasy as I cry out.

My mind becomes a frenzied storm, an intoxicating mix of violence and eroticism. I let out a shuddering moan, my breath hot against his ear, his teeth grazing my tender breast. I am addicted to his touch, the way he mercilessly pounds into me, filling me completely with his thick, pulsing cock. Every nerve ending in my body bursts with pleasure, tears streaming down my face from the sheer intensity of it all. The pain, the pleasure, the sin of it all. I am drunk on the sensations that I crave with such reckless abandon.

Enraptured by his desires, he had an insatiable craving for me. I was consumed by him, taken by the passion that had eluded me until now. My body surrendered to his every whim, relinquishing control as he possessed me completely. His touch claimed not just my flesh, but my very soul - he had made me his own. The surrender was sweet, yet dangerous; it was the ultimate sacrifice of desire. I ran my hand through his hair, relishing the sensation as every thrust took me closer to the edge.

As he quickened his pace, my mind was blown beyond reason. "I want to see you come apart for me," he whimpers softly. His hips moved fiercely, taking me closer to the brink. "Saint." I moaned his name, the sound desperate and raw. As the searing heat crested through my body, I cried out in ecstasy, and Saint was there to answer. A symphony of gasps and grunts surrounds us as Saint claims me like a savage. His primal hunger and raw passion leave me breathless - a lost cause in his powerful embrace. My senses reel as his thrusts pick up speed, pushing me to the brink of ecstasy.

I cling to him, surrendering to the erotic chaos he brings. Saint's hard length pulses inside me, tearing down my defences and filling me with primal lust. His feral whimpers reverberate through my body as we reach the peak together, my screams mingling with his. My skin is on fire as Saint bites my breast, sending a jolt of pain and pleasure through my body. My heart beat drums out of control as I tremble, bursting with sensations I have never known before. Saint's possessive hold on me never wavers as the aftershocks of our passion shake his body. I'm left dazed, trying to catch my breath, and when he finally kisses me, I'm reduced to a quivering mess.

"Saint, stop," I beg between gasps, but he just chuckles, lost in his own carnal world. "P-please stop it's too much." Picking me up with ease, Saint's kiss on my forehead is gentle and tender, a stark contrast to the fierce eroticism of just moments before. With a gradual deceleration of his movements, he moans into the hollow of my neck before sliding out of me.

"You might need some assistance walking for a while Doe but I am more than willing to bear the burden." I playfully swat his shoulder as a retort. "You're such a pain in the ass." no Saint gives me a quick peck on the cheek. "I know."

"And all the food I made went to waste," I point out, glancing at the messy table. He meets my eyes and smiles apologetically. "I'll make it up to you." He scoops me up in his strong arms, cradling me as he carries me toward the bedroom. With one hand, he nudges the door open and gently places me on the plush bed.

"I'm going to run a bath for you," he says softly. I nod, watching him head to the bathroom, and soon after, I hear the water running. A moment later, he returns, wraps his arms around my waist, and lifts me again. My legs wrap around him instinctively. "I can walk, you know," I tease.

"Can you?" he smirks, raising an eyebrow. I look away, smiling despite the soreness. "That's what I thought," he says, carrying me into the bathroom, where the scent of lavender fills the air. The lights are dim, and the large tub is filled with warm, soapy water. He helps me in, and I quietly thank him as I sink into the soothing bath.

"Join me," I suggest, looking up at him.

"Are you sure?" he asks, a hint of nervousness in his voice. I giggle.

"Come on, the water's nice." For the first time, I notice a flicker of hesitation in his eyes, which makes my heart flutter. His cheeks flush slightly as he gets in behind me, his long legs on either side of me. I snuggle closer, and he wraps his arms around my stomach. I turn to look at him.

His expression is serious, but when he catches my gaze, it softens. The way he looks at me is different from how he looks at everyone else. "Why do you act like this menacing character when you're nothing like that?" I ask, unable to hold back my curiosity. His fingers gently sweep my hair away from my face, making my heart race.

"Because, Doe, that's who I am," he replies. I shake my head, unconvinced.

"No, you're not. You're broken, and you won't admit it. You collect scars because you want proof you're paying for whatever sins you think you've committed." The room falls silent, and his eyes darken slightly.

"I understand that you want to believe in a romanticized version of me," he says, "but I'm no hero. I am who I am, and I'll never be anyone's saviour."

"Why?" I press, challenging him. A dark grin spreads across his face as he chuckles.

"Because the tragic hero always chooses the world over their lover. But I'm not a hero, Irena. I'm the villain. And the villain always chooses to save their lover at the cost of the world." My heart aches with both sadness and fascination. I reach out, cupping his face gently.

"I want to see all of you, Saint. The good, the bad, and the ugly. Just be real with me." He exhales deeply, closing his eyes as he allows himself a rare moment of vulnerability.

"I'd rather you fix it first," he murmurs.

"Fix what?" I ask, confused. Slowly, he opens his eyes and locks them onto mine with intensity.

"Fix me, please."

CHAPTER 41

SAINT DÉ LEON

I was taught from a young age to be stone-cold and self-reliant, to hold myself high and poised. Sin has stained my bones, fires have scorched them, betrayal has broken them, loneliness has left them cold, and they've been soaked with blood. I wonder if I told Irena about the darkness within me, would she still see me as her dark knight in shining armour, or would she recognize me as the villain in my own story?

In the darkness, I can sense her presence behind me.

Her breath teases my neck, sending shivers down my spine. I'm bound, vulnerable. Beads of sweat gather on my forehead, my nakedness making me feel exposed. In a flash, a sting first grazes my back, then erupts into sharp pain. I can't help but wince as my body recoils.

"You've been a naughty little boy, Saint," she purrs into my ear. Another strike to my back, each one as intense as the last. "You know what happens when saints become sinners?" she taunts, a sinister gleam flickering in her hazel irises. I feel my throat tighten in fear.

"They get punished," I whisper, my voice barely audible. Her lips curl into a dangerous grin. "Badly," she hisses, bringing her whip down on my trembling body once more. The sting in my flesh is overwhelming, and tears begin to blur my vision.

Irena's melodious voice breaks through the silence and pulls me back to reality. I shake off the haunting memories of my childhood and meet her curious gaze with a blink.

"Good morning, Doe," I murmur, planting a kiss on her smooth cheek and pulling her closer. Her chuckles perforate the stillness of the night. "It's the dead of night, Saint," she retorts. I glance at the clock, which shows 4:23 AM, and scoff. "It may be dark, but it is morning," I reply, watching as her eyes roll dramatically. Her groan interrupts the silence as she shifts uncomfortably. "Did you sleep well?" I ask, turning to face her. "Well enough to squeeze in three hours and nurse the excruciating pain between my legs," she sighs. Concern furrows my brow. "Want me to kiss the pain away?" I offer with a lopsided grin. Irena's cheeks flush, and she shakes her head.

"No." Brushing my thumb over her lip, I meet her gaze again. There's something about Irena that I can't resist. Maybe it's the way she exudes danger like she's always on the brink of doing something reckless. Or perhaps it's her angelic innocence, a stark contrast to the dark energy pulsing through her veins. But whatever it is, I know one thing for sure: I want her. No, I need her, desperately.

I don't want anyone else to have her. Her heart, her lips, her arms—that's my place. When she's near me, all my frayed edges start to smooth out. If peace were a person, it would be Irena. "I'm ready," I blurt out. Her smile fades as she cocks her head inquisitively.

"Ready for what?"

"To tell you about my past," I reply. Irena shifts next to me, propping herself up on one elbow. Taking a deep breath, I exhale slowly, steeling myself for what's to come. "I was raised to be a fighter," I begin, my voice barely above a whisper. "To be the one with bloody knuckles and shards of glass.

They wanted people to be afraid of me, and for a long time, I wanted that too." I pinch the bridge of my nose, trying to dispel the memories flooding my mind. But Irena's hand on my arm, firm yet gentle, reminds me that I'm not alone anymore. Somehow, that makes it a little easier.

As I struggle to catch my breath, a metallic taste fills my mouth — I'm bleeding internally. Suddenly, Gabriel's voice booms through the air, jolting me out of my daze. "Get up, Saint!" he shouts, and I flinch at the force of his words. I was just twelve, lying on the ground after a brutal beating from my father. The silence in the gym was palpable, broken only by the whispers of those around me. I strained to push myself up, my arms quivering with effort. The pain was excruciating, but I refused to show weakness. Gabriel's menacing gaze bore down on me, his eyes dark with anger. "You fucking disappoint me," he growled, stalking toward me.

I could feel my heartbeat racing as he advanced, ready to strike again. With a blood-stained forearm, I wiped away the trickle of blood from my nose. Gabriel's eyes glared down at me with pure fury. A sharp sting jolted through my body as his hand made contact with my face, sending me stumbling. Blood spilled from my mouth as I coughed in agony. As I raised myself, Gabriel flexed, his bulky body radiating power. He rolled his neck before announcing,

"Get the hell out of my face. We start again tomorrow." I sprinted out of the gym, all eyes on me. Dashing upstairs, I bumped into Abel. "Are you okay?" His innocent, childish tone floated toward me like a feather on the wind. "I'm fine," I muttered. "Training was rough." "I need to clean up, so go play or whatever," I said, walking away. Climbing the stairs, I noticed the maids' pity and heard laughter from my mother's room. Freezing at the familiar voice, I wanted to run, but Angeline spotted me. "Saint, come here and let me see you!" she slurred, her voice unsteady. I hesitated but entered the room, my heart pounding. Angeline was as drunk as ever, her emerald green eyes gleaming with mischief. "Don't be a stranger, Saint," she purred, taking a swig of wine. I noticed her bruised face and shook my head.

Her sister, Noona, sat nearby, her eyes gleaming with forbidden desire. Angeline excused herself, leaving me alone with Noona. My heart pounded as she pulled me into an embrace. Her touch turned inappropriate, and she whispered, "Your mom won't be back for a while. Behave, or I'll punish you again."

The memories of my childhood molestation terrorized me, leaving deep scars. The hurt flooded me, but I buried it. Irena's voice snapped me back. "When did the anger take over?" I chuckled bitterly. "Oh, around the time I was four. My father had a quick temper, but it was my mother who fanned the flames. Their relationship changed after my baby sister Grace died, just an hour after she was born." "You had a sister?" Irena asked, wide-eyed. I nodded. "Her death broke them.

Gabriel's violence escalated, and my mother drowned herself in alcohol. Things got worse after Abel was born. My mother wanted to abort him, but Gabriel stopped her. She tried to kill him in secret, but Gabriel kept her locked in her room until Abel was born. When Angeline couldn't care for us, Noona moved in." I paused, and Irena's touch on my cheek grounded me.

"You don't have to, Saint," she whispered. "I know, but I want to," I replied. "When Noona moved in, I was seven.

She played the role of a second mother at first. But one night, she came into my room. I was terrified. After that, I cried myself to sleep, hoping it was a nightmare. I tried to tell Angeline, but she hit me and threatened to harm herself and Abel if I spoke. Noona's abuse lasted for a decade." Irena nibbled on her lip, her voice soft. "What happened next?"

"I killed her. Then Gabriel. Abel killed Angeline. I took over," I said quietly. "I've done things I carry with both pride and shame," I admitted. Irena asked, "What are the shameful things?"

"I found myself doing to others what Noona did to me. It disgusted me, but it also thrilled me. That's the shame I carry." Before I could continue, Irena kissed me — soft, tender, and full of understanding. It wasn't pity; it was a promise that she'd fight my demons with me. She pulled away, pressing her forehead against mine. "I was worried you had no humanity left," she whispered. "I am the villain I claim to be," I said. "But I've accepted the darkness. I'm not alone anymore. I have you."

"You, Irena Dé Leon, are the first to see my demons and still smile. My heart is yours, to do with as you please. Break it, tame it, bleed it out. I'm yours for every second I have. Even after I'm gone, I'll belong to you." Tears shimmered in her eyes. "You're mine, Saint. I'm not going anywhere," she said, her voice steady.

"Till death do us part," she added quietly. In a rush, I seized her lips, pouring all my passion into the kiss. She's my lifeline, my tether to the world. She knows all my secrets now, except one…

She's my lifeline; my tether to the world. She finally knows all my secrets, except one; *that I am madly in love with her.*

CHAPTER 42

IRENA NOWAK

After my shower today, I noticed bruises all over my body—my inner thighs, breasts, stomach, ass, and legs. Saint wasn't kidding when he said he would mark me; he practically branded me.

Bite marks everywhere, like I was his canvas. I didn't mind, but what bothered me was how long it would take for them to fade, and the effort it would take to cover them up. "When did you learn to play the piano?" I asked, twirling as Saint's soft whistle accompanied his melody.

The soreness in my body lingered, but I could manage it, especially since Saint usually carried me around the house. I might complain, but secretly, I loved the attention. "I took lessons when I was 10," he explained.

"Not sure what drew me to it, but it comforted me in a strange way." My heart ached when I thought about everything he went through as a boy. Saint deserved the world, even if he didn't think so. He wasn't evil or ruthless for the fun of it—he was a broken soul who found comfort in his darkness, made his own hell a home. "So, you're passionate about the piano," I pointed out.

"Yes, along with slow dancing and sports cars," he added, still playing the piano. It was snowing outside, so Saint decided we'd stay in for the weekend. His back faced me as he sat there, his hair messy and fluffy, dressed in a simple white t-shirt and grey joggers. He was lost in the music, and I found myself grinning like a fool, watching my husband play my favourite instrument. If someone had told me three months ago that I'd find peace through Saint, I would have laughed in their face. Now, I hadn't touched a drink in a month, and I was the happiest I'd been in a long time, all because of him.

"Saint," I called softly. He stopped playing and turned to face me. "Thank you," I said. He tilted his head, searching my eyes before smiling. "Come here." I walked over to him, and he pulled me onto his lap, pressing a kiss to my forehead. "You're welcome, Irena."

"I really mean it," I squealed. "I haven't had a drink in a whole month, and I'm so happy." His eyes brightened, and he mumbled, "I'm proud of you," before running his fingers through my hair, kissing me all over my face. I giggled like a child until he pulled back and frowned. "There's still blood in your hair," he pointed out, showing me a strand that was stained. I sighed. "I thought I washed it all out this morning."

Saint inspected my hair. "I could wash it for you. Maybe braid it too?" My eyes widened in shock.

"You're kidding, right?" I laughed, but he shook his head. "What can't I do?" he teased. "No, it's just—you, Saint Dé Leon, want to wash and braid my hair?" I asked in disbelief.

"I see no problem with that," he shrugged. In one swift move, Saint picked me up, and I giggled as he carried me to our bedroom. He slapped my ass playfully, and I squealed. Once we reached the bathroom, he ran the water and grabbed a chair, along with the hair products. I smiled, amused as he made me sit. Tilting my head back, he rinsed my hair with warm water, then applied conditioner that smelled like coconut, massaging my scalp.

"Feels good?" he asked.

"Mhm," I hummed, shivering as his low chuckle sent a wave of warmth through me. Butterflies fluttered in my stomach. These simple moments with him meant everything. He would burn the world for me, but what I cherished most were moments like this—playing piano together, or him washing my hair. I used to want to disappear, not realizing all I ever wanted was to be found. Saint found me. After he finished rinsing my hair, he wrapped it in a towel and led me back to the room. I changed into a green jumper since my shirt got wet.

When my hair was dry, Saint sat me down. "Are you sure you know what you're doing?" I asked, doubting him. "Yes," he said confidently. "Now let me work my magic." I sat quietly, feeling silly as he braided my hair. It felt like we were best friends at a sleepover.

"You make me feel like I'm at a salon," I joked. "I love that little laugh of yours," he said. "It's cute—and it'll probably get you fucked at some point," he added casually.

Clearing my throat, I felt a familiar ache between my legs, imagining him following through with his words. After some flirting and jokes, he finally finished braiding my hair. Excited, I rushed to the bathroom to look at myself. My jaw dropped. Where the hell did Saint learn to braid like this? My hair looked gorgeous. Turning to him, I jumped into his arms, crashing my lips to his.

"You did amazing! Where did you learn this?"

"I always wanted a daughter, so I watched videos when I was younger," he said simply, making me smile. He might have a reputation as a monster, but I was starting to think he was more like a fallen angel.

The guards opened the double oak doors, leading us into Abel's foyer. As we turned left into the glass room library, we stopped dead in our tracks. Abel was standing between Nirali's legs as they made out passionately. "Abel," Saint scolded. Abel lazily raised a finger, signalling for Saint to wait. Saint folded his arms, waiting impatiently while I chuckled quietly. Eventually, Abel and Nirali pulled away, and Abel whispered something to her that made her giggle before they turned to us.

"You want a taste too?" Abel mocked. "Each time you open your mouth, more shit comes out," Saint retorted, rolling his eyes. Nirali approached me with a smile. "Let's go before more of them show up." Saint turned to me. "If you need anything, I'll be in the office," he said before I followed Nirali. As we walked toward the bar, Nirali suddenly stopped and eyed me suspiciously. "What?" I asked. "Why are you walking like that?" she questioned. "Like what?" I replied dumbly. She raised an eyebrow. "Holy shit, did you — you had sex with Saint!" she squealed, excitement gleaming in her eyes. I shushed her, dragging her to the bar. Nirali grinned.

"You've got that after-sex glow, and you're wobbling," she teased. I laughed, shaking my head.

"Okay, we did, but—"

"That explains the turtleneck and coat you're wearing," she smirked.

"So, how big is he?" My face flushed. "Too many inappropriate questions, Nirali," I giggled.

"We're both adults here!" she brushed me off with a wave. I sighed, rolling my eyes playfully.

"Yes, Saint is good, and yes, he's big, but I'm not discussing his size with you. You're married!" I pointed out, making her blush.

"On a serious note, though," her tone shifted. "He's not forcing you into anything, right?"

"Why would you ask that?" I frowned. "He's trouble, Irena," she said. "I just want to make sure you're safe." I smiled softly.

"I get it, and I appreciate you looking out for me, but Saint is different with me. We click in a way that makes sense. At first, all I wanted to do was run, but he showed me there's no need. He taught me to stand my ground and battle my demons. We fit together in ways no one else can see." Nirali sighed.

"It'll probably get worse," she muttered.

"I knew that the day I said my vows," I smiled.

SAINT DÉ LEON

"Holy shit did you. Ah! You had sex with Saint!" I hear Nirali's voice squeal with excitement outside of the library.

Prince stares at me as he fixes himself a glass of whiskey. "Not a single word," I demand, and he cocks a brow. "I didn't say shit." He spat.

"You didn't have to. I could smell your comment from a mile away." I declare, and he smirks, ignoring me, then continues to pour the whiskey into the glass. Zoltan plops himself on the couch running his hand hair through then asserts.

"Explains the way she's walking." I glare at him and he chuckles. Abel plops himself beside Zoltan and slaps him on the back of his head. "Joke all you want about it, we all know that you can't please your girl to that extent," Abel comments, and I almost smile as Prince lets out a light chuckle as leans against the wall and sips on his drink. "Please, I can take one good look at any woman, and they'd be creaming their pants." Zoltan grins proudly. We all remained quiet and stared at Zoltan blankly. I swear the shit that comes out of his mouth is twice the bullshit that comes out of Abel's mouth. Although I suspect them and would gladly confront them now with a gun pressed against their temple. I had to pretend as if everything was alright. Prince clears his throat.

"Anyway back to Saint. I never thought you would have a woman wrapped around your finger." He states. I fold my arms and shake my head.

"She's got me wrapped around her finger." I corrected him, and Zoltan choked on his drink. "The day has come when Saint has finally fallen in love." He states sarcastically. I stare at him seriously. "I am in love with her." The room silenced. All eyes are on me.

"Shit, Saint." Abel blurts out. "I fucking knew it." he brags, and I roll my eyes. He takes pride whenever he is right, which is fucking irritating.

I take a seat across from him and run my hand through my hair.

"Funny how dangerous it is to finally have something worth losing," I utter.

"When did you realize that you're in love with her?" Prince questions, popping out a cigarette and lighting it, then puffing.

I lean back, my arms spread on the head of the couch.

"When I took her to kill those three shitheads," I told him. Prince chuckles, appearing beside me. "It hasn't even been 6 months. Do you know any shit about her?" I turn to look at him, irritation boiling in my veins.

"I know enough. She's fucking impetuous. Glowing with madness, she's chaos and honey all things messy, sweet, and fucking lovely.

I love her Prince, all of her but the dark side of her Jesus Christ.

Any girl can play innocent, but her demons are what drove me wild; her secrets, her pain, her darkness, that's what made me fall madly in love with my wife." She tastes like every dark thought I've had. Like the moon, Irena had a side of her that was so dark that even the stars couldn't shine on it, but a light brighter than the sun that I'd be happy to burn an eternity under her blinding beauty. And if her poison apples don't kill me, her beauteous soul and insanity will.

CHAPTER 43

SAINT DÉ LEON

Aimer et être aimé.

To love and be loved. Have you ever experienced the captivating allure of a blooming rose?

Its petals unfurl in a mesmerizing dance that leaves you drunk with its sweet fragrance.

The dew-laden leaves, trembling with the excitement of a new romance, seduce your senses. Have you ever longed for a rose, even while it wounded you with its prickly thorns?

Irena was that once-in-a-lifetime flower coveted by reckless hands that never intended to cherish her. Now, she's a dead rose in my grasp.

But even in her fading state, I find a unique beauty transcending mere petals. Her wilted petals remind me that, even in death, love and beauty live on. Enraptured, I observe as she dives headfirst into baking. The intoxicating aroma of chocolate and vanilla fills the air, causing my mouth to water with longing.

Her tresses are neatly tucked up into a bun while she dons a cosy forest-green sweater and a pristine white apron.

Suddenly, Irena strides over to me and extends a spoon brimming with chocolate mix.

"Open up," she commands, and I oblige, allowing her to spoon feed me.

With a quick swipe of my tongue, the perfect balance of sweetness and texture is revealed to me. Irena's eyes light up with anticipation as she eagerly awaits my critique. "It's delicious," I respond, eliciting a broad grin from her beaming face. "Alright, I'll just pop these babies in the oven and let them do their thing," she announces. Swiftly spinning around, she retrieves the tray from the counter and slips it into the scorching oven, before firmly closing the door. After dusting off her hands, Irena removes her apron and sets it aside before approaching me. "You'd be an amazing mother, Irena," I blurt out, and Irena nearly loses her balance. I swiftly grasp her wrists and draw her onto my lap with ease. "Where did that come from?" she giggles, her eyes gleaming with delight. "Don't you believe you'd make an excellent mother to our children?" I ask. She laughs again, ignoring my probing stare while twirling strands of my hair between her fingertips.

"No, it's just that I never expected we'd be contemplating starting a family. It was the farthest thought from my mind." I shrug, enveloping her in a warm embrace. "Are ready to have children?" I inquire, and she finally holds my gaze. "Are you?" A soft snicker escaped from my lips as I revealed my deepest desire.

"I've always dreamed of having a little girl…someone I can shield from the world's harshness, tuck into bed at night, and spend mornings creating playful hairdos with. I want to engage in all the quintessential father-daughter activities," I explained with a wistful gaze. Irena let out a heavy sigh and tenderly cupped my cheek. "When the time is right, Saint, I promise to give you the gift of fatherhood. But for now, I want to indulge in the freedom I never had growing up - enjoy every moment life has to offer."

I was determined to make her every wish come true. "Alright, tell me. What is it you want to do? Whatever it may be, I'll make it happen right now."

"I understand that you have the ability to do it," Irena nods, chewing on her bottom lip. "However, I want to savour every moment and not rush into anything. We have all the time in the world." She explains how she desires to visit her family in Tanzania and immerse herself in her mother's culture. She looks forward to exploring the neighbourhood, listening to her parents' stories, having bonfires on the beach, dancing to Moroccan music, and indulging in fresh fruits and fish. With a glimmer of hope in her eyes, she muses about how she longs to feel entirely liberated. "Am I in the picture?"

"Of course you are."

"But right now-" As she begins to articulate her thoughts, I silence her words with the tender press of my lips against hers. My mind is consumed by the intensity of the moment as her fingers entwine in my hair, eliciting a guttural moan. I reluctantly break away, knowing that succumbing to my desire would only complicate matters.

"Doe, there's no need to expound. Take all the time you need, and I will be here eagerly awaiting the moment your dream becomes our reality." Because for Irena I'd do anything, anything to make her happy.

I drove through the gates of Abel's mansion with a mix of apprehension and determination. As I pulled up beside his fleet of luxury cars, I wondered what awaited me inside.

I knew my unannounced visit would catch him off-guard, but the latest developments with the notorious drug lord in the western hemisphere couldn't wait any longer. Exiting my sleek Mercedes, I braced against the biting chill of the season. Dressed in tailored trousers and a crisp white tee under a trench coat, I ignored the cold as the guards at the entrance gave me a brief nod before opening the imposing doors. The moment I stepped inside, a stillness engulfed me. The mansion, bathed in shades of sombre grey, felt frozen in time.

"Abel?" I called into the emptiness, my voice echoing. Silence. My footsteps felt heavy as I ventured deeper into the house. "Abel?" Again, no answer. Unease crept in, but I kept moving. I swept through the library, the bar, even Nirali's painting room—nothing. Finally, I reached Abel's bedroom. Hesitating for a moment, I knocked lightly and, without waiting, pushed the door open. Inside, Nirali sat on the bed, her face streaked with the telltale signs of recent tears.

"Oh, hey," she mumbled, hastily wiping her face. "I didn't hear you."

"Where's Abel?" I asked, scanning the room. "He's out," she replied quietly, avoiding eye contact. Something was off. I could feel it.

"Why are you crying?" I finally asked, my brow furrowing. Nirali hesitated but eventually reassured me that Abel hadn't done anything wrong. Despite our frequent clashes, over time Nirali and I had developed a sibling-like bond, though I'd never admit it. Sensing her hesitation, I urged her to open up.

"You can trust me," I said softly. She fidgeted for a moment before standing up, frowning deeply. "I need a drink for this," she muttered, walking toward the bar. She poured herself a glass of wine and offered me one, but I declined. She shrugged, filling her glass halfway. As she sipped, her eyes betrayed the storm of emotions brewing inside her.

"I don't know if Abel told you, but we've been trying to have a baby," she began, her voice wavering. The confession hung heavy in the air as she continued, her words turning into sobs.

"It's been eight months, and I—I went to the doctor. Saint... I can't get pregnant." The words came out broken, a choked laugh accompanying the tears as she added, "I'm infertile." Her voice cracked, and I felt the weight of her pain.

"Irena doesn't know," she quickly added. "She's dealing with enough already. Please don't tell her."

"I won't," I assured her. Nirali sighed, her gaze dropping to the floor.

"I feel like I've let everyone down. Abel, my parents, myself." I paused, choosing my words carefully. "It's natural to feel that way, but infertility isn't a failure. It's a challenge, and one you can face together." Her pained eyes met mine. "But it's not just about that. It's the emotional toll, the feeling of emptiness."

"I get it," I nodded. "But you're not alone, and this doesn't define you. Abel loves you, and that won't change." Tears welled up again. "Why me? Why do I have to go through this?" she whispered.

I gently took the glass from her hand and drew her into my chest. "Life's unfair sometimes, but you're strong. You'll get through this. You have Abel by your side."

"All I ever wanted was to be a mother," she murmured into my chest, her sobs quieter now. Meeting Irena had unlocked a new side of me, and I found myself more empathetic, wanting to offer comfort where before I might have brushed things off. Seeing Nirali, my sister-in-law, so broken stirred something protective in me.

"You're strong, Nirali. Don't let this defeat you. You've come so far. But you need to talk to Abel. He deserves to know." She looked up at me, her eyes brimming with tears. "I know," she sighed, her gaze dropping to my now damp shirt. "Sorry about—" I waved it off.

"Don't worry about it."

"Thank you," she whispered, offering a small, grateful smile.

"If you need anything, I'm always a call away," I reminded her, hoping it brought her some comfort. She nodded, her smile growing a little more genuine. "Okay." She wiped her face, her usual mischievous glint slowly returning.

"Let's keep this between us," she quipped, a playful light in her eyes. I smirked.

"God forbid the world finds out we can actually stand each other." We shared a small laugh, the tension easing.

"Thanks for being here," she said softly, her voice laced with gratitude.

I nodded. "You're stronger than you think, Nirali. You'll get through this." She sighed again, a small glimmer of hope flickering behind her eyes.

"I hope so," she whispered, but for the first time, I believed she might actually start believing it herself.

CHAPTER 44

IRENA NOWAK

With his black platinum card in hand, Saint urged me to indulge in whatever my heart desired. "Go ahead, buy an entire jewellery store if you want, Doe," he declared. His words were overwhelming, but I appreciated the gesture. Saint was going to be busy for a while, and this was his way of apologizing, which I found utterly endearing.

I invited Nirali to join me for some shopping since I knew it was her favourite activity, but she declined, saying she wasn't feeling well.

Lately, she's been avoiding me, and though I wanted to visit her, she asked for space. I respected her wishes and waited for her to feel comfortable talking to me. Accompanied by my 13 bodyguards, I strolled through the mall, browsing cute and sexy outfits. Feeling thirsty after walking for a while, I stopped at a smoothie stand and ordered a strawberry coconut smoothie. After a few minutes, the lady handed me my drink, and I thanked her before taking a sip, enjoying the refreshing taste. I hadn't realized how much time had passed until I glanced at my phone—three hours had flown by. Out of the corner of my eye, I noticed the guards keeping a safe distance, dressed in regular clothes to blend in.

Despite their intimidating demeanour, guilt washed over me as I realized they'd been carrying all my bags. One more stop, and they could finally head home.

While heading to the next store, a notification appeared on my phone, and my face lit up when I saw the sender's name.

Opening the text, a broad smile spread across my face as excitement bubbled within me.

A flutter of butterflies stirred in my belly.

His sweet treatment always sent me spiralling with delight.

Saint: You having fun with our money?

Me: You did say I should spoil myself... and maybe buy a whole jewellery store?

Saint: I'm teasing, Doe. You okay, though?

Me: Yeah, just picking up perfumes and handbags. How's everything at work?

Saint: A lot of shit going down, but all I can think about is being in your arms when I get back.

Me: :(

Saint: I'll give you whatever you want tonight.

Me: Oh really? What exactly are you offering?

Saint: Not sure, but make sure you ' re naked too.
I ' d prefer that.

I giggled as his reply came instantly. Saint: What's that surprise?

Me: You wouldn ' t want me to ruin it, would you?

With a grin, I made my way to the perfume counter, picking a scent that exuded luxury and elegance. Next, I grabbed three designer bags, relishing in Saint's command to indulge.

Suddenly, my phone rang, and I glanced at the caller ID: Saint. Smiling, I silenced the call, slipping my phone into my purse before heading to the checkout counter.

After a quick swipe of my card, I secured my purchases and headed for the exit. Just as I was leaving, one of the guards appeared by my side, offering to carry my bags. His Scottish-accented voice was rugged yet polite.

"Let me help you with that, Mrs. Dé Leon." My heart fluttered, and I couldn't resist smiling as I handed him the bags. "Thank you," I said, and he nodded, stepping back respectfully. As we reached the parking lot, the guards formed a protective shield around me. A black SUV pulled up, and one of them opened the back door. I slipped inside, greeted the driver, and soon we were on our way back to the mansion, followed by the convoy of security vehicles.

Anticipation hummed in my veins, and my mind raced with possibilities as I waited for Saint to return home. With his dominant tendencies temporarily relinquished, I was left with an unfamiliar but thrilling sense of power. The possibilities seemed limitless, but I decided to start small—a simple request that he prepare dinner instead of me. And prepare he did. As I entered our beautifully set dining room, my eyes widened in awe. He had thought of everything - the table was adorned with fragrant flowers and flickering candles, my favourite Merlot glistening in the light. And the food. Oh, the food. My mouth watered as I admired his handiwork, grateful for the chance to luxuriate in the fruits of his labour. Enraptured by the exquisite aroma, my mouth waters as I gaze admiringly at the feast my dear husband has prepared. The flaxen and alluring braids of my hair dangle tantalizingly over my naked shoulders, and my eyes glimmer like stars in the intimate glow of candlelight. Saint's passionate hunger is palpable as he moves forward to embrace me, but I silence him with a sultry whisper.

"First feed me, then fuck me," I murmur, my voice honeyed but authoritative. My words are like sweet torture to my beloved, who groans in dismay before pulling out a chair for me to sit on. I cross my legs coquettishly, ensuring my knees are raised high by my heels, and rest my hands in my lap. Saint resumes eating, and I watch him with a teasing glint in my eye, head tilted to the side as I arch a brow. "What are you doing?" I questioned him in a tone as if scolding him.

"I'm eating. Then I'll feed you," he replied, locking his eyes onto mine.

"I told you to feed me, and that's what I want. Remember the deal for tonight. I get whatever I want." Saint amused himself with a light chuckle before repositioning his chair to my side of the table. As he began to feed me, I savoured each bite as if it were a divine delicacy. My slow and seductive movements with the fork added to the moment's intensity. With his eyes fixed on my every movement, Saint's admiration grew with each passing second.

His expression darkened with a newfound hunger as he watched me lick my lips satisfactorily. My every move captivated him, eagerly anticipating what else the night would bring. As I savoured the sensual display, I detected his escalating arousal and then his bulging erection, yet he persisted in feeding me until I was satiated.

When I completed my meal, I took a sip of wine and found it a delicious accompaniment. Saint unexpectedly commented, "You're incredibly sexy when you boss me around." I responded with a sweet smile, kissed his cheek, and whispered, "I want a bath. Bathe me, Saint." Saint reacted with a shaky whimper and a throat-clearing, which raised the hairs on the back of my neck, filling me with an intense and unsettling sensation. I accepted Saint's hand, and he led me back to the bedroom. "Please wait here. I'll be back," he murmured as he disappeared through the door. I perched on the edge of the bed, my legs crossed daintily and tried to control my racing heart. Suddenly, the unmistakable sound of running water filled the room, and I knew he was back. I didn't have to wait long as Saint returned, catching me in a sultry pose, my leg playfully kicking up as I wiggled my foot at him.

Moving towards me with poised grace, Saint approached me and knelt before me, his fingers deftly undoing the buckle of my pencil heel. With a swift motion, he reversed my legs, lifting the other shoe, the one cloaking its sister in sensuous mystery. His gaze burned hot against my silky skin, sending shockwaves down my spine, heating my bones, and leaving me shivering with want. With just a gentle nudge, the sensation of his touch alone threatened to leave me breathless. But I remained composed, taking in every moment as he gracefully slid the stocking down my sculpted leg to my dainty ankle. Ever so gently, he lifted my foot and like a true artist, rolled the stocking off my heel. The other was removed with equal finesse, and I regained my footing.

There Saint remained, an adoring worshiper at the altar of my beauty, as he went about unzipping my skirt. A festive pair of red thong panties delicately trimmed with lace were revealed as they slid down my legs with his tender help.

His hands roamed passionately up the curve of my thighs, over my hips, all the way to my waist, holding me firmly in place as he stood. With great effort, he started undoing the corset, which tumbled to the ground along with the rest of my clothes. I stood bare before him and could tell that he was eager to have me as he nibbled on his lower lip. He embraced me and made a move to kiss me.

"No, no," I declared as I backed away and shook my finger in his face.

"Bath first."

"Fuck Irena this is pure torture," he complains, and I smile as I walk into the bathroom. He helped me into the tub and then knelt beside it. I handed him a bath, sponge and body wash. He carefully soaped and rinsed my luscious body.

My slippery, wet skin felt like silk. He raised each leg in turn and soaped and rinsed them as well. He cleans my pussy and I moan at the sensation of his hand gliding over my bare skin and then between my lips. After bathing me, Saint towelled me off, and then we moved back to the bedroom. "I'm going to go change. Stay here," I instructed. Saint's eyes were bright and eager, but he kept a neutral expression. I went to the walk-in closet and immediately put on the lingerie. Staring at myself in the mirror, I couldn't help but feel pleased with how the delicate fabric clung to my curves. I made a few adjustments and ran my fingers over the faint stretch marks on my rear end. I wasn't trying to brag, but I knew I looked desirable. I couldn't wait to see the expression on Saint's face when he returned. He loves to tease me so now it's my turn to have fun. I covered myself up with a robe and wandered through the closet.

My fingertips brushed over the fabric of the expensive suit jackets and trench coats. I stopped in front of the drawers and pulled them open individually. Each of them is used to store socks, watches, cuffs, ties, and more. Until I came to the last drawer. I pull it open and my heart drops when I see what's in front of me.

Cuffs, whips, and different sorts of knives are neatly laid out.

I picked up the silver cuffs, analysed it carefully then placed them back down then my fingertips brushed over the silk of the whips then traced over the silver of the knives. I'm not shocked, no I am intrigued. Has Saint been storing these for me or he had them before we even got I don't think twice as I take the cuffs and blindfold. When I stepped out of the closet Saint's gaze trialled down to the stuff in my hands.

"You went through my drawers." he points out casually, his voice is low and tone calm and collected but the raging storm swimming in his darkened green pools says otherwise. A long beat of silence as I drew closer. "Why do you stash cuffs, whips, and knives?" I changed the subject. Saint's jaw ticked. I walked over to the bed and tossed them on it. "Do you use these?" I question, turning to face him. His features are sharp and tipped with malice. A prickling sensation that webs my nerves. I look directly into those green eyes. "I used to," he answers truthfully. "But the ones I used are no longer here. Those are new. I was planning on using them on you." I nod. I bite down on my lower lip, approaching Saint. I fluttered my eyelashes and smiled innocently. "I want to use them..." I pause, Saint's gaze darkened with amusement.

"On you." He raises a perfect brow, a wicked grin gracing his sinful lips. Removing the robe, I allow it to slip off me and Saint's Adam's apple bobs up and down as he runs his hand through his hair.

"You're going to remove all your clothes and I want you to lay on the bed," I ordered. Saint tilts his head to the side, his eyes admiring my body. He lets out a low chuckle before unbuttoning his shirt.

My mouthwatering when his defined muscles are in view, tossing the shirt away he does the same with his pants, shoes, and socks and stays in his briefs. He walks over to the bed and climbs on it. Laying on his back with his hands behind his head as he watched me with intimidating eyes. With a smile on my face, I took hold of the handcuffs and blindfold then got onto the bed, crawling towards him. I secured him to the bedpost, and he wriggled his wrists before locking eyes with me. He gazed at me with passion-filled eyes and groaned. Trying to escape the cuffs, he struggled but was unsuccessful, and eventually let out a frustrated sigh. I crouched down, moving sensually, feeling the warmth of his exposed skin on my thighs, the strong muscular contour against my bare ass. "You're enjoying this, taunting me?" he questions darkly and I let out a light giggle. "Far than you can imagine." I spread myself wider and ground my strapped naked skin into the bunched cloth, his arousal a bar of heat between my spread butt, rising, twitching along my hip. "Let's get something straight here," I said sternly.

"Today I get anything I want, right?"

"Right," he answered.

"Well, what I want is you. I own you. I can do whatever I want to you and you'll do whatever I say, right?"

"Right." This was something I never knew I was capable of; forceful, dominant, and sexually aggressive.

It scared me, but I liked it. Before blindfolding him, I lowered and licked his hard erection. The only thing that was separating me from suffocating on his big dick was the briefs he was wearing. My pussy throbbed as I freed his beautiful cock. Unable to stop myself, I immediately bent to take it into my mouth, luxuriating in the width and hardness of him and knowing that it was all mine to play with.

Moving my head up and down, I fucked him rhythmically with my mouth and heard him gasp as I pushed his cock deeper down into my throat with each movement. "Fuuuck." Saint groaned as I did my magic. I slid my lips down his shaft, continuing my exhilarating assault on his glans with my tongue. I gripped his balls as I sucked at him, feeling the blood pulsing as his excitement increased. His whimpering got louder as his body jerked. He thrust up into my throat and I moaned when his tip hit the back of my throat, hard. "Irena." Saint whimpers, indicating that he is close. I immediately pull away his cock slipping out my mouth with a sloppy pop. I licked my lips, savouring the pre cum then crawled up Saint. Pushing my thin fabric aside to reveal my pussy. A buzz of desire had held me in its thrall, moisture had clung to my pussy lips. "Open your mouth and stick out your tongue," I ordered. Saint jerks his wrists and groans.

"You're lucky I'm cuffed to the bed." He utters to himself, heat licks every nerve in my body. Saint opens his mouth and sticks out his tongue. My legs are resting on each side of his face as I hovered over him. I hold onto the bedpost and lower my inner thighs onto his face. Groaning as I felt his tongue lick my entrance. His tongue takes lazy licks up my slit, before entering me, fucking me. My long braids swish against my breasts as I move against him. My clit had never ached like this. It was swollen and needy, and he was driving me fucking crazy.

"Yes, fuck yes." I bucked my hips up at his face.

"More." I whimpered. His hot tongue tugged at my folds, the bareness of my vagina feeling extra sensitive. I arched against the bed. The bed post screeches as I dig my nails into it. Tingled in my fingers as I gripped for purchase. My body felt electric like at any moment I would fly off into the air. Divine pressure massaged me, and I tensed as he bit down on my sensitive cunt before he plunged his tongue in my entrance again, flicking my clit like a savage-teasing the opening of my cunt. A loud moan ripped from me. His lips seemed to smile, so smug and pleased with the noise he evoked. He drew my labia into his mouth, gently squeezing them between his lips and running his tongue over the tips. "That's it, Saint," I yelled, thrusting my hips forward, stopping and shuddering in ecstasy. He plunged his tongue into my vagina as deeply as he could manage. My muscles tensed and my thighs squeezed together when he slurped me up. I bucked again, and again his tongue sent me to see the stars.

"I need you inside me," I moaned and turned around to straddle his hips. Then I lowered myself onto his cock and began bucking back and forth and up and down with more enthusiasm than ever before. We both shuddered in pleasure. I felt the walls of my vagina constrict around his cock as I stroked up and down his thick long length.

A tear formed in the corner of my eye as the head of his dick taunted me, over and over, just barely nudging my sweet spot. "You're... driving me insane." he moans.

"Please, fuck let me see you." Finally giving in I remove the blindfold and meet his intimidating gaze as I bounce on his cock. My hands were on his chest, my cheeks clapping with each thrust.

Tears blissfully streak down my face at how deep it is, how good it fucking feels to ride him. How he filled me up. It felt like home. He smirked, licking his lips. "I know, baby. And it feels good, doesn't it?"

He groaned and leaned his head back. His hands clenched whilst he cuffed to the bedpost. "You feel so fucking good Doe." he praises, butterflies fluttering in my stomach. I whimper and groan. "You're doing so good riding my cock like my greedy whore." The way he praises and degrades me sends shivers trailing up my spine with pleasure. Heat swelled in my cheeks and along my chest. I gazed down and admired how he looked with him buried inside of me. I leaned toward him.

Our tongues danced together as our bodies melded into one. Kissing me passionately as his cock plunged to new depths. We clung to one another. My hands wandered over his smooth skin, never knowing where to stop, or what to touch. All thoughts left my mind. I held on tight as I rode him.

"That's it, baby. Fuck me." The ridge of his cock stroked my front wall, sending melting warmth through me, gasping and loving the way his hair framed his face.

Heat trickled down inside me once again, our bodies shook and tensed, meeting a climax together. Silence fell over us as I softly kissed him. Slowly, he regained his breath and I stroked his cheek.

"You are desirable." I gasp with uncontrollable laughter, pressing my lips to his once more even as he remains inside me. Instinctively, my fingers seize the keys and unshackle him in one swift motion. In response, Saint lifts me effortlessly off his dick, pivoting me around to all fours.

I clutch the sheets tightly as he seizes my hips, urging me to arch my back and submit myself to his penetration once more. For a moment, my senses are overwhelmed by the sheer pleasure, and I can't help but whimper and bite my lip. He grips the nape of my neck with one hand, pulling me close enough to kiss me tenderly, his cock still pulsing within me. Without warning, Saint smacks my ass with his free hand, eliciting a gasp that turns into a moan of pleasure as he slams into me again.

Desperately, I grind against him, my eyes rolling back as he quickens his pace and fucks me relentlessly from behind. "You feel so fucking good." As Saint moaned, it was as if I were lost in a misty dream world. My mind became consumed with carnal desires that I struggled to control. With each forceful thrust, a lustful euphoria enveloped me and rendered me powerless to resist. The sensation of his balls slapping against my skin with each effortless slide of his body into mine was surreal.

My body was drenched in sweat, my breath laboured as though I'd just run a marathon. I bit down hard on my lip until it nearly bled, so intense was the pleasure. The groans, moans, and whimpers we emitted were like a divine chorus, and every note was my favourite as Saint took me apart. And in the moment everything collapsed as we both reached the euphoria. The pleasurable bliss washing over us. I cried out as Saint whimpered uncontrollably. As he ejaculated in me, the feeling of warm liquid oozes out of my entrance, trailing down my inner thigh. Our bodies sweating and tensed as we allowed the feeling to take over. In the last moments, we try to control our breaths

My mind was still reeling when Saint leaned in, his lips finding my neck in a fiery kiss. His strong hands cupped my breasts, squeezing them with just the right amount of pressure to make me shiver.

Lifted, I pressed my back against his chest and wrapped my hand around his neck. While I'm still inside of him. Eager to meet his gaze, I turned to face him, locking eyes for a brief moment. His smile was like sunshine, his single dimple making an appearance as he pinched my nipples between his fingers. A shudder ran through me, and I knew that sleep was out of the question tonight.

"There's no sleep tonight," I breathed, my lips meeting his in a hungry kiss.

He pulled back, grinning against my lips. "And as promised, I'll ruin you in the best way possible tonight."

A gentle knock echoed through the room. "Enter," I chimed, sliding on the diamond earrings that Saint had presented to me the week before. Today, Saint and I were going out, but I had no clue about our destination. He even gifted me a dress for the occasion; it was sheer, bejewelled with diamonds, and covered in delicate rose patterns that hugged my body and highlighted my curves. My braids flowed down my neck, and my subtle makeup was only amplified by the contrast of my daring red lipstick. The door opened, and one of the maids stepped into the room. She seemed to be in her early forties, her silver hair framing her face. "The car is prepared, ma'am," she announced.

"Thank you very much," I murmured appreciatively, and she gave me a courteous nod before exiting. I wear my coat and rise from the chair.

I exit the room and stop on my feet when I notice white petals on the floor. I smile and follow the trail of petals which lead me outside and a black Mercedes waits for me and Saint in a dressed suit.

As the chill of the wind kisses my cheeks and the sky transforms into a gentle shade of grey, all living beings seem to disappear into hiding. The world around me, once vibrant and full of colour, now appears barren and lifeless. However, this transformation also brings with it the anticipation of something magical: snow. With its graceful descent from the heavens, snowflakes fall like angels, each one unique in its shape and form. Gently, they land on the earth, creating a soft white blanket that covers everything in sight. Snow is a true wonder to behold - a sight that fills the heart with joy and wonder. For those who never get to witness its beauty, they miss out on a true marvel of nature. My eyes grow wide as he reveals a beautiful full bouquet of white roses. "Saint, these are beautiful." I gasp as he hands me the bouquet, and my eyes grow wide. These are heavy. He approached me, his 6,2 height hovering over me as he placed a kiss on my forehead.

"You look stunning. I can't wait to rip this dress off you tonight," he mumbles and I'm greeted by heat flushing my cheeks. I playfully roll my eyes. The maid from earlier reappears and I step back. She smiles. "I will be taking these ma'am and setting them in the kitchen." She states and walks away with the beautiful bouquet of white roses. I've grown fond of them since Saint always gets me white roses. As he presents me with a stunning bouquet of white roses, my eyes widen in awe.

"These are beautiful, Saint," I gasp as he hands me the bouquet, my arms straining under their weight. Towering over me at 6'2", he leans in to place a tender kiss on my forehead.

"You look stunning. I can't wait to rip that dress off you tonight," he murmurs, causing my cheeks to flush with heat. I roll my eyes playfully. Just then, the maid from earlier reappears and I step back as she takes the bouquet from me.

"I will be taking these, ma'am, and setting them in the kitchen," she smiles before walking away. I've grown fond of white roses, as Saint always gets them for me. Saint helps me into the car and buckles me up before rounding the car and taking his place in the driver's seat. The engine roars to life as we drive away in silence for 20 minutes. Finally, I break the silence. "Where are we going?" He chuckles. "Do you know the definition of surprise, Doe?" I scowl at him and he shakes his head, squeezing my thigh with his free hand as the other controls the steering wheel. "I've been clueless for weeks and the suspense is killing me," I complain, staring out the window at the winter wonderland outside. As the wind begins to nip at my face and the sky turns a light grey, I can feel the anticipation building.

Snow is a magical thing, fluttering down from the sky with grace and elegance, softly landing on the earth to create a white blanket covering the ground. Snow is truly a remarkable sight, but those who never see it regularly miss its beauty. Soon, the Eiffel Tower comes into view, lit up by dozens of spotlights arranged along its girders. Cones of light highlight the structure and reveal it in a new light, both from the bottom and from the second level, where the tower's curved silhouette serves up an unbeatable view.

"We're here," Saint proclaims, gesturing to the tower. My eyes widen as it looms larger and larger in the window.

"The Eiffel Tower?!" I squeal, and he nods as the view gets closer by the second. "I rented the whole tower just for the two of us," he calmly states, and my heart drops in amazement.

Speechless, I can only admire the historic building as Saint helps me out of the car. We walk together to the tower and climb into the elevator as it lifts us up. The breathtaking city of Paris spreads out before us, and I can hardly take it all in. "This is beautiful," I breathe.

"And it's all for you, Doe," Saint says, placing a kiss on my forehead. As the elevator comes to a stop, the doors slide open and we are greeted by the heavenly smell of garlic and butter.

My mouth waters as we enter the restaurant located inside the tower, and a waiter approaches us with a huge smile on his face. The wood floor of the indoor restaurant complements the white painted ceiling, with black chairs and tables lit by candles and red roses scattered across the floors. To my left is a huge window that shows the view of the city, with the towers' poles crisscrossing each other to add an extra effect.

"Mr. and Mrs. Dé Leon, it's a pleasure to have you with us. My name is Louís, and I'll be your waiter for the rest of the night," Louis introduces himself in a thick French accent.

"Let me show you to your table." Saint and I follow Louis to our table, where two menus are already waiting for us. Saint helps me into my seat and takes his seat.

"This place is beautiful," I tell him as Louis walks away. Saint tucks his phone into his jacket and watches me intently, causing me to shift uncomfortably. Finally, he speaks. "How did you pull off renting the whole tower?" I ask, still in disbelief.

"Irena, have you forgotten that I can buy you a whole city if you'd just ask?" he states matter-of-factly, causing me to flush. Sometimes I forget how insanely rich Saint is, and how he can use his own money to disappear from society.

Louís arrives once more, quietly opening the bottle and pouring the wine before leaving it aside again. While taking another sip of my beverage, Saint observes me with an intense level of intimacy by tilting his head slightly to the side.

Rising from the chair he adjusts his suit and gestures his hand for me to take. "Aren't we going to order food first?" I question. "We have all the time in the world." I smile, placing my glass down. I place my hands in his and our hands lock together as he guides me to a different room. The room is illuminated with candles and fairy lights. Soft music hums in the air, white glowing roses are scattered on the floor, and the city night view of Paris is visible through the glass windows. The candles provide us with a soft, flickering reflection as Saint slips me into his arms. I enjoy the softness of his touch and the spicy masculine smell of him. The sensual song sets emotions on fire, emotions so deep and tender that we savour each touch and human sensation of a long, slow dance. I look up, meeting his eyes. The colour of forest green, paved with a path that I'll take forever. They say green is the strongest colour because it ignites the new season after the passing of wintry days, and in that, his eyes were born strong, beautiful, and dangerous.

We move quietly in each other's arms. My head rests against his chest. Each heartbeat is in sync with mine. The wine pulsates through my veins, casting a warm glow upon me and allowing the magic of true chemistry to expand between us. I draw him even closer and allow him to feel the warmth in my strength. We do not hurry this dance, but take pleasure in being close and knowing we will have no boundaries between us during, or after the slow dance ends. He lifts my face to him to search my eyes in the soft candlelight and gently tastes his lips. I love the smell of his skin and let him feel the touch of my lips and breath against his neck. He moves closer, and my body responds to the kiss. My breasts press against his chest as my hands move up and down his back. His fingertips trace through the skin on my neck, followed by gentle kisses. My body responds to his touch as he brings my emotions higher in the night.

My hands move to his face to kiss him softly and see the passion in Saint's eyes. "Je T'aime. Te Amo. Eu amo você. Phom rak khun. Ana ahibuk. Te quiero. Ya lyublyu tebya. Kocham cię. I love you, Irena. I love you in any language, I love you in any form. I love you in every universe. Far more than I can figure out how to put in words. Loving you with my madness is the best way to keep me sane," he whispers.

My heart thunders as I look at him with so much emotion. He smiles, stroking my cheek.

"You don't have to say it back, though. I'm just telling you to make sure that what I'm feeling is real." And just like that, realization dawns over me.

Saint is in love with me.

CHAPTER 45

IRENA NOWAK

Snow, a wondrous gift from nature, possesses a magical quality. It descends gracefully from the heavens, like an angel, gently blanketing the earth in a pure, white layer. As the wintry breeze sends shivers down my spine, I take a sinful sip of hot chocolate. Suddenly, the sliding door creaks open, interrupting the peaceful silence with the sound of heavy boots crushing frost-covered ground. A familiar, comforting aroma fills the air, and my heart skips a beat as I recognize the scent I adore.

Saint's velvety voice comes from behind, "You'll catch a cold out here." His touch grazes my skin, sending electric waves through my body. I turn to meet his gaze, feeling his lips brush against the side of my neck, igniting butterflies in my stomach. "I'm snuggled under a blanket," I reply, my eyes still on the pristine winter landscape.

A peaceful silence falls between us. I feel like the frost covered leaves, frozen in place, the chill in my veins stilling my thoughts. I could grow accustomed to this calm.

Saint breaks the quiet. "Tonight, I'm attending a poker event with some men like me. I want you to come with me." I glance at him, surprised. "So, you want me to join an event filled with people like you?" I ask, suspicion creeping into my tone. He rarely invites me to these types of gatherings—so why the change?

"Even though I don't usually bring you to these events, I'd feel better with you there tonight. Besides, I'd love to have you by my side," he explains. "Why the sudden invitation?" I ask, raising an eyebrow. "Shall I remind you of the last poker game?" I add, recalling the chaos. He shrugs. "As long as no one oversteps their boundaries with either of us, there won't be any issues." I shake my head. "I question your principles, Saint."

"Regardless, I want you to come," he says, resting his chin on top of my head. "Abel's going, and Nirali doesn't want to be alone, so Abel asked me to bring you along."

"It's amusing how you're asking me now," I remark, half-smiling. "Normally, you'd exclude me or keep me in the dark."

"Doe, I know Nirali's your friend. The choice is entirely yours," he replies confidently. It has been a while since I've seen her.

With a playful smile, I respond, "Oh, look at you—"

"Don't even start, Irena," Saint warns, but I can't help snuggling closer to him, resting my head on his chest. "Honestly, I want to make sure Nirali's comfortable, so count me in," I confess. I could say I also want to spend time with him, but I'd rather not inflate his already large ego.

"What time are we leaving?" I ask. "Around ten," he replies. As I think about what to wear, I remember the stunning dresses Saint has bought me. Letting out a small sigh of frustration, I decide to seek his fashion advice—after all, his style is impeccable.

SAINT DÉ LEON

"Wait a fucking minute," Zoltan exclaims with a glimmer of excitement in his eyes. "You're telling me poker night is at an upscale strip club?"

Prince raises an eyebrow. "Are you really enthusiastic about being surrounded by provocatively dressed women when you've got a partner waiting at home?"

Curiosity piqued, Nirali chimes in. "Zoltan, do you have a girlfriend?"

Zoltan grins mischievously. "Does it look like I have a girlfriend?"

Nirali assesses him, tilting her head. "No, definitely not."

Zoltan's smile fades. Irena stifles a snicker beside me, earning a subtle glare from him. An innocent smile dances on Irena's lips.

"Be careful how you look at my wife, Zoltan, or I'll make sure you never lay eyes on her again," I say firmly.

Zoltan dismissively shakes his head and rolls his eyes. "Are you really affected by her words?" Prince teases, earning a sharp reply.

"Shut up," Zoltan snaps before hurriedly leaving the limousine.

"Marriage isn't in his future," Abel declares, making us all turn to him with raised eyebrows. He playfully covers his mouth. "Oops. Did I say that out loud?"

Nirali nods solemnly. "Poor Zoltan. He habitually suppresses his emotions, even if it means a lifetime of loneliness."

Prince emerges from the shadows with a gleam in his eye. "What about me?" he eagerly asks. "Do you think I'll ever find love?"

Nirali hesitates. Abel steps in, quickly adding, "I'd rather keep my opinions to myself on that one."

Nirali chuckles softly, a weight lifted off her shoulders.

Prince glares at Abel. "Hell must be packed with people like you," he spits, flinging open the limousine door and disappearing into the night, leaving us stunned.

"Well, you two put a damper on things," Irena observes, trying to lighten the mood.

Nirali shrugs, an enigmatic smile tugging at her lips. "They might be grown men on the surface, but deep down, they're still just angsty teenagers—with all the mood swings and sensitivities."

Stepping into the chilly air, I pulled my coat closer. Irena, de- spite the cold, looked utterly glamorous in her silk gown and fluffy coat. Meanwhile, I stuck to my trusty black tux and gun holster—prepared for anything.

The building's exterior exuded grandeur, its black-and-white marble façade speaking of wealth and power. As we approached the entrance, security conducted a thorough check of my credentials before allowing us in.

Inside, the immaculate black tiles reflected the subdued lighting, adding to the club's dignified elegance. The walls, a sophisticated grey, perfectly complemented the ambiance.

Old married men occupied booths with their wives, watching strippers dance on their laps. Other patrons discussed business, puffing on cigarettes, while the hushed music vibrated discreetly through the walls.

"Dé Leon," a voice called behind me. I turned to see Ace, a figurehead in the western hemisphere's drug trade, scrutinizing me with his deep-blue eyes.

"Ace," I greeted. Ace was a key player in international shipping and drug smuggling, and an important ally in my past life. Our relationship was cordial.

Ace grinned and extended his hand, but his attention quickly shifted to Irena. "Do I have the pleasure of being introduced to this beautiful lady?"

A surge of envy coursed through me, but I introduced her. "Irena, my wife," I said firmly, tightening my grip around her waist.

Ace nodded. "I never thought I'd see the day Saint settled down. You're a lucky man."

Ace smiled at Irena. "It was a pleasure meeting you."

"Nice meeting you too," she replied cordially.

Ace walked off, and Irena commented, "Compared to the people you've introduced me to, Ace seems okay."

I responded concisely, and we proceeded to our table.

"This is so erotic," Zoltan chirped, and Prince rolled his eyes.

The waiter interrupted the silence, offering cigarettes. We all declined except for Prince, who savoured his smoke with a contented moan.

"You're smoking again?" Zoltan asked worriedly.

Prince turned slowly. "I was smoking last night, and oh look, I'm still smoking today."

"Why is it a problem that he's smoking?" Irena asked.

"Well, he's so addicted he'd choose it over sex, money, or po—"

"Okay, Nirali, we get it. Thank you," Prince cut her off, taking another drag.

"I ask all of you to consider the importance of shutting the fuck up," I said firmly.

"Okay, Daddy dearest," Zoltan joked playfully, making Nirali laugh loudly.

I groaned, massaging my temple. Irena stroked my arm gently. "Come on, Saint, can't you cut them some slack?"

I turned to her. "Do you have any idea what it's like being in the same room as them?"

She furrowed her eyebrows. "No, I don't."

"Then you'll soon find out why I prefer your company over theirs," I said, causing her shoulders to droop.

Before she could respond, the waiter returned. "May I take your order?"

"A whiskey and a martini," Abel ordered.

Irena asked for a glass of wine, and I added, "Whiskey for me."

Prince interjected, "I'll have whiskey too." Zoltan followed with, "Martini."

The waiter inquired, "Anything else?"

Zoltan remarked sarcastically, "How about a glass of virgin blood?"

The waiter shifted uneasily, and we all stared at Zoltan.

"That's not funny, man," Prince retorted.

Zoltan shrugged. "We all have our flaws."

"That will be all, thank you," Irena told the waiter, who walked away.

"How does your poker event usually unfold?" Irena asked.

"We wait for everyone to arrive, then gather upstairs. Some bring their wives; others don't. The ladies can watch or leave whenever they want," I explained.

"Why are we in a strip club?" she asked.

I explained that a different person hosted each year, and this year's host likely had ulterior motives.

"Have you ever hosted?" she asked.

I shrugged, recalling a half-hearted attempt. "I dabbled in hosting but passed it off to Abel."

As the minutes ticked by, the strip club filled with revellers. A woman clad in scarlet lingerie beckoned us to follow her to the second floor.

The upstairs room was dominated by a magnificent mahogany bar and cozy tables, retaining the same aesthetic as downstairs but more impressive.

"Alright, shitheads, the moment we've been waiting for has arrived," Zoltan smirked, finishing his whiskey.

We made our way to our designated booths, seating ourselves with our significant others. I pulled Irena onto my lap, and Abel did the same with Nirali. Agu, a master of arms trading, shuffled and dealt cards. The tension in the room was palpable, like a battlefield. Only one soldier would emerge victorious.

I picked up my cards—2 hearts and 8 hearts. "Like I expected anything better," I muttered.

Abel called out, "100,000 euros," revealing a suitcase full of cash. I glanced at his cards—Ace of Diamonds and Ace of Spades.

Nam-Gil, sitting beside me, fidgeted nervously, his leg trembling as he reached for his deck.

Agu lit a cigar and laid down the King of Hearts and Ace of Clubs, a victorious smirk on his face. Nam-Gil's poker face remained unreadable as the smoke from Agu's cigar enshrouded him.

"You alright?" I asked Irena, who quietly observed the scene.

"Yes, but I don't understand what's happening," she replied.

I gave her thigh a gentle squeeze. "I'm going to get a drink. Can I get you anything?" I ask Irena, smoothing my tie. She casts a glance at the bar, then shakes her head as I plant a kiss on her forehead. "I'll be back in a minute," I murmur, heading toward the direction of Nirali and Abel.

Upon reaching the bar, I leaned in and muttered, "Something strong," to the bartender. As he busied himself, I closed my eyes and massaged my temples. A presence beside me made me open my eyes, curious.

Out of the corner of my eye, a familiar figure catches my attention: Anatol.

Paris isn't exactly his usual haunt, so I can't help but wonder what in the world he's doing here.

"How's your brother, Grzegorz?" I casually ask, my voice laced with a sinister undertone. Truth be told, I took great pleasure in breaking a few of his bones, and I'm not at all ashamed of it. Anatol clears his throat, fidgeting with his tie. "He's... regaining his strength," he finally manages to stutter out.

Anatol is one of the quieter members of the Nowak family, but don't let that fool you: he's as manipulative as they come. "I'm just here to check on my niece," he informs me as he subtly glances at Irena, deep in conversation with Nirali. His gaze then snaps back to me, and I can't help but feel a chill run down my spine.

"Tell me, how has she been treating you lately?" he inquired, a hint of smugness in his voice. Suppressing the urge to lash out, I sipped on my drink, letting the liquid courage flow through me.

"Her behaviour towards me is not your concern," I retorted, my words razor-sharp. His response was a chuckle, one that grated on my nerves.

"Ah, but our relationship is stated as per the agreement you signed," he reminded me, condescending. My hands clenched into fists, the anger bubbling within me.

But then, a realization hit me, and I made a decision. I would no longer be beholden to the Nowak brothers or their schemes. It was time to take my life into my own hands. My feelings towards Irena have changed. I do not intend to ruin what we have.

I respect Irena's wishes, so I will not act out on the agreement I shared with them. Three months ago, the esteemed Nowak brothers provided invaluable assistance rescuing my business from a potentially ruinous situation. Unbeknownst to me, an unknown source had successfully breached the firewalls of my global trading and money laundering operation, putting a staggering 10 billion euros in jeopardy. Despite my best efforts, I could not resolve the issue alone. Then, I turned to the Nowak brothers, known for their expertise in dealing with complex security breaches and hacking.

The Nowak brothers had provided invaluable assistance, for which I felt indebted. To show my appreciation, they recommend- ed that I marry their niece. Initially, the idea did not appeal to me, but when I learned that the potential bride was Jan's daughter, my dear friend and supporter, my initial reluctance faded. Given Jan's significant contribution to my achievements, honouring his memory by marrying into his family appeared appropriate.

Although a union was formed, there was a condition attached. Given her prominent status, the elders of the Nowak family arranged for Viktor to marry someone of their choosing to produce an heir to continue the family's enterprise. It was highly necessary that she become pregnant and give birth to ensure the legacy of the Nowak empire.

But plans changed when Irena killed Viktor. Fate took a turn, and we got married as per our agreement that I would impregnate her and pay her one million euros.

"I'm no longer included. I'll pay fifty million dollars and recommend a replacement for Irena without interfering with her life," I replied, sipping my drink. He objected, "That was not part of our deal."

I confronted him, feeling increasingly angry. "It doesn't matter to me. I won't make her pregnant. She has expressed opposition to having kids, and I respect her wishes," I asserted resolutely. He scoffed, "When have you ever respected a woman?"

As the glass met with the wooden surface, an involuntary movement rippled through my jaw, betraying the inferno of rage that burned within. "I've always been a bastion of respect towards women. But you and your wretched siblings? You treat them as mere objects of desire, with no regard for their dignity. Your ostentatious posturing is nothing but a sad display of your insecurities." With each word, my voice quivered with the effort of restraint.

Anatol's eyes flashed with fury, the tension between us palpable like the tremors of an impending earthquake.

"If you don't keep your promise, we'll find a replacement for you as the father of her children, whether she agrees or not," he threatened harshly. With a swift and unfaltering motion, I grasp Anatol by the collar. Rage ignites within me like a bolt of lightning striking the earth.

"Let me be clear: if you think so much about interfering with our marriage, the consequences will be swift and brutal. Your very essence will be stripped bare, leaving you in a world of unparalleled torment. The precision and elegance with which I will carry out your punishment will leave even the most astute observer convinced that your death was beyond the realm of natural causes." The atmosphere seemed to quiver with the intensity of my threat, like a blade honed to perfection.

Anatol's facade of composure wavers, and a faint glimmer of fear flickers. "You're in love with her, aren't you? You'd rather put your entire livelihood on the line than risk losing her," he observes with keen insight, leaving me speechless. A sly grin spreads across his face.

As I release my grip on his collar, Anatol brushes off his suit and straightens his shirt, avoiding eye contact. I can feel the tension in the air.

"Well, Saint, if that's how you'll play it..." He trails off, stealing one last glance at Irena before locking eyes with me. He leans in, his voice low and measured.

Anatol's words cut like a knife as he spoke them with conviction. "Believe me when I say this, I genuinely hope Irena dies." He gracefully stepped back, spun on his heel, and strolled away.

CHAPTER 46

SAINT DÉ LEON

Abel gawked in disbelief. "It's so weird to look at," he muttered, shaking his head. Nirali snickered beside him, but Irena rolled her eyes. "How can it be so strange that Saint is showing his caring side?" she asked, her voice cutting through the tension. Abel stroked his stubble and stared at us with a watchful gaze.

Suddenly, Abel spoke up again, an accusation hiding behind his words. "I mean, it's questionable that you stayed, and to top it all, you fell in love with him." His tone was laden with suspicion, and Nirali and Irena exchanged a wary look as they both knew what he was implying.

My brother loves to spike me off. I wanted to reach out for the wine bottle on the table, ready to bash him over the head for daring to question our relationship.

However, Abel noticed the subtle exchange between them and leaned back against the couch. "What?" he demanded, crossing his arms over his chest. Irena cleared her throat before speaking up, finding courage in her glass of wine as she tried to hide her face from view.

"What is it?" Abel persisted, seeming unaware of how offensive his words were sounding. Nirali glowered at him, warning, "Abel, I love you, but you must learn when to read the room." My brother may have been powerful, but he wasn't powerful enough to face two angry women. He shrugged and gave a small smile before continuing in a lower voice.

"It's just me questioning how Saint managed to make Irena fall in love with him?" he trailed off. All eyes were upon Irena now, who shifted uncomfortably in her seat before finally responding, "I haven't told him that I love him yet."

Abel seemed taken aback by this response and pushed back his hair before asking the obvious question, although whether it was out of genuine curiosity or because he wanted to cause more trouble was unclear.

"Do you love him?" he questioned quietly, though thunder roared in my ears as all eyes were upon Irena and me, awaiting an answer.

"Well-" she clears her throat, fidgeting in her seat.

"I care for him," she utters, uncertainly meeting my gaze and pulling them away just as quickly.

Abel leans forward, arching a curious brow. "Well, does it ever concern you that maybe you will eventually be like Saint one day? Doesn't it occur to you about all the fucked up things he did?" I watch as Irena's face contorts with confusion and fear. She straightens her posture as she responds, "I already know about Saint's past." trying to hide how much Abel's words have shaken her. Nirali meets my gaze and gives me an apologetic look, but I can tell she's thinking the same thing as Abel.

"Woah, back up. Saint told you about Noona?" Abel inquires, his eyes sparkling with intrigue. Irena nervously chuckles as she nibbles on her bottom lip. "Abel. Enough." I warn him sternly, knowing exactly where he's going with this. But he dismisses me with a wave of his hand. "Relax, brother. I'm just shocked that you finally shared your past instead of dealing with it in an unhealthy manner. I'm proud of you," he says before pausing to chuckle with disbelief. "Irena did he also tell you that I killed my mother." Abel smiles wickedly as he delivers this bombshell with a twisted sense of humour. "I was eight."

Irena remains silent, not knowing how to respond or react to Abel's confession. My stomach tightens into knots as I realize the full extent of what we're all dealing with here.

"Abel," I warn again, hoping to cut off any more damaging revelations from him. But he dismisses me once again.

"That he killed Noona, Gabriel, and his child." The room falls silent as Nirali gasps and covers her mouth in shock. I look at Irena, now white as a sheet, and my heart breaks for her.

"What?" Irena exclaims in disbelief. My mind races as I try to come up with a way to explain everything, but it feels impossible.

Nirali slaps Abel on the shoulder, trying to snap him out of his twisted game. "Leave." She tells her husband firmly. "Nira-" Abel starts to protest, but Nirali cuts him off with a fierce glare and a raised hand. "You've done enough running your mouth, Abel. Leave." She demands, and finally, he sighs and rises from the couch before exiting the library.

"Saint?" Irena questions softly, her voice cracking with emotion. Her words strike me like a knife to the gut, and I feel helpless to offer any comfort or explanation. I pinch the bridge of my nose as I struggle to keep my emotions in check. The weight of everything feels heavy on my shoulders, and I'm not sure how much longer I can carry it alone.

"I should probably be going," Nirali declared, standing from her chair. She brushed herself off before pointing to the other side of the room. "I'm going to sit over there for a bit. I can't miss out on this fight." She crossed her legs as she eavesdropped on our conversation with a smug expression on her face. I couldn't help but roll my eyes, annoyed that my brother had found someone like him. "You killed your child and never told me. What's worse is that not so long ago, you told me that you wanted to have children with me. Are you going to kill them too?!"

My whole world was pushed away when a dark, vivid memory flashed in.

As I trace my fingers along the glittering blades of the knives, my pulse quickens, and a raw, animalistic urge awakens within me. At only 16, I've yet to experience the thrill of my first kill, but each day, my hunger grows more ravenous. The pent-up fury and frustration I've bottled up for so long is bubbling to the surface, threatening to consume me completely.

Suddenly, the click-clack of stiletto heels echoes through the room, causing me to jolt upright. I tense up, the hairs on the back of my neck standing at attention as the intoxicating scent of lavender fills my nostrils. It's her - Noona.

As she moves in close, wrapping her arms around me, I can feel the heat of her body mingling with my own. For a moment, I'm transported back to when she was my protector, my guiding light. But something has shifted - I've grown taller, stronger, and more powerful than her.

Noona is a vision of age-defying beauty, with a radiance that belies her 40 years. In just a handful of months, she'll blow out 41 candles with her signature grace and poise.

"Are you hiding from me?" Her voice instigates a visceral response as if my entire being recoils at her presence. I close my eyes and take a deep breath, trying to swallow down the nausea that churns within me.

I hate her. The intensity of my hatred courses through my veins, burning like a wildfire that refuses to be extinguished. The pain she's inflicted upon me is unforgivable.

"I was trying to," I say, my voice heavy with contempt. She laughs, a sound as grating as nails on a chalkboard. She reaches out and tugs cruelly at my hair, and I steel myself against the urge to lash out at her. "What happened to the sweet boy I used to know?" she asks coyly, though her cruel intentions are transparent. Refusing to engage her, I fixate my gaze on the gleaming

blades that shimmer in the light, inviting and dangerous all at once.

Her voice, a mere whisper, grazed my neck. "Ignoring me, are we?" My skin erupts in goosebumps. Stepping back, I watch as she teeters on her feet. Facing her, I finally meet her gaze. The dark- ness in her eyes is almost palpable. "Have you for-"

"No, I haven't. I'm tired of you taking advantage of me. I don't care if you twist the story and tell Gabriel that I forced myself on you. Do whatever the fuck you want Noona, and if Angeline wants to kill herself, she can go ahead and be selfish. I will take Abel with me and protect him from all of you." I blurt out. Tears began to sting the corner of my eyes. Noona frowns, tilting her head to the side as she stares at me in disbelief. "Your father is not home, and your mother is drunk on the couch. That means I can do whatever I want to you, and I will ensure I discipline you so we can get your attitude in check." She

states as she approaches me, and I push her away; she stumbles on her feet again.

Her eyes grow wide, a wicked smile dancing on her lips. "You're going to regret that." Unexpectedly, Noona delivers a stinging blow to my cheek before she latches onto my throat, squeezing with a ferocity that steals my breath away. Gasping for air, I can feel spots swirling before my eyes as my body quivers in fear. Reacting instinctively, I clutch at the first object within my grasp.

"You need a lesson in how to treat a woman with a child," she snarls venomously, but before I can stop myself, I thrust the sharp blade deep into her stomach. Instantly, her eyes widen, tears of fear welling up as she stares deeply into my soul.

And then, it hits me like a ton of bricks. She's carrying my child. "What?" I whisper incredulously. "I'm pregnant." Her hand reaches out to grip mine, desperation flashing in her eyes. "The baby is ours," she cries out, a glimmer of hope returning to her torn face. "Forget everything, and let's raise our family together... with Abel, too. Just save me, Saint." she pleads before a gush of blood erupts from her mouth, staining her lips a crimson red.

Rage courses through my veins, overpowering any hint of disgust. How After years of suffering through endless abuse, grooming, and the unspeakable horrors of rape, she still has the audacity to propose we raise a child together.

With a steady hand, I press the blade deeper into her flesh, listening to the-

"Saint?" Irena calls out, pulling me out of the trance. I chuckle darkly.

"Answer me, Saint. Are you going to kill my children too?" I shake my head. Meeting Irena's hurtful gaze. "No, it's different. You wouldn't understand." I utter. "Then let me understand. You had a secret child. You killed your baby. How do you live with yourself knowing that you killed your first child?"

"And this is my cue to leave." Nirali interrupts and then walks out of the library.

My heart beats, aching in my chest. "It wasn't my baby. It will never be my baby."

Irena scoffs in disbelief. I reach out and try to touch her, but she leans back. Another stab to the heart.

"Irena..." I trailed off slowly. "Why?" She questions softly. "It was Noona's. When I stabbed her, she told me that she was pregnant and I was the father, Hoping that it would change my mind, but that only gave me another reason to kill her. I didn't care if she was carrying my child. If I allowed her to live and give birth to the baby. I would despise the child as much as I despised the mother."

"What that woman has put me through, Irena." I suck in a breath, fighting back the tears as all the emotions that I've been bottling up come crashing into me in one big wave. "What she has put me through, one knew how much I cried that day, and till this day, I still can't escape her. I can't escape the shit she has put me through. People would always say, "But it made you stronger." I was a fucking child. A child. I didn't need to be stronger. I needed to be safe."

"I never had a childhood because of her. I never experienced love and safety because of her. She ripped away all my self-respect and left me with nothing. She's the reason I'm like this. So tell me, Irena, why would I want the gruesome sound of her choked screams? As I twist, her eyes widen with raw panic.

"You and the baby can rot in hell for all I care." She does not know the pain and regret I've been through till I had to fall on my knees and beg God himself to heal me.

"I'd rather die than be a father to someone who turned me into a monster?"

Irena remains silent, not knowing what to say. "I'm not angry at what you did. I don't have the right to judge. I killed my husband, for crying out loud. What bothers me is that you didn't tell me, and what makes it worse is that it was your child." I nod in understanding. Taking Irena's hands into mine, she sighed. "I am many things; I've done many things, but when it comes to you. I will never forgive myself, knowing that I've done something to hurt you. Your trust means more to me than anything else in this world. I value you more than I value myself. You come first, our children come first, and I will protect you and our children from this world. From myself." I held her face. "Do you think I care about anything but you, Irena?"

Irena searches my eyes. Her gaze finally softens. "I know you do, Saint. You and I have been through a lot. It's hard for us to trust and attach ourselves to people. So you hiding all these secrets won't make it easy for me to break down my walls for you. I want your honesty. Show me all the darkest parts of you, and let me love you anyway; all it takes is your honesty. That's all." Irena looks at me with her soft gaze. She strokes my cheek, her head tilting to the side. "It scares me sometimes, seeing the emptiness in your eyes."

Irena leans in, kissing my lips tenderly, pressing her forehead onto mine. "Someone wise once said I kiss your scars away and replace them with mine." She whispers, and I smile. I sigh. "When I was young, I used to say I would never get up this way." I scoff. "Now look at me. How can you care for me when I'm all fucked up on the inside. You need someone who will help you heal. You deserve someone who will share their light with you. Not me.

All I can offer you is my darkness." I ventilate. "No, no, I don't. I need you. You're powerful, violent, devastating, and utterly magnificent and in some fucked up way. I find comfort in it. So no, Saint, I don't want a happy, bubbly person to fix me. I prefer my chaotic storm that will destroy anything in its path."

My heart clenched, and butterflies erupted in my stomach. "I love you so much, Irena."

Irena smiles as she pulls me into a warm, comforting hug. Her warmth tangles well with my soul.

I've finally found my home.

"Do you have to go?" Irena murmurs with a heavy heart, her eyes shimmering like precious jewels.

With a deep sigh, I feel disappointed that I must leave Irena for a week. Tenderly, I tuck a wisp of her braid behind her ear and caress her face with warmth. As I drop a kiss on her forehead, she clutches me with all her might, fearful of letting go.

"Just one week," I assure her. But she scoffs and crosses her arms, glaring at me with a fierce scowl. "One week is like an eternity when it comes to you. You can't bear to be away from me for a day." She accuses, jabbing her finger at me. I can't help but grin, knowing that she's right.

I chuckle and press my lips against her, the sensual feeling dancing in my stomach as she clutches onto my shirt and pulls me closer. Our tongues were touching, and our lips were moving delicately.

In a sinuous motion, I snake my arm around her waist, holding her in my embrace. Her body pressed against mine, Craving to tangle her into the very fibers of my soul. Irena has captured me completely; there's no chance of me ever letting go. She possesses every inch of me, body and soul.

I am devoted to her beyond measure, willing to follow her to the farthest ends of the universe.

If she dives into the ocean, I'll jump right in after. Even if she takes off into the cosmos, I'll be beside her. If she meets her end, I meet mine. She holds the key to my very existence. She is a deity, a goddess to be worshipped with fealty and reverence.

She is my religion, and I'll bow before her for eternity.

As Irena and I pull away from each other's embrace, a shy smile spreads across her face as she extends my luggage towards me. The air between us crackles with unspoken emotions my heart swells with love, urging me to confess what lies heavy on my tongue.

"I love you," the words spill out, catching Irena off guard. Her cheeks flush a deep crimson hue as she manages to steady her voice.

"Be safe, okay?" she insists, brimming with concern. I nod, closing the gap between us one last time to savour the taste of her lips. Then, with a heavy heart, I climb into the car, leaving Irena behind with nothing but a final, longing glance. The engine revs to life, and I drive off, carrying a piece of Irena's heart with me.

It's just one week, yet it feels like a whole fucking eternity.

CHAPTER 47

SAINT DÉ LEON

Abel settled into the seat opposite me and inquired, "Does she know about it?" My eyes were fixed out the window, contemplating the peaceful fluffiness of the clouds drifting by.

With a sigh, I loosened my tie and downed a gulp of whiskey, savouring the scorching sensation as it warmed my insides. "No, it's best she remains in the dark," I replied with a pointed remark.

Abel nodded, his fingers tapping away at his phone, providing me with a moment to retreat back into my own thoughts.

If only she knew the truth behind our marriage, I fear Irena would never allow herself to fall in love with me. Our bond has grown strong, and I refuse to let one dark secret unravel every- thing we've fought to build. The mere thought of her hating me sends chills down my spine.

But there's so much at stake. The Nowak brothers must be taken down, I must do it in a way that doesn't raise suspicion from the other crime families. If the truth ever came out about me killing my wife's family, I'd lose everything, my connections, my trust.

I won't back down. If the Nowak brothers refuse my offer of 5 million, they better prepare their deathbeds. No matter what it takes, I'll protect my wife.

"How are things between you and Nirali?" I inquire, hoping to shift my focus elsewhere and to see if Nirali told Abel about her being infertile. I've been mired in my worries and haven't had the chance to discuss his situation.

Abel lifts his head from his phone, his eyes widening at the mere mention of his wife. He stealthily stashes his device as he clears his throat, ready to answer.

"We're doing well," he says, his words hanging in the air. My brow quirks upward inquisitively. I'm guessing she has not told him yet.

"Only well?" I press, watching as he clears his throat and adjusts his crisp suit. A faint blush dusts his cheeks as he leans in to confide, "We're trying to get pregnant."

My eyes widen in surprise for an instant before I compose my- self and cross my arms over my chest. "Ready to take on parent- hood, are you?" I assert, watching as he nods resolutely. I promised Nirali I wouldn't tell Abel, so I'll act like a mindless sheep. "I'm more than ready to be a father," he says firmly, "and she's beyond excited to be a mother. We both want to start a family." A small smile tugs at the corners of my mouth, feeling a glimmer of joy in my heart for their bright future ahead.

Who knew Abel would fall in love with a woman who appeared out of nowhere? I sure didn't see it coming. They sure did come a long way. "What are you hoping for, a girl or boy?" I asked curiously, watching as he nervously bit his lower lip before running a hand through his hair. "Honestly, as long as the baby is healthy, I couldn't care less," he replied nonchalantly. "And Nirali?" I probed, curious about what she wanted to have. "She's hoping for a son," he answered with a shrug.

With a nod of understanding, Abel and I shifted the conversation to the latest developments with the Nowak brothers. Our minds were focused on the upcoming meeting with global bosses in New York, where we planned to discuss ways to expand our territory and catch up with old acquaintances. As the plane touched down, we readied ourselves for the challenges and opportunities ahead.

A clandestine gathering of the most notorious and powerful names in organized crime was held at the imposing abode of mob kingpin Nelson King, nestled in the elusive 625 McFall Road in Apalachin, New York. Amongst those present were Abel and I, the Dé Leon, the ironclad Lansky's, the menacing Costello, the cunning Mogilevich's, and the fucking Nowak. The agenda was as weighty as it was dangerous, the rampant and turbulent affairs of loan sharking, narcotics trafficking, and gambling were being discussed at length. However, the most pressing concern was the occurrence of the shadowy and anonymous hitmen destroying our shipments and informing the feds. Little did I know I wasn't the only one facing these problems. With stealth and cunning, the bastards have brazenly set targets on those gathered in this very room, including me - placing not only our business but families at great risk. Rest assured, should we catch them, they will rue the fucking day they dared to trifle with us.

A scowl creases Nelson's face as he voices the growing unease of the local authorities, who have noted an influx of flashy foreign vehicles sporting dubious license plates.

I note how Krzysztof and Anatol exchange furtive glances in the uneasy silence that follows. Sitting next to me, even my brother senses the mounting tension in the air.

"The issue can wait. Our priority now is to locate the audacious fuckers who dared to cross us," Carlos Costello commands, his hand crashing down onto the table in determination.

A sly grin dances across Kirill Mogilevich's face as he takes a deep puff from his Cuban cigar. Nelson shoots a scowl in Kirill's direction. "Do you find this amusing?" he snaps irritably. Kirill nonchalantly shrugs, his Russian accent lingering in his words. "It's sad that you fools haven't realized the truth yet."

I lean in, desperate to hear his thoughts. Kirill's weathered brown eyes analyze us before locking onto my own. My words escaped with a tinge of impatience, "Realise what Kirill?" The wisps of smoke issuing from his cigar danced dispassionately in the air. Sighing heavily, he cast his gaze toward me with a resigned shake. "It's beyond belief that someone as intelligent as you hasn't yet connected the dots. Your razor-sharp mind and firm resolve have always been your forte. However, it appears that something is distracting you from the situation."

My brows furrow. Kirill cocks his head to the side. "It is not suspicious that these fuckers know every single detail of our shipments and manage to mess up the security system and break into our very homes without getting caught. When we always discuss a well-proofed plan to catch them, they are one step ahead of us for some strange reason. We are looking for some- one we least expect it to be. Someone we trust. Someone sitting in one of these chairs disguising themselves as a victim." Kirill points out, blowing a puff of smoke

Abel and I exchange looks. It's neither Abel nor me, so we are off the table.

Everyone else in the room exchanges looks, wondering who the rat may be. "But why would they sabotage us, knowing that we are one of the high-class crime families?" Nelson questions. "For more power," I utter, and all eyes shift to me.

"The most cowardly of all of us would be the person who might be behind the chaos of our business. They take us out one by one, starting off with the one who is the highest in power and money, then finish off with the weakest and once they have all destroyed us, they take what's left and build something even greater to improve their name." I explain.

"Saint and I are off the list, including Kirill, so it leaves the rest of you," Abel states. Anatol scoffs, catching our attention. "How do we know it's not you guys trying to trick us? After all, you guys are the big men in this room."

I frown, meeting Anatol's gaze. "What if it's you? It makes sense since the Nowak family fell off the rank after Jan died.

Krzysztof scoffs. "Please, we know our boundaries, Saint, plus why would we sabotage a business for our so-called son-in-law?"

I roll my eyes at his lies. One day, I'll expose them for the disgusting double-crossing bastards that they are.

I gaze at all the photographs I've been gathering for the past month.

I scrutinize each detail, ensuring that nothing is overlooked.

I haven't had proper sleep for the past two days. All I've been preoccupied with was trying to locate the rodent.

And so far, my leads have been as fruitless as a parched well. All I could think of was Zoltan and Prince. After the occurrence at my residence, they haven't displayed any signs of suspicion, and everything has been quiet, which raises suspicions for me. And to make matters worse, I have to concern myself with the Nowak brothers and the agreement, not to mention that it's floating somewhere out there with someone ready to ruin my marriage with Irena and potentially undermine ten per cent of my work that I've built around the criminal organization.

As someone who possesses as much authority as me, being ineffectual is extremely frustrating.

I cannot allow anything to be disclosed, but the individual I'm dealing with is more intelligent than I anticipated, and it's the first time in my life to acknowledge this, but I'm afraid I may not have the advantage.

Which is why I'm finished waiting. I'll have to take matters into my own hands and interrogate Zoltan and Prince until one of them gives in.

CHAPTER 48

SAINT DÉ LEON

I can't sleep. I've been tossing and turning in my bed as a myriad of thoughts race through my mind.

I suspect that the Nowak brothers are responsible for the sabotage ordeals, as well as the personal issues I have with them, including my marriage.

I groan, running my hand over my face as I drape the blanket over my body. Closing my eyes, I attempt to compel myself to sleep. I am completely drained and I desperately need rest be- cause tomorrow is going to be a gruelling day.

Fuck, why am I suddenly unable to sleep? Normally, I would fall asleep effortlessly after a long day with Irena-Irena. That's why I can't sleep. I sleep peacefully when I am with her.

She's like my security blanket.

Without hesitation, I reach for my phone that is resting on the dresser.

Unlocking it, I immediately dial one of my employees. After the third ring, they answer.

"Hello, sir," they greet. "Kas, I need you to prepare the private jet," I inform them. "Where to, sir?" they inquire. "Paris," I reply. "Okay, sir, I'll send a car to your penthouse in thirty minutes to pick you up," they confirm, and I end the call. Rubbing my eyes out of sheer exhaustion.

Once I have Irena by my side, I'll finally be able to get some undisturbed sleep.

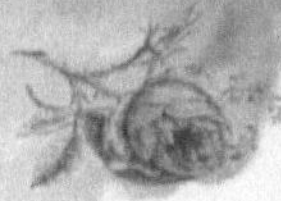

The 8-hour journey was tiring. I attempted to rest, but I was awake like an energetic child on a Saturday morning.

I step out of my car and secure it, inserting my keys into the lock I unlock the door and enter the dim silent house. My foot-steps reverberate with each stride as I make my way upstairs.

Upon reaching our bedroom, I gently push the door open and walk quietly.

The moon casts a glow of glistening light in the room. Planting kisses on Irena's soft skin as she slumbers. Though her eyebrows are slightly furrowed and tension lingers on her face. Taking off my clothes and leaving only my briefs, I stealthily slip into bed. Pulling Irena close to me. Her warm embrace put me at ease and her delicate vanilla scent caused my heart to skip a beat.

She groans, fluttering her eyes open. Her brows furrowed as she met my gaze in confusion. Gently pinching my face to check if I was real.

"Am I dreaming?" She softly questions herself. I chuckle, placing a kiss on her forehead. "No, I'm here for real," I utter, my voice hoarse and raspy. Her cheeks blush as she pulls me closer.

"What happened to wait a week to see me?" she asks in the nape of my neck.

I inhale her scent and sigh. "I missed you and couldn't sleep," I answer honestly. She pulls back, meeting my gaze as her eyes widen in realization.

"You flew across the globe because you couldn't sleep without me?" She clarifies.

"If you put it that way, then yes," I state. She smiles softly. "Oh Saint, that wasn't necessary. We could have called or video chat- ted." she declares. I shake my head.

"Not enough of you to lull me to sleep. I needed to hold you." She plays with my hair, planting gentle kisses on my face. "Well then I'm here, you can sleep now," she whispers.

Like a spell, my body relaxes and my heartbeat slows down as sleep finally takes over.

I R E N A   N O W A K

My fingers extend in search of Saint but grasp only air. With a heavy exhale, I open my eyes to find nothingness beside me. Saint left, but traces of his scent linger, taunting my senses. Lying on my back, I gaze upward and release a soft moan, lost in thought. The flutter of delicate wings within my gut ignites memories of last night, and Saint's words dance among them.

With the world at his feet, he flew across oceans to wrap me in his arms. His sense of urgency was palpable, and his desire to be near me on this momentous occasion was impossible to ignore. Not every day does someone go to such lengths for someone they care about.

His love knows no bounds, soaring beyond what mortals could ever conceive.

I am left in awe of his devotion, wondering if I can match it in return.

When my eyes set on him, my entire being is enveloped in a surge of euphoria that leaves me breathless. He has mastered the art of leaving me speechless within seconds.

My name glides off his tongue like a sweet melody laced with the tenderness and passion of his affection. How his eyes search mine unwaveringly makes me feel like I am the only one who matters in his world. Whenever his fingers brush against my skin, it feels like a delicate trail of soft kisses, waking up every nerve ending in my body with a jolt of electric sensation.

My entire being thrums with an electric pulse, my heart racing with my feelings for him. But no matter how deeply I feel, I can't help but think that his love reaches heights I can't even fathom.

Whether it's fear or denial that holds me back from saying those three words, I can't quite say. But one thing is certain: my world revolves around this man, heart, and soul.

"I'm so sorry for calling you to come here at such short notice." I let out as I stepped aside for Nirali to enter.

She removes her coat and hangs it on the hanger before dusting the snow off her clothes. I shut the door behind me and nervously nibble on my bottom lip.

"Reena, feel free to call me at 3 am, and I'll hurry over despite still wearing my pyjamas," she jokes, and I grin.

She looks at me and her smile disappears. "What's the matter?" She asks.

I exhale, pulling on my hair's roots. "I'm freaking the hell out, Nirali," I confess, and she gently leads me to the kitchen while placing her hands on my back.

"Calm down, Irena. Talk to me." Her reassuring presence washes over me like a soothing balm. Inhaling deeply, I observe intently as she gracefully strides into the wine room and returns with a bottle of wine and two elegant glasses. As she deftly prepares our beverages, I feel the butterflies in my stomach fluttering nervously.

Finally, she delivers my drink with a gentle smile, and we clink our glasses together. Downing my wine in one swift gulp, I place the glass on the counter and summon my courage to reveal my innermost thoughts. "I think I'm falling in love with Saint," I spontaneously expressed. Nirali was startled and almost sprayed her wine across the room while staring at me with an astonished expression. She then removed the remaining wine dribbling from her lips before pouring me another serving of the drink. "You might need this more than I do," she announced, to which I responded with a shaky chuckle.

"Never thought you would fall in love with him," she states, and I shrug. "Although I'm scared, Nirali. I don't know why, but something keeps pulling me back." I uttered, taking a sip from my wine.

"What do you feel when you're with him?" She questions. "When I was looking at him last night, I sensed something magical stir- ring deep within me. The power of love surged through my veins and wove tendrils of warmth and affection around my heart. My emotions were a riotous swirl of passion and devotion, surging to the surface and flooding my senses. His very presence filled me with a joy so profound, I couldn't help but let out a giggle. Watching him slumber peacefully, I knew that this sensation was what true love was all about. It was as if the sweetest whispers of love were drifting through the universe, showering us with promises of forever."

Watching him sleep with a peaceful smile, I knew that this was what true love was meant to feel like.

A love that whispered promises of eternity and beyond, evoking a sense of pure bliss that soared toward the heavens.

Lying there beside him, I chuckled, knowing that this was the love that would last a lifetime.

My heart beats with a fierce, unconditional love for Saint, yet fear grips me tight.

"Wow, you do love this man." she asserts with a heavy sigh. "I don't know..." I trailed off, pinching the bridge of my nose. "Maybe I'm afraid because it's difficult to imagine someone being in love with me." I scoff. "I can't even picture myself loving myself if I hadn't met Saint," I utter, tears not beginning to shimmer in my eyes.

Nirali's shoulder sag, and her eyes soften in sorrow. "Awh babe, I think you feel this way because you had to endure a lot of hate in your past, which caused these insecurities," she states, setting her glass down and around the counter as she stands in front of me.

"Irena, look at me," she demands gently, and I lift my gaze, meeting her beautiful brown eyes.

A single tear caressed my cheek, and Nirali blindly brushed it away. When she realized that she had touched me, fear framed her eyes.

"Loving yourself can be challenging at times, but the alternative of not loving yourself and believing that you are unworthy of love is an even tougher battle. You must end the self-deprecation caused by your past. Irena, from the moment I met you, it was evident that we were kindred spirits, and we were. The universe dwells within you, and you are a truly stunning, empathetic, resilient, and genuinely extraordinary person. Your wounds are finally beginning to heal, not simply because of the aid of Saint, but because you have allowed them to mend themselves. Though your cuts and bruises may leave scars-" she stops and glances at the faint marks on my wrist before returning her gaze to mine, a tiny smile playing on her lips. "These scars serve as a reminder to you of the abyss that you fell into- the one where you suffocated yourself, convinced that you'd be lost forever. And then, unexpectedly, someone shared their love with you, and from there, it transformed into something even more beautiful."

"When you truly accept yourself for who you are, you'll be ready to tell him. Together, you'll embark on a wild and magical adventure, with your souls twirling amongst the shining cosmos. It'll be a beautiful chaos, filled with endless possibilities and infinite love."

A lone teardrop traced its path down my face as Nirali tenderly brushed it away, her touch tentative and hesitant. Upon realizing her action, a glimmer of fear flickered in her eyes.

"I I'm-I-uh I'm sorry-" Without a word, I embraced her tightly, cutting off her apology mid-sentence. She stood still momentarily, her muscles taut with surprise, before melting into my arms and returning the embrace with all her might.

"It's fine," I assure her, and she relaxes, pulling away. I breathe out and smile. "How have you been? You seem distant lately."

Nirali bites her lower lip and sighs, and I search her eyes. "Nirali?" I ask, my voice gentle with concern. Nirali starts to tear up, quickly wiping away her tears and forcing a smile. "I'm sorry, forget about it," she says, and I shake my head. "Hey, hey, talk to me, love," I urge, taking her hand in mine.

Nirali nibbles on her lower lip. "You know Abel and I have been trying to conceive, right?" she asks, and I nod as she continues. "Well, I recently found out that I'm unable to have children," she blurts out, and my heart sinks. "Who else knows about this?" I ask, shocked. "Just Saint. I haven't told Abel yet," she admits, and my eyebrows furrow at the mention of Saint. She notices and weakly smiles. "I know. I would have told you, but you have so much going on. I don't want to burden you with my problems."

"No, Nirali. Don't think like that. You're my friend, and I would drop everything to listen to your problems," I reassure her. "This is a difficult time for you, and you need all the support you can get, especially from Abel," I tell her, and she nibbles on her lower lip. "What if-" I shake my head, interrupting her. "Stop thinking about the 'what ifs'. He is your husband, and he loves you unconditionally. Your inability to conceive won't change the love he has for you. Not now, not ever."

I smile softly as I meet her gentle gaze. "You are a strong woman, Nirali.

Emotionally and physically. But with this, you shouldn't face it alone. I advise you to push away that nagging voice and tell him. Together, you can explore other alternatives. Hold onto that glimmer of hope, and maybe, by some miracle, you'll become the wonderful mother you're meant to be," I state as I watch her tears trickle down her face.

I extend my hand and brush away the tears. Immediately, she lures me into a hug.

"I love you, Nirali," I murmured into her hair, overwhelmed by my gratitude for her unwavering friendship.

"I love you, Irena. Thank you for being you." As her head nestles onto my shoulder, her muscles surrender into a sweet surrender. "I really needed that," she murmurs, and my heart blooms joyfully. A woman like Nirali does not deserve this type of pain, and as her friend, I'll do everything I can to support and give her comfort through this difficult journey.

The path to true self-love starts here, and once I am sure I can rely on myself emotionally, I will share my feelings with Saint.

CHAPTER 49

IRENA NOWAK

Three days later

With a tune on my lips and a twirl in my step, I go to the kitchen to whip up some chocolate chip cookies. The counter is littered with a few stray utensils, but I pay them no mind, for the melody that fills the air from my classical playlist far outshines any mess.

As I whisk away at the eggs with effortless grace, I tie up my hair in a messy bun, my white sweatshirt hugging my frame. A true baker's outfit.

Lost in my baking haven, my phone's ringing jolts me out of my reverie - the caller ID reads "Saint". Untethering it from the counter, I answer.

"Bonjour biche," a rich, velvety voice murmurs, sending shivers down my spine.

"Hej kochanie," I answer, his chuckle causing my heart to flutter.

Every molecule of his being has a hypnotic hold on me. "How is my beautiful wife doing?" he questions. "Well, your wife is baking some cookies," I tell him, and he sighs.

"Have I mentioned that you're the most extraordinary baker in existence? I'd do anything for those fresh, mouth-watering cookies right now." he laments, eliciting a light chuckle from me. "I'm flattered Saint. When you return, I'll happily whip up another batch and serve them to you hot off the oven," I assure him as I expertly mix the eggs with other wet ingredients. The tantalizing aroma of the dough diffuses through the kitchen, a delicious testament to my culinary prowess.

"Well, I would love that very much, but I'd prefer you bake with only an apron on and feed me while I fuck you on the kitchen counter." As he utters those words, I freeze, my cheeks ablaze with a surge of warmth that spreads deep into my body. "I'd appreciate you having your sex talk in the other room, Saint.

I'm working here." As I listen to Abel's grumblings echoing in the bellowing background, my chuckles escape with a sweet taste of blush.

Amid distant shuffles and the thud of a door shutting, he smoothly interrupts our conversation. "Ignore him. But let me continue my promise of how badly I want to fuck you while you innocently offer me your cookies..."

Despite being completely alone, an unsettling sense of unease washed over me. I couldn't help but clasp my thighs together and nibble on my lower lip as his words sent my imagination into overdrive.

It hit me then… Nirali's words had been eerily prophetic. My insatiable lust for Saint had transformed me into an absolute sex fiend. I craved him like nothing else. You do become a sex addict once you're doing it with someone you can't get enough of.

I can't help but let out a mischievous laugh at the mere thought. "Well, if I may say, I'd love that very much. Can you imagine the heavenly aroma wafting from the kitchen as I stand, wearing only an adorable apron? I'll be perched on the kitchen counter with my legs wrapped around you while you energetically thrust into me, all while I feed you piping-hot cookies fresh out of the oven." I taunt playfully, barely able to contain my excitement." I tease, "Fuck, Irena are you trying to get my balls blue," I shrug, acknowledging that he can't see me, and respond, "You started the conversation; I'm just assisting you in visualizing it."

He groans, making me grin like a crazy person. I gently set the ingredients bowl down and saunter over to the cabinet, eagerly reaching for the sack of baking flour. A sultry voice breaks through the silence as I measure the perfect amount.

"I miss you," he whispers, stirring up a flurry of butterflies in my stomach. A smile spreads as I respond, "I miss you too. Just two more days until you're back in my arms."

As I extracted the luscious bar of chocolate from the frosty fridge, I took an impulsive stride toward the counter, my fingers grazing over the shiny handles of the knife holder. My thoughts drifted briefly to a sizzling time here Saint used the knife on me. I shook my head and peeled away from the tantalizing reverie. Swiftly, I selected a different blade with a sleek steel handle, clearing my throat to banish any lingering diverting thoughts. With deft motions, I settled the rich bar of chocolate onto the smooth chopping board, ready to masterfully slice it into delectable pieces. "Oh, so you've been keeping track? I'm thrilled to devour your cookies and you, of course," he proclaims, and I can't help but shake my head. "Psh, I've been having a blast while you were away," I fib.

"Have you been pleasuring yourself?" he asks, his voice tinged with a yearning that inflates my confidence. "Yes. Every night, I've sprawled out on the bed with my legs spread and fucked myself," I tease, and he lets out an agonized growl, an expletive slipping past his lips.

"Do you hear that?" I asked Saint, my tone laced with worry. His voice turned serious as he quizzed me, "Who do you think it is?" I hastily dusted my fingers and laid the gleaming knife on the counter. "I have no idea," I replied, my heart pounding uncertainly. "Are you expecting someone?" He asks. "No."

As I tug on the door handle, my heart plummets, and I am met with a familiar set of piercing blue eyes. My uncle Krzysztof grins devilishly, clad in a nonchalant grey suit that hangs off his chiselled physique as he holds a large black envelope in one hand.

My throat tightens as I stutter, "W-what are you doing here?" Suspicion ripples through me as I observe him adjusting his tie with practised ease.

"I just came to check in on my favourite niece, and it seems you're doing quite well," he responds smoothly, casting a slow appraisal over my form that sends shivers down my spine. Only when our eyes meet do I realize I've been caught in his wicked game.

"And I have a meeting with your husband Saint. Is he here?" he questioned. "No, but he will be back soon. I'll let him know you dropped by." I lied, though my reasons were unclear. Maybe I didn't want to reveal that Saint was out of the country, or perhaps I found it odd that he hadn't rescheduled the meeting.

So Krzysztof is lying.

His foot halts my progress as I attempt to close the door, and he forcefully nudges it back open. "I'm in no rush, not to mention the snowstorm outside is ferocious. Besides, the way the snow is sprinting down outside is hardly optimal for a slick drive back to my penthouse. The roads are just asking for an accident. Best to stay put," he elaborates, casually sauntering in. My throat cleared uncomfortably, and the entire room became tense as the atmosphere shifted.

"Finally, now that we're alone, I have the opportunity to catch up with you," he stated, and I forced a smile while pursing my lips.

Noticing that I had forgotten my phone in the kitchen, I lead him there but remembered that Saint was still on the phone. "Would you like some water?" I inquired.

Krzysztof rejects my offer of kindness, tossing the envelope on the counter. "Why are you here Krzysztof?" I question. He cocks his head to the side, grinning mischievously. "I'm here for Saint," he replies, his tone dripping with insincerity.

I refused to believe his words and crossed my arms in defiance. "You're lying."

His expression remained unfazed. "Ah, the disrespectful back- talking is still your go-to defence mechanism, I see." Despite the fear that began to take hold in my chest, I refused to let him see me falter. My heart was pounding, but I held my composure.

"I am not being disrespectful. I merely expressed my personal belief that you may be untruthful. It is important to understand the difference." I assertively declare.

With a deep breath, Krzysztof slowly advanced towards me. But I refused to budge an inch as I met his intense stare head-on. He paused a few feet away from me.

"Hmm, Irena, Irena, Irena." tsking my name and shaking his head in disappointment. "Careful now, sweet Irena," he warned, his voice laced with an imposing tone, "you wouldn't want to see what happens when you cross me again, would you?" A wave of rage washed over me as he trailed off, and I could feel the fiery passion bubbling beneath my skin.

"Allow me to jog your memory, Krzysztof. I am no fragile maiden and certainly do not quiver at the mere sight of you. If you have come seeking a brawl, rest assured, the consequences will be yours to bear, not mine. After all, you wouldn't fancy ending up like poor Grzegorz, would you now? My husband may take matters into his own hands and teach you a lesson for your impetuous intrusion." My words were laced with icy authority as I clarified who held the real power in this scenario. "Maybe he'll cut your tongue out worse, kill you." Krzysztof merely chuckled with a hint of amusement dancing in his eyes. My voice is laced with a dark warning as I confront Krzysztof. "You know he'll be back, so it's probably best for your safety if you leave now." But Krzysztof doesn't seem to take me seriously. His eyebrow raised smugly. "Last I heard, he's still in America. Should I ring him up? Saint! Saint!" he calls out mockingly, his words ringing in a deafening silence. Suddenly, his tone changes, and he approaches me menacingly. "To be honest, I'm here to warn your precious husband. He will regret it if he doesn't pull through on our deal."

The words are barely out of his mouth before he grabs my hair, brutally slamming me onto the kitchen counter. As I looked on, my view became hazy, with specks dancing before my eyes as a persistent buzz droned in my ear. My sight faltered, and I staggered back, sensing a warm trickling that went down my cheek.

"You, my dear, are his weakness. With you in our grasp, we can attain anything from him." He declared, seizing my throat as his grip tightened.

As the glint of the knife caught my peripheral vision, I lunged for it and launched myself at my uncle with a ferocity that felt like wildfire coursing through my veins. In a frenzy of rage and adrenaline, I let out primal screams that reverberated off the walls as I relentlessly stabbed him, his skin yielding to the sharp blade with each brutal strike.

FUCKYOU!
STAB
FUCKYOU!
STAB
KYOU!
STAB
FUCKYOU
STAB
FUCKYOU!
STAB
FUCKYOU!
STAB
FUCKYOU!
STAB
FUCKYOU!
STAB
CKYOU! *STAB*
FUCKYOU!
FUCKYOU!

His chest ripped, ribs broke, and pulled out with violence. He gasped, his eyes bulging in disbelief. From his open mouth came gurgling, sputtering sounds. He wanted to cry out for help, but he could get no volume. The soft melody from earlier still played, a cruel juxtaposition to his fiery agony.

The pungent aroma of iron and the sound of flesh yielding to my blade around the air in my lungs.

Gasping for air, my eyes filling with tears, my head throbs with excruciating pain. His overpowering strength keeps me in place despite my efforts to push him back. "You're nothing without him," he sneers, his voice dripping with venom. "Always have been and always will be. Just a pathetic girl responsible for the death of her parents doomed to never find love."

For a moment, I nearly lose consciousness. But then my eyes fall on the knife, still lying on the counter from when I'd been chopping chocolate. With a desperate grab, I snatch it up and de- liver a deep, swift wound to his gut before finishing him off with a vicious kick to the balls.

As Krzysztof falls, coughing and helpless, I refuse to hesitate. With the blade still in hand, I repeatedly stab him, venting all my anger and pain into each piercing blow.

"ROT IN HELL!" I scream plunging the knife into his soft rip- ping flesh.

Blood painted my face and clothes. My every nerve was electrified by the adrenaline coursing through my veins. His throat was the final strike, and I watched as his life seeped from his body, terror-stricken eyes locked in my gaze until the very end.

With a heavy exhale, I let the knife fall, crimson drops cascading from my features as I rose to my full height. I snatched the phone from the nearby counter, only to find the line was still open.

My trembling hand raises the phone to my ear, hearing his frantic voice on "Irena, Irena, speak to me. Are you alright!!?" His words oozing with concern. With a quivering voice, I respond. "Saint," I whisper hoarsely, causing the weight on his chest to dissipate.

His tone lightens with relief. "Thank God. Irena, are you okay?" My eyes dart to the lifeless body at my feet. Krzysztof cold, dead gaze meets mine, surrounded by a crimson puddle.

Taking a deep breath, I confess, "He's dead, Saint."

CHAPTER 50

IRENA NOWAK

"You fucking pieces of shit you had one job! One fucking job!" Perched atop the stool like a bird of prey, I couldn't pry my gaze away from the macabre display of blood that clung to every surface. My hand - stained scarlet, left a grim reminder of the deadly exchange that had taken place.

"He showed me evidence that his family, sir," the guard stuttered, his eyes wide with terror. But Saint only laughed, a low, wicked sound that reverberated through the silent room, his fingers tracing the rough scratch of my stubble face.

Saint's piercing gaze locked onto the security guard as he demanded, "Recall the instructions I delivered to you before I took off?" His tone was full of fury and impatience. As the guard coughed nervously, Saint pressed on, "Restrict entry to only the family members who have previously been here."

He didn't stop there. "Can you find any indication of Krzysztof Nowak visiting through the sign-in logs?" The guard shook his head negatively. This only made Saint's anger flare up further. "Use your fucking words!" he snarled.

Saint's grip tightened on the guard's shirt as he pulled him nearer. "You're lucky that she's still breathing, but, unfortunately,
I entrusted you to keep her safe, only to find out she suffered an injury to the head." He gritted his teeth as he spoke, a dangerous glint in his eyes. "I-I'm sorry sir I promise it won't happen again," he asserts.

"I know you won't." With a low growl rumbling in his chest, he shoves the guard away with a force that leaves him stumbling. "Thank you si-" The grateful words that were about to spill from the man's lips never see the light of day, cut short by Saint's sinister actions. In one fluid movement, he draws his gun from its holster and fires three quick shots into the hapless guard's skull. The sound of the man's body hitting the floor reverberates through the room, and Saint barely flinches as a spray of blood splatters across his face. With the weapon safely back in its rightful place, he strides over to me, his movements both fluid and menacing.

There he stands, nestled between my parted legs, lowering his head to rest on my thighs.

"I'm so sorry, Doe." His soft murmur grazes my ears as I remain motionless, transfixed upon the crimson blood of Krzysztof on the floor.

Suddenly, Saint withdraws, his hand reaching up to delicately grasp my chin, coaxing my gaze towards him. "Are you okay?" he queries with tender concern.

I slice my gaze to him, and his eyes soften when we make eye contact.

My mind was swirling with uncertainty. Was everything okay? My heart thudded in my chest, and I couldn't shake the ominous words that had just been spoken. "I don't know if I'm okay. He said he wanted to kill me, Saint, that all my uncles promise to kill me if you don't fulfil your end of the deal." My brows furrowed. "What deal, Saint?" I ask, voice shaking.

He gazed at me, an edge in his eyes that I couldn't quite place. "It's a dangerous world, Irena. Everyone has their motives." His hand brushed my cheek gently, a stark contrast to the grimness of our conversation. "But I won't let anything happen to you. You're everything to me."

My pulse was racing, and my thoughts were in disarray. What kind of deal had he gotten himself into? And what could I do to help? I knew I had to trust him, but the gravity of his words weighed heavily on me like a dark cloud hovering above. It was just business, he said, but things were never that simple when it came to family. And I was right in the middle of it. "I am afraid I've only made things worse by killing Krzysztof Saint," I confess, my voice trembling with fear. The weight of danger now rests heavily upon us both. Saint shakes his head, his reassuring gaze com- forting me. "Do not worry, Doe, I will ensure nothing harms you," he assures me. My emotions bubble up inside me, threatening to overflow like a violent tsunami.

Suddenly, I blurt out the insecurity that has been gnawing at me for far too long. "Do you think I am worthy of love?" Saint looks at me with concern, furrowing his brow. "Why would you doubt your worth?" I shrug, feeling foolish for even asking. "It's nothing, forget I said anything," I mumble through my tears, brushing them away hastily.

"Irena, do you know the depths of love I hold for you?" he whispers, staring into my eyes with a passion that ignites a flame. "Words fail me, my heart overflowing with adoration for you. In my eyes, you're the shining star that lights up my world, and for as long as I exist, you'll always be my cherished one. Nothing can break the bond we share. It's unbreakable, unshakable, as pure as the divine heavens above us." He takes my hand, caressing it with tenderness and a loving smile. "You're deserving of all the love in the world, Doe. You always have been and always will be. Don't you believe any lies or hurtful words your uncles uttered? You are a treasure, a gem that shines brighter than the sun itself."

With his soothing words, a sense of comfort washes over me, my quivering lips now no longer trembling but curved upwards in a smile. My eyes quickly dart to the envelope that Krzysztof brought. I silently wondered what were the secrets that were hidden in the file. Gently, he kisses away my tears, distracting me from the curiosity that is eating me up. His lips trailing a path of sweet kisses, filling me with a warmth that envelops me entirely. My lips meet, a melting of hearts as if nothing else in the world existed but this moment.

"Do you ever feel like this world is just too much?" he asks, his eyes piercing mine. I nod, knowing exactly what he means. "What you need, Doe, is a break. A chance to escape, to find peace in solitude." His hand reaches out to hold mine. "I have the perfect place in mind. Let me have the maids pack your bags, and we'll disappear together, just you and me." A smile spreads across my face as I lean in, my hand resting on his neck. "Yes, let's go," I whisper. He gently kisses my cheek before enfolding me in a warm embrace.

As I gazed out the passenger window of the Range Rover, I felt as though I had been transported into a winter fairytale. The trees bowed elegantly under the weight of the snow, causing an arc of glittering crystals to powder the ground. The azure blue sky was a dazzling backdrop for the pristine skiing conditions, making it difficult to contain my excitement for the upcoming weekend at the cosy log cabin with Saint. My attention shifted to the side of Saint's chiselled jawline, and I was struck once again by his remarkable handsomeness.

It was almost surreal to believe that he was my partner and that our relationship was thriving with each passing day.

"Almost there," he murmured, his eyes fixed on the winding, snow-covered road ahead. "Are you ready for some excitement?"

"Excitement?" I echoed. "Skiing," he grinned mischievously. "Oh, right. Of course," I replied, my heart quickening with anticipation.

His expression softened. "I'm sorry about Krzysztof. I'll make sure that I take your mind off of it."

"It's alright," I reassured him. "But I am looking forward to skiing." He placed a reassuring hand on my knee. "Me too, and once we reach the cabin - secluded and serene -with a crackling log fire and a plush fur rug, I plan to keep you naked and writhing in pleasure for the entire weekend."

"I'm not sure about that," I felt a flutter in my chest, and my stomach tensed.

Whenever Saint mentioned anything sexual or what he wanted to do with me, I couldn't help but react this way. He was phenomenal in bed, the best I've ever had. With him, I never had to worry about not reaching a climax; it was only a matter of how many times. His thick cock always brought me to orgasm, and he had great finesse with his fingers and mouth too.

I shifted in my seat. Oh God, I need help. Just a few hours ago, I killed my uncle, and now I'm feeling aroused while sitting next to Saint. I need to control myself.

As he navigated the winding road, he took a moment to trace his fingers up my soft thigh before firmly grasping the steering wheel again. Finally reaching our destination, I eagerly donned my cosy black earmuffs and slung my skis over my shoulder, noticing that Saint had followed suit with his jacket left ajar.

The light snowfall, rustling branches, and frigid air failed to mar our excitement as we made our way through the wintry landscape. The crunching snow beneath our steps was like music to our ears. "I adore this," I proclaimed, grinning from ear to ear as we journeyed deeper into the frosty forest. "Me too. I came here in my early twenties to escape the world."

"I wouldn't blame you. It's so peaceful here." Grieving the path to the lodge was impossible, with the path wholly covered. "Are you sure we won't get lost?" I questioned, and Saint chuckled.

"I know it like the back of my hand," he reassures. As we strolled shoulder to shoulder, a sudden rustling jolted me, and I turned my head to spot a feathered beauty flitting about the branches to my right. A flurry of snow it dislodged sparkled in its wake, cascading to the ground like a cascade of glittering jewels.

"How wonderful. I feel a million miles from Paris. And it's so quiet, too. Peaceful."

"Come on, we still have a long way ahead of us." My weary groan melted into a contented sigh as Saint led me deeper into the mountain, chatting effortlessly about nothing. He had been right all along. The crisp air and breathtaking scenery had done wonders for my frazzled mind. I laughed and bantered with him as we ascended, forgetting all my troubles. We reached the top quickly, and the stunning winter vista took my breath away. A wide smile spread as I took it all in, grateful for Saint's thoughtful gesture. There's nothing quite like the rush of knowing you're about to defy gravity, soaring to nearly two miles high on a crickety seat dangling from a cable before rocketing down on a pair of skinny plastic strips. The entire ski experience is a thrill ride that starts with the chair lift, culminates at the peak, and then picks up speed on the way down. At the bottom, I gaze up at the colossal mountain that tested my skills. I snap my boots into my skis, clutch the poles, and slice through the pack toward the chairlift. Excitement buzzes through the crowd- some, like me, are eager to conquer run after run, while others feel trepidatious, facing the slopes for the first time.

"Are you okay?" Saint asks, his cheeks rosy from the nippy air, his beanie, goggles, and heavy clothes snuggling his body as a shield against the wind. I'm a bit nervous, to be honest," I reply. "Don't worry," he assures me. I'll stick by your side and keep you safe."

"Just you and me," I beam, feeling my jittery nerves settle as our camaraderie fills the chilly mountain air. "We're going to have a blast!" A shiver of apprehension ran down my spine as I gazed upon the lost belongings scattered amidst the snow. The mere thought of my skiing poles slipping from my grasp scurried through my mind, arousing my anxiety. Nevertheless, as we glided upwards, I was astounded by the expanse of the sloping terrain that steadily revealed itself. Initially, the skiers and snowboarders below us implausibly appeared in no hurry as they lei- surely slalomed down the incline. However, as we climbed higher, so did the proficiency and swiftness of those descending. As our ascent continued, the shroud of trees that once shielded us from the biting wind faded away, and we were mercilessly bombarded by it, leaving us feeling like hundreds of needles were pricking us.

Despite the distractions, my thoughts are captivated by the skiers and snowboarders deftly carving their way down the mountain. My heart quickens as I recall my own thrilling descents from past trips. As the chair lift reaches the summit, I dismount gracefully and pivot toward the path I've plotted. Despite the biting cold, I barely feel it beneath the multitude of clothing layers embracing me. The mountain was blanketed by a vast blue sky, which held the sun like a shiny medal above it. Sunlight poured into the valley, making colours sparkle and radiate with life. Beneath the sky, a sea of pure white snow stretched like a sheet, tempting the lift sitters with its serene beauty. As eyes roamed further, the snow became scarce, leaving jagged rocks and blemishes.

It was early winter, and the snow was a delight to behold. It seemed to embrace every inch of the mountain, covering its scars and flaws while enhancing its beauty. Rusty red rocks and gentle brown hues peeked out from beneath the snow, painting a picture of contrast and harmony. Young trees emerged from the snow as if bursting from their cribs with vigour and eagerness. Even resilient weeds refused to be silenced, becoming the mountain's unshaven stubble.

Nature and weather were locked in a fierce battle, but their efforts yielded nothing short of extraordinary beauty. Looking out at this spectacle, it was a battle to be forever remembered.

Gazing in wonderment, a chilling breeze danced through my locks. The aroma of fresh pine sent my senses on a journey as I took in the breathtaking panorama of untamed terrain. With my sturdy boots anchored in the snow, a tremble crept over my body. But as I gracefully glided through the pristine powder, calmness transformed into invigorating gusts, tinting my cheeks rosy. The adrenaline rush proved a potent cure for the frigid bite of ice and frost. The living metaphor couldn't have been more conspicuous- my inner warmth and ebullient spirit were my best allies.

As I picked up the pace, the wind was a formidable foe, pushing with all its might, but my trusty jacket thwarted its malevolent designs. A quick glance and I saw Saint, emboldened by the sheer joy of skiing. For him, it was nothing short of his raison deter, lighting up his world just that little bit more.

As we reach the end, my heart races excitedly, and Saint suddenly appears by my side. I remove my goggles with a beaming smile, followed by Saint, who does the same.

"Absolutely breathtaking," I exclaimed, still catching my breath. Saint pulls me towards him and places a tender kiss on my forehead, his touch sending shivers down my spine. "Shall we walk to the cabin?" he proposes, leading me into the forest's depths, the trees towering over us like ancient guardians.

As we go through the wilderness, I notice a structure peeking through the trees. As we draw closer, the cabin comes into full view. It has a snow-covered roof, windows that look like glittering jewels, and a chimney that pokes at the sky like a proud soldier.

"It's magnificent," I breathe in awe. It's like something out of a Christmas fairytale." He took my hand. We're going to have a great time."

"I know." "Starting now?"

"What?" He set down his skis. "Doe, here you can make all the noise you want, and only the deer and birds can hear you," he utters, his gaze darkening sinfully. I flustered.

I gazed into his striking green eyes, flecked with glints of gold and bursting with an unmistakable passion. I had grown accustomed to deciphering his thoughts, and it was clear that his mind was fixated on one thing. "You're thinking about sex, aren't you?"

"Guilty as charged." My laughter filled the crisp air as I raised my hand to catch a snowflake.

"So, we'll stand under here." He took my skis from me and stepped towards the cabin under the wooden overhang. "And I promise you won't be cold."

"Saint," I warn. "Okay, what if someone comes and sees us?" As we stood there, engulfed in a sea of serenity, he gazed off into the distance with a casual air. "No one can hear us, my love. We're miles away from any prying ears."

He gently wrapped his arms around me, pulling me closer into his embrace. As his warm breath graced the nape of my neck, I inhaled the spicy scent of his cologne, sending shivers down my spine. "But what if..." I began to say before he silenced me with a tender kiss on my neck. Then, he gradually lowered himself to plant a kiss on my chest.

As his lips trailed over my skin, my nipple perked up, and my pussy ignited with a fiery hunger for him. His touch was electric, sending bolts of pleasure straight to my core. I yearned for more of him, craving everything he offered me.

I ran my hands over his hair and then to his cheeks. "A dog walker might come by or..."

"I've never known anyone to just show up here." He kissed me, his mouth soft, his dark stubble brushing my chin. "But I promise I'll keep a lookout."

I kissed him back, stroking my tongue onto his.

"You won't regret it," he murmured, his voice low but a playful smile dancing on his lips.

"I know." I grinned.

As his lips met mine once more, I felt a jolt of desire surge through me. His hands eagerly cupped my breasts, and the absence of a bra only heightened the thrill. Peeking through the fabric of my top, my nipples were taunting him to continue his exploration.

With each kiss and nibble, I became more and more breathless. My fingers greedily clung to his jacket, my yearning building to a fever pitch. There was no denying it, my panties were already saturated with lust, and there was no turning back.

He declared, "You're incredibly irresistible," and held me tightly as our lips collided in a passionate kiss. "I won't ever lose my desire for you."

"Good." I encircled my arms around his neck and pressed myself against him, detecting the outline of his erect cock beneath our clothes.

He let out a low growl and pulled me nearer. "Fuck Doe" he proclaimed while placing his hand into the waistband of my black pants.

I parted my legs and relished the sensation of his cool fingertips sliding under my panties to touch me. "Oh... Saint." I breathed out.

"Hot and wet, just how I like you," he murmured, stroking my pussy. "I need you." "Come closer," he commanded, his voice low and seductive. As I turned to face the cabin, every nerve in my body was alive with excitement. My back pressed against the cool, rough-hewn wood, my heart pounding in my chest.

With a swift movement, he had my trousers down around my knees, and the cool air rushed over my bare skin like a wave. I felt his eyes on me, drinking in the sight of my curves and contours.

"You have the sexiest ass I've ever seen," he breathed, his voice full of heat and desire. His teeth nipped at my skin, and I moaned softly, relishing the sensation.

As he pushed my white bodysuit aside, his fingers tracing the curve of my hip, I knew that I was his. The anticipation was almost unbearable, but I couldn't wait to feel him inside me, taking me to the heights of passion.

With an exclamation of pleasure, I felt him kneel behind me, his mouth kissing and caressing my butt cheeks with fervour. The sensations sent shivers through my body and set my arousal ablaze. His lips and tongue explored every inch of my curves, making me moan and tremble in delight.

"Saint," I whispered, my voice cracking with desire. "Please, don't stop."

He didn't. Instead, he gently parted my ass to reveal the warmth between my thighs. His hot breath teased my most intimate areas and I gasped as his kisses grew deeper, more intense. I lost myself in the wicked pleasure, my body bucking and writhing against him.

And then, his tongue was on me, delving deep into my sex with sinfully erotic precision. I cried out, my senses consumed by the rawest pleasure I had ever felt. My pussy ached for more, for more of Saint's incredible touch.

He tipped me forward, his eyes devouring me as he took in my flushed, wet body. "You're so beautiful," he murmured, his fingers finding my clit and sending me over the edge. I moaned, my entire being consumed by waves of pure bliss.

"Yes," I panted. "Ah, Saint. More." And he gave it to me, every sensual inch of his body dedicated to fulfilling my deepest desires. With each touch, each kiss, each thrust, I lost myself in the rapture of his passion, utterly and completely consumed by ecstasy.

My body shook with an intensity that threatened to bring me to my knees, my toes curling within the confines of my sneakers. The sensation of his deft fingers working my clit in small, rapid circles sent me spiralling toward ecstasy. His tongue was abruptly replaced by four fingers, plunging deep into my innermost depths.

This was only the beginning of what I craved; I surrendered completely to his cadence, uncaring of who might witness our passion. With my back arched sinfully and my pants pulled down around my ankles, my bare ass presented to him, my husband continued to work his fingers relentlessly, driving me to the brink of insanity.

As he moaned in pleasure, I felt every fibre of my being grows weak, the need driving me to the brink of collapse. His voice, gravelly with desire, wafted to my ear. "Do you want me, baby?" he breathed, his arms wrapping solidly around my waist.

The plea was all it took to send me tumbling over the edge. I gasped and moaned breathlessly, barely holding on as pleasure overtook all of my senses.

"Yes, please."

The velvety head of his engorged cock pressed against my entrance, radiating intense heat. The urge to feel him inside me was insatiable, and he reciprocated my eagerness, plunging deep with one audacious thrust. The slippery wetness that coated me made it an effortless descent.

He groaned in pleasure, "My God, you're amazing. So hot, so tight."

Cupping my breast in one hand, he gripped my hip with the other, setting a ferocious, unrelenting tempo. Each time he with- drew from me, I was left breathless until he plunged back in, jolly my entire body.

"I want everyone to hear how good I make you feel," he grunt- ed in my ear, urging me to stand, back to his chest with his entire length still inside me.

"Scream out how amazing this is."

"I thought you said no one comes around here." I managed to say.

"I lied."

My senses took flight as if I were traversing a constellation a cosmic explosion igniting every inch of me. And while I wasn't furious in the slightest, I was giddy with anticipation at the possibility of being caught.

"Oh my..." My breath hitched as his fingers deftly sought out my pleasure center. Writhing under his spell, I surrendered willingly. The intoxicating grip he had on me, like I was his to claim, made the heat in my body surge.

The pressure built within my core, my sensitive nub expanding, the brink of ecstasy teasing me.

Undeterred, he focused on his task with unwavering determination, urging my release to spill forth with each passing moment.

With a shuddering cry, I gasped in the frigid air, knowing that the moment of no return had arrived. The intensity grew, and my body ignited like a roaring inferno. Ecstasy coursed from my clitoris down to my aching core, urging me on to the ultimate peak.

"Sweetheart," he whispered, skilfully working my swollen bud, inching me closer and closer to the edge. With an explosive release, I collapsed into his strong arms, my body convulsing with unrivalled pleasure.

His breaths were short and fervent as he hugged me tight, never wanting to let go. I was still gasping for air, but would forever remember this moment of pure rapture.

"You're incredible," he breathed hoarsely.

Lost in a whirlwind of passion, I turned to face him, my cheeks flushed with excitement. And then, I whispered those words that I never thought I'd say.

"I want you... to come."

"I'm going to, but it's all about you Doe."

With a gentle touch, he cradled my breast, sending waves of cool pleasure across my heated flesh. Our bodies intertwined in a symphony of ecstasy, as we surrendered to the indescribable sensations that consumed us both.

With renewed vigour, he plunged his rock-hard dick deep inside of me. Each thrust sent aftershocks coursing through my body, my pussy still tightly gripping him. As his pace quickened, I could feel his impending release. His cock was throbbing and steely, his breaths coming in jagged gasps.

He sucked in the air faster, his eyes screwed tightly shut as he blissfully fucked me. His cheeks had flushed deep red, and his grip on the back of my neck grew tighter. Suddenly, another burst of pleasure overtook him. He cried out unholy praise to the heavens, thrusting deep inside of me as hot liquid spilled out and mixed with my own release.

Exhausted and spent, Saint held me close, his still-erect member buried deep within me. "I could stay like this forever," he whispered in my ear, wrapping his arms tightly around me. I giggled in response, utterly content in his embrace.

"Come on, let's take this inside," he murmurs, catching me off guard as Saint effortlessly lifts me up, our bodies still intertwined as we make our way to the cozy cabin. His lips pressed against mine with fervour, an insatiable hunger driving us forward.

CHAPTER 51

IRENA NOWAK

A blissful hush enveloped the cabin, the only sound being the warm and comforting crackle of the fireplace. The gentle flickering of the flames illuminated Saint, and I nestled cosily beneath a thick, fluffy blanket.

"Tell me," I prompted, gazing up at Saint with genuine curiosity. "What's your favourite memory of us?"

Saint's honey-green eyes glimmered in the light of the fire as he pondered my question, his face buried in his hands.

"There are so many..." he mused before flashing me an impish grin. "But if I had to pick just one, it'd be anytime we fucked the life out of each other."

I groaned in jest, playfully swatting him on the arm. "Ugh, come on! Give me a real answer."

A smile of contentment stole over Saint's face as he fell deep into thought.

"Well, I remember a moment when I was playing the piano with you. It's like we became these raw, unguarded versions of ourselves..." his voice trailed off wistfully, and a tender smile slowly spread across my face.

"Turns out I love watching you sleep," I tell him almost half the truth.

Saint gently brushes my cheek with the pad of his thumb. "Not to be cliché or anything, but I also love to watch you sleep. You, on the other hand, drool like a baby." He teases, and my cheeks flush from embarrassment. Pushing his hand off, I lightly slap him on the shoulder.

"No, I do not."

He scoffs.

However, he continues mocking my sleeping habits, even going so far as to imitate me in slumber. I push him away but cannot help but giggle as he rewards me with a melodious laugh, his eyes crinkling with joyful mirth.

Nothing is more delightful than basking in this man's warmth and affection, even in the quiet moments of rest. I was utterly captivated, unable to peel my eyes away from him as he was consumed by his infectious laughter. Watching him filled me with a sense of joy that I had never known before. At that moment, I understood what it meant to witness pure beauty.

His eyes glimmered like molten honey in the firelight as he pondered deeply.

"Although, I treasure every moment we've spent together," he adds. I couldn't help but chuckle, realizing we were both experiencing the same intense connection I shared, feeling his arms wrap around me. His curious gaze lingers on me as he asks, "And what about you?"

As I gaze into his eyes, a rush of memories overwhelms me, but one image stands out.

"Remember when you flew across the world just because you wanted to hold me in your arms, and I helped you fall asleep?" I trailed off, and his eyes gleamed. "How could I forget?" I lightly chuckled. "I was watching you sleep. You are an adorable sleeper with light snores; sometimes, your body twitches. I find it cute." I explained, and his cheeks flushed. "Why is it your favourite?"

Because of the realization that I was profoundly and irrevocably falling for you.

"Oh," I falter, sensing his intention. "But... we don't have the necessary ingredients..." I protest, already imagining the delightful aroma of my famous cookies. A smile dances across Saint's lips as he deftly opens the refrigerator and searches through the cupboards. My mouth drops in wonder as he produces everything I need with ease. "I must say, you're quite remarkable," I chuckled, and he responded with a smug grin. "Do you need a hand getting undressed, Doe, or should I simply admire the view?" he inquired, causing my body to tingle with excitement. "I'll let you watch, but that's all you're getting," I retorted, whisking the. It was as if time stood still as I gazed into Saint's enchanting eyes. His emerald irises shimmered like a sea of precious stones, delicately weaved with strands of golden honey. Each time he laughed, his eyes would light up like a constellation of stars, creating an other- worldly glow that radiated from within.

In his eyes, I could see the secrets of the universe and the wonder of creation. There was a magic there that I couldn't quite put into words. It felt like I was staring into eternity, and I was grateful for every second I got to bask in his presence.

Saint leans in, cupping my face as he captures my lips. He pulls me onto his lap, and my hand snakes around his neck as I deepen the kiss by tugging on his hair. He squeezes my waist, kissing me slowly and passionately. It's not the usual kisses we share. This one is different, far more intimate. Oddly, we express our love for each other through this kiss. My heartbeat slows down, and everything around us falls away. I feel like I'm floating into space while Saint and I passionately kiss.

He hoists me up quickly, seamlessly, and I melt into his tender, rose-coloured lips. "Where are you taking us?" I breathe barely above a whisper. "To the kitchen," he retorts with confidence, and before I know it, I'm perched on the inviting wooden counter. Saint withdraws, pausing in thought. "Hang on," I muse, leaning towards him curiously. "What is it?" I ask. "I want to create a new treasured moment for us," he calmly offers, deftly grabbing a cute apron embroidered with charming floral accents. A warm, rosy glow rushes to my cheeks.

I know where this is going.

I shed my clothes and threw on the apron without wasting another moment.

Saint's gaze lingered on my exposed skin as he picked up my discarded clothes and carefully placed them on a nearby chair. As he gathered the ingredients for our baking venture, I couldn't help but feel a growing desire for more than just cookies on this chilly evening. "Shall we begin?" he smirks, puffing out his chest as if leading the way was some grand feat. I couldn't help but roll my eyes, brushing past him to gather the ingredients. As I slice the butter with deft precision, Saint's palm collides with my back- side, making me yelp.

Whirling around, I hold the knife directly to his face, daring him to make another move. "Don't push your luck, Saint," I warn. With a mock salute, he sets to work on the dry ingredients whilst I fire up the stove. The unsalted butter sizzles as I brown it to perfection before pouring it over a sinful brown and white sugar mixture. Let the baking games begin. The cosy cabin was filled with a bustling bakery's warm, inviting aroma. My eyes traced Saint's skilled hands as he meticulously chopped the luscious bar of chocolate into tiny bites. Grinning to myself, I whipped the eggs, vanilla extract, and other ingredients until they combined into a silky, decadent caramel mixture.

As Saint deftly sifted the flour, baking soda, and salt, he sauntered over to my side of the kitchen. I dipped a spoon into the wet mixture, allowing Saint a taste, and his approving nod only heightened my excitement.

After some playful banter, we combined all the elements, and Saint carefully folded in the chocolate. The dough was left to rest and grow to its full potential, and once the moment arrived, I deftly shaped each cookie before placing them in the oven to bake to perfection.

Just as I turn around, Saint takes me by surprise. He twirls me around, dips me low, and plants a deep kiss on my lips before hoisting me up into his arms. As he holds me close, I can't help but grin, my hands instinctively resting on his solid chest.

But then I notice the unfairness of our situation - I'm standing there naked while he's fully dressed in a black tee and grey joggers. I pout, and Saint chuckles before giving me a quick peck on the lips and pulling off his shirt. My eyes widen as I take in his chiseled abs, and I can't help but smile in approval. "Better," I say, wrapping my arms around his neck. As I tilt my head up to meet his eyes, Saint's gaze is intense, and I can feel the weight of his words before he even speaks them. "I could stay here with you forever," he says, his voice deep and severe. "Leave everything behind and just start a new family."

I hesitate, knowing there are so many things we have to con- sider, but at the same time, there's something so tempting about the idea of starting a new life with him. "Saint..." I begin to say, but my voice trails off.

"What about...?" I never get to finish my sentence as Saint cuts me off with another kiss, his passion taking over as we both lose ourselves in the moment. "Abel can take over. I can step down. All you have to do is say the word," he announces, searching my eyes as honesty drips from his words. I frown, yet a small smile tugs at the corner of my lips.

"But you love the mafia," I told him. "Not as much as I love you, Irena." Unexpectedly, Saint drops down to one knee, leaving me speechless. My eyes enlarge as he effortlessly retrieves a small, mysterious box from his pocket. "Saint, what's going on?" I gasp, feeling as though my heart may flutter out of my chest. With gentle sincerity, he replies, "I'm doing it the right way," his gaze overflowing with adoration.

With the grace of a prince, he caresses my right hand, effortlessly removing the suffocating ring my uncle once forcefully placed on my finger. As if unwrapping a treasure, Saint unhurriedly opens the plush box before my eyes, revealing a breathtaking sight.

I gasped in amazement, astonished by the five magnificent diamonds elegantly arranged on the white gold band. The stones twinkled like stars in the night sky, enchanting me with their beauty, and I shuddered with excitement. Saint's eyes met mine, and I sensed the depth of his love for me in his gaze.

Tears of joy begin to well up in my eyes.

As my emotions surged like a tidal wave, tears cascaded down my face in a deluge. But between spasms of laughter and nods of agreement, I found the words to express my heart's desire.

"Yes!" I cried out, "I'll marry you!" Saint slipped the ring onto my finger and, with unparalleled vigour, sprang to his feet.

He pulled me close.

Is this a dream, or is it a reality?

All I know is that the ring, the diamonds, the moment... it's all perfectly fitted for me. "My dearest Irena, as I look into your eyes, I am reminded of how lucky I am to have you. Your love, friendship, and companionship lift me up and make me believe in something greater than myself. You are more than a partner to me; you are the soul mate I've searched for all my life. And so, I offer you this ring as a symbol of my commitment, not just to be with you for a day, a year, or even a decade, but for every moment of my life." He pauses, searching my eyes. "Remember when I told you that two things can have me, you and death itself well scratch that. Only you can have me, Irena; not even death can separate us." He utters, and my heart completely melts.

"I know we both eschew the idea of fairy tales, but let's not miss out on our chance to create one. I want to be your knight in shining armour – to protect and shield you from the pain that has touched your soul. I promise to you that I will stand by you no matter what, holding your hand in the storm and drying your tears when they fall."

"I will be the goofy husband that makes you laugh every day and the passionate lover that takes your breath away. Most of all, I will be the steady partner who listens to your worries, fears, and hopes. With you, I want to scale the heights of musical harmony, dance upon the rooftops of Paris, stir pots and pans while cooking up a storm, feel the sun on our faces as we drive off into the sunset, and laugh until we can no longer laugh. With you, my heart desires to create a beautiful family we could both be proud of."

"Therefore, Irena, my love, my best friend, my soul mate, let me say it: I will spend the rest of my life in your loving embrace." With that, he felt the world stand still.

"Will you marry me?"

"Yes! Yes! Yes! A thousand times yes."

"Good, because I wasn't going to take no for an answer, " he points out seriously, and I roll my eyes as a light giggle escapes my lips. Where will we even get married? When will the wedding be!?" I question as panic takes over. Relax, you told me that you'll finally feel free when you visit Tanzania," he reminds me with an impish smile. The mere mention of the lush island destination quickens my pulse.

"Wait, are we really getting married there?" I blurt out, my eyes sparkling with excitement. He nods, a low chuckle rippling through us both. "Yes, and while we're at it, why don't you finally connect with your roots and invite your long-lost family?" he suggests, his voice awash with warmth and promise.

I erupted in uncontainable euphoria, peppering his face with dozens of affectionate pecks. He chuckled, encircling me in his arms.

But my excitement was cut short as I suddenly recalled the batch of cookies baking in the oven.

Hastily slipping out of Saint's grasp, I scurried over to the stove, greeted by the toasty warmth embracing my skin and the heavenly aroma of just-baked treats.

Leaning back towards Saint with a grin etched on my face, I announced, "The cookies are finally ready!"

SAINT DÉ LEON

With a seductive sway of her hips, Irena pivots to reveal golden-brown cookies fresh from the oven. My lips curl into a smirk as I watch her exquisite form move with grace and dexterity. With nothing but an apron delicately hugging her form, my mind races with sinful thoughts of nibbling on her luscious chocolate derrière. Suddenly caught in my stare, Irena quirks a mischievous brow, shifting her weight ever so slightly.

"You have quite the staring problem," she playfully chides, offering me a plate of cookies. I simply shrug in response. "Can you blame me? You look absolutely delectable," I confess, unable to resist her charm. Irena giggles and shakes her head, her innocent smile making me weak in the knees.

With a sly grin, she coquettishly whispers, "It's time for you to taste my delicious cookies." My heart races as I know her words hold a deeper meaning.

Without hesitation, I scoop her up in my arms, balancing the plate of cookies between us, and lead us back to the couch.

Sitting on the plush couch, Irena perches herself on my lap, and I gently take the plate from her. We stare into each other's eyes as the fire crackles in the background, casting an orange glow and enveloping warmth. The air between us thickens with a passionate tension that's ready to ignite at any moment.

Irena delicately lifts a single cookie and takes a bite, eliciting a soft moan as it effortlessly dissolves in her mouth. A surge of desire courses through me in response. With her hooded gaze fixated on me, Irena gently feeds me the delectable treat. The cookie sends my taste buds into a state of bliss as its sweet and creamy flavours envelop my senses. As the last crumb passes my lips, I pull Irena closer for a tender kiss. My heart flutters as I taste the sugary sweetness on her lips. Entranced, I lift her up and draw her intimately closer.

Her sigh of satisfaction echoes against my mouth as we kiss.

"Don't stop feeding me, Irena," I whisper enticingly as she assists me in slipping out of my pants and briefs, revealing my eager erection yearning to indulge in her dripping entrance. Irena delicately presents another cookie tempting my taste buds, and in a moment of perfect synchronization, I fervently devour the treat while sinking my cock into her depths of pleasure.

Irena's body trembles with pleasure as she nibbles on her lower lip, savouring the sensation of our intimacy.

"Ride me, Doe," I whisper, and she complies with a seductive sway, feeding me her most delicious cookies. Looking into her eyes, I see a depth of emotion that suggests I am more than just a passing fancy.

In her gaze, I am her universe.

As I gaze up at her, I'm mesmerized by the way her eyebrows furrow and her lips part in a perfect O. The intensity between us is palpable as she moves slowly, savouring every moment of our intimate embrace. With my hands firmly gripping her hips, I feel a deep desire to do more than just have sex.

No, what I really crave is to connect with her on a soulful level, to become intertwined with her being in a way that transcends physical pleasure.

This is not just sex…it's an act of surrender, a merging of two souls in a dance of passion and devotion. Tonight, I don't want to just be with her - I want to become one with her in a symphony of divine ecstasy.

Our emotions were a wild blaze of passion, fuelled by the intensity of our desire for one another. As she threw herself into my arms, her every touch sent shivers down my spine. Our bodies swayed in perfect harmony, like two stars swirling in the night sky, united in a cosmic dance of love and lust.

I knew Irena was lost in the moment, as her hips rocked back and forth, pressed tightly against mine. My hands gripped her waist, feeling her every movement as if it were amplified a thousand times over. The heat between us was palpable, as we spiralled deeper and deeper into the dizzying abyss of our shared desire.

"Saint," she murmured, my name a sensual warning on her lips. I could feel her teeth nipping at my shoulder, her fingers tangled in my hair. Every inch of my skin was alive with fire, a thousand suns burning bright within me.

This was no mere physical encounter, this was a meeting of souls. A cosmic collision of two beings, fused together in a moment of pure, unadulterated bliss.

I embraced Irena fervently, my heart racing with anticipation as our climax approached.

"God, Irena, I love you so much," I whispered, overcome with emotion. She let out a primal cry of pleasure in response.

In an instant, our passion ignited like two celestial bodies colliding, creating a dazzling explosion of pure, inner bliss. It was a beautiful, chaotic dance of desire that left us both breathless and spent.

"I enjoyed the cookies," I whisper and she laughs breathlessly. "Yeah, the cookies were amazing."

We weren't talking about the cookies.

Playing the piano with Irena was like breathing in fresh air on a crisp autumn day. Our fingers aligned perfectly on the black and white keys, forming a seamless melody that captured the essence of our bond. Each note was a gentle caress on my ears, leaving me lost in a world of pure emotion.

As we continued to play, our souls became intertwined like two vines wrapped around each other. Irena's smile was evidence of the magic in the air, and I knew this moment would live forever in my heart.

Together, we allowed the music to speak for us, our eyes locked in an unspoken understanding. It was a moment that transcended time and space, a beautiful memory I knew I would one day share with our children. For at that moment, as our fingers danced across the keys, Irena and I connected in a way that only the art of music could allow.

There's something magical about playing the piano with her. It was our first exchange of words, the moment we lowered our defences and truly connected. As our fingers danced across the keys of the smooth white piano at home, I knew I had found a kindred spirit.

But it wasn't until we found ourselves nestled in our cosy cabin, surrounded by snow-capped trees and the gentle fire glow, that the true magic happened. We sat side by side, our hands effortlessly gliding over the keys of the rustic old piano. As the sweet melodies filled the air, my heart leapt with joy, and butterflies fluttered wildly in my stomach.

Sceptical of soul mates, I never thought I'd find my match.

Irena and everything changed. She's the puzzle piece that fits seamlessly with mine.

My perfect soulmate.

CHAPTER 52

IRENA NOWAK

"And that's how he proposed." I end of the story. My weekend with Saint was nothing short of magical. Just the two of us lost in our own little world. We shared laughter, cuddles, and intimate moments that made my heart skip a beat. We bonded over baking and indulged in the heavenly treats we created together.

As the weekend drew to a close, I couldn't help but feel a sense of sadness looming over me. I wanted it to last forever, but reality beckoned us back.

Nirali wipes her tears and looks at me in disbelief. "Who would've thought Saint had such a romantic side to him. I never saw it coming." I nod in agreement, equally surprised by his hid- den depths.

"Irena, have you been hiding in some secret, mystical realm? You would have been my saviour when I first encountered him. This guy was a total jerk, and I was at a loss. Whatever you did to him, keep it up because he's far less grumpy these days - almost reverent of you like Abel."

"Okay, okay," I laughingly interrupt as my friend rolls her eyes. "But honestly, it's true. He's transformed into a new man thanks to you, and it's all too evident that he admires you in a way that's both sweet and awe—inspiring." With a hint of bashfulness, I take a sip of my drink. "When and where is the wedding taking place?" she inquired. "Tanzania," I revealed, watching her eyes bulge with intrigue. "On the sun-kissed shores?" she exclaimed elatedly, causing me to chuckle. "Yes, on the beach, Nirali."

It's a sensation that still bamboozles me; the fact that he asked me to spend forever with him, despite surrendering everything else, just to call me his. All it took was a single affirmative answer.

"Nirali," I began, locking eyes with her as I took a deep breath. I relinquished the mounting anxiety that was slowly creeping up on me. "I'm ready to declare my feelings to him." I paused. "That I love him."

Nirali clutched my hand with glee, a joyous expression spreading across her face. "Irena, this is such wonderful news! It may seem like a small step, but for someone like you, it's a giant leap. You're finally letting go of a part of yourself to embrace some- one you love," she exclaimed.

I couldn't help but smile at her encouragement. "Yes, Saint has been so supportive. He's ready to lay everything on the line for me," I replied, feeling a warm flutter in my chest.

Nirali's eyes widened in disbelief, her voice quivering with astonishment.

"You mean...he's willing to give up the mafia, just for you?" she gasped, and my heart swelled with fondness for my devoted partner.

"Yes, he's willing to make that sacrifice for our love," I murmured, my lips curving into a grateful smile. "I'm torn, really," I confess to Nirali. "He's talking about starting a family, and I'm not sure if I'm ready for that kind of commitment. But then again, maybe it's the next natural step for us." She nods, understanding the weight of my words.

"For now, though, I think we'll focus on enjoying the little things, like planning our wedding and creating a life together," I say, feeling the warmth spread through my chest with the promise of our future.

Nirali smiles in agreement. "Imagine the joy of taking our future little ones on family getaways and watching them grow up," she breathes out wistfully, lost in her fantasy.

Just as the air is filled with the excitement of possibility, my phone interrupts, signalling an incoming call. I grin upon seeing my Saint's name flash on the screen, and Nirali can't help but giggle at the happiness that radiates off of me.

"Hey," I answer. "Hey, Doe, I'm so sorry I can't pick you up. Some- thing came up, but my driver is on the way," he announces, as the hum of hushed conversation floats by in the background. "It's okay, what time will you be back home?" I asked. "Probably around 10," he states. With my heart in my throat and a smile tugging at my lips, I nibble on my bottom lip as I summon the courage to spill my news. "There's something I need to tell you, but I want to do it in person," I confess, my nerves getting the better of me.

"Are you okay?" he asks, concern etched in his voice, and I can't help but let out a light chuckle.

"I'm more than okay, Saint. I just can't wait to see you." The promise of his arrival sends a shiver down my spine, and I feel my cheeks flush as he murmurs, "Just a little while longer, and I'll be holding you in my arms." I could talk to him for hours, but I know our time is limited.

"I've got to go," he sighs, disappointment colouring his words. "But I'll see you soon." He says. "Bye Doe."

"Bye," I whisper, a hint of affection as I hang up the phone. "Your cuteness levels are off the charts, it's making me nauseous," quips Nirali, feigning disgust by dramatically gagging. I playfully nudge her shoulder, rolling my eyes. "Shut up."

Suddenly, my phone buzzes, and a message from Saint flashes across the screen.

Saint: He's here.

I approach, the driver gets out of the car and opens the door for me. But before I hop in, I return to Nirali and wrap my arms around her warmly.

"I'll text you, okay?" I whisper, burying my face in the crook of her neck. "Okay," she answers, with a deep sigh as she pulls away. As I emerge from the comfort of Nirali's house, I am met by a biting gust of frigid weather that stings my cheeks. The driver greets me with a hasty nod as I slip into the car, his fingers deftly closing the door behind me. He circles the vehicle with agile steps, gracefully slipping behind the wheel and bringing the engine to life as we depart from the curb.

As I sit back in the plush seat, a small smile spreads across my lips and I press my temples against the icy glass, gazing out at the lifeless trees that blur past us. But as the minutes tick by, my nerves begin to take hold. It's just three simple words I have to confess to him, so why am I so breathless with apprehension?

All I need to say is that I love him…nothing monumental, right?

But despite this knowledge, I let out a heavy sigh of defeat. Why am I making this so difficult?

As I arrive at my house, I am greeted by the silence. I take off my coat and slip out of my heels.

Saint won't be back for a while, so I have the house to myself for now.

I'm exhausted and want to sleep, but first, I need a drink. I head to the kitchen and pour myself a glass of wine. As I take a sip, my mind drifts to the image of Krzysztof's lifeless body lying on the floor, sending shivers down my spine. I don't feel guilty for killing him, but the fact that I feel nothing unsettles me. I remember that day vividly. Every word he spoke fuelled my thoughts. And then, my curiosity was piqued when I noticed the black envelope he had left on the counter.

I wonder what's inside that envelope?

It must be something important since he brought it with him to meet Saint. But I can't shake the feeling that whatever is in the envelope is more significant than I initially thought.

Biting my lip, I refill my glass and head to Saint's office. I have an urge to uncover the contents of that envelope because my curiosity is consuming me, and when I set my mind to finding something out, I always uncover the truth, sooner or later.

I push open the door to Saint's office and switch on the light, revealing the stillness of the room. As I approach his desk, I place the glass of wine on the table and begin searching. I pull open drawers and sift through files, finding background information on people and potential locations for Saint's business expansion. I analyze his drug trade and illegal weapon smuggling activities. Reaching under the desk, I pat for hidden compartments and come across a gun. Clearing my throat, I sigh and continue my search. After five minutes, I reach the last locked drawer.

It may be stuck. I exert all my strength to open it, but it re- mains locked.

That's when I realised I'd hit the jackpot.

I quickly leave the office and rush to the kitchen, grabbing a knife before returning to the office.

Now this is where my craftsmanship comes in handy. Back when I used to live with my uncles. They would always secure their alcoholic beverages in the cupboard and due to my dependency, I would always utilize tools to break into their supply and steal alcohol, replacing it with water so that they wouldn't notice. They would always change the brand because the taste of it was bland, but they didn't know that I would refill it with water.

As I used the blade to nudge the drawer open, it didn't work, but after many unsuccessful attempts, it finally budges.

I toss the blade to the side and pulled the drawer open; my heart sank when I finally saw the dark envelope. I pick it up and opened it, pulling out the documents inside.

I expected more, to be honest.

As I stand up, I grab my glass of wine and take a seat in Saint's chair.

Quietly, I read through the documents. My heart sank when I saw my name, and the realization hit me. This is Saint's and my marriage agreement. I set the glass of wine down and continue to read through it, my heart sinking with each sentence as each word fills me with anger and anguish.

As I flip through the pages, everything suddenly makes sense, and everything I believe about Saint is now in question.

I hadn't realized how long I'd been rereading the agreement until I heard the door creak, and Saint walked in.

I raise my teary gaze to meet his. His smile immediately vanished when he noticed the documents in his grasp. The bunch of white roses in his hands slipped from his fingers and fell to the ground.

"All this time-" I trailed off with my hoarse voice. "No, I-" I interrupted him by leaping to my feet. "Y-you married me not for the sake of your reputation or my family's, but to exploit me as a means to bear children for my uncles. To use me for — you were planning to kill me..." Tears now streamed down my face like a river. Saint attempted to approach me, but I seized the glass of wine and hurled it at him. The glass shattered into countless pieces as the crimson liquid stained the walls. "Irena, I was going to tell you after I terminated the agreement with your uncles," he explained. "You're lying, you intended to keep this hidden from me," I declared, unable to halt the tears. I grabbed the documents and read them aloud. "It is stated here that I, Saint Dé Leon, here- by agree to the terms with the Nowak family to fulfil my obligations and, in return, will receive a payment of 100 million euros, as well as owning 20 per cent of the Nowak family's organization to expand the French drug trade unit in Poland. The stipulations are to impregnate the niece of the Nowak brothers, Irena Nowak, with a maximum of three children after each birth. And once fulfilled, you agree to take matters into your own hands and kill her so that she has no legal rights to claim over the Nowak business, and instead, her children will inherit it!" I exclaimed. And as I flip further through the pages I find my medical record indicating my health to have children.

Everything now revolves around Viktor. His actions have start- ed to become clear. He is unable to have children, which is why he repeatedly raped me, just so he could fulfill the agreement. However, since he never disclosed his inability to my uncles, they would dismiss my claims of abuse and rape by my deceased husband.

"Irena, let me explain," Saint says, but I shake my head. I need to escape from here. "No, Saint," I say, rushing out of the office with him following behind. I quickly make my way to the door, grab-bing my coat and heels before heading towards the garage. Saint grabs my arm and pulls me towards him.

"No, let go of me!" I scream. "Irena, please let me explain," he pleads, his voice cracking.

I struggle in his grip and scream at him to release me, but he refuses, begging me to stay. Beads of sweat form on my forehead as tears continue to stream down my face. I resort to my last option and slap him across the face, pushing him away before rushing towards the board with car keys. I grab a random green key, pressing the open button as a car beeps three times. I press the garage button to open it and quickly make my way to the car. As I enter the vehicle, I lock eyes with Saint. Once the car starts and roars to life, I shift the gear into reverse and back out of the garage without sparing another glance towards Saint. As I drive away from the driveway, my mind becomes overwhelmed with past and present issues. All the lies, secrets, and betrayals hit me all at once. I don't know where I'm going, but I just can't be with Saint right now.

In one fateful moment, my heart was torn from my chest with a single blink as the car careened off the road and plunged into the deep, unforgiving ditch below. My world spun wildly out of control as the bumper collided with the earth, propelling the car into an aerial chaos of death-defying flips, finally landing on its roof with a sickening thud. The windows shattered into a million razor-sharp fragments, slicing through my skin like Swarovski crystals. In the distance, gunshots shattered the intense silence, pierced only by urgent shouts. As I struggled to regain my shattered senses, I gasped for air, but searing rib pain made it impossible to breathe. Dangling upside down, the suffocating seat belt relentlessly squeezed my already tight chest, as I frantically tried to make sense of the chaos around me.

Suddenly, a desperate voice shattered through my confusion, cutting through the deafening ringing in my ears. "Get the girl," it exclaimed, sending shivers down my spine.

With a wave of pure agony coursing through my body, I shut my eyes as tightly as possible. A sudden slap jolts my senses back to reality, as I spot the silhouette of a figure outside my window, face obscured by a daunting black mask. In front of me lie cold hazel eyes, brimming with malice and menace. "Mhm, she's still breathing," growls the voice, deep and rough. "Alright, let's get her out of here."

Panic slowly creeps in through my veins until I can barely resist. In a weak voice, I ask, "Who are you?" as I swat away the figure's hands.

With a small click, I hear him mutter, "Don't even think about it, lady."

With one motion, he pulls me through the side window.

All I can manage now are weak whimpers as my vision starts to fade. "No, please," I plead, only to be silenced by another cruel blow.

Darkness takes over, enveloping me in an eternal slumber.

PART THREE

SOMETIMES GOOD THINGS FALL
APART SO BETTER THINGS CAN FALL
TOGETHER

CHAPTER 53

SAINT DÉ LEON

I've been searching for Irena since she left, and there's no sign of her vehicle. Four hours have passed, and panic begins to seep into my veins. She couldn't have gone far; if she wanted space, she would have gone to Abel's place. But when I checked there, she wasn't around, which only fuelled my unease. Maybe she turned back home and didn't find me. As I drive, I pray to anyone who can hear me that Irena is indeed home and that I can explain everything to her so she can forgive me. Originally, I hadn't planned to tell her, but fate took matters into its own hands, and she found out. I knew I should have burned that awful contract before we left, but my foolish self didn't think Irena would pay attention to the mysterious folder her uncle brought over.

As I enter the gates of my house, I quickly exit the car and rush inside. Peeling off my coat, I fling it onto the hanger and scan the silence that stretches before me. The walls seem to be holding their breath, and the only sound is the rush of my own blood.

My heart stumbles in my chest, as if it knows something I don't. "Irena!" My voice echoes through the halls but is met with silence. A knot forms in my stomach as I reach the bottom of the stairs. Please be home.

Before I can climb the stairs to investigate, a sharp knock at the door steals my attention. Vin, one of my guards, stands on the other side with a mysterious brown file in his hands. "Who's it from?" I demand, eyeing the unmarked package with suspicion. Vin shakes his head. "No sender, but it has your name on it." I take the package from him, my mind racing with possibilities. "Did my wife return?" I ask suddenly. Vin's piercing gaze meets mine as he delivers the sobering news: "Regrettably, Mrs. Dé has not made it back yet." My heartache is palpable, and my mind scrambles to make sense of what's happening. I acknowledge his report and shut the door on Vin's steady presence.

Fumbling with the documents, I flip through the piles of photographic evidence. Reality crashes around me like an avalanche as I land on a set of devastating images of the very same vehicle Irena drove out with, preceded by a ghastly car crash. My breath hitches as my eyes flicker to the next snapshot. That's when time stands still. Irena is stripped down to just her underwear and a bra, her body marked with purple and black bruises that stretch across her skin, her head hanging low in shame.

As I scrutinize the picture for any hint or clue, I find nothing. The background is bleak and blurry, while she is the unmistakable focus of the image. My heart aches as I see her crumpled on the cold, filthy concrete floor; her eyes swollen shut, her lips split and bloody. "Fuck!" I explode, flinging the photographs away from me with frustrated force, slamming my fist violently into the wall until my knuckles bleed. My hair is in disarray as I pace the room, overcome with guilt and a rising wave of panic that crashes through my mind. A vortex of despair begins swirling within me, draining every last ounce of vitality from my being.

Suddenly, darkness eclipses my sight, and an overwhelming wave of fury hits me like a tsunami. I ball up my fist. "FUCK! FUCK! FUCK! FUCK!" With a thunderous roar, I shatter anything near-by. Who the hell had the balls to take her away from me? Where could she be? With unbreakable determination and a fierce sense of justice burning within me, I vow to track down those bastards and make them beg for mercy before their souls are doomed to eternal damnation.

I grab my coat and storm out of the house. I unlock my car, slide into the driver's seat, and start the engine as it roars to life. Shifting into gear, I press on the gas pedal and drive off with speed. "Call Abel," I order coolly. "Calling Abel," the AI assistant intones, dialling my brother's number. After two rings, the line clicks open.

"Talk to me," he grunts, his voice gruff with irritation.

"I need you to arrange a meeting. Now. The warehouse. Ten minutes." I bark into the car, my eyes darting to the timer on the dashboard. Without waiting for a reply, I end the call, gritting my teeth and gripping the wheel until my knuckles turn white. With a ferocious growl, the car hurtles down the empty road, so fast that the scenery outside becomes a blur.

I won't stop until I find you, I promise. I'll bring you back home, safe and sound, and we will make everything right.

"Wake them up," I commanded as my two guards removed the sack from the men's heads and then doused them with icy water. Their bodies jerk and they meet my gaze.

I push myself away from the wall as I toyed with the torch in my hand. "What the hell is this?" Prince questions as his gaze shifts back and forth between Zoltan and me. Zoltan attempted to break free as I securely bound him to the chair with chains and did the same with Prince.

I pinch the bridge of my nose and then take a deep breath to calm myself. Zoltan had droplets of sweat forming on his forehead as Prince glared at me with confusion. "Irena has been abducted." Was the first thing that escaped my lips. "What does that have to do with us? Why are we restrained instead of assisting you in finding her?" Zoltan questioned as he attempted to break free from the chains but fails. I lift my gaze to meet his, my jaw clenching as the venom seeps into my veins. "Because I've been suspicious of both of you. You know how we've been searching for the mole. All the evidence I've personally gathered has led to both of you. Normally, I am a patient man when it comes to discovering a traitor but Irena has disappeared and I cannot waste any time." I declared. "So, whichever one of you it is should make things easier and confess now. Or I could take my sweet time with roasting you alive until you finally surrender." I uttered, flicking the torch on as the golden hot flame danced in front of my face.

"Come on, man, why would we be the betrayers? We have known each other for nearly two decades and have been in this profession for ages, man!" Prince exclaims and I shrug nonchalantly. "People change."

Rolling my neck, I groaned in satisfaction as the cracking sounds of my bones reach my ears.

"Who do you work for?" I inquire, my eyes scanning their gazes and they look at each other. "Saint, you can't be serious," Zoltan scoffs and I raise my eyebrows as I inquire. "Oh really?" In an instant, I turn on the torch and move the flames over his skin. Zoltan maintains eye contact as he starts to tremble, his skin bubbling and slowly tearing, causing him to turn red. "Let me ask again." I declare. Turning to face Prince, I switch on the torch and instruct my men to expose his neck to me. "Who do you work for, Prince? Why does all the evidence I've gathered lead to both of you? Are you the one who kidnapped Irena?" I question, the anger inside me ready to explode, but my tone remains calm and composed. As his flesh bubbles, his screams reverberate within the concrete walls and he shakes uncontrollably in the chair. "I could continue for hours. You know how I operate. You wouldn't want me to reach that level with you guys." I state, and they both look at me as sweat starts to trickle from their pores. I sigh, pulling back as I hand my torch to one of my men. I roll up my sleeves, and after a moment of silence, I strike Zoltan across the face.

His head jerks to the side, and a second later, I do the same with Prince. My fist flies back and forth between the two until my skin tears, and so does theirs.

I grab Prince by his face, blood now staining his mouth as he glares at me.

"It's not me. I would never betray you, Saint. Not now, not ever. It ain't me, man." He declares, and I squint my eyes, searching his face. Pushing him away, I turn to Zoltan and grip his face. Examining his expression, I ask. "Is it you?" A moment of silence passes, and he finally responds, meeting my gaze. "No." He states.

And that's all it took for me to understand who it was. "Take Prince to the adjacent room," I order my men. The three of them hoist the chair Prince is bound to and leave me all alone in the cell with Zoltan.

I chuckle to myself, pushing my hair out of my face as I gaze at Zoltan.

"You cunning bastard."

Zoltan spits out the blood onto the floor and looks at me with a groan. "Who are you working for?" I inquire again, peering down at him. "I'm not working for anyone Saint." He retorts bitterly and I chuckle to myself before striking him across the face with all my might, moments later a tooth flies out of his mouth. "I don't collaborate with anyone." He declares through clenched teeth. "I work alone. Everything I've done was solo. To eliminate you. The failed shipments, that was me. The betrayal to the police, that was me. Convincing individuals to turn against you was me. Ever since that woman of yours, Irena, entered your life, you've become weak." He groans.

"You used to be ruthless Saint. Slaughter dozens of men in cold blood. But now you've become a coward. You're feeble, a damn romantic and it's sickening."

My jaw clenches as I glare at him, my anger reaching its peak.

"You want my personal perspective on the entire situation regarding Irena...?" He pauses, a cruel smile spreading across his lips. "I'm glad she was taken from you; that way, you can return to your old ways. Our old ways. We can-"

In an instant, I find myself on top of Zoltan, the chair thrown to the ground as I continue to strike him across the face. Again and again and again until he is unrecognizable, blood splattering onto my face, his skin tearing open as he gurgles on his own blood. I was consumed by the rage that I hadn't noticed Abel entering. Until he called out my name.

"Saint?" He calls out, I turn to look at him, breathing heavily. "Bring the flamethrower."

Abel glances at Zoltan, sighing before he exits. I stand up, lifting the chair that he was tied to.

"I'm not finished with you," I mutter. He's going to regret ever uttering those words.

CHAPTER 54

SAINT DÉ LEON

"Any leads on who might have been involved in taking her?" Ace inquired, about a temporary replacement for Zoltan until I can get someone trustworthy enough to take his place. For now, I reached out to Ace asking for his assistance to help me find my wife, and immediately, he booked a flight to France the next day. "Not a single shred of evidence. The vultures that snatched her just vanished into thin air," I hissed, my anger simmering just beneath the surface. Meanwhile, Abel furrowed his brows and typed away with annoyance etched across his face.

The accident that caused Irena's disappearance was captured on surveillance footage where a mysterious van was involved. The perpetrators concealed their identities behind black masks with no registration plate in sight.

Abel and Prince are hard at work, scouring through street and security

cameras to track down the perpetrators. But it feels like a nail-biting waiting game that we may not win.

"Thus far, we've tracked the van's course as it cruised along the freeway, but we lost it when it vanished into the shadows after passing under a bridge," Prince reveals with a strained tone. Tension builds within me, manifesting as a fierce migraine and an unyielding sense of agitation. My desperate desire to rescue Irena boils within me, clawing at my skin like fire.

Suddenly, Abel's words cut through the apprehension like a razor, a glimmer of hope amidst the chaos. "Hold on, we found it again," he announces, his eyes narrowing with focus as he delves into the city's labyrinth of street cameras.

As Abel was mid-sentence, a disturbance from my pocket interrupted, drawing the attention of the room towards me. The buzz was incessant, generating an uneasy air that permeated the space around us. I cautiously reached for my phone and observed an unknown on the display, prompting me to answer with trepidation. "It's been a while Saint," warped voice rasped, concealing its identity with a chilling effect. "Who the fuck is this, where is my wife? I swear to," I spat vehemently with a clenching of my fists but then interrupted. A chuckle escapes the person's lips. "Your promises are as empty as a desert, Saint. Don't forget, I have her in my clutches. Any attempt to vex me will result in her paying the price," the fiend spits venomously over the receiver. My grip on the phone stiffens until it almost crumples beneath my fingertips.

"She's got spirit though," he adds with a chuckle, but the humour only fuels my wrath. My blood simmers like molten magma. "Listen closely, Saint."

"Meet me at the abandoned Grand Moulins factory, precisely at this hour tomorrow. I urge you to come alone so that we may converse. Bring 500 million euros. Who knows, you may even lay eyes upon her once more," the voice on the other end of the line declared before abruptly ending the conversation.

As the phone call concluded, my eyes shut tight and my composure crumbled. Like the final grain of sand in an hourglass, my grip on the situation had slipped away and all that remained was uncertainty.

My entire being succumbs to an abyss of menacing blackness, a suffocating void that engulfs me wholly. There is nothing, not a glimmer, not a spark, just pitch-black emptiness.

Echoes of raucous shouting fill my ears as my body is suddenly seized by multiple hands, and unceremoniously slammed onto the unforgiving table. Trapped and struggling, I raise my voice in a desperate shriek, but the darkness enveloping me hinders my attempts to fend them off.

My struggle soon comes to a halt as my hands are twisted into uncomfortable angles, and my head is pressed onto the rigid wood. As the world around me fades into an eerie silence, I realize that I am no longer in control.

But I'm not about to surrender to their will. Gathering my strength, I strike back with a swift kick to one of their balls.

In a fluid movement, I rise to my feet, seize one of them by the collar, and press the barrel of a cold metal gun against their skull.

Then with a sudden burst of red, my senses ignite with a frenzied intensity.

I leap into action, propelled by a fury I cannot control. My chair hurtles across the room, a deafening clash echoing as it collides with the shelves, books cascading to the ground in a flutter of pages. A second chair flies into the bar, the smash of glass shards mingling with my desperate cries.

An ominous cry rips from my soul, the intensity of it causing me to convulse and tremble uncontrollably; its mournful linger tapering off into a deafening silence. Another burst of emotion ignites within, a thunderous howl that shreds my vocal cords, and I unleash my fury on the surrounding objects. My eyes cannot bear witness to the destruction my hands are causing, but my heart palpates fiercely within my chest, urging me on. A flat- screen TV is the first to shatter under the weight of my rage, and I grab the first thing in my reach, a delicate vase sitting peacefully on a nearby table, and hurl it towards the window. A crash echoes throughout the room as the glass shudders and cracks under immense pressure. Like an astronaut in outer space, I am suddenly deaf to everything around me. The absence of sound amplifies the depths of my despair as my hands blindly grope for more things to destroy. My fingers clutch and tear through anything within reach, violently sending these items into a state of oblivion as they shatter upon impact with the floor.

It's all my fault. All my fucking fault!

"Fuck Saint. Jesus calm down!" I hear Ace call out. As I gaze into the emerald eyes of my brother, my nostrils flare with anger

and my chest convulses with emotion. My eyes blur with tears, their glimmer a reflection of my inner turmoil.

"Saint, calm down," my brother murmurs, endeavouring to soothe me. But his words fall flat in the face of my overwhelming guilt.

I am no longer the person I once was. I cannot calm the storm raging within me. She's gone because of me. Fear and pain are her only companions, all because of me! With careful precision, Abel plucked the gun from my grasp and gently nudged me aside. As I hung my head low, he concealed the weapon behind his back and rested a comforting hand on my shoulder. A flurry of emotions coursed through me, and I struggled to keep them contained. The words that emerged from my mouth came out cracked and ragged. I clamped my eyes shut and fought back the urge to shed tears. With a lump lodged in my throat and my chest tightening, I found it impossible to draw a steady breath.

In the face of my distress, Abel stepped forward to offer guidance. "Saint, pull yourself together," he said. You can't afford to act rashly if you're blinded by your emotions; it makes your thoughts destructive; they'll only lead you down a dangerous path."

I felt my heart skip a beat at his words, and I tried to interject. "I-"

"Listen to me," Abel interrupted. "We'll get her back, but we need to be smart about it. They're not going to make it easy for us, so we've got to devise a plan to outsmart these bastards."

Clenching my hands I nod. I will not rest until the fuckers heads are in my hands.

As I glanced at my clock, the piercing sound of the chimes echoed through the air. 11:45 pm, the exact moment that asshole had called me the night before. My heart raced with trepidation, wondering what sort of disturbance he would inflict upon me this time. The frigid winter weather outside only added to the ominous atmosphere of the night. Shrouded in the gloomy clouds, the moon added a foreboding feel to the already eerie setting. I felt a sense of unease permeate my being as if something terrible was about to happen. Sitting across from the window, I stared out into the darkness, lost in thought.

Suddenly, Abel's voice crackled in my earpiece, breaking my concentration.

"Saint, all snipers have taken their positions. We're ready for anything." The reassurance of my team's preparation was the only thing keeping me anchored in the midst of the brewing storm.

"Copy that," I answer. As I grasp the handle, my hand quivers with anticipation as I unlock the briefcase containing the 500 million euros. With eyes glued to the towering stack of green, my heart races with each bill I count. For a chance to have her back, I'd give everything I own without a second thought.

As I snap the briefcase shut, I exit my vehicle and confront the ominous building. The cold piercing air sends a chill down my spine, but my determination persists. As I approach, the outline of a figure and a crimson car catches my eye. Hastening my pace, I halt abruptly as I approach the vehicle, feeling the weight of the money heavy in my hand.

The person in front of the car is a stranger to me. He has broad shoulders, tanned skin, and muscles that could make anyone feel small. However, his attempt to intimidate me is in vain.

As I see him, I feel a burning fury inside me. "I'm here, where the hell are you?" I ask calmly, though my voice is laced with venom.

The door of the car opens and shiny black shoes hit the ground, followed by the sight of his tall physique. When I look into his brown eyes, I cannot hide my bitterness.

"It's you," I say, clenching my jaw. Grzegorz smirks and adjusts his suit. "Ah, well, well, well, Saint. Good to see you too."

I willed every muscle in my body to remain calm and collected as I approached Grzegorz. "So, how are the shattered bones holding up?" I quipped, trying to hide the panic in my voice. He shrugged nonchalantly, studying his left arm with a critical eye. Despite the bruises marring his features, it was clear that his wounds were on the mend.

"Must say, you've really done a number on me, Saint," he drawled; his demeanour was surprisingly cool. With a snap of his fingers, a hushed whisper to his accomplice, and a momentary pause, a white van materialized before us. My stomach lurched as the doors swung open and two burly men shoved a woman out, her head shrouded in a bag. She stumbled to the ground, her half-naked form exposed for all to see. And then, in a flash of recognition, I realized who she was.

Every inch of her caramel-coloured skin was tainted with cuts and bruises, a sight so painful my heart ached to even glance at her.

"Get rid of that filthy covering," Grzegorz ordered, his voice dripping with malice. With swift action, the two men unveiled the bag from her head. Blinking back tears, Irena's eyes struggled to adjust to the cars' lights.

I felt a fiery anger seething within me, coursing through
my veins like hot lava. My entire body shook with rage, my jaw clenched tightly, my eyes growing

darker by the second, and my head pounding harder than ever before.

"Remember our little chat over the phone about what I'd do if you made me angry?" Grzegorz sneered his words like venom. "Irena here has been my punching bag ever since."

With an ominous stride, I advance closer, my briefcase slipping from my grasp. "I swear on my life, Grzegorz, lay a finger on her-"

The air crackles with tension as henchmen appear from every corner, brandishing guns aimed straight at me. But it's Anatol who steals my focus, emerging from the van, weapon in hand. However, it's not directed at me; it's trained on Irena's temple, her terrified expression all too apparent.

"Saint," Grzegorz sneers, the sound of my name on his lips sending shivers down my spine.

"I'll say it again, just for emphasis," he drawls, a smirk playing on his lips. "I want you to open it and show me. I wouldn't want to risk my face being blown up.

With a pounding heart, I pried open the briefcase and unveiled the hefty stack of cash. The corners of his mouth upturned into a wry smile before he signalled to one of his henchmen to take the briefcase from me with a resounding click.

"As smooth as butter," he drawled with a sly smirk. "Nice doing business with you, Saint."

My blood boiled at his arrogance. "You're not leaving with Irena," he sniffs the air. "Cross me, and Irena pays the price. Lay a finger on any of my loyal men? Irena gets hurt. Think about taking a shot from your snippy sniper. Well, guess what? I'll personally make sure Irena takes the bullet instead." The joy in his tone is matched only by the darkness glinting in his eyes.

"But here's the kicker…if any of your snipers even so much as aim my way, my men and I will unleash a fury that'll see Irena's life snuffed out on my behalf. And it'll all be because of you." He adds with a venomous smile.

In one swift movement, Anatol seizes Irena by the hair and wrenches it back, causing a heart-wrenching scream to erupt from her lips. "Now, the money," he demands, all pleas for mercy falling on deaf ears.

My jaw was clenched and my heart was pounding when I uttered those words, "If I bring the money, Irena will be safe," But instead of a serious response, Grzegorz laughed, his tone laced with amusement. "Hold your horses, buddy. Let's be clear here. I never promised to leave Irena alone just because you gave me the money. I only said I'd bring her to you if you paid up," Grzegorz clarified with a sly grin. His expression turned menacing as he leaned in closer. "So, my money." With a fierce glare, I dropped down and snatched the briefcase from the ground. As I rose to my feet, I thrust the case in his direction, only to have it flung back toward me in disdain.

"Do you think I'm some kind of idiot?"

Yes.

Grzegorz raised a brow, amusement sparkling in his eyes. "Oh, Saint, you speak of deals when you never kept yours. Do you remember our little agreement? Get Irena pregnant and give us the baby? It seems like all your promises were just a load of hot air."

Irena's exclamation pierces the air like a sharp blade as tears begin to form in her once-hopeful, now lifeless brown eyes. I finally raise my gaze to hers, and the betrayal I see there sends a sharp pang of pain through me. I'm so sorry doe.

My throat tightens unable to speak to her in her current state, feeling a wave of guilt washed over me like a suffocating tidal wave.

As I try to explain, I see the pain in her eyes deepen. "Don't take it to heart kid." Grzegorz asserts, bracing myself for her reaction. "We were selling you off to get you pregnant with Viktor at first, but things didn't go as planned. Fate had other ideas, and we ended up making a deal with Saint instead."

"I know everything." Irena declared through gritted teeth as she looked at me with pain in her eyes.

My chest tightens with emotion as I continue, a sickly feeling growing in my stomach. "Good because, Irena after Viktor passed away, God rest his soul. Saint, the one we thought we could trust, signed an agreement to fulfil the agreement, but he went and broke the deal. All because he claims to 'love' and 'respect' you. It's pathetic, really." Irena's eyes widen, and I can see the glimmer of an emotion I recognize all too well. It's the same emotion she had when we made love in the cabin: a mix of wonder, trust, and desire. And I know at that moment that I've lost her.

A glimmer of hope illuminates her pallid features as she whispers, "You do see me as worthy." Her uncertain yet hopeful expression warms my heart.

Anatol's disappointment seeps through his voice as he laments, "It's a shame really, considering his impeccable standing in society."

"So I'm taking matters into my own hands and remarrying her to an underground lord who I found in South America. Obviously, I will not be giving away his identity knowing you will kill him in less than 24 hours." Grzegorz explains. "I'll send the divorce papers. Fill them, and we will be going our way, and you can carry on with whatever floats your boat." he casually proclaims.

"Oh, but wait," Grzegorz chuckles before whipping out his gun and firing mercilessly at Irena's leg and arm.

The sound of the gunshot cracks through the air like thunder and my heart seizes within me. The sight of her writhing in pain on the ground brings me to my knees, tears cascading down my own face in empathy. As she screams out in anguish, it's as if every fibre of my being is screaming with her. My eyes lock onto Grzegorz's, a fiery rage burning within me. The world around me fades into nothingness as my vision turns pitch black, consumed entirely by unbridled fury.

My mind was a raging inferno of all the punishments I'd inflict on Grzegorz. Irena's cries were stifled as one of Grzegorz's troops hoisted her up, threw a bag over her head, and shuffled her back into the van.

"I'm going to crash your head onto the ground, causing it to splinter into shards. Then, with my own hands, I'll extract your eyeballs from their sockets and offer them to you as a ghastly appetizer. After all that I'll use a machete with a black handle to slice your fucking guts out!" I yell as a promise.

"Empty promises, empty promises." He utters. My eyes are pools of shimmering tears, and my body shakes with boiling

anger. I glare at Grzegorz, who looks back at me with sadistic pleasure, a wicked smile playing on his lips.

"Two bullets for Irena," he says, his voice dripping with malice. "For the fractures in my bones and the death of my brother. And don't even think of following us, or I'll do the same thing you did to me, breaking Irena's bones."

With one final, cold glance my way, Grzegorz turns on his heel and strides to his car. The others slink away into the darkness, some disappearing into the back of a waiting van.

The engines roar to life, and the two vehicles speed away, leaving me alone in the silent night.

CHAPTER 55

IRENA NOWAK

Three months later

As I languished in a vast, opaque void, something rudely roused me from my slumber. The sharp pang of agony lanced through me once more, and I winced in response.

"Irena. Wake up." The voice echoed ominously through the abyss, smearing fear across my nerves. The shadowy expanse seemed to pulse with foreboding energy, warning me of impending danger.

With a jolt, something yanked at my arm. "Get up, you useless sack of bones!" A rough hand shook me again, jarring me from my trance.

Suddenly, a cascade of frigid water surged over me like a waterfall, shattering my half-conscious state like a bolt of lightning. My body plunged into spasms and shudders, as every shard of pain converged into a single, searing force.

My heart is on the brink of bursting through my chest, hammering against my rib cage with the tenacity of a battering ram. "Rise and shine, time to meet your match." The harrowing voice echoes through the eerie darkness, followed by a sudden flicker of light that blinds me momentarily.

As my eyes adjust, I come face to face with Anatol - a snarling demon, features now distorted with an icy coldness that reeks of decay. A graveyard of a man, devoid of any soul or warmth.

But I refuse to be his prize. My fury engulfs me like a tempest, blackening my heart as it devours my being. "I'm not going anywhere with you," I hiss with conviction, spitting my defiance at the tomb before me. The pain is a sudden, jolting burst that rips across my cheek with razor-sharp precision. My eyes widen in disbelief, but my reflexes are too slow to avoid the inevitable. I feel the fire surge on the side of my face, and my hand flies up to clutch at the raw, smarting flesh. Blood trickles down my nose as I stare at my own fingertips, stained with evidence of my vulnerability. A sickening cocktail of disgust and fury churns in my gut, threatening to overwhelm me. But I remain silent, locked in a precarious situation without any room for recklessness. My body is frozen, my mind slipping back into the darkness that claimed me months ago. The Irena I thought I left behind is clawing its way back to the surface. Frail. Terrified. Vulnerable. Adrift. With a snap of his fingers, Anatol summons two men who enter the room with a bundle of clothes in hand. "Dress her," he commands, before striding out of the room. The two men move towards me, one sporting a wicked grin and the other a copper mane. "Hold her," the raspy-voiced man instructs his accomplice, eyeing me hungrily.

With hair like the finest copper, he pushed me forcefully onto the musty mattress, pinning me down with an unrelenting grip. He swiftly removed my baggy T-shirt, stained with my blood and specks of dust, casting it to the ground. In a moment of audacity, he disrobed me entirely, replacing my modest attire with a blue dress of his choosing. I squirmed, desperate to escape his clutches as a chorus of screams burst forth from my throat. He hoisted my head against my will, determined to subdue me completely.

I cried out in agony as his knee pressed into my gut, exerting a crushing weight that made every breath a struggle. My eyes brimmed with tears, each one a testament to the unyielding pain that wracked my body. Beads of sweat rolled down my forehead from all the fighting. I could feel their calloused fingers on my skin, eliciting a deep-seated revulsion that had plagued me for years. That all too familiar feeling had returned, the feeling of being touched against my will, a feeling that robbed me of my humanity.

As they completed their task, I gasped for air as an unwelcome mist of perfume engulfed me. It was a peculiar blend that reminded me of a grassy forest scattered with pine cones. How anyone could find such a scent pleasing, I couldn't fathom. "And her hair?" The man with chestnut locks inquired the cooper-haired accomplice. He simply shrugged and responded with a lackadaisical "I don't know, man. Her braids look alright." The brunette-haired man nodded in agreement, and with my head bagged, they effortlessly hoisted me out of the dingy basement.

My heart is crushed in agony, and a solitary cry breaks free from my lips. I cannot bear to endure this anguish once more. Not now.

My newfound joy is but a flicker in the grand scheme of things. I refuse to have it snatched away from me by the cruel hands of fate. A lump lodges itself in my throat, and I struggle to swallow as the reality of my circumstances sinks in.

The soft, trembling voice creeps into my mind like a tiny spider, spinning its web of doubt and fear. I shake my head, determined to silence it.

Saint is my saviour. He has promised to protect me, to cherish me forever. I am not alone.

But the voice persists, growing bolder with each passing moment. You are nothing, Irena. A mere burden on society, a cursed child who brought about the demise of her own parents. No one cares for you, no one loves you. You are doomed to be lost forever.

I feel myself slipping, the tendrils of anxiety and self-doubt wrapping around me like a tightening coil. I must resist, I must believe in Saint's love.

No one will ever find you.

But the voice whispers on, a haunting melody of despair and hopelessness that threatens to consume me.

In an instant, I'm hurled onto the couch and a sharp gasp escapes me as the stitches from my gunshot wound are stretched to the limit. Darkness engulfs me, but the thump of heavy foot- steps echoes like a snare drum in my ears. The door creaks open, and I hold my breath, waiting for the worst.

A deep voice booms, sending tremors through my body. "Is this her?" The question is laced with a thick Mexican accent, and I can sense a cold, sinister presence lurking nearby.

Grzegorz, ever the lapdog, replies without hesitation. "Yes, González." The air thickens with tension, and I can't help but won- der what these people want from me. Suddenly, the rough fabric of sackcloth is ripped away from my face, and I blink back the glare of the dimly lit room. My eyes dance from Anatol to Grzegorz and, finally, land on the face of the man who's about to be my new husband.

My gaze locks onto his pitch-black eyes, drilling into them like I'm staring down a notorious villain. He huffs heavily, his wrath painting a ruddy hue across his face. His eyes themselves seem lifeless as if his entire being is animated only by his nefarious intentions.

"Sure, she's a looker," he sneers, his tone dripping with arrogance. "But next time, Grzegorz, I'd appreciate it if she wasn't dressed like she'd gone ten rounds with Muhammad Ali. And would you care to explain why she's bleeding?" His finger jabs at the crimson stain seeping into my blue dress, rendering it unrecognizable.

Grzegorz chuckles, a knowing gleam in his eye. "Just a little mishap, Manuel. She ran away and it was difficult to get her back."

Manuel nods, his hands sliding into his pockets as he steps toward me. There stands Manuel with an air of maturity in his mid-forties, bedecked in intricate tattoos that wrap around his tanned, chiselled frame. His effortless style is a spectacle to behold as he dons a white and black shirt, unbuttoned just enough to reveal his chest hair peeking out from under a shimmering gold chain. Completing the look are his sleek black jeans and polished shoes.

As I rise to my feet, Manuel's hands make a beeline for my womanly curves.

His fingers trace the contours of my breasts before inspecting my hair and face with cold scrutiny. Before I can comprehend what's happening, he hauls me around like a rag doll to grope my ass, leaving me gasping in shock. A sharp smack resounds through the room, sending me yelping in discomfort.

"She's a natural. Good," he comments, turning to face Grzegorz with a smirk. "Once she's healed, I'll sign and deliver my end of the bargain in a month's time. But for now, I'll take the five-hundred-million payout."

"Rest assured, she'll be in the best of care," Anatol assures him. "I don't give a fuck what you do with her." His unfeeling tone tells me everything I need to know about his lack of concern for my welfare. Meanwhile, Grzegorz merely grins, clearly amused by the proceedings.

"As long as you call me once she's ready," he drawls. His cavalier attitude makes my stomach turn with disgust.

As I lock eyes with Manuel, he smirks, his gaze devouring my form. "I'm about to have a blast with you," he murmurs in a mysterious voice, sending chills cascading down my spine at the mere idea.

Where are you, Saint?

SAINT DÉ LEON

Fury. It's a force of nature that we underestimate. The power it holds is beyond what we can imagine.

The boundaries of human ability no longer constrain us , with just a few sparks of my anger, entire cities could crumble into oblivion. The black flames within me threaten to burn everything in sight to ashes.

But for now, the destruction is directed inward. My own reflection glares back at me, suffused with violence on a cosmic scale. The universe was built on chaos, and now two black orbs of wrath reflect back at me, reminding me of that primal force that rages inside us all.

SHE'S GONE BECAUSE OF YOU!

My clenched fist smashes into the mirror, causing it to quake with fear. Its delicate surface tries to hold on but eventually crumbles into a million tiny shards that rain down like a storm of emotions. Each one reflects the state of my shattered soul.

I couldn't care less about the physical pain, what's breaking me apart is much deeper than that.

With a growl escaping my lips, I continue to pound my fist into the mirror. Once, twice, thrice, until only a crooked few remain. But even as the broken pieces scatter across the floor, the echoes of her cries still haunt me.

Her brown pools of pain flickering in my memory, I drop my head in defeat. It's only been a week, but it feels like a lifetime since I've felt at peace. My spirit is cracking under the weight of my heavy heart.

Inhaling a lungful of air, I exhale it with measured precision. A resolute determination courses through me, fuelling my unwavering resolve to leave no stone unturned until Irena is found.

CHAPTER 56

SAINT DÉ LEON

"I just found the bastards that were responsible for Irena's car crash." Able declares while I pore over the printed-out images of the van.

"Tell me their names," I commanded. "They go by Adan and Amari Jacobs, notorious twins from South Africa who go by the moniker Brother Hunters, the very hitmen the underworld hires for their assassinations," he elaborated.

"So they are the fuckers who were hired to steal Irena from me," I mumbled to myself.

"By combing through clues, I've successfully traced the whereabouts of the van's last use. Curiously, it appears that Irena was transferred into the care of Grzegorz at a deserted hospital, and the culprits swapped their ride from a van to a stylish green BMW i7. Tracking their movements, it's been discovered that they've recently settled at a location, waiting for their next instruction," Able disclosed with a flourish.

I slump back in my seat, my hands massaging my face as I try to wrap my head around the latest development. "Do you have a location?" I ask, my voice cautious.

"They seem to have taken refuge at 3 Rue du Chantier in Marseille," Able answers promptly.

I spring out of my chair, feeling the adrenaline hit me. "Then let's make our way there. Book a flight to Marseille," I instruct.

Without missing a beat, Able's fingers fly furiously over his laptop as he types away. "Already taken care of," he confirms.

The moment I lay my hungry claws on those treacherous brothers, I will finally get the information I need that will lead me straight to Irena. And with the devilish duo, Grzegorz and his odious sibling Anatol, in my grasp, I will ensure that they pay in full for their foul acts.

Four days later

The flight from Paris to Marseille took about an hour and a half, and the ride to the location took at least forty minutes because I was driving over the speed limit.

A cop stopped us, and he was wasting my time, so I bribed him with a thousand euros to leave us the fuck alone, and of course, he took it, knowing that this would be the only time where he would get fast money.

As I parked the sleek rental car a few blocks away from the towering building, I couldn't help but feel a surge of adrenaline course through my veins. With my trusted duffel bag in hand, I turned to find Abel following closely behind. Together, we strode purposefully toward the hotel entrance, ready to embark on our covert mission.

Upon arriving at the front desk, we were met with a steely receptionist who seemed hesitant to divulge any information. But with a well-timed reference to our connection with the brothers, her guard was quickly lowered. With a flicker of a smile, Abel and I made our way to the elevator and ascended gracefully to the 7th level.

Finally, we arrived outside room 6C, and my heart rate spiked as I gritted my teeth and balled my fists. Calling forth all my alpha energy, I pounded on the door with a ferocity that could wake the dead. Yet there was only silence, mounting my frustration to near-unbearable levels. Desperate for answers, I pounded again and again until finally...

"Who the fuck is it?!" Shouts one of the brothers, his voice dripping with one of the many South African accents you can encounter. The country boasts such an array of flavours in speech, after all.

I give the door another thunderous knock, sending shivers through the wood.

Suddenly, the entrance swings open, revealing piercing auburn eyes which quickly furrow with suspicion. The bastard glances at Abel, then my duffle bag, but before he can reach for his firearm, I come at him with a headbutt that sends him stumbling back- wards.

"What kak is this, Amar-." His words were cut short as I snatched his brother's gun and turned it against him.

"Take a seat," Abel commanded, while Adan snickered. "I won't sit down for crap," he argued. I rolled my eyes.

Why do they always have to make it difficult?

Grinning wickedly, a surge of venomous anger courses through my veins, and my heart pounds against my chest like a runaway train. "I didn't do anything, man, I only-" His pathetic plea is cut short as I deftly reach for the pliers, my mind made up. With a rough tug, I feel his teeth give way as they tear from their gums with a sickening pop. Blood dribbles from the gaping hole left in their place as his screams pierce the silence, but I silence him with a swift clamp of his jaw. Pink skin now angry and tears glistening in his eyes, I revel in his tortured state. I hold up my trophy, his teeth, wrenched free couch. Swiftly, I placed it over Amari's face, muffling his screams as I suffocated him with the soft fabric. With one hand holding down the pillow, I pressed my pistol to it and pulled the trigger. The blast echoed through the room but was slightly muffled by the cushion's fluffy embrace. My eyes stayed fixed on Adan, watching as his breathing grew ragged and his eyes widened in horror. He could do nothing but bear witness as his younger brother's life was snuffed out before him. With a hollow thud, Amari's body crumpled to the ground, and a pool of crimson began to spread from the bullet hole between his lifeless eyes.

"What the hell man!" Adan's cry of disbelief echoes around the room like a gunshot. My neck and shirt are now spattered with his blood, a messy reminder of his weakness. I calmly retrieve my handkerchief from my pocket and wipe away the evidence, letting it fall carelessly onto the lifeless body. With my duffle bag on the table, I unzip it slowly, my eyes scanning the contents with a revolting satisfaction. Each tool brings to mind the agony and suffering I will unleash onto Adan, and it sends a sickening thrill through my entire being.

The pliers are my weapon of choice, deceptively simple yet efficient. As I approach my victim, my eyes roam over his features, taking in every detail. His jaw is the first thing I grasp, holding it tightly as I force his mouth to open, studying his pearly- white teeth with an almost grotesque fascination. My voice oozes with menace as I utter a question he knows the answer to all too well.

"Do you have any idea who I am?" I growl, watching as realization slowly dawns on his face. The spark of fear in his auburn eyes is like sweet nectar to me, and I relish in the power it gives me.

There it is.

"See this tooth, I'm going to do this again and again until the truth escapes your lips. And when your death comes, it will come slowly, painfully, and with a beauty that only I can create. Or, you could save us both the trouble and fucking tell me now and make your death as quick as your brother." My words leave my lips like venom, and I can feel the darkness churning inside of me. I am a force to be reckoned with, a natural disaster waiting to strike.

"Let's try this again." As his screams echoed off the dingy walls, I pulled back on his jaw and demanded answers, my fingers slick with the blood and saliva that dripped from his mouth.

With a pained groan, he finally spits out a name, his words tangled with snot and terror. "It was some Polish guy. He promised us a cool million if we grabbed a certain girl. Goes by the name of Irena Nowak."

"When was this?" I demanded, my voice low and dangerous. "It was a month ago," he replied, his words dripping with disdain. "We've been keeping tabs on her for weeks."

The revelation stoked my anger even further. A month of tracking?

Unforgivable.

My anger boiled over at his nonchalance, and with a swift movement, I wrenched open his jaws and yanked out his lower incisors. Blood spurted from the wounds like a majestic whale emerging from the sea, eliciting a scream of pure agony from my captive.

The putrid odor of blood wafted up to my nostrils, sending a rush of satisfaction through me. Darkness enveloped me with its inky blackness, erasing any trace of light or humanity from my being. But as the memory of the Saint who had passed away four months ago surfaced within me, I knew that I had to act. They had taken my doe, and I would stop at nothing to get her back. Casting aside the tooth I had just extracted, I turned to Adan, my eyes boring into his like a drill. He gazed back at me as if he had seen his worst nightmare brought to life.

"Please, please!" he pleaded, his body quivering uncontrollably. "I didn't know she was yours." "Where did you take her?" I asked in a calm and composed manner. His face twists in discomfort, "It was a sketchy joint, some abandoned structure off the beaten path. We thought we were meeting Grzegorz, but instead, he sent us to meet some dude named Diego."

A shiver runs down my spine at the mention of the enigmatic Diego. "Diego Fumero?" I trailed off slowly and Adan nodded. "Yeah him." Of course, he's also in this. Motherfucker. The way he looked at Irena when she met him at the ball, and the disrespectful comments he made...

I should have seen it coming from a mile away. That slimy snake has always been lurking in the shadows, praying for my inevitable tumble. And now that he's got a hold of my most vulnerable spot, he's strutting around like he's got the biggest brass balls in the universe.

"So, where do I find this dipshit?" I demand, fixated on his blood-spewing mouth.

Adan shoots me a sideways glance, his eyes ablaze with rage. "You took out the only person who knew where he was, remember?" he snarls, spittle flying. I roll my eyes in disbelief.

Bullshit. With a flick of my wrist, the pliers went flying across the room like a bullet.

My hand instinctively went for the blade, snugly strapped to my ankle. The metallic glint of the razor-sharp edge promised sweet revenge. In one swift motion, I grabbed him by the ear and sliced it off with a single, clean cut. The blood gushed out like a geyser, painting the walls red. Adan's eyes rolled back in agony, but the fear pulsated from him like a palpable energy, filling me with dark satisfaction.

My fingers grip his jaw and yank him towards me, his cries falling on deaf ears. "Diego," I murmur calmly, a sick smile playing on my lips. Adan's wide eyes practically bulge out of his head as I tease him with his own ear, dangling it like a piece of meat in front of a ravenous beast. Tears flow down his cheeks like a deluge, but I'm oblivious to his pain, sucked in by the thrill of the chase.

I take in his fear, delighting in the sight of it, as I demand answers. "Where is he?" I whisper, flicking his ear again. The pain shoots through him, but I can't resist the satisfaction of seeing him suffer.

"F-fuck man he's in Poland." He stutters out a reply, and I know I'm close.

"Address?" I demand, and his guilt-ridden head gestures toward the lifeless body of his brother. I motion my Abel over, and he goes through Adan's pockets, fishing out a folded piece of paper.

My eyes dart across the page, the thrill of victory coursing through me as I spot the address of Diego's location. A curt nod from Abel is all I need, and I let go of Adan, ready to claim my prize.

He begged for mercy, stuttering incoherently as I grabbed a handful of his hair and yanked his head back. The blade made another luscious arc, slicing through his vulnerable neck. Flesh gave way to steel, and blood rained down on us both, drenching me in a crimson shower. His eyes bulged in terror, and blood bubbled out of his mouth as he choked on his own life force. Watching him die filled me with a sickening pleasure. I tilted my head, gazing deep into his lifeless eyes, as the last vestiges of his soul drained away.

His last gasp rattles through the room, his body wracked with convulsions as his final breath escapes him. The thick, red river of his blood spills from him like an offering to some dark deity.

With a heavy sigh, I release his head, leaving him to crumple onto the couch. The once-pristine fabric is now stained with his life's essence.

I inhale sharply, feeling the blood of my enemy staining my skin and ghosting across my senses. Pulling out my phone, I feel the sticky slickness of it as I punch in the passcode and dial Ace's number. The third ring connects us.

"I want you to send the cleaning crew over here," I order, my voice ringing out sharp and clear. "I'll send you the location."

"Consider it done," comes the reply, and I hang up, my mind already moving on to the next challenge.

I pivot around and face my brother, breath catching in my throat. "It's time for me to journey to Poland solo, but know that I'll call on you, if I need backup," I declare with conviction.

Abel's arms fold, his expression filled with reluctance. "Are you positive you don't want me to accompany you?" he hesitates before adding, "I'm here to support you either way."

My focus remains unswayed. "No, I have to do this on my own. I need this." Comprehension dawning on his face, Abel nods. "I understand. I'll stay behind and keep watch in case you require my help."

I nibble at my lower lip, absently sweeping a strand of hair out of my eyes. "You'll get her back soon." he blurts out and I lift my gaze to meet his. "I just-"

"You don't have to explain yourself, Saint. I know," he asserts, implicitly referring to Nirali.

I take a deep breath. "Let me take a shower and after, I'll track down Diego once I land in Poland," I tell him.

Abel heads for the door. "I'll meet you in the car," he says before exiting and shutting the door behind him. Silence engulfs the room, but my thoughts are far from tranquil. I cannot rest until Irena is reunited with me, and then, and only then, will I find peace again.

One week later

My boots bear witness to my fierce resolve as they trudge through the thick red pool of blood that lines my path to Diego's house.

The bodies of his hired protectors lay strewn about, all 12 of them, their blank stares fixed upon the twinkling stars above. They were merely obstacles in my way, and now they have paid the ultimate price for their allegiance to the wrong man.

I spare not a thought for their grieving families, nor do I waste a single tear on their shattered lives. The only thing on my mind is justice, and I will stop at nothing to achieve it. With a mighty kick, I shatter the front door and confront the startled occupants.

Diego's opulent mansion is a marvel of green and white, adorned with medieval artifacts that speak to his immense wealth. Two grand staircases stand tall on both sides of the house, leading up to a magnificent half-moon balcony that wraps around the structure. The man of the hour emerges from above, a wild gleam in his eyes, flanked by two bulky guards.

His salt and pepper mane is a dishevelled mess, strands standing at attention, but his eyes widen in surprise as soon as he spots me. I arch a single eyebrow, daring him to flinch. "Am I interrupting something?"

He stammers for a moment too long, unable to process my sudden arrival, when I take out my gun and fire two swift rounds, one for each guard.

It's almost too easy. Does he think those bumbling bodyguards could keep me out? I bet they were Grzegorz's men.

The guards slump to the ground- silenced before they even realise what hit them.

Diego's men crumple to the floor in sickening thuds, blood seeping into the ivory tiles below. His eyes fly open in terror, darting around like a cornered animal. But my voice stops him in his tracks. "Don't even think about running, Diego." Slowly, he turns to face me, quaking with fear. There's a distinct odour that hangs around men faced with their own mortality. They're brave until they're not, and then they're just scared. Diego's no different. He knows he's going to die, no matter what he believes in.

"Don't even try to touch me and-," he snarls. I roll my eyes. "Shut the fuck up, Diego. You know better than to piss me off."

He grits his teeth, but he knows better than to pick a fight with me. Sweat drips down his temples, his fists clenched so tight they're shaking. His self-assured facade is cracked, and he knows it.

As I gazed up at Diego, his haughty demeanour pushed me to take action.

With measured footsteps, I ascended the grand staircase, determined to show him the error of his ways.

Oh, how foolish he was to think that the ultimate victory was dying with his head held high.

Stopping mere inches from his towering frame, I envisioned him bowing before me, remorseful and contrite. With lips pressed against my boots, he would pay the price for his insolence.

"Where is she?" I demanded, my voice steady and void of emotion. Diego's eyes darted nervously, his Adam's apple pulsating as he struggled to speak. "I wasn't informed of her whereabouts." A wicked laugh escaped my lips, laced with venomous malice. "Do not try to deceive me, Diego," I hissed. "Your connection to her captors is all too clear." His eyes widened with shock, and I saw him struggling for words. But it was too late. The truth had been unveiled.

Grzegorz will take my life if I breathe a word," he blurts out. I stare at him in disbelief, my eyes narrowing with contempt. "Well, Diego, it seems that you're already a dead man walking just by being in my presence." I point out the harsh truth.

"What's the use of all this? She's vanished, gone," he adds with an exasperated sigh. Suppressing a grin, I purse my lips, the scars on my face contorting with a frown, and slowly approach him like a predator sizing up its prey. The rush of adrenaline and satisfaction floods my veins as Diego stiffens up beneath my scrutiny. "You're going to regret the day you crossed me, Diego," I warn him in a low growl.

In a swift motion, I hurl him over the railing, his screams piercing the air until they dissipate into a sickening thud when he hits the ground. The sound of his bones snapping and cracking fuels my dark desires, and I allow myself a twisted smile.

As I descend the stairs, I hear the pitiful sounds of Diego's agony. I observe his broken limbs that seem to be twisted in unnatural angles, his left leg's bone protruding out. Hovering over him, I catch a glimpse of his terrified eyes.

"Where is she?" I repeat my question, hoping that this time might be the last. He remains silent, his teeth chattering, tears streaming down his face.

As Diego trembles before me, his fear palpable in the air, I feel my disappointment rise like bile in my throat. He hesitates to speak, and I'm left with no choice but to take matters into my own hands. Without a second thought, I kneel before him, my fingers digging into his flesh until I feel the bone beneath. He screams, the sound music to my ears, and I twist it, watching as his body jerks with pain.

"I could make this quick," I offer, relishing the power I hold over him, "or..." I pause, twisting even harder now, blood staining my hands as he gasps for air.

"O-okay, p-please j-just..." he stammers, his entire body shaking beneath me.

My eyes lock onto his, and I tilt my head to the side, waiting for him to spill the necessary information.

"They're currently in Rybakowo," he blurts out, the sound of his fear ringing in his ears, "but you have to make it quick since they'll leave for Mexico soon."

I rake my eyes down his trembling form, my stomach lurching at the sight of him pissing himself.

"Where in Rybakowo?" I inquire, my voice low and menacing. He inhales shakily, sobs breaking free from his chest.

With a swift and powerful slap across his cheek, he grits his teeth and suppresses a yelp before spitting out: "Łąkowa, 66-416 Rybakowo."

I stand up and brandish my gun, aiming straight at Diego's arms. "Bleed out," I hiss.

Without wasting a second, I dial Abel's number, and he picks up immediately. "I know where she is," I declare into the phone, savouring each syllable like a piece of rich, indulgent candy.

I'm finally going to get back my wife.

CHAPTER 57

IRENA NOWAK

Emotions surge within me, clogging and drying my throat like a desert wasteland. Disgust, anger, and terror intertwine in a tangled web of misery. The mere thought of remarrying makes every inch of my body recoil, twisting my stomach with revulsion. I clench my fists, trying to contain the hot tears that well up in my eyes.

Days blur into one another, lost in a suffocating loop of mind-numbing sameness. There's no joy left, no light in my life. But as I lay on my bed, I close my eyes and force my mind to my happy place, Saint and I playing the piano in our cabin.

"Stay strong," I tell myself, drawing on every ounce of willpower I have left. And at that moment, I hear a soft whisper, *"I'll find you, doe. I'll bring you home."*

The celestial echoes of his voice lull me into a sense of calm, filling my lungs with the air of comfort. My mind is transported to a time of pure bliss when we were together. It's in these moments that I find the strength to carry on.

But then, the cackle comes back, piercing through my momentary peace.

The voice needles at me, probing at my vulnerabilities.

With a determined breath, I squeeze my eyes closed, mustering all my strength to push back against the voice sneaking into my mind. The door bursts open, and heavy, ominous footsteps draw nearer to my bed. Though my back is turned, I stay completely still, pretending to be slumber less.

"Is there anything else you require, sir?" one of the maids' ventures. Shivers of fear ripple through me as rough, calloused hands ghost over the contours of my body. I'm barely dressed in a pristine white tee that doesn't quite reach my rear, but thank-fully, a cozy blanket shields me from the intruder's gaze. "Leave us alone," the voice reverberates through the room, sending chills down my spine. It's Manuel; that unmistakably threatening tone could only belong to him. I observe as the door slams shut, blocking any glimpse of light that might offer me protection. I curl up under the covers, concealing myself from him as if my life depended on it.

But there's no way out. Soon he's removing the covers, exposing me to his cold, calculating stare. I keep my eyes closed, refusing to meet his gaze.

I sense the warmth of his body as, he leans in closer, his scent of tobacco and cologne overwhelming me. I can barely maintain my composure as he plays with me, his thumb tracing my hair. My body trembles, but I refuse to display any vulnerability.

And then he steps back. "I know you're awake." He declares softly, and my eyes flutter open as I turn to meet his calculated stare. He tilts his head to the side. "What do you want?" I inquire quietly. "I want to familiarize myself with you. After all, chica, you will be the mother of my children." He states, and I scoff sarcastically. "Why bother? You're going to end my life after I fulfil you and my uncles with enough children." I spat bitterly, and he gazed at me as if solving a complex puzzle. "Perhaps you can provide me with a reason not to kill you." He proclaims, and I sigh, averting my gaze. "Don't. You're not strong, you pathetic bitch. No one is going to save you. It's time to wake up from your delusional world.

waste your words on me, Manuel," I utter, turning my back to him. "After all, I'm worth nothing except for being a procreator." I pause. "Do us both a favour and let me be to drown in my sorrow." Dread tightens in my stomach, and I tense up.

After a tense silence, I hear his footsteps fade away, followed by a creak of the door and a gentle slam.

Suddenly, a creaking sound emanates from the darkest corner of my room, jarring me from my deep, inexorable slumber.

My senses are invaded by an unsettling feeling that grips me in a vice-like hold, as I jolt awake, drenched in a cold sweat. Be- wildered and disoriented, I am confronted with utter darkness, my only source of comfort being the pale luminescence of the moonlight creeping through the narrow crevices of my window. The subtle strands of light struggle to penetrate the inky shadows that engulf my room. Through the haze of my unconsciousness, a shiver runs down my spine, and I become acutely aware of the ominous presence surrounding me. My breathing grows ragged, and my chest pounds with an intensity that makes my heart feel like it could burst out of my chest. It takes me a few moments to gather my bearings. I pull myself up from the bed. A shiver creeps down my spine as I sense an unseen presence lurking in the shadows. My skin prickles with goosebumps, and I know without a doubt that someone is watching me.

Gritting my teeth, I force myself to sit up, ignoring the pulsing ache between my legs. The darkness is oppressive, pressing in on me from all sides. I glance out of the window, watching the raindrops trickle down the panes.

A sudden bolt of lightning illuminates the room in a blinding flash, and I seize the opportunity to scan my surroundings. No one is there. Or are they simply hiding in the shadows?

The feeling of being observed is so strong that I can almost detect a physical weight on my skin. With a sinking heart, I slide out of bed and rush to the door, pounding it with all my strength.

Finally, the door creaks open, and I come face to face with Grzegorz. My fury is like a raging inferno, consuming me from the inside out.

"What the fuc-"

"Tell me," I pleaded, the words dripping with angst. "Why are you doing this?"

Grzegorz scoffed, crossing his arms with a haughty air. "Doing what Irena?" My frustration boiled over, spilling into a forceful shove towards Grzegorz.

But his dark eyes were unmoved by the fresh wounds painting my skin. As the realization dawned on me, a painful lump lodged in my throat.

Grzegorz truly is an evil heartless bastard.

"You-" A strangled sob caught in my throat. "Why?" I screamed. "Why are doing this to me!?"

My voice echoed in the emptiness of the room, ringing with the agony that clawed through my heart.

"Why, I thought we were family. I am the daughter of your dead brother?!"

I pleaded without hope, feeling the weight of devastation closing in.

With tears flowing down my cheeks relentlessly, I prod Grzegorz with every fiber of my being, desperate for answers. In response, Grzegorz barks fiercely and unleashes a slap that makes me stagger and crash onto the hard floor.

Looking up at him, my heart clutches in a vise as he glares down at me with an ice-cold stare.

My voice trembles as I cry out, unable to contain the torrent of emotion inside me. "WHY?!" I cry out, sobbing uncontrollably. "I-I was getting better. I really was. Now I'm here wondering what I did wrong to deserve this?"

"W-what did I do to be unloved by you?" my voice cracks at the end and Grzegorz stares at me. Not a single trace of emotion shimmering in his eyes.

"Why am I not loved by any of you?" I add, my voice cracking as I stare at Grzegorz. His eyes remain devoid of any emotion, intensifying the overwhelming sense of pain that grips me.

I don't know how to anymore, Saint. I don't fucking know how. In the eerie silence of the night, Grzegorz was ready to abandon me to the dense chasm of darkness. But in an instant that changed, as I caught the shrill echoes of a thunderous eruption from the outside, followed by a volley of aggressive gunshots and distressing screams that echoed through the shadows. Grzegorz's eyes widened abruptly, overwhelmed with surprise and panic. My heart skipped a beat, and the world around me became an indistinct blur.

"I can't even sleep, I can barely eat. I'm miserable because of you!" I scream, letting the anguish inside me take over. "This isn't just depression anymore, Grzegorz. You've drained every inch of my energy, leaving nothing but a shell of who I used to be. I can't even bring myself to look in the mirror anymore because I don't recognize the person staring back at me. I'm ashamed of what I've become."

A peal of choked laughter escapes my lips as I lock eyes with Grzegorz. "I'm sick of fighting. Every day, every moment is a struggle. But I still keep going because of him." I pause, my voice reducing to a whisper. "But now, I'm just tired. So, so tired."

"Why? What could I have possibly done to warrant this punishment?" I murmur, my fragile voice trembling with each syllable.

"You're a constant reminder of that bastard we call our blood. You're nothing but a burden we're forced to bear," he spews, his eyes boring into me with seething hatred. "What has my father done to make you hate me so much?" I inquired, tears spilling out of my eyes. He leans in close his eyes burning with hatred. "He took everything from us. I was supposed to be the rightful head of the family. I was supposed to be the one who ought to have made my father proud but your bitch of your father was the favoured one. Making us follow in his footsteps. And now that he's gone we can reclaim what was rightfully meant to be ours. The only problem is you are the crucial element for us to have complete authority to inherit the family enterprise once we are finished with you. Everything Anatol and I have laboured for will finally be justified." He pauses and seethes into my ear. "You are just as pathetic and worthless as Jan Irena. A fucking mistake, like he was."

Keep fighting, baby. Keep fighting.
Saint.

CHAPTER 58

SAINT DÉ LEON

The sky was a gloomy casket-black that sent shivers down my spine. As if on cue, thunder roared and clouds gathered, heralding the arrival of rain.

"Three guards have been neutralized on the east side. The pathway is clear,"

Abel's voice sounded coolly in my earpiece.

With determination fuelling my steps, I strode into the heart of the main area, the sheer enormity of the space overwhelming me.

Abel and Prince were our skilled overseers, their watchful eyes trailing our every move. Meanwhile, Ace and I kept a careful vigil on the 35-foot soldiers who were tasked with providing us cover.

My heart races as I step into the yard, my gun gripped tightly in my hand like a lifeline. My eyes dart from corner to corner, ready for whatever danger lurks in the shadows. Suddenly, Ace materializes before me with two other men, his face etched with unmistakable anxiety. "What's going on?" I demand my senses on high alert. His reply hits me like a punch to the gut: "They know we're here."

Before I can even begin to process this news, a deafening explosion rocks the air. We huddle together, bodies trembling, as debris rains down around us. The force of the blast nearly knocks me off my feet, but I catch myself just in time, my eyes scanning the area for any sign of the enemy. And then they come, bullets raining down on us like a lethal hailstorm, the voices of our adversaries echoing through the air in a foreign tongue.

Frustration coursed through my veins, tightening my muscles and leaving me restless and eager for action. I clench my fists, determination etched on my face as I prepare to face whatever danger lies ahead.

"Looks like you've got company,"

"Five men are heading your way," Prince spoke through the window earpiece.

I stretched my neck, savouring the release of tension as my bones clicked into place. The task ahead would be no walk in the park – taking down five men would require finesse and speed. I'd had it easier when I'd snuck past the guards positioned around the dilapidated house.

The tapping of heavy boots on wet pavement echoes through the otherwise chaotic night. I stand half-hidden behind a thick tree trunk, my finger poised on the trigger of my gun. In the distance, two figures emerge from the mist, their intention clear. I take a deep breath and step forward, firing my weapon into the air. Both men stumble, their bodies crumpling like ragdolls.

But before I can celebrate my victory, a third figure emerges from the shadows. This one is armed with a gleaming hunting knife, its sharp edge glinting menacingly in the pale moonlight. I dodge his first swing, then quickly take him down with a swift kick between the legs. As he falls, I use his own weapon against him, piercing his neck with the blade. But my moment of triumph is short-lived. Bullets whizz past me, and I know I'm in trouble. Desperate, I grab the dead man's body and use it as a shield, feeling blissfully sickened as blood oozes over my hands. Finally, my attackers stop firing and I use the brief respite to dart behind a nearby wall.

It's then that I hear it…the unmistakable sound of gunfire. I peek cautiously around the corner, only to see the assholes drop to the ground mere feet away. Someone else has taken them out, leaving me to wonder exactly who I'm dealing with.

Ace's welcome was laced with a smug smirk that nearly made me roll my eyes to the back of my head. But we had a job to do, so I gathered my wits and led the way to the door. The hinges groaned in protest as we pushed our way in, my men chomping at the bit to put their skills to work.

Commanding them with swift hand signals, they dispersed, their footsteps ringing out in the empty halls like pealing bells. Suddenly, gunshots shattered the air, and I braced myself for whatever chaos was to come.

As I turned to face the action, a man came hurtling towards me with a vicious right hook. I felt my head snap back in pain, blood filling my mouth, and knew I had to retaliate. Gathering all my strength,

I grabbed the attacker, flinging him to the ground with an earth-shattering thud.

But even as I went in for the finishing blow, someone tackled me from behind, knocking my gun out of reach. I scrambled to my feet, determined to finish the job by any means necessary.

The wretched dickhead scrambled to his feet, his movements desperate and uncoordinated. He charged towards me, butted me in the chest like a wild animal. With a vile sneer, he raised a stiff thumb, aimed it at my eyes. I deftly rolled his head away and retaliated with a left to the wind. Spinning around, I delivered a thunderous right that ripped his ear and unleashed a shower of hot, sticky blood. Before I could catch my breath, the first guy charged at me again, swinging two bone-breaking blows to my head. Pain exploded in my skull, leaving me reeling and disoriented. The brute continued to hammer at me with both hands, his fury fuelling each blow.

Clutching his shoulder for stability, I countered with a head- butt that knocked him out cold.

The sudden rush of adrenaline surged through me, and I shifted into high gear, another guy rushed towards me, dodging his attacks with lightning, fast reflexes. I missed a crucial right but compensated by launching my body towards him, my arm snaking around his thick neck. In one swift motion, I grabbed his left wrist and jerked upwards, breaking his neck with a deafening snap. Running up the stairs, the chaos around me fades away as my sole focus is finding Irena. My heart races as I scour every empty room on the second floor, desperate for any sign of my baby. Suddenly, I sense her presence behind one closed door. With a powerful kick, the door flies open, revealing Grzegorz holding Irena hostage with a knife to her neck.

My heart pounds so loudly, drowning out the sounds of Irena's muffled cries. Upon closer inspection, I am consumed with pure, unadulterated rage. Dry streaks of tears painted on her face, dark, hollow sockets where her eyes once shone brightly. She has been starved, beaten, and bruised, the evidence of her torture marked across her skin.

"You're stupid for coming here," Grzegorz spits through trembling lips as the sweat pools on his forehead.

"You're an imbecile for taking her away from me," I hiss menacingly, baring my teeth.

With a lightning-quick motion, I draw my minigun from the holster, flaunting the silvery weapon in Grzegorz's face. He flinches back, fear etched on his face like a permanent marker.

Irena, held hostage by Grzegorz, trembles in terror, her heart racing with fear.

To my relief, he wasn't smart enough to use Irena as a shield. I hold my ground, aiming Grzegorz's shadowed shoulder blade, his Achilles' heel.

With a burst of courage, I pull the trigger, and the bullet ricochets through my flesh with a sickening crunch. Grzegorz screams in agony, and the knife clatters to the floor as he releases Irena from his grasp.

At that moment, nothing but darkness enveloped me, a whirl- wind of unchecked rage and fury. Great balls of fire burned with- in me, the weeks of bottled-up indignation finally erupting like a silent volcano.

With a fierce tug on his hair, I snatched the blade resting at his side and plunged it savagely into both his eyes, the sockets bursting as if they were just rotten eggs.

Gooey blood spilt out from where his vision once was, painting the floor like a grotesque canvas. But the symphony of his agony was the sweetest melody to my corrupted soul, sending shivers down my spine and awakening every twisted impulse within me.

I snarl, feeling the rage course through my veins like lava. "Death isn't enough. He took everything from me, so I'll take it all from him." With each word, I plunge the knife deeper, letting the twisted pleasure wash over me like a tidal wave. My hands shake as I remember her screams and the way he laughed as he broke her.

But now, with each stab, it's as if a weight is being lifted from my soul.

The darkness inside of me is finally finding its release, and I let it take over completely. The smell of death and decay fills the air, and I can't tell if it's coming from him or from within me.

Finally, when I can't lift my arm another time, I stand, breathing hard, covered in his blood. I feel his life draining away under my feet, and I smile, knowing that justice has been served. But then, I hear her voice, and I remember that justice isn't always enough.

"Saint, he's dead," she spoke softly. As she enveloped me in her embrace, a new world was born. Her touch ignited a warmth that suffused every fiber of my being. My heart quickened, nerves tingling like they had been asleep for ages, now awakened by her touch. Finally turning to her, I traced her delicate features with my fingertips.

Her eyes — oh, her eyes — shimmered with unspoken secrets and emotions. My lips parted to speak, but her voice cracked first. "I-"

"Shhh," I murmured, silencing her with a finger to her lips as the world around us vanished. "I'm sorry about everything Irena. I'm sorry about the contract, I'm sorry about hurting you that single thought shatters me in ways that I cannot describe."

Gazing into her eyes, everything else seemed insignificant, unimportant. She smiled weakly, her fingers tracing every line on my face, and it was as if angels had touched me with their kisses. "It's okay. You've come all this way for me."

The words "You're here" fall from her lips as tears roll down her face like tiny streams. But my heart is full of warmth and love for Irena as I take her in my arms and repeat softly, "I'm here."

At that moment, my heart swells with joy that I've finally found her, even though I can't help but feel pain that she's in this state. Yet, knowing that she's finally safe in my arms, I feel a sense of relief wash over me. I want nothing more than to whisk her away to a place where we can make a new start together. "I lo-" Suddenly, her words are interrupted by a deafening gunshot that shakes me. Frantically, I pull Irena close to me and try to shield her from the bullet. As I brace myself for the pain, I feel nothing.

That's when I realize…I'm the one who's not been shot. Gasping for air, Irena clutches her stomach as blood seeps through her fingers. Her eyes widen with disbelief as she turns towards me, searching for answers that even I don't have. Suddenly, my attention is diverted to Anatol. He's propped up against the door, crimson red blood oozing from every wound. I raise my gun in retaliation, but he slumps down to the ground, his weapon clattering to the floor.

Irena stumbles and I rush to catch her, praying that she'll make it through.

She mutters something incomprehensible through laboured breaths.

"Saint," she whispers, her voice barely louder than a whisper. My heart aches at the sound of her voice cracking.

"S-saint-" she breathes. "No, no, you're going to be okay Doe. You're going to be okay." I soothe her with words, promising her that she'll pull through.

But my quick fix isn't enough. Her blood loss is getting worse by the second. I rip off pieces of her shirt to try and stop the bleeding.

Irena's eyes shine with tears as she gazes at me, her delicate hand brushing against my cheek. Her brown irises are filled with pain, yet they remain stunningly beautiful.

"Saint," she whispers, her voice trembling. My heart clenches in my chest, threatening to suffocate me as I gaze back at her. "No, my love," I utter, my emotions choking my words. "I won't let you slip away. I just got you back."

Panic courses through my veins as I contact Abel through the earpiece.

"Abel, are you there?" I shout, desperation overshadowing my voice. "Yes, what's going on?" he responds, his tone laced with concern.

"Irena has been shot," I exclaim, the fear in my voice palpable. "Get the car started. We need to get her to the hospital."

As I reach out to lift her, she winces in pain and stops me. "I have to—", I begin, but she cuts me off with a firm resolve.

"No," she breathes, tears now blurring my vision. "There's no use." With a long, melancholic sigh, Irena pulled at my shirt and drew me closer.

Her lips met mine in a gentle, affectionate kiss as she pressed her forehead against mine, her eyes locked onto mine.

Tears welled up in my eyes as I choked out the words, "I-I just got you back." Irena nodded, her lips trembling. I could feel her struggling to catch her breath. "I know, my love. I-I know."

"But t-that does not matter what matters is that you made me feel like a person...Saint, I love you unconditionally," she whispered. "My only regret is that I wished I had told you sooner."

My world shattered into a million pieces. I tried to speak, but my throat was choked with emotion. I had rebuilt my life to have her back in it, only to have it collapse again. No, I couldn't bear it. My world had crumbled once before when I lost her, and I refused to let it happen again. She was my soulmate, the very reason why I existed in this world. Without her, I was nothing but a mere shell of a man, a lifeless ghost roaming the earth.

Her life force was intricately woven into every fiber of my being, inseparable and irreplaceable. If she were to die, then death would undoubtedly claim me too. As I held her in my arms, I could sense her life force slowly ebbing away. My heart felt as though it was being crushed under the weight of a thousand boulders. I gripped her hand tightly, hoping it would be enough to keep her with me.

As I draw Irena nearer, her petite hand finds mine and guides it to her chest. The melody of her heartbeat dissolves into a heart- breaking symphony of slowing beats, causing my own heart to fracture into a million tiny fragments.

Moments later Abel comes rushing in, he pauses in his tracks when he meets my gaze. Then his eyes slowly move towards Irena, and he's shoulders fell in defeat.

"Shit."

"I love you, with all my bruised heart, and after that. I'll still love you, Saint. My heart is yours. Tame it, break it, bleed it out. It's finally yours." she breathes out a smile tugging on her bruised lips.

Her words slice me open, a declaration of love that transcends time and space, and with it comes the haunting realization that she is saying goodbye. Yet, despite the bruises and ruptures that come with love, she gently asks me to conquer and claim her heart as my own. Just like I asked her to do with mine two months ago.

As she breathes out her final utterance, a gentle smile lifts the corners of her lips, My own breath catches in my throat as I feel her tender fingers release their hold on mine, slipping away like a dream, a moment too fleeting.

"Irena," my voice trembles with desperation as I shake her gently, hoping for a response. "Doe, you can't leave me now. Wake up, please." Tears well up in my eyes, threatening to spill over. "You're everything to me. My heart, my world, my everything," I whisper brokenly. "No, no, no, no, fuck please no."

Holding her close, I rock back and forth, my heart heavy with the fear of losing her once again. I refuse to let her slip away from me. Not after everything we've been through. Not after finally finding her again.

"I just got you back," I cry out, my voice raw with emotion, "Please don't leave me now."

Please.

CHAPTER 59

SAINT DÉ LEON

Silence surrounds me as I huddle in the corner, lost in thought. My mind yearns for your presence, desperately hoping for your return.

But deep within, I know it's a wishful dream that can never come true.

My tears fall like raindrops, a soft, gentle drizzle that masks the deep sorrow that grips my soul. I can sense your presence beside me, silently holding my hand and comforting me in my pain.

This grief has taken over my life, leaving me drowning in a sea of despair.

An endless abyss of loneliness and heartache. I'm torn be- tween the acceptance of your death and the anger of why fate chose to take you instead of me. It feels like a selfish emotion, but it's hard not to feel it.

Everything around me is still, but a fierce storm of emotions rages on within me.

In a desperate plea to Fate, I raised my voice to the heavens, beseeching death to take me in her stead.

Irena deserved to chase her dreams, to bask in the warmth of the sun while I lay six feet under. The silence that followed only amplified the rage and disbelief within me, tearing at my heart and soul.

With tears streaming down my face, I held you in my arms as you exhaled. My heart shattered into a million pieces, unable to reconcile the fact that you were truly gone. Every fiber of my being screamed that this was just a horrific nightmare, a twisted figment of my imagination.

But it was not so. The piercing agony of reality settled in, mercilessly tormenting me with the knowledge that the love of my life had been taken from me. During that pain, I couldn't help but remember how your skin glowed with a golden radiance, basking in the sun's warm embrace — a stark contrast, now, to the ashen hue that coated your fragile form.

My soul mate was gone, leaving behind only the nightmare of grief as a cruel reminder that life is both beautiful and unpredictable.

The enigma behind why you had to leave remains an unsolvable puzzle.

Even if someone attempted to explain it, the chaos it would bring to my heart would remain unchanged. The fragility of love has dawned upon me, leaving grief and longing to fill its place. The memories we shared and the once effortless moments have ceased to exist, living only in my mind. As I try to numb the anger, the longing for you remains constant. The reality of my predicament is painfully clear, and I refuse to live this way. Each day I wake up, aware that I won't be able to hear your infectious laugh or feel the tenderness of your gentle touch. The absence of those brown eyes, which shone like honey under the sun, seemed to darken the days. I miss making love and savouring your delicious cookies. I miss bringing your favourite white roses daily.

As I stand under the moon talking to you, I know you won't answer me. We had envisioned our future: happily ever after. A picturesque scene of us ageing gracefully on a tropical beach as our children frolicked in the shimmering waves. It was a vow we had made to each other, etched in our hearts.

Yet, fate had other plans, refusing to grant us what we yearned for, what we craved, what we needed…what was meant to be.

Each step I take towards you is heavy with overwhelming grief, my heart aching to feel the warmth of your embrace once again.

As I gazed upon her face, serenity took hold, bringing a gentle smile that seemed to dance across her frigid complexion. Drawn by her calm, I leaned in for one final embrace, my lips connecting with hers as I savoured the moment.

As we lingered in our embrace, memories cascaded through my mind, each one a treasure to hold close. My eyes drifted to the ring that glimmered on her finger, a symbol of our grand plans for a wedding in Tanzania, now reduced to this final goodbye.

You left too soon, Irena; I wasn't done loving you. Her eyes stole my heart; her smile gave me life.

Her presence made me high and her touch left me breathless. With her captivating eyes, smiling lips, and mere presence, Irena captured my heart. Her touch made me weak in the knees, leaving me breathless and reeling with love.

But this is not the end. As I promised, we will meet again in echoes where the end begins. A place where your soul and mine will intertwine, forever united.

Dressed impeccably in a sleek black suit, I stand tall and proud, emanating the essence of a refined gentleman on this unforgettable day.

My chest trembles with emotion as I hear the doors glide open, and I behold the sight - the pristine white casket bearing your earthly remains, lifted with the utmost care.

Their movements are measured and harrowing, and each step is wrought with reverence as they set you down at the altar. The lid, concealing you from mortal sight, is gently hinged open for all to pay their respects.

The sacred chapel glows with tranquil beauty, adorned with the sweetest scent of your treasured white roses.

Our story did not end in bliss. It was just a mere fantasy, a figment of our imagination.

But despite the sadness that enveloped us both, I couldn't help but feel a sense of peace settle over me, knowing that she had found solace in her final moments.

She finally confessed her love to me, and that will be the one thing that I'll carry proudly to my grave.

Staring at her, I sigh. My heart ached at the sight.

This was my wedding day, and this was her funeral.

CHAPTER 60

SAINT DÉ LEON

As the hours turned into days and the days into weeks, Abel and his wife, Nirali, stood steadfastly by my side, witnessing the devastating toll that grief was taking on me. With every passing moment, Nirali endeavoured to be my comforting presence, offering solace in the gentle touch of her hand and the soothing power of her words. Although her attempt failed, she didn't understand that the complexity of grief was an ever-changing beast that gripped my heart and mind in its relentless grasp. But she listened patiently to my tales of my beloved Irena's past and cherished memories, understanding how each cherished memory was, simultaneously, a double-edged sword.

Nirali's intentions were good, her words filled with hope for a brighter tomorrow. Yet, her comprehension of my pain often left me feeling misunderstood and isolated. How could I possibly get over the loss of my soulmate, my reason for existing? How could the void she left be filled when her absence was a constant, haunting reminder?

These questions gnawed at my mind, dragging me deeper into the dark abyss of depression. I yearned for the pain to subside, for the wounds of grief to heal, but the weight of loss grew heavier with each passing day.

In moments of solitude, I found myself grappling with conflicting emotions. On one hand, I longed to honour Irena's memory by cherishing our love and the life we had built together. On the other, I felt a growing guilt for even considering ending it all. It was a battle within myself, a seemingly impossible entanglement of love, loss, and loyalty.

My world has been plunged into a suffocating darkness that seems to have no end. It has been a constant battle against the overwhelming weight of grief that consumes every ounce of my being, leaving me gasping for air in this vast ocean of despair.

Irena was not only my wife; she was my soul mate, who under- stood me completely and brought light into the darkest corners of my soul. Her loss has left an immeasurable void within me, an emptiness that cannot be filled no matter how hard I try. Her absence is a constant ache, a haunting presence in every corner of our once-joyful home.

The memories of our times together bombard my mind with relentless force, like a never-ending slideshow of happiness and laughter. From our first meeting, Irena had captivated me with her facade of innocence, snappy tendency, and remarkable dark side, but apart from her dark side, her radiating warmth could melt even the coldest of hearts. We embarked on a journey of love and companionship, weaving a tapestry of shared dreams and aspirations that painted the canvas of our lives together.

But now, I find myself trapped in a desolate landscape where the colour has faded and the vibrancy of life has been stripped away. Each passing day is a torturous reminder of the happiness we once shared, now cruelly replaced by the gnawing agony of grief. The silence in our home is a constant reminder of the laughter and love that have forever disappeared, replaced by an echoing void.

How can one's heartbeat be when the essence of one's existence has been extinguished? The world continues to turn, bustling with the routines and joys of others, while I remain trapped in this tumultuous whirlpool of sorrow.

The simplest of tasks become monumental challenges as I navigate through life without my guiding light. Even the most mundane activities, such as cooking or simply dressing up, are now reminders of the intimate moments I shared with Irena. Once filled with her infectious energy, the empty bed space be- side me now mocks my solitude and amplifies my anguish.

The nights are the hardest, as darkness envelopes my weary soul and amplifies the reality of her absence. I lie in bed, longing for her comforting presence, for her touch that used to chase away all of my fears and doubts. The pillow still carries the faint fragrance of her hair, a bittersweet reminder of our love. How can I possibly endure a lifetime of nights spent alone, haunted by the memories of what once was?

CHAPTER 61

SAINT DÉ LEON

Melodies are dancing in my mind as I enter a musical realm. The ebony and ivory colours gleam, igniting my dexterous fingers with unparalleled ease.

My senses are emboldened as the fiery elixir courses through my veins, beckoning me to let go. The melodies of the music pulsate within me, carrying me away into a delirious state. The amount of liquid courage I've consumed is a mystery, but one thing is certain, I've drunk so many amounts of alcohol to smother the agonizing ache deep within my soul.

It's in this moment, it's through the piano, that I feel a certain tranquillity, akin to the feeling of being near my beloved Irena.

A memory from our last duet together floods my senses, setting a foundation for my emotions to flow freely.

As a sweet voice echoes in my ear, my breath catches in my throat. It's our favourite part, she reminds me. I can feel her presence, almost tangible, and my heart skips a beat. "I miss you so much," I whisper into the night, desperate for her to hear me.

And then, as if by magic, she's there. Sitting beside me, bathed in moonlight, her skin glowing with an ethereal radiance. Her dress, a white as pure as her soul, hugs her curves and I am lost in her beauty. Her hair, a wild tangle of curls that frames her face, further accentuates her loveliness. But it's her eyes that capture me, brown as warm as a blazing fire that promises an unending comfort. Her lips, full and soft, beckon me closer, and I want nothing more than to drown in their sweetness.

In the flickering light of the moon, Irena is a constantly shifting canvas of browns. From her long, black lashes to her defined brows, everything about her evokes a sense of tranquillity.

I know it's only a mirage, a figment of my imagination. Yet, I cannot help but hold on to the hope that this is not the world's cruel way of taking her away from me.

As the moon casts a dreamy glow on her face, she grins, her eyes twinkling like stars.

"*I miss you too Saint.*" she whispers, holding my gaze for a moment. "*But we'll be together again. You know what you must do.*" With a tender and refined tone, she vanishes in a flash. The cushion beside me where she liked to sit while we made music on the grand piano stood bare as if she was never there.

With each heartbeat in sync with the rhythm, I feel my soul's alignment. It's a moment of pure connection, a connection that I use to communicate the most profound parts of my love for Irena.

With my eyes closed, I let the gentle notes of the music carry me away, imagining her sitting beside me. Our fingers dance together on the piano keys, weaving a tapestry of raw and beautiful emotions. Here, at this moment, I am saying goodbye to the world and embracing my love.

The memories we share are a salt sea that will never evaporate. They are etched in my mind and forever engraved in my heart. I will carry each cherished moment with me until the end of time.

As the final cadence of the song reverberates through the room, I reluctantly open my eyes, mesmerized by the serene beauty of the moonlight peering through my window. The twinkling stars in the night sky offer a welcome respite from the harshness of reality.

As I delicately pluck the pristine white rose from the piano, my fingers can't resist twirling it, feeling its velvety petals brush against my skin. The thumping of my heart creates a symphony in my chest, signalling that you are close. I gently place the flower back down, and instead, my hand finds the cold metal of a single bullet.

I trace your name, lovingly imprinted by my own hand on the bullet and solemnly load it into the gun. You will be the last thought on my mind, the final image to pass through my soul.

With eyes closed, I bring the pistol to my temple, my fragile spirit in striking contrast to your broken one. I loved you with unwavering passion, but it's cost me everything. And now, I will join you in peace, finally together forever.

Summoning every last ounce of bravery within me, I squeeze the trigger and the bullet pierces through my skull.

Aliah Darkrose

Where ever you go, I follow Irena.
Not even death can do us part.

527

THE END

527

ALTERNATIVE ENDING

4 YEARS LATER

SAINT DÉ LEON

There she is.

My beautiful wife.

We were blessed with a sight that few have seen, a sunrise-gold beach that sparkled with divine magic. The sea was a lazy spectator, ebbing and flowing with such gentleness that it seemed to be at peace with itself, draped in robes of Neptune blue. The sand beneath our feet was soft and plush, like a giant blanket of candy floss. It was bordered by towering cliffs, like a scythe slicing through the beach. In the vast ocean, pulsing light streams painted the surface in a breathtaking golden haze. The silence was almost sacred, and this Babylon of beaches could have been paradise. As we looked towards the horizon, it was embroidered with a delicate line of silver.

Irena basked in the warm Brazilian sun, her hair cascading in luscious curls that danced in the wind. Her skin glimmered like the finest gold, and her white floral dress fluttered like a butterfly in the breeze. As her toes wiggled in the sand, I felt a smile slowly tug at the corners of my lips as I watched her play with Noémie.

There is a precious gem in my life, my two-year-old little girl named Noémie. She is the spitting image of her mother but with a few of my traits, like the sparkle in her lively eyes. And let's not forget the charm in the little gap between her pearly whites, an inherited characteristic passed down from her grandma on her mother's side.

After I saved Irena from her uncles, I knew it was time to relinquish my position and let Abel take over. My violent takedown of the brothers brought the Nowak family business to a halt. Fortunately, Irena salvaged whatever was left and put it in her name.

As we pledged to each other, we headed to Brazil to start anew. Little did I know that Irena's mother's relatives would become our newfound friends when we visted Tanzania three years ago. Although I'm not one for mixing with the locals, I find these sweet-tempered folks bearable. The biggest surprise came when I decided to show my appreciation by blessing them with three million euros, allowing them to swap their humble village living for a life in the city.

After we decided to leave to Brazil, Irena and I worked on con- structing a seaside retreat on a remote island. Two years after our successful project, my precious Noémie was born, bringing us great joy.

Now I live in paradise with my doe and little dove.

It was a gruelling year for Irena as she tried to repair the pieces of her shattered soul. The once lively spirit I had rescued was now a mere shadow of herself, consumed by a dark cloud of depression. Her appetite waned, and conversation with others was out of the question. She never cracked a smile for four long months, and I could sense she was barely holding on.

One day, I stumbled upon a devastating sight - Irena cutting herself. I was at a loss for words as she begged for forgiveness, and I held her tightly, promising to nurse her back to health no matter what it took.

The journey was challenging, but Irena was worth it. I made sure to give her the time and space she needed to heal, and for over a year, we didn't engage in physical intimacy. My priority was to help her rebuild her self-esteem and sense of self-worth; inch by inch, she began crawling out of the abyss.

It was a tough road, but when I saw the first flicker of a smile return to her lips, all the sacrifices were worth it.

I put my life on hold. Stepped down, and Abel took over.

It was one of the best decisions I've made because it was the only way to ensure Irena's safety and bring her back.

My task was to rekindle the light within her, just as she had ignited my soul with a mere match strike. That spark has grown into a wild inferno, a blazing desire that only she could quench.

"Papá!" a tiny voice erupts as my little angel races towards me. Two perfect white roses adorn her pigtails, like soft clouds tied to her head. Her strawberry jumper hugged her tiny frame, making her look like a candy cane come to life.

As her proud hairdresser, I stretch out my arms in anticipation, ready to catch her. With a contagious giggle, she jumps into my arms, and I toss her up, grabbing her just as quickly. Her giggles fill my heart with such overwhelming love and happiness.

But as Irena comes into view, my little dove hides in the safe- ty of my embrace, peeking out fearfully as if she's lost in a dark forest, searching for light.

"Mamá cookie monster," she whispers. "Mamá is the cookie monster?" I question, and she nods.

As Irena draws closer, she folds her arms and playfully shakes her head, fixing me with a mischievous gaze. "Guess what? I'm also the cookie monster. Ready to gobble down on you!" I respond with a playful growl, sweeping Noémie into my arms and peppering her tummy with kisses, sending giggles cascading from her lips.

Noémie squirms in my embrace, calling for Irena to rescue her from my relentless tickling. "I'm the cookie monster too!" Irena chimes in, her voice low and throaty as she playfully pinches Noémie's cheeks and smothers her in a flurry of sweet, tiny pecks.

"No! No, cookie monster!" Noémie's high-pitched laughter echoed as she nimbly pushed us aside with her dainty hands. We relentlessly tickled and showered her with kisses until she finally gave in, delivering a playful slap to my chest before sulking.

"Not fair," she declared, her little button nose scrunched up. Irena leaned in and bumped her nose with a finger.

"To even the playing field, would you like to help mamá with baking yummy cookies?" Irena inquired, causing Noémie's vibrant emerald eyes to twinkle with excitement.

"Papá, can we play fairy tea party?" With a grin, she turned
to face me eagerly, her eyes shining with excitement. I couldn't help but let out a half-chuckle at the sight of her eagerness. "Yes, my little dove," I replied, "We will play fairy tea party after we've helped mamá bake yummy cookies." Her face lit up with glee as she wiggled out of my arms and dashed towards the house.

"Don't run too fast!" Irena called out, watching us dart into the house with a smile.

As I turned to face Irena, I couldn't resist pulling her close
by her waist, feeling her warmth meet mine. "You

know," I whispered into her ear, a sly grin creeping across my face, "after I tuck Noémie into bed, you can join the cookie monster and let the stars sing to you."

"God, you're so corny," Irena snickered, wrapping her arms around my neck.

I raised an eyebrow, feigning shock. "You really think so?" I teased.

"Absolutely," she replied, her eyes sparkling mischievously. "You being a father has turned you soft."

But as I gazed into her eyes and felt her arms around my neck, I knew that perhaps being soft wasn't such a bad thing.

I lean in, grab her ass, and bite down on her neck. "So you want me to fuck you instead as you gaze upon the stars, doe? "I murmured, my voice low with lust. I felt her breath tickle my skin, and blood rushed straight to my dick.

Her breath washed over me like a warm breeze, sending shivers down my spine and setting my blood ablaze. "Maybe," she whispered, her voice breathless. I smirk. "I love how easily your body surrenders to me."

Irena withdraws, placing her palms on my chest and clears her throat delicately. "My body is not one to surrender easily," she protests.

I cock my head to one side, slipping my hand under her dress. My fingers trace the outline of her panties before sliding them aside and inching along her moist slit. She quivers uncontrollably, nails digging into my flesh as she bites down on her lip in ecstasy.

"You reacted just as intensely when I first touched you at the ball," I murmur by her earlobe, drawing close. "I said it before, and I'll repeat it. Your body is a terrible liar then you are."

Releasing her, I withdraw my damp fingers and savour the tangy taste of her essence.

I cannot wait to fuck her tonight.

With bated breath and a fluttering pulse, she waits in anticipation.

"Fuck you." She spat, hating that I was right. As always, I smirk. "I love you too doe."

"Now let's bake some cookies, so you can feed them to me later," I tell her. I pecked her on the cheek and walked away.

As always.

Irena: 0

Saint: 1

Irena furiously brushes past me. "After you fuck me, you're sleeping on the couch tonight." She declares, then walks past me without looking back.

With a mischievous grin, I observe her make her way into the house, steam practically coming out of her ears.

My amusement grows.

It's no secret that Irena despises being corrected or having her opinions challenged, but even in moments like these, I can't help but marvel at the fierce passion she brings to everything she does.

I take a moment to reflect on what we have.

With complete certainty, I know that ours is the kind of love poets wax lyrical about and dreamers spend their nights pining for.

This was my happily ever after.

ACKNOWLEDGMENTS

I am absolutely honored by the overwhelming support and love you've shown for Death Due Us. It has been a journey writing a story that so many of you have embraced with open hearts. The passion and excitement you've shared has truly touched me.

As many of you know, Housewife was written with a certain intensity that some readers thoroughly enjoyed, while others may have found it too bold. After listening to your feedback and reflecting on the diverse tastes within this wonderful community, I've decided to create a clean version of Housewife for those of you who prefer a story without the smut.

This decision comes from a deep appreciation for every one of you—whether you love the raw, unfiltered version or are looking for a story that focuses more on the emotional journey without the steamier details. Your unwavering support has made this possible, and I feel so fortunate to have readers who connect with my stories in their own unique ways.

Thank you for being the reason I continue to write, and for allowing me to grow and explore new facets of storytelling. I am beyond grateful for each and every one of you.

GET TO KNOW THE AUHTOR

To know Aliah better and communicate with her or be updated about her work you can find her on her socials that will be listed below.

INSTAGRAM:
@authoraliahdarkrose
TIKTOK:
@authoraliahdarkrose
FACEBOOK:
@authoraliahdarkrose

www.ingramcontent.com/pod-product-compliance
Lightning Source LLC
Chambersburg PA
CBHW030916120726
47906CB00002B/361

* 9 7 8 1 0 3 7 0 6 9 8 6 4 *